ALSO BY MELISSA GOOD

Dar and Kerry Series
Tropical Storm
Hurricane Watch
Eye of the Storm
Red Sky At Morning
Thicker Than Water
Terrors of the High Seas
Tropical Convergence
Stormy Waters
Storm Surge: Book One
Storm Surge: Book Two
Winds of Change: Book One

Other Titles
Partners: Book One
Partners: Book Two

Winds of Change
Book Two

Melissa Good

Yellow Rose Books
by Regal Crest

Texas

ISBN 978-1-61929-232-1

First Printing 2015

9 8 7 6 5 4 3 2 1

Cover design by Acorn Graphics

Published by:

Regal Crest Enterprises, LLC
229 Sheridan Loop
Belton, TX 76513

Find us on the World Wide Web at
http://www.regalcrest.biz

Printed in the United States of America

Chapter One

KERRY LEANED BACK in the deck chair and put her feet up on the aft well wall of the boat, idly watching the sun sliding toward the sea as they traveled along. Chino was curled up in a ball on her bed nearby, and Mocha had just given up watching the spray and was snuggling up next to her.

It was later than they'd planned, and Dar had the gerbils scrambling, trying to get them down to the cabin before it got dark. If she tipped her head back the other way, she saw Dar's back as she sat at the console, hands on the throttles and bare feet curled around the captain's chair's footrest.

Was Dar ready for some coffee? Kerry felt like she was, so she got up and went into the cabin, holding the door open as Mocha noticed her leaving and bolted after her. "Want to help me get your other mommy coffee, little man?"

"Yap!" Mocha seemed amazed at everything. He skittered across the boat's deck, barking at the moving sunbeams, astonished when the surface under him rocked suddenly as Dar moved across a wake. He looked at her with wide eyes.

Kerry started laughing. "What's it like to be so brand new, huh?" She went behind the counter in the galley and got some coffee working. "Everything's just so cool."

Mocha came behind the counter and sniffed everything, including her feet, with earnest thoroughness. He sat down and looked up at her, his tiny tongue hanging out.

Kerry reached down and picked him up, cradling him in her arms. "Oh, you're so cute." She scratched him behind his ears and examined his brown paws with their inky black pads.

A big shadow crossed over the boat and she glanced outside, seeing them moving past the bridge that linked the mainland to the start of the Keys. "Ah, we're crossing into the gulf." She put Mocha down. "I need to get some coffee upstairs, kiddo. Don't start chewing anything."

Mocha bounced off and found a Chino sized Nylabone that he pounced on and claimed with a paw, applying his baby teeth to the partially chewed surface.

"Good boy." Kerry filled the thermos with sugar, milk and coffee and capped it, then shook it vigorously to mix the ingredients. Then she hung the container around her neck by its strap, and went to the door, slipping out and then climbing up the ladder.

Dar was just putting her sunglasses on, since they were heading into the westering sun, and she turned around as Kerry arrived, her face creasing into a grin. "Hey, beautiful."

"Flattery will get you hot coffee every time." Kerry slid into the chair next to her and uncapped the thermos. "Almost there."

"Almost there," Dar repeated, taking the cup and sipping on it. "That was nice, today."

"It was." Kerry took a mouthful of coffee directly from the thermos. "I enjoyed just hanging out with all those folks and talking like we were just regular people." She pondered the horizon. "I lost count of the people who came up to me and told me how sad they were to see us go."

"Me too." Dar adjusted the throttle a little. "But the new guys may make a go of it. Different outlook. Might not be all bad."

"You said you knew the guy taking your place?" Kerry asked. "Higgs? I think I read about him in one of the industry papers. Seemed like he was pretty well regarded."

"Met him at a conference last summer," Dar said. "Reminded me a little of Bob. Very status conscious, spent a lot of time talking about his Mercedes Benz."

"Nice." Kerry sighed. "What did those people do to deserve that?"

"The other one, who's taking your position, Mark sent me a brief on him," Dar said. "David Willerson. He's from the oil industry. Was the CIO of some drilling company who's got family ties to Higgs."

Kerry sighed again. "I don't care what happens to the company. I do care about what happens to some of those people. Especially the ones we managed."

"Mm."

"On the other hand, maybe rearranging everything we did there will keep them too busy to care about what we're doing," Kerry said. "And I hope they have some kind of success, Dar, because I'd like all those people there to keep getting paychecks."

"Because we can't harbor all of them," Dar said, pragmatically. "I have to tell you, though, Mark said whatever it was that pushed him to come talk to us that night we left was pure karma. He's so damn happy."

Kerry smiled.

"He said he'd been wanting to make a change, to go in a different direction, but it was hard to take the risk. This forced him to." Dar fell silent and put the thermos cup to her lips.

Kerry waited a bit, but there seemed to be nothing more forthcoming. "Hit home a little?" she asked.

Dar shrugged. "Not really. Because we'd already made that choice, Ker. I keep losing sight of the fact that before they fired us, we quit." She laid on a turn to the left, a lazy arc that would bring them around the end of Key Largo and into Blackwater Sound.

The water here was flat and calm, typical of the Gulf side. The water was alive with boats though, crisscrossing through the shallows, many coming back from days out fishing.

That never caught Dar's interest. Going under the water always seemed preferable. Spending her time watching the fish and seeing the coral structures was far more enticing than sitting on the boat waiting for a bite.

"Want to do a night dive?" Dar asked. "Just off the dock? I'll turn the big lights on and we'll see if we can find your earrings."

Kerry grinned, her face reddening a little. "Sure. I still feel like an absolute idiot for having them in that pocket," she said. "I'd love to go on a little treasure hunt with you."

Speaking of lights, Dar turned on the boat's, though the sun was not quite near the horizon just yet. She checked the channel markers and aimed a course down the center of them, lifting a hand and waving at a sailboat turning off and going in toward shore.

"Is that Marvin?" Kerry asked. "I owe him a half gallon of milk."

"Since when do we ever get milk in half gallons?" Dar inquired.

"We don't. It's all he had." Kerry patted her on the back. "Let me go downstairs before our puppy decides to chew a hole in the fiberglass." She filled up Dar's cup from the thermos, kissed her on the lips and then retreated down the steps to attend to the frantic yelps that were coming from the boat's cabin.

Dar smiled, looking ahead to the horizon where she could already see the spit of land that held their cabin and the dock she was aiming the Dixieland Yankee toward. She took another sip of the coffee, convincing herself she could taste the love Kerry put into the making of it.

She could, right?

"Dar?" She cocked her head as the boat's intercom crackled, and Kerry's voice echoed softly through it. "Yep?"

"Did you know this new gizmo has a piece of software that lets me control the systems in the cabin?" Kerry said. "I just turned on the aircon and the lights."

Dar shaded her eyes, and chuckled. "Yep, you sure did." She saw the dock halons popping on. "That's pretty cool. I forgot to do that from the condo."

"Heh." Kerry clicked off.

The sunset spilled across the hull as she slowed for the approach to the cabin, the bow coming down in the water as she cut power. The dock itself was just big enough for the Dixie, and she maneuvered carefully past it, putting the engines into reverse to bring them to dead slow, then letting the mild current carry them back against the wooden pylons.

For a moment she let herself imagine a life where she piloted a boat for a living instead of what she actually did.

No high tech, no conference calls, no miles of wires to worry about. Just day after day of laying down float plans, and keeping the boat in good condition

It was enticing, but she knew enough about herself to know that it would be interesting only for a little while, and then she'd wish she was doing something more challenging. There were only so many routes, so many soundings, so many people to take out fishing, or diving or just sightseeing.

Dar smiled, as she heard Kerry come out on deck, already reaching for the lines. Just a daydream. But it was a nice daydream, and since she was lucky enough to own a boat that required a little skill to drive, she got to indulge in it from time to time when docking the yacht in places like this. She put the engines into drive and held the boat against the dock while Kerry walked along the side wall and tied them up to the standing posts.

Easier than floor based cleats. "We tied?"

"Yep." Kerry came back to the rear of the boat and then went to the door, opening it to let Mocha and Chino out. Chino immediately recognized a favorite place and leaped out onto the dock and trotted toward the cabin.

Mocha was too short to follow, and he stood up and scrabbled at the fiberglass, hopping a little bit until Kerry picked him up and stepped shoreward with him. "Take it easy, Mocha." She put him down and watched him ramble off the wooden pier, starting a through sniff fest of the sandy backyard.

Kerry followed him, pulling the keys to the cabin from her pocket as she joined Chino on the porch. She unlocked the door and pushed it open. "G'wan, madam."

The cabin was already a comfortable temperature, and the lights were on. "Second home sweet home." Kerry entered their bedroom and took a deep breath of the scent of clean linen. "Want to grab a sandwich before we go diving, hon?"

Dar was busy in the kitchen. "Sure. Just giving the mooch pooches some grub."

Kerry took a swimsuit from one of the drawers and traded her shorts and shirt for it, then added a light dive coat that went to her knees.

It was terrycloth lined with a water resistant exterior, a good compliment to a night dive in chilly weather. She walked back out and found Dar watching the dogs hoover up their kibble with an indulgent smile. "I have some pita pockets. You up for a couple of gyros?"

"Yum," Dar said. "I'll go get the gear ready."

Kerry flipped on the music system and went to the fridge, removing two carefully packed bags of shaved lamb from the freezer. She tossed them in the microwave and punched defrost. Then she got a container of chopped tomatoes along with a can of fried onions and a bottle of ranch dressing. "Sort of gyros, anyway."

"Yap!"

She looked down to find Mocha attentively at her feet, with Chino sitting behind him, her tail sweeping over the tile floor. "Excuse me? Your other mother just fed you."

"Growf," Chino responded, sniffing the air as the lamb defrosted.

Kerry chuckled, taking the lamb out and opening the bags into the pan, already hot with a little oil. She quickly warmed the meat, then assembled the pocket sandwiches with their personalized substitutions, putting the fried onions in instead of chopped fresh ones, and drizzling the definitely un-Greek dressing over it. "Sorry kids. No gyros for you."

She went to the fridge and got two bottles of root beer, putting them in her coat pockets before she picked up the sandwiches and headed for the door, both dogs trotting after her.

It was now twilight and the dock was lit up. The Dixie's white hull gleamed and reflected into the water. Dar sat on the side of the boat, her phone to her ear. As Kerry got closer she heard a wary tone in Dar's voice.

"That's the general idea, yes," Dar said. "The idea is to build intelligence into the filters so you can let the processors do the heavy lifting and deliver possible vectors to your analysts."

Kerry handed over a sandwich and sat down on the gear locker on the pier, gaining an instantly attentive pair of soulful eyed watchers. She took a bite of her gyro and took a piece of the lamb out, offering it to Chino.

"Right, I get that, but it's a fire hose," Dar said. "There's such a thing as too much data. You need to find a way to channel it so you're not looking at every byte."

Kerry thought it was probably the government. She wiggled out a tiny piece of the lamb and handed it over to Mocha, who was standing up with his front paws on her knee. She knew Dar sent over a rough top level plan several days back, but having her get a call on a Saturday about it was surprising.

"Right." Dar paused, then nodded. "That's what I...yes." She took a bite and chewed as she listened, then hastily swallowed. "I'm due up to see Gerry Easton on Wednesday. I can stop by." She listened again. "Exactly. You got it. Bring them in and we can white board the whole thing."

Kerry heard relief in Dar's low tones and if she turned, she knew she'd see that tall body relaxing. Sure enough there came the soft thumps of Dar's heels idly hitting the side of the boat.

"Okay, then, see you on Wednesday afternoon," Dar said. "Thanks for reviewing the plan and getting back to me." She closed the phone and took a big bite of her gyro. "Yum." She hopped off the side of the boat and took a seat beside Kerry. "Looks like I get to deal with both our government clients next week."

"So I heard." Kerry contentedly munched. "I have four potential new clients scheduled for that day or I'd come with you." She took a sip of her root beer. "By the time you get back we might not need that contract if they give you a hard time."

Dar gave Mocha some of her lamb. "Did I tell you recently you rock my world?"

Kerry put her head against Dar's shoulder and grinned.

"These are really good." Dar indicated her pocket. "I love those fried onions."

"I know," Kerry said. "Okay, let me get these guys inside while we go diving. We'll end up chasing them around in the water the whole time otherwise." She stood up and displayed a bit of remaining sandwich. "C'mon, kids, first one back to the cabin gets a treat."

Dar dusted her fingers off and went back to the equipment storage locker that was built onto the dock along with the housing for the air compressor to fill the tanks. She removed two of the tanks and checked their pressure then jumped on board the boat to go and get into her swimsuit.

By the time she finished and came back out, Kerry was there, checking her mask. She joined her and they geared up in companionable silence, pulling on full wetsuits and in Kerry's case, a hood.

"Polar bear." Dar settled the back of the hood under her suit, and zipped it up. "For someone from the frozen north you sure put on a lot of rubber."

"Pfft." Kerry stretched her arms out to settle the neoprene. "I haven't spent half my life in the ocean, Dardar." She sat down and got her arms into her BCD, clipping everything up and fastening her camera in its case to one of the D rings. "Especially not in the middle of winter."

Dar stood up in her minimalist rig and tightened the straps, then picked up her fins and walked to the end of the pier, regarding the water. She reached over and flipped the underwater lights on the structure, then held on with one hand and put her fins on with the other. "Let me go check things out first."

"Yes, grandma." Kerry smiled, though, and continued to rub no fog on her mask.

Dar inserted her regulator, put her hand over that and her mask, and stepped off the dock, landing in the water with a healthy splash.

The depth off the end was about fifteen feet. Dar went down about half of that before she leveled out and relaxed, floating in mid water as she adjusted the fit of the gear and tightened everything down. The lights outlined the rough coral formations just off shore. Startled and bewildered fish were flitting around, not expecting the return of the sun quite so soon.

It was nice, with very little current and relatively clear. Dar inflated her vest and went to the surface, sticking her hand up and giving Kerry an okay sign.

Kerry was seated on the edge of the dock in her gear kicking her fins. Seeing the sign, she leaned forward and just tumbled into the water with a less spectacular splash, sinking down to join Dar as she dipped again below the surface.

The water was cool and it penetrated her wetsuit quickly, but just as quickly it warmed to her body and she relaxed as she felt the chill fade. The lights under the dock made the bottom as visible as daylight would have and she adjusted her gear and followed Dar as she moved over to the end point of their part of the beach.

They slowly searched the bottom, drifting along side by side as Dar gently fanned the sand with her fingers.

Kerry didn't expect to find anything. She'd already written off the baubles, marking it down to something she'd know better about the next time, so though she dutifully peered in all the crevices and used her hand light to inspect the holes in the coral, her enjoyment was mostly based on spending time at one of her favorite hobbies with her very favorite person.

So it was fun for her to spend as much time watching Dar as she was hunting. She unclipped the camera on her shoulder and spent a few minutes taking pictures, getting shots of the coral in this unusual light before she casually swung the lens at Dar.

Dar had divined her intention and was now lying on her side at the bottom on a sandy area, body fully extended, hand propping up her head.

Oh, nice. Kerry cheerfully shot the pose, getting a nice stream of tiny bubbles trickling up from the regulator in Dar's mouth. Then Dar cooperatively gave her another shot, by taking the regulator out and sticking her tongue out of her mouth as far as it could go.

Kerry managed to capture it, then she started laughing, bubbles emerging from her own gear in thunderous spurts.

Dar grinned and replaced the mouthpiece, then elevated off the ground and started hunting again.

They were now directly under the pier where once upon a time Dar had gotten bitten by a fish. The illumination beyond it was broken up by the large shadow cast by the Dixie.

Dar pointed as she spotted a lobster darting across the coral, hurrying out of sight as they cruised over it. Dar put on a burst of speed and stretched one long arm out, getting a hold of the creature mid shell.

Its tail flicked rapidly, but Dar's grip proved its match and she stuffed the animal in a mesh bag clipped to her BCD.

Lobster linguine for dinner, Kerry reckoned. She was about to swing around and go back under the pier when a flash caught her eye and she hovered, spotting something shiny from where the lobster had emerged. She dove down and got her hand flash out, flicking it over the rocks and finding the item.

Hot damn. Kerry was truly surprised. She felt Dar come over the top of her, and she pointed with her light at the sparkle, reaching down to capture it with her hand.

A spurt of surprise came out of Dar's regulator, a cloud of bubbles heading upward as Dar tilted her head to examine her find. Then she made a double okay sign and grinned visibly.

Kerry held both hands out in a motion of mock modesty and put the earrings, which were tangled together, and stayed that way, safely into the palm of one hand and closed her fist around them.

Dar pointed her thumb upward and raised her eyebrows.

Kerry nodded and they started up for the surface when they both paused, hearing boat engines nearby. Engines that didn't move past, but circled in an idling motion complete with a sudden, powerful beam of light that pierced the already halon lit depths.

Dar sighed visibly and moved closer to the pylon, clipping her lobster bag to a ring before she breached the surface of the water.

Perfection, it seemed, was too much to ask for.

DAR PULLED HER mask off as she climbed up the dive ladder onto the pier, spotting the Coast Guard cutter idling offshore. She took the time to go sit on the gearing bench and unclip her BCD, putting her fins down and standing up in her wetsuit and booties.

She ran her fingers through her wet hair and walked to the end of her dock, putting her hand on the last pylon as the searchlight swung over and, to her mind since she was fully lit by the dock lights, unnecessarily blinded her.

She put her hand up to shield her eyes, opening up the radio box mounted near her hand and punching in the Coast Guard frequency. "Cutter offshore bayside MM 98, can I ask what your problem is?"

The search light cut off and now she saw figures on deck. The cutter swung around and motored over, as Dar heard Kerry divesting herself of her tank behind her. She put the radio handset back onto its holder and waited as the vessel eased closer.

"Did we do something wrong?" Kerry asked, handing Dar a dive jacket.

Dar shook her head. "No. Lobster's even in season. I just left it down there because I wasn't sure how long this was gonna take and I like mine fresh killed."

Kerry grimaced just slightly.

The cutter dropped a small rubber boat with two figures in it, and it roared over and came to the end of the dock. "You people have permission to be diving out here?" The taller of the two figures asked.

Dar glanced around then back at him. "I own the dock, the land, the cabin up there and this boat." She indicated the Dixie. "Who am I supposed to be asking for permission?"

The figure relaxed. "Okay, no problem. Can we come up?"

"Sure."

Kerry zipped up her jacket. "I'll go make some coffee and get out of all this wet rubber." She patted Dar on the butt and retreated down the pier, heading back to the cabin where dog barks were now loudly evident.

"Sorry about that," the Coast Guard officer said, as he got to the top of the ladder and stood up. "We've had reports of trespassing up and down this area and weren't sure what was going on." He held a hand out. "Lieutenant Davis. And you are?"

"Dar Roberts." Dar gave his hand a shake. "Sorry for the wet."

"We're used to it." The man smiled. "So were you folks doing work under there? We saw the lights."

Dar shook her head. "Just looking for something we lost the last trip," she said. "What kind of trespassing? We don't get down here a lot. I have an alarm, but there's always a way to get around that."

The Coast Guard lieutenant was already nodding before she stopped talking. "This area's got a lot of unlived in coastline just up north of here. Got people living wild, and after 9/11, we don't like that so much anymore."

"Ah."

"Not that everyone's dangerous, but you don't know, and we're not in a mode to take anyone for granted," he said. "Even nice ladies like you."

"Got it," Dar said. "Well, we've got some identification inside. Want to see that and have some coffee?" she asked. "The last thing we want is to have you guys think we're troublemakers."

The lieutenant and his petty officer attendant grinned and followed her to the cabin. "Can't be too cautious, right?" the lieutenant said. "Bet you make a better pot of coffee than our cook does."

Dar grinned wryly at the mild flirting and took it for the compliment it was. She led the way up the walk and opened the door, standing back for them to enter. "Careful of the dogs. They lick."

Kerry already had the coffee perking and was dressed in a pair of sweatpants and a hoodie, her wet hair brushed back to dry. She smiled as they entered and indicated the stools at the breakfast bar, which they took after unzipping their heavy sea jackets.

"I'm going to get out of this suit," Dar said. "Give them our ID, wouldja?"

"Sure." Kerry went over to the messenger bag she'd taken off the boat and rooted in it while their visitors fixed themselves some coffee. She removed their driver's licenses, and Dar's captain's license just in case, and brought them back over. "Here you go."

"That's good coffee," the lieutenant said. He took the IDs and studied them. Then he handed them back. "So this is a weekend place for you gals?"

Kerry took a cup for herself and leaned against the counter. "Something like that. We work and live up in the city. It's nice to get away from there sometimes."

"Where you live? That's not the city." The lieutenant smiled. "I've been to the Coast Guard functions out there."

"Close enough. We work in Coconut Grove." Kerry, however, lifted a hand and half shrugged in acknowledgement. "It's still way more laid back down here."

The petty officer hadn't said anything, but now he nodded in agreement. "My family's place is ten minutes down from here. I liked it growing up. Just long summer nights of cracking open coconuts and grabbing land crabs for dinner." He had the flat, not quite accent that some Miami natives did, and by the faint smile, the memory was a good one.

Kerry couldn't quite imagine doing that, though she knew Dar had. "It's nice here in Key Largo. I like the small town feel to it. I grew up in a fairly small place in Michigan."

"People here know you," the lieutenant said. "That's what we want to key into, if you catch my drift. We want people to tell us when things are out of place. Someone saw the lights on here and called us. Didn't know what was going on."

"We just had the lights put in a few months ago," Kerry said. "Sorry if it alarmed anyone. I didn't really think about it."

Dar emerged from the bedroom, pushing the long sleeves on her t-shirt up past her elbows. "So you're crowd sourcing info?" She came over and stood next to Kerry.

"Something like that," the lieutenant said. "We've only got a limited set of eyeballs. If people knew what to look for, they might have noticed things like those men getting pilot's licenses, you know?" he said. "So we're asking citizens in the area to keep their eyes open and let us know when they see something they think doesn't look right."

Dar nodded. "That could make people say things that might not be true about neighbors they just don't like," she said. "People can be assholes, that way."

"It's true. But the last time we had too little information. It's better to have too much. Well, thanks for the coffee, ladies. Sorry to have bothered your diving. I'll make a note in our logs that you checked out so if we get a call next time, we can let them know not to worry." He lifted a hand and he and the petty officer headed back to their ship.

"Huh." Kerry eyed Dar. "I get his point, but why do I feel like that's not a good thing?"

Dar took a sip of her coffee. "Calling the authorities on your neighbor because you think they may be a terrorist isn't a good thing, Ker."

"Unless they really are a terrorist."

Dar grunted, and nodded. "I'm going to go get our lobster. Got your earrings?"

Kerry pointed at the two items on the counter. "I can't believe we found them."

"Glad some fish didn't swallow 'em." Dar ambled out of the

kitchen. "Or maybe they did." She winked at Kerry as she opened the door. "And that's just where they got pooped out."

"Oh." Kerry regarded the two items. "Well, they can always be washed." She picked them up and went into the bedroom, pausing as she saw both dogs snoozing comfortably on their bed. Chino was curled up in a ball, and Mocha was tucked up next to her, his head resting on her elbow.

Aw. Kerry put the earrings down and picked up her camera instead, freshly released from its watertight case. She took several shots, then went back into the living room just as Dar entered with the lobster bag. "Pan fry it and toss it with linguine?" Kerry asked, getting a grin in response. "You get to kill it."

Amiably, Dar did, and about twenty minutes later they were seated on their couch with two very attentive dogs, sharing a plate of seafood pasta.

"You don't get any of this," Dar informed the watching dogs. "This spicy sauce will make you both sick to your stomachs." She put her feet up on the coffee table next to Kerry's. "This is awesome."

"Thank you, my dear." Kerry absorbed the compliment with a smile. "I'm always happy to try and make something yummy from your hunting and gathering."

Dar chuckled. "I'm going to finish this then see if I can work up a presentation for the feds."

Kerry turned her head and gently nibbled Dar's bare shoulder. "Really? Let's not start working on the weekends so fast, huh?"

"You have something else in mind?"

"Matter of fact I do." Kerry finished up a final bite of dinner and put the plate down on the table. "Starting with a hot shower to get the salt off and a tumble into our very comfortable bed."

They heard a clank and looked over to see Chino placidly licking out the plate, Mocha scrabbling with his paws to try and get at the edge of it.

"But first we rescue the crockery." Dar got up and swiped the plate. "Stop that you pirates." She straightened up and went into the kitchen, rinsing the dish off and putting it on the drain board as Kerry came in behind her, circling her with both arms and laying her head down on her back.

Dar turned around and returned the hug, absorbing the intensity of the affection almost radiating from her. "Kerry," she warbled softly. "You're the best."

"Not sure about that, but I am the luckiest." Kerry exhaled in contentment. "C'mon. I can taste the salt on you." She licked Dar's collarbone then released her and led the way to the shower.

The hot water and scrubby sponges felt good. Dar's sensual touch felt even better and in a well choreographed movement from the shower enclosure to the towel rack ended with both of them wrapped in a bath sheet, pressed together.

Steam from the shower, cool air from the cabin. Kerry felt like she was on something of a sensual overload as Dar's fingers laced behind her neck and she circled her waist with her arms and pulled her closer, savoring the emotional and physical charge as their bodies meshed.

Dar half turned and tried to move, but the towel was binding them. Half laughing she removed it and they got from the bathroom into the bed in a tangle of arms, legs and comforters.

The lights were dim and they had the windows open, allowing the fresh breeze and the sound of the sea to wash through the room, brushing over their bare bodies as they stretched out and started a leisurely exploration of each other.

Only to be interrupted by a wild yapping and an invasion of paws and tiny teeth, which nearly made them levitate off the bed. "Holy crap!" Dar yelped. "He bit my —"

Kerry started laughing, burying her face in Dar's shoulder as she got hold of Mocha and lifted him up and over her body.

"Stop that ya rug rat!" Dar tapped him on the head. "Who said you pups were allowed up here?"

Kerry, who was still laughing, rolled onto her back holding her stomach as Chino sniffed at her in puzzlement.

"What the hell is so damn funny?" Dar sat up and defended herself from the wildly tail wagging puppy. "Mocha, cut that out!" She picked up the animal and put him on the floor. "You too, madam!" She pointed at Chino. "Down!"

Chino obediently hopped off the bed and barked at Mocha, who was balancing on his hind legs trying to get back up.

Mocha fell over onto his back, with a yelp of surprise. Then he pounced on Chino's paw and started biting it.

Kerry was still laughing. She wiped the tears from her eyes and sat, bringing her legs up crossed under her as she leaned her elbows on her bare knees. "Sorry, hon." She put her hand on Dar's back. "I don't know why that struck me so damn funny but it did."

Dar sighed and got up as the dogs both raced out into the living room and went to stand by the back door, looking expectantly at her. "Want to have some warm milk and start this all over again?"

"Sure." Kerry got up out of the bed and pulled on a t-shirt, handing one over to Dar as she followed her out the door. "It's a little early for bed anyway and at least I'll get a chance for my hair to dry or I'll look like a Chia Pet in the morning."

Now Dar snickered. "Kerry the Chia Pet. I think I'm going to add that to Gopher Dar."

"Wench."

"I'll make it a hedgehog," Dar said, as she went to let the dogs out into the fenced area in the back that led towards the pier.

"Stay away from the water."

"A hedgehog?"

"Sure. They're adorable."

Kerry gave her a skeptical look. Then she turned and went into the first of the two offices in the cabin, turned on her PC and waited for it to boot. She brought up a browser and did a search for hedgehogs then bit off a grin and went back to the living room. "Okay." She joined Dar at the doorway. "You're right. They're really cute."

Dar affected a mock hurt look. "You didn't believe me?"

"I just had no idea what they looked like. They're cuter than gophers."

"As they should be since you're cuter than I am." Dar whistled softly. "C'mon guys."

Kerry circled Dar's body with her arms and leaned against her. Then she gave her a kiss on the shoulder and retreated back to the kitchen, getting out the fixings for some honey laced warm milk.

"I'm going to end up chasing that dog into the water," Dar said. "Mocha!"

Chino paused in the act of trotting back over to the door and barked at the puppy, who was snuffling at something on the beach. "Growf!"

"Whose idea was this?" Dar asked, sighing as she went down the steps to the sand.

"That would be yours, Dixiecup," Kerry said to her retreating back. "But I agreed to it, so I guess next time I get to chase down the little sucker."

She got the cups out and warmed them, then filled them with milk and popped them into the microwave, leaning on the counter while she waited for them to heat. The living room was a comfortable place, couches facing the windows so they could watch the sunset and a television mounted on the wall to one side.

They had cable here, but seldom watched it. They occasionally turned on the news, or, when it was that season, watched the hurricane coverage. Cabin time was mostly spent on the water, near the water, enjoying the town, riding the bike —

Dar's yell spurred her to come around the counter and head for the door, poking her head out. "What's up?"

Dar had Mocha under one arm and she was slogging through the sand heading back up to the cabin. "He was fighting with a damn land crab!"

Kerry stifled a laugh as Dar arrived at the porch. "Did he get hurt?"

"No, but the damn thing bit me when I tried to save it from him." Dar gave her an aggrieved look and displayed a lurid red mark across the knuckle of her index finger. "Ow!"

"Woow," Mocha let out a puppy yodel.

Kerry bit the inside of her lip to keep from laughing again. She leaned over and gave the spot a kiss. "Aw, my brave Dardar. You saved the puppy."

Dar came inside and put Mocha down. "Stupid crab." She went over to the sink and ran cold water over her finger. "It was guarding its hole," she said. "Mocha was trying to play with it."

Kerry eased around her and got the cups, adding some honey to them and mixing the liquid. "Well, he's a puppy," she said. "He's never seen a crab before. Or a beach, or most of anything else. Can you imagine what it must be like to be so new and not know what anything is?"

Mocha recovered from his crab battle and pattered over to the water dish, licking at it with somewhat erratic enthusiasm.

"No, actually I can't." Dar dried her hand off.

Kerry took her cup and went over to the couch. She sat down and stretched her legs out across the tile floor. "What do you think about an electric fireplace for the corner there?"

Dar took a seat next to her and sipped at her cup. "Sure. So long as we puppy proof it. We don't want to come back in to find our dog with no eyebrows."

"Point taken. I was listening to an infomercial the other morning and I saw these little fireplaces that are supposed to be handmade by Amish people."

Dar turned and looked at her. "You don't for one second actually believe that, do you?"

"No. I don't. But it gave me the idea of getting an actual one for here," Kerry said. "And hey, I completely forgot this, but I meant to tell you about it. I was walking around the back of the office building and I found a break in the bushes."

Dar remained silent, sipping her milk.

"It looked like something big was going in and out of there behind the hedges where that other property line is. I think maybe something or someone went through there."

"Behind the hedges?"

Kerry nodded.

"You think it was the homeless guys?"

Kerry shrugged. "I don't know. It just looked weird."

"Okay, let's have Marcus check it out next week. I'm pretty sure he doesn't want to have people living in his bushes." Dar eyed her. "So that's why you put those leftovers from the cart on that iron table in front." She saw the blush rise on Kerry's face. "You sneaky little bugger."

"Well, it was better than leaving them for the bugs inside," Kerry muttered. "The cleaning people had already been through."

Dar chuckled and draped her arm over Kerry's shoulders. "It's fine. It'd just end up in the garbage, and besides, I had them put all the server crates out in the back with the pallets, too."

"That's enough wood to make a Huck Finn raft." Kerry watched the stars outside twinkle. "You know, we're sitting here in this nice cabin and pretty much anything in the world we need taken care of, not to mention having each other, and..."

She paused, and shook her head.

"We're lucky people," Dar finished for her. "You and I."

"We are."

Mocha put his paws up on the couch and looked at them expectantly.

"And you're a lucky puppy." Kerry put her cup down and picked him up, putting him in her lap and scratching his ears. "He's so darn cute."

Chino jumped up on the couch on the other side of Dar and put her head down on her leg, letting out a long sigh.

"So what do you think about the little punk, Chi?" Dar asked, stroking her head. "You jealous of all the attention we're giving him?"

Chino's eyebrows twitched and she peered up at Dar soulfully.

"Don't worry." Dar smoothed the fur over her soft ears. "You're still our favorite girl." She smiled when Chino's tail thumped on the surface of the couch. "I'm sure you're gonna enjoy him a lot more when he gets a little older and stops chewing on you."

Mocha looked up from chewing Kerry's fingers.

"And you, too." Dar leaned over and gave her a kiss on the lips.

"Mm. Feel like I'm floating in a big vat of marshmallow goo." Kerry sighed. "Between those two pairs of Labrador eyes, and you kissing me, I almost expect to hear the theme from the Love Boat starting up any minute." She looked up to find one round, blue eye peering at her, the other obscured by Dar's hair. "Yes?"

"Is that a good or a bad thing?"

"Being completely surrounded by love? What do you think?"

Dar smiled. "So." She tickled Kerry's ear. "Valentine's Day."

"Mm?"

"Pack a bag for three days."

"Really." Kerry nibbled Dar's shoulder. "What do I pack?"

"Beads."

Kerry's eyebrows hiked. "Beads?"

"We have reservations in New Orleans for the last weekend of Mardi Gras. That okay with you?" Dar noted the look of delight on Kerry's face with satisfaction. "Good surprise?"

"Hell yes!" Kerry bounced up and down in her seat, making Mocha yelp and bat at her with his paws. "Oh my god, Dar! I've always wanted to go!" Her eyes lit up. "You are awesome!" She put the puppy down and threw her arms around Dar. "Eeeeee!"

Dar drained her cup and put it down, very pleased with the reaction to her plan. "Now." She turned and cupped Kerry's cheek, leaning over to kiss her. "Where were we?"

"In the bedroom." Kerry tugged her upright and gave her a nudge. "Go go go."

Chapter Two

MARK STUCK HIS head into Kerry's office. "We got phones," he said. "And let me tell ya, Mayte's rocking it as a PM." He entered carrying a desk phone and put it down on her desk. "She's got those guys controlled."

Kerry put her pen down and shifted her attention to her new phone. "Oh. Nice." She waited as Mark ran the cable down and plugged it into the second network jack under her desk. The phone lit up and started through its boot up process. "I'm glad Mayte's doing well."

"So, it's got a built in phone book." Mark perched on the desk and pressed the buttons. "And we're all in it. They got this module we can use to link it to email. So you can see who's online or not."

"Do we want to do that?" Kerry asked.

"We can play with it. Sure would be slicker than me using Pinger to see if you guys were here."

Kerry chuckled. "That's true. Okay, put it in. What the hell. If Dar doesn't like it she'll just hack into it and re-write it or something."

"Yup." Mark got off the desk. "So that's it. I'm running all the phones out on the carts. I got two guys maybe starting tomorrow so I can get back to some planning stuff again." He waved. "Later!"

"Thanks." Kerry amused herself for a few minutes punching the phone's buttons and looking up names. She hit the entry for Dar and heard the phone in the next office start to ring.

"Yes?" Dar's voice rumbled through the speaker. "Playing with your new toy, Kerrison?"

"Can I record you saying that and use it as my ringtone?" Kerry asked. "I'm getting into these ringtones."

Dar started laughing, audible both through the phone and through the open doorway. She hung up the line and a moment later appeared at Kerry's side, dropping onto the window bench that had become one of her favorite spots. "Like the phones," she said.

"Me too," Kerry said. "Did you get your travel all sorted out?"

"I did. Maria set up a deal where we get first class upgrades in return for ten hours of consulting time a week with a travel agent consortium she knew of."

"Hon, I wouldn't book you anything but first class anyway, even if I had to bake and sell cupcakes on Brickell every week to support that," Kerry said in a mild tone.

Dar smiled. "I know. But Maria did a great job with the negotiation, so as much as I love your cupcakes, we won't need them." She winked. "I'm off to my first programming team meeting. Wish me luck." She got up and cracked her knuckles, then wandered out.

"You need no luck, Paladar Katherine." Kerry chuckled to herself as she sorted out the listings of service offerings she was developing. "All you need are those brain cells and the baby blues. Everything else falls in place around you like metal filings around a magnet."

"Pardon?" Maria poked her head in. "Were you speaking to someone, Kerrisita?"

"Just myself." Kerry scribbled a note. "Great job on the travel account, Maria." She glanced up and smiled at the older woman, who danced in place and snapped her fingers. "That's exactly the kind of thing we need."

"You are very welcome," Maria said. "I am having such the good time here, Kerrisita, you have no idea." She continued her little dance out the door, salsaing away in her UGG boots and leaving Kerry with a big grin on her face.

"Now that's cool," she said, resting her hands on the desk.

Her new phone buzzed. "Huh. Already?" Kerry glanced at the device and pressed the answer button. "This is Kerry."

"Yes, ma'am," the receptionist downstairs said. "I have a visitor for you? He says he has an appointment, a Mr. Bott?"

Kerry checked her calendar. "Yes, please walk him up, Angelina, thanks." She released the button with a feeling of satisfaction, then reached for her cup of tea and sipped it, sitting quietly until she heard the sounds of approaching footsteps outside.

A soft knock came at her door. "C'mon in."

"Hello, Miss Kerry?" A doe eyed, dark haired girl opened the door cautiously. "Someone is here to see you."

"Thanks, Zoe," Kerry said, giving their new junior admin a smile. Maria's family friend had turned out to be a gentle, slight girl, as shy as Maria had said she was, with a look of perpetual astonishment on her face.

She had a slight speech impediment and she limped a little. Kerry noticed several reasons for her to be a little on the wallflower side. But she was sweet and very willing to learn. So far she'd done all right.

A man entered behind her and crossed the floor, extending his hand to Kerry as she stood to greet him. "Hello there."

"Mr. Bott? Thanks for coming over." Kerry indicated one of her visitor chairs, and she seated herself as he did. She studied him briefly. He was a little above average height, with curly brown hair and hazel eyes, and a tapered, athletic frame. "I appreciate it."

"No problem at all," he said. "Your message said you were looking for some security services. That right? How can I help you? My company doesn't do the traditional security guard kind of thing if that's what you're in the market for."

"I know," Kerry said. "I wasn't really looking for security guards." She got up and went to the door, closing it before she came back to her desk. "After all, it's not that big a building and we don't transact in cash."

He nodded, but remained silent.

"What we do is provide IT services." Kerry sat back down. "To some very average clients, like Dade Paper, and some not so average ones like the Federal Government."

"Ah." He nodded again.

"So I need some help in developing a security plan that will keep our intellectual property secure," Kerry said. "I need someone to strategize with us about how to put in place data security also."

Now Bott smiled. "Well good. Then I see you did your homework before you called me." His eyes twinkled a little. "Because that is what we do. So let me do my sales spiel and lay out what our services are and then we can decide if we can do business with each other."

Kerry nodded and leaned on her elbows. "Pitch me. Just one thing — don't put any software into the sales job. My partner won't allow any third party in here."

He paused and regarded her. "You write all your own?" He seemed surprised. "That's unusual, even for a tech company."

"That's unusual, especially for a tech company," Kerry said. "But that's how it is."

Bott shifted and hiked one knee up, resting his arm on it. "Fair enough. So let's start at the beginning with physical security."

"Let's."

DAR WAITED UNTIL the chatter died down and then regarded her little pack of programmers.

Mixed bag. Mostly young, though one of the most recent hires was an old timer, a grizzled gray software architect with a long history of project work. Mostly a little restless and outspoken, none of them so far afraid to voice an opinion.

All of that pleased Dar. She suspected the attitude was likely going to rub her the wrong way at times, and she also suspected she would need to earn her stripes with this new group, but she much preferred that to a bunch of earnest yes men.

Or women, as it were, since two of the coders were.

"Okay, folks," Dar said. "Let's get this going and keep it short."

The gang amiably settled down and focused on her.

Dar cleared her throat. "First off, welcome to the company. At this point, most often you'd be given a little rundown on the history and all that, but we don't have any history. The company started up a few weeks ago, so we have to kinda make it up as we go along."

She paused and everyone looked at her in silent attention. "Any questions about that?"

Mostly head shaking.

"Okay," Dar said, "our first project is going to be in two parts. One, a universal database, and two, an enterprise service bus that will feed into it from a variety of different systems." She paused. "The project is enterprise grade and has to handle a very high rate of throughput."

The programmers all exchanged glances. Most of them had started just that morning and were still getting settled into their cubes. One of the females held her hand up. "Which database are we using for that?"

"We're writing it from scratch," Dar responded with a faint smile. "But I have a base code for it."

Another one raised his hand. "And the ESB? Are we writing that from scratch, too?"

Dar nodded.

"Wow," he said. "Can I ask why?"

"Sure," Dar said. "Because the customers who come to us are looking for something that's very specific and designed for them. Not a product that's off-the-shelf components stitched together. And the other reason is some of our customers want one hundred percent assurance that every line of code is known."

"Like...for security?" the woman asked.

"Something like that, yes," Dar said. "Sometimes the contracts we sign require confidentiality. Sometimes you do it to make it a differentiator between us and our competitors."

"So another company can't come in and tell your client — hey we can do that, too, only cheaper," the older man spoke up. "Custom. I like that."

Dar grinned at him.

"Company I was at last, they did it the other way," he said. "Put together some off-the-shelf stuff, then sold it with a support package cheap enough to convince the customers they'd be saving a lot of money." He shook his head. "Didn't work out. Fifty percent of us got laid off after eight months."

Stan, was his name. Dar recalled. Stan Ruffelhouse, who had worked for one of ILS's competitors and probably had some small idea of who she was.

"Company was all about sales. What's the next sale? How can we sell more?" Stan said. "Never about keeping the customers, just getting new ones."

"Sales is like that," Dar said. "It's part of the culture."

"Here, too?" the woman spoke up. "You need sales, right?"

Dar paused and considered a moment before she answered. "Right now, Celeste, we don't have a sales department. To be honest, I never got along with sales in my prior job. But you do need to put your products out there if you expect your company to grow. So we will have one, but I'll have to figure out how to do that."

"If you...I mean, we, don't have a sales department how'd we get a project?" Stan asked.

"Long story," Dar said. "But that's why we don't have a sales department yet. I've got enough projects lined up to keep us busy until that all gets sorted out."

The door bumped open and Chino wriggled into the room, trotting over to Dar and nosing her knee.

"Hey, Chino. You coming in to hear my lecture, too?"

The Lab wagged her tail, going over to the corner and settling down into a ball there.

"That's a nice dog," Celeste said. "It's cool you bring her here. Can we bring animals, too?"

Dar leaned on the back of her chair. "I love animals," she said. "But if your animals are going to take up more time to watch after, or chase after, or keep from fighting than your work does, we've got a problem."

Celeste smiled and lifted her hands. "Point," she acknowledged. "I was thinking more like a small fish tank."

"Fish are fine. I have some in my office," Dar said, taking her seat again. "Since that came up, let's talk about work hours." She leaned her elbows on the table and tapped the wood lightly. "I expect people to be productive." She let her eyes track to each new face. "So you'll all have delivery dates and product schedules."

They nodded in understanding.

"Generally speaking, the doors'll be open from seven or eight a.m. to seven or eight p.m.," Dar said. "So figure out how you can get your work done in the hours we're open. Everyone understand me?" she asked. "Not everyone's a morning person. As we continue to build the company the hours will change and get later, depending on support groups."

Slowly, faces creased into smiles.

"Don't work from home, though," Dar said, after a pause. "One, we don't want the code out of the building, and two...." She felt her lips twitch. "You should have a life outside work."

Stan leaned back in his chair with a satisfied expression. "And if we like being early birds?"

"Have at it," Dar said. "I am."

"Good," he said. "So lemme ask you. All this about security and all that. Who's the customer? For this project, I mean?"

"Department of Defense," Dar said in a mild tone. "You probably guessed that from the security clearance requirement."

"Wow," Celeste murmured.

"But we have other customers that are a lot more mundane," Dar said. "So don't worry about it."

She waited for more comments, but there were none. "So, here's how it's going to work. We'll start on the database. The raw code is already in the repository, and I'll be posting a structure plan there on what needs to be coded to work. Everyone will check out an assigned section, code it, then check it back in."

She studied the group. "Any questions about that?" She paused and then went to the white board, picking up a marker. "Let's go over the basic data structure so you'll have an idea of what we're aiming at."

KERRY RELAXED IN the outdoor chair, one of several they'd bought and put into the central garden area. She kept one eye on Mocha's scampering while she waited for Dar to arrive, enjoying the sunlight as it counteracted the cool breeze.

A lot nicer than going down to the cafeteria. It felt like she was taking time out in the middle of the day, and the outdoor space felt relaxed and private. She did suspect it would lose some of its appeal once the weather turned hot.

But for now it was lovely. She let her hand rest on her denim clad knee and took a deep breath, exhaling as she heard a set of distinctive footsteps heading toward her from the back alley. She tilted her head and looked, spotting Dar strolling across the grass with Chino in tow.

Mocha spotted them and raced over, yapping excitedly as he reached Dar and went in circles for a minute, then fell down.

Kerry chuckled as she watched Dar carefully step over Mocha, her hands full of paper bags that held their lunch. "Hey, hon."

"Hi." Dar put the bags down on the stone table nearby and took the seat next to Kerry. "How'd your meeting go?"

"Pretty good," Kerry said. "I think I want to interview a few more companies, though, before doing a contract. This guy talked a good game, but there were a couple things he said that made me wonder." She folded her hands over her stomach. "I have two people from county government coming over this afternoon about a traffic light synchronization program. Can we do that?"

"Sure." Dar fished around in the bags and pulled out a sandwich, handing it over. "But are you telling me those lights I always suspected were completely roll of the dice random really were?"

"Apparently."

"Nice." Dar removed her own sandwich and sat back, extending her legs and crossing them at the ankles. "Mark tells me we need to get a few help desk people on board already," she said. "So I have the HR team looking for them. I figure we can put them in that small office next to the server room."

"Did his new assistant start?"

"Yeah," Dar said. "I saw him running cables in the programmer's cave. Nerdy little guy."

"Oh, he'll be out of place here." Kerry took a bite of her curry chicken salad and enjoyed the crisp bite of granny smith apple in it. "How's your skateboarder doing? I saw him bringing in his iguana this morning."

"He's doing all right," Dar said. "This is his first job. He's never had to code on a schedule before. I've got him doing small code sections and then running tests on them."

"And he's writing a game?" Kerry seemed bemused at this.

Dar waggled her hand. "It's more of a gaming system," she said. "It's a framework you can use to underlay different kinds of games. Once he's got to a certain point, I'll write a controller console for it and we'll see if we can get some game people on board to market it."

Kerry chewed thoughtfully. "That wasn't something I saw us branching out to," she admitted. "I never even saw you play a video game."

Dar's face creased into a brief grin. "I did in my younger years. Just ask Mark." She offered a bit of her sandwich to Chino and immediately got a very attentive puppy clawing at her kneecap. "I'm not sure we want to go into the games themselves, but the system could be interesting."

"Okay, so. I got an email earlier from the local small business group. They've got a convention next week. They know it's short notice but were wondering if we want to participate? I guess someone gave them our names," Kerry said. "I've got the booth prices on my desk, they're not bad."

Dar looked thoughtful. "We ready to go public like that?" she asked. "I wouldn't mind going, but I don't know that I want to put a booth up."

"Really?"

She shook her head. "Booth makes you one of many," she said. "Give them a call, see if they've got any panels or talking opportunities. Look for a place where we can stand out and shine."

Kerry stopped chewing and regarded her. She swallowed and washed down her mouthful with a sip of the bottled tea Dar had brought her. "Y'know, you still manage to surprise me sometimes," she said, seeing the wry twinkle in Dar's eyes. "This is going to sound ridiculous, but sometimes I forget who I'm married to."

Dar chuckled. "That's because you're used to me sending a gopher to torment you and singing in your ear." She looked pleased with the compliment anyway. "All jokes aside, if you get me an opportunity to do a keynote or something like that, it would work better for us."

"Absolutely, maestro," Kerry said. "I'll give them a call when I go back inside." She succumbed to the entreating green eyes at her knee and fished out a piece of chicken. "Only a little bit, you monster." She offered the piece to Mocha, who nibbled it.

They ate together in companionable silence for a few minutes. Then Dar got up and balled up her wrappings, putting them in the bag she'd brought. "I'll be upstairs building my presentations for Wednesday." She moved behind Kerry and leaned over, kissing the top of her head. "Later."

"Later." Kerry smiled, reaching behind her to pat Dar's leg as she moved off. She slowly finished her sandwich, sharing bits of it with her two attentive friends as she listened to the snatches of salsa music coming out of the windows.

That lasted all of five minutes, then another pair of footsteps approached her little haven and she looked up to see their landlord coming at her at a trot. "Hey, there."

"Hey there!" Marcus sat down in the seat Dar had so recently abandoned. "So, you asked me about the homeless guys around here, right?"

"Right."

"Are you having a lot of problems with them?" Marcus asked. "I know the cafe said they were causing some issues around here."

Kerry sipped her tea, watching his face. "To us? Well, it's just that they were fighting with the maintenance men and then with each other. I don't want the people who work for us to be nervous going in and out of the building. Especially in the evenings."

Marcus was already nodding. "I know." He looked uncomfortable. "It's just hard, if you know what I mean. I don't want to get a rep that I'm against vets, or anything."

"No one does," Kerry said. "Dar's from a military family. I'm just not sure what the deal is. People are having to deal with them being rude and yelling and all that. Even the cafe gals are nervous about walking to their cars at night. I'm not against vets. I'm just for civil behavior."

Marcus sighed. "See, those guys, there's like, six or eight of them, right? They grew up in the neighborhood and most of them went off into the service together. They were in my brother's high school class, in fact. So everyone around here knows them."

Kerry continued to sip her tea. "And? Does that give them a free pass to harass people?"

"Well." Marcus glanced around and then back at her. "Yeah, actually. People are sort of...they feel bad and they're sort of embarrassed, because their families kinda moved off when they went into the Army and left them no place to go."

Kerry blinked. "What?"

Marcus nodded. "It wasn't like a planned thing," he said. "I mean, it's not like they moved away and didn't tell them, but there were some houses and the shopping center bought them up, you know? The families all moved upstate."

"And they didn't want to go with them when they came back?" Kerry stared at him. "So they just stay here on the streets?"

"Yeah," he said. "Scott, that's the guy in the wheelchair, says this is his home. He's not going up to Melbourne. He hates it there. That's where the family moved to. His buddies call him Wheels. I think he kinda hates it."

Kerry was still a little stunned. "Yeah, I can see that. Like if they were calling him Stumpy or something. So isn't there something that can be done for them? The military can't do anything?"

Marcus shrugged. "I have no idea. Not my area of expertise. I think he likes living on the street, to be honest. He said he tried programs and things like that, but everyone there told him what to do and he doesn't want anyone to tell him what to do. He gets a check from the government and all that."

She remembered something Andrew had once told her, way back when, at the very beginning of their relationship and she nodded thoughtfully. "Well, so what are we supposed to do then? We tried talking to them. Told them to stay clear of the building."

Marcus's eyes widened. "You did?"

Kerry nodded. "I don't want to call the cops on them. I just don't want our staff to be uncomfortable leaving at night. I've got some younger women working for me that I don't want hassled."

Marcus looked thoughtful. "Let me talk to them. See what I can do. They don't usually listen to me, though, they think I'm a punk."

Kerry folded up her wrappings and put them in the bag Dar had left. "Marcus," she said. "Just between you and me? Try to get them to see reason. Dar's father is on a trip right now, but when he comes back, if they're still causing a problem he'll make them wish they hadn't."

"Okay," he said. "I'll try. Gotta keep my clients happy." He got up. "Wish me luck."

Kerry waved as he trudged off, looking apprehensive. "Good luck."

DAR ADJUSTED A frame on the screen, studied the result, then shifted it a bit with her mouse. She compiled and ran the little script she'd just finished and observed the motion on the monitor, nodding after a minute in satisfaction and saving the presentation.

It was dark outside and quiet in the office. She heard the soft rattling of Kerry's typing next door, and near the window curled up in the big dog bed, Chino was in a Labrador dream, paws twitching and faint grunting whines coming from her chest while Mocha was sprawled across her legs in blissful abandon.

The music system in the corner was playing a soft tune and she absently started singing along to it as she transferred the presentation from her desktop system to her laptop, starting the program up to make sure it would run correctly on the new machine.

While it was moving through its assembled bits, she took out the hard copy of her proposal and thumbed through it, scanning over the pages to make sure she didn't misspell anything and that the sections were in the right places. With a nod of approval she closed the folder and put it in her backpack.

She heard the faint sound of the zipper on Kerry's soft sided briefcase, shut down the laptop and got ready to leave.

Outside she heard the wind in the trees, and now that the building was empty there were shifts and creaks in the walls and floors that belied the age of the building. She glanced out the window and saw the branches bending, indicating the storm that the weather channel predicted had, in fact, arrived.

"Glad we brought our jackets," Kerry said, shrugging into hers as she came to stand in the doorway between their offices. "Nasty out there."

"So I see." Dar slid her laptop into the backpack. "Oh well. Even Miami has to have winter storms sometimes." She got into her own jacket and shouldered the pack. "Let's go home."

They got the dog leashes arranged and walked down the steps, snapping off lights as they went. Kerry walked over and armed the building alarm, giving a nod as she keyed it.

Dar opened the front door, hearing the long beep as they went through and she locked it behind them. "You think we'll be twenty-four-seven at some point, Ker?"

"Depends," Kerry answered as they walked down the path to the parking lot. "Do we in source a NOC and support desk, or outsource it? How many accounts do we need to make it economical to keep it in house? I know you don't like outsourcing."

"Never did," Dar said. "No one cares as much about your business as you do."

"And yet we were the outsource for so many support areas."

Dar smiled. "I was arrogant enough to tell customers that we did care more about their business than they did. And in some cases, that was true."

"We were different."

"That's what I told myself," Dar said. "And you know, if you're not a technology company, there's a point to paying a technology company to do your technology for you."

"True." Kerry opened the back door to her car and put her case inside. "But we are a technology company so...c'mon, Chi, up you go."

"So it probably behooves us to watch our own stuff," Dar said, sliding into the passenger seat and setting Mocha on her lap. "But not just yet. Let's wait 'til we deliver some product first." She settled back and glanced out the front windshield of the Lexus. "Ah."

Kerry closed her door and looked up, following Dar's gaze. "Ah," she echoed. A group of figures were huddled near the street lamp. "Well at least they aren't fighting." She started the engine and flicked the lights on. "Nasty night to be out, huh?"

"Mm." Dar studied the ragged looking group. Two of them turned and looked at the car, then turned back around and put their back to the light. After a moment they all turned and walked down the path between their building and the next, quickly disappearing past the hedges. "Did you tell me you saw a break in the leaves around back there?"

Kerry nodded, resting her hands on the steering wheel. "You think they're hiding in the trees back by that other building?"

"Maybe," Dar said. "There's enough space there for a shelter, sort of."

Kerry drummed her fingers. "What do we do about that?"

"They're not hurting anything being back there, are they?" Dar asked as Kerry shifted the SUV into gear.

"Maybe we can talk to our security vendor about it once we have one," Kerry said. "Changing your mind about having guards in the building?"

"Mm." Dar propped her elbow against the window and resting her head against her fist. "I don't know, Ker. I can secure the data, that's not a problem."

Kerry left off the questioning and concentrated on driving instead. She wasn't in the mood to start a disagreement with Dar, and she sensed they were on sort of different sides on the question. "We'll work it out," she said after a brief silence.

"I'm sure we will." Dar wriggled into a more comfortable position. "Feel like Italian tonight?"

Did she? Kerry pondered the idea as she headed east along the causeway toward the ferry base. "Yeah," she said. "Seafood pasta maybe and a salad. It's kinda late to start cooking."

"Meatballs," Dar rumbled, going nose-to-nose with Mocha. "You want meatballs, Mocha?"

"Yap!"

"Growf." Chino poked her head between the seats, as they pulled onto the ferry.

"See what you started?" Kerry put the car in park and relaxed. "Now you have to cough up the meatballs, darling."

"We can order them some."

"Spoiled dogs."

"Along with ice cream for me," Dar said.

"Spoiled human."

TWO DAYS LATER Kerry pulled into the parking lot early, after letting Dar off at the airport. She got her laptop case and closed the door behind her, having left the two dogs in the condo since she lacked enough hands to wrangle them without Dar's help.

It was very quiet. She unlocked the door then slipped quickly inside to turn off the alarm, kicking the front door closed behind her as she went past. The receptionist wasn't due in for another half hour, and she hesitated, then left the alarm off as she went up the steps to her office.

It felt strange to be in the place all alone. Kerry shrugged off her sometimes admittedly overactive imagination and dropped off her laptop bag, then went to the little kitchen on the second floor to put some water on to heat.

She was aware of the silence around her and wished she'd brought at least Chino along to keep her company. The Labrador wasn't a watch dog, but she was big and had a loud bark. "Am I getting paranoid?" she asked aloud, putting a teabag in her cup and pouring the hot water over it. "I hope not."

She carried the cup back to her office and put it down, pausing to start up her PC before she sat. She took a sip of the tea, then paused when she heard the door downstairs open and close.

Her heartbeat picked up. She got up, pulled her cell phone from her pocket and walked to the top of the stairs before calling out. "Hello?"

No answer. Kerry cursed silently at herself for leaving the door open and paused, trying to decide what to do. She retreated back into Mayte's space and quickly texted Dar a message, then went into her own office, locked the connecting door between her space and Dar's, and then went back into the outer room and stood in the entrance, giving her a view of the upper corridor and the stairs.

Her throat was dry and she felt her heartbeat speed up. She strained her ears to see if she could hear someone moving around below. Her device buzzed gently in her hand and she glanced down, thumbing open a message from Dar that said

```
Called the cops. Lock yourself in your office.
I'm getting a cab.
```

"Oh, Dar, no." Kerry started to dial then stopped when she heard a creak on the stairs. She hesitated, caught between wanting to see who it was and being afraid it was someone she didn't want to see.

Macha overrode common sense and she abruptly walked forward and went to the top of the stairs, bracing her legs at shoulder length apart and looking down. "Hey!"

The figure walking up stopped and stared at her. He was a man of medium height, with a muscular body and short, almost crewcut brown hair. He was dressed in old, faded camouflage pants and a black shirt, and there was an expression she could only describe as insolent on his face.

Okay, so now she was glad Dar had called the cops. "You're trespassing," she said.

He spread his arms out to either banister. "You the bitch who told that fag to tell my friends to stay away from this place?" He had a deep, husky voice. "Are ya?"

Kerry kept her voice even with a good deal of effort. "Yes," she said. "I told our landlord we don't want people fighting outside the door."

He started climbing up toward her again. "I don't appreciate that."

"I don't actually care," Kerry shot back. "You're not above the law any more than the rest of your friends are."

He stopped again about three steps down from her. "You call the cops?"

"Yes," Kerry said.

"I didn't hear anyone call the cops." He stepped up one more step toward her. "Bitch."

"That's not my problem, asshole." Kerry wasn't entirely sure where all the faux courage was coming from, but at least her voice wasn't shaking and her knees were holding her up so far. "You've got no business being in this building. You're trespassing and the cops are on the way to haul your ugly ass out of here."

He stared her in the eye. Kerry stared right back, hoping like hell her legs would both continue to hold her up and obey her if she had to do something crazy like defend herself.

She had the skill to do that, a little. Her mind knew what to do, or at least, she hoped it did.

He stepped up one more step and his head was even with hers. "You've got more guts than sense, you know that?" he asked. "I could rape you blind before those fat fucks at the doughnut shop could get here."

"You can try," Kerry replied in a quiet voice, barely hearing her words over the thundering of her own heartbeat. She felt the fear winding up in her and it was hard to keep her breathing even.

Then the door slammed open and a moment later Mark's voice was yelling out a wordless warning, as he came barreling into the office on his way toward them.

The stranger stepped back and held his hands up. "All right, take it easy buddy."

"Take it easy?" Kerry suddenly felt her fear turn to outrage. "You come in here and say you're going to rape me and you want us to take it easy?"

"Get the fuck out of here!" Mark yelled, at the same time. "Who the fuck do you think you are coming in here, jackass!" He had just taken his motorcycle helmet off and was swinging it from one hand, coming up the steps like a homicidal care bear.

The door opened again and a breathless Mayte and Maria half walked, half ran in. "Merde!" Maria yelled. "What is this? I will get the police! Mayte! Get the baseball hat and go there!"

The intruder kept his hands up and slowly slid down to sit on the stairs. "Okay, people," he said. "Don't get all civ crazy on me. I'm not going to do anything."

Kerry relaxed as Mark scrambled up to stand in front of her, looking as dangerous as a thirty something nerd could. "Thanks, Mark." She patted his shoulder. "Glad you came in early."

"Early hell!" Mark said, catching his breath. "Dar called me. I broke like twenty red lights getting here. The damn cops are probably going to chase my ass right through that door."

Mayte climbed up the steps and was now standing next to Mark, and they all turned to stare at the intruder. He was sitting quietly, his hands on his knees, looking from one of them to the other.

Kerry put her hands on her hips. "You're messing with the wrong people, buddy," she said. "We don't intimidate easily."

"Yeah I get that," the man said. "I thought you were just a bunch of nerds."

"We are," Mark said. "So you shouldn't mess with us. We can do shit like send your food stamps to Tibet."

The man's eyebrows hiked up. "Shut up."

"We can. And you should be glad we showed up before her SO did," Mark said, pointing at Kerry.

The door opened yet again and Maria re-appeared with two policemen behind her. "There!" She pointed. "That is him."

The intruder sighed. "Fuck."

"You?" The first policeman headed up the stairs, hauling a pair of handcuffs from his belt. "You stupid son of a bitch. We told you to keep your nose clean."

"I'm just trying to protect my guys," the intruder said in an angry tone. "Why can't you all just leave us the fuck alone? Why do you all have to be such assholes?"

The policeman grabbed him by the arm and pulled him upright. "Because we have to enforce the law, inconvenient as it is for you. So your 'guys' can't just do what they want and you can't just go into offices and threaten people." He yanked the man down the steps. "Sorry about this bubba, folks," he said. "We'll take him down and get him out of your hair." He glanced at Kerry. "You want to press charges?"

"Absolutely," Kerry said. "Especially since he threatened to rape me."

The cop glared at the intruder in disgust.

"I was just trying to scare her!" the man yelled. "I wasn't gonna touch her! I could have already done it if I wanted to long as it took you to get here. Might as well have since—" He stopped as the cops and his progress was halted by Dar entering and coming to a halt right in front of them.

"Excuse us, ma'am," the second cop said, reaching around Dar to grab hold of the intruder. "We're just getting this guy out of here."

For a moment Dar didn't budge. She stared hard at the intruder, who met her eyes for a second, then looked away. "Thanks," she said in a clipped tone. "I'd like to make sure he doesn't come back so whatever you need from us, we'll do it."

The cop nodded. "Yes, ma'am. We'll put him in the car, then we'll be back to take some statements." He maneuvered the now silent intruder out the door, his partner following him.

Dar exhaled. Then she trudged up the steps, clapping Mark on the shoulder as she came even with him. "Thanks." She half turned.

"Thanks Mayte and Maria, too."

"Anytime, boss." Mark wiped the sweat from his forehead. "What a way to start the morning."

Dar reached Kerry and opened her arms, enfolding her in a hug as she bumped her backwards off the stair verge. "I'll book a later flight," she said as Kerry leaned against her. "Son of a bitch."

"Dar, I will take care of that for you." Maria patted her arm and slipped past into her office.

"Ugh." Kerry finally took a deep breath and released it. "My stupid fault. I left the door unlocked when I came in. I feel like such a jerk."

"Don't." Dar bumped her further back away from the stairs as the door opened and voices started echoing through the hall again. "But bet your ass we're going to have physical security here before the end of the god damned day," she said as they cleared the doorway into Kerry's office and she closed the door behind them.

Then Dar simply held onto her. "I think I'm going to throw up. You scared the shit out of me."

"Sorry." Kerry rubbed her side gently. "Dar, I'm so sorry." She felt the shivering in Dar's tall body and it brought on a flood of intense shame. "So sorry."

Dar took a breath and released it. "It's okay." She rocked them both back and forth a little. "I'm pretty sure I left some kind of security panic behind me at the airport." She sniffled a little. "I'd just gone through x-ray when I got your text."

Kerry winced. "Oh boy."

"Knocked over a bunch of TSA agents and the x-ray machine, and a line of stanchions," Dar said mournfully. "I bet I'm on some list now."

"Dar." Kerry rested her head against her collarbone.

"But you're okay," Dar said. "And believe me, that's all that matters to me right now."

A knock came at the door and they reluctantly parted. "Let's get the cops out of the way, then we can go tell HR to get us some big, beefy security guards," Dar said. "You were right about that."

"I'd much rather have been wrong," Kerry muttered as she went to the door and opened it. "Stupid jerk." She exhaled. "Hi, officers. C'mon in."

The cops came in and one of them took out a pad. "Sorry about that, ma'am. We've been having a lot of problems with these guys lately."

"Yeah, we've seen them around a lot," Kerry said. "Is that guy one of their old captains or something? He seemed to be responsible for them."

"That guy?" The cop snorted softly. "Lady, he's a priest."

Both Dar and Kerry swung around and stared at him in unabashed disbelief. "Uh...what?" Kerry managed to get out. "That guy?"

"Well, he's a chaplain, from the service or something," the cop said.

"That's what he says anyway. He was over in the Middle East with them, and I guess he's working at the halfway house down the road trying to get them some help or something."

"I think he's the one who needs help," Dar said. "Is he nuts?"

The cop shrugged. "Hard to say. You know, those guys had to deal with a bunch of stuff over there, not real nice stuff. My brother went through that. It's tough. They come back and no one gives a damn, you know?"

"My father's retired Navy."

"So you get it," the cop said. "They did service, then they come back and no one wants to help them out."

"No, I don't get it," Kerry said. "It's no justification for him coming in here and threatening to rape me." She had gathered some of her wits around her. "So we are going to press charges."

The cop was making notes. "We can probably get a restraining order to keep him away from here," he said. "Thing is, these guys feel like they're owed." He sighed. "So, let's hear what happened."

Kerry went to her desk and sat down. "Sure." She folded her hands as Dar took a perch on the windowsill behind her. "I came in early...around seven. I opened the front door and came inside, and about...I guess ten minutes after that I heard the front door open and close."

"Uh huh."

"So I went to the stairs and called out. I thought our receptionist had come in a little early, or one of the other staff, but no one answered."

"Right."

"So a couple minutes after that, I heard someone on the stairs. I went to the top there and found this guy coming up toward me."

The cop regarded her. "It occur to you to lock yourself inside the office?" he said. "And call 911?"

"Actually, not really, no," Kerry said. "I did close up the back door so there was only one way into the office here. But then I saw him and he started threatening me."

"So you called the police," the cop said.

"I called the police," Dar interjected quietly.

The cop looked over at her. "You were here at the time?"

"No. I was at the airport."

The cop blinked at her in confusion.

"I texted her when I heard that sound downstairs," Kerry said. "And Dar sent the cavalry. He just stayed on the stairs yelling at me and saying he was going to hurt me until Mark showed up and then everyone else did, too."

"Uh huh." The cop nodded. "So we got this guy in the car, and we're going to take him down to the station. His story is, he was just trying to scare you off from complaining about his buddies." He studied

Kerry's pale face. "He said that they should be able to go on the sidewalk if they want to, you know?"

"They can walk all over the sidewalk," Dar said. "We objected to them fighting with each other on our doorstep. Not to mention rummaging in our garbage, and giving the maintenance guys a hard time when they complain about the mess they're making."

The cop nodded and his partner nodded as well. "Yeah, okay. I know they do that a lot. We'll see what we can do about it," he said. "For the record I don't think he'd have hurt you. I've known these guys for a few months." He glanced at Kerry. "And besides, he said the scaring didn't work. Thinks you have brass ones, no offense."

"Well," Kerry said. "I've met my share of assholes. But if it was one of our staff, it would have been different, and I'm not going to subject them to that. They have a right to come to work and not worry about that."

The cop nodded again. "Fair enough. We'll be in touch." He lifted a hand in goodbye, and he and his partner left Kerry's office, closing the door behind them.

Kerry sighed, and turned to look at Dar. Then she got up and went to perch on the sill next to her. "Big beefy guards, huh?"

"A dozen of them. One of them right outside your door." Dar wiped her hands off on her jeans. "Jerks."

Kerry rested her head against Dar's shoulder. "Next time I'll lock the damn door."

"OKAY, LET'S TRY this again," Dar said, as they pulled up to the airport for the second time that morning. "Do me a favor?"

"Anything." Kerry put the car into park. "Have I said how sorry I am about being so dumb?"

"A dozen times." Dar leaned on the console between the seats. "Please don't be the last one out tonight." She studied Kerry's face. "Please?"

"Okay." Kerry put her hand on Dar's cheek. "I promise."

Dar covered her hand and then gently kissed it. Then she released her and got out of the car. "Let me go talk to someone in security. Hopefully they won't try to arrest me." She put her hands on the door frame. "See you tomorrow."

"Call me when you get there," Kerry said. "And good luck, hon. Though I don't think you need it."

Dar smiled briefly and reluctantly turned her back on the car and trudged into the entrance of the airport.

Kerry sighed and watched her disappear, then she put the SUV into drive and maneuvered her way out of the drop off area and onto the exit road. She was still somewhat sick to her stomach from the morning's events and she took a sip of water from her water bottle as she eased into traffic, trying to settle herself.

She was glad Dar was only going to Washington overnight. She already missed the convenience of the private jet they'd enjoyed and she pondered the possibility of managing their own in the relatively near future.

Less stress, less trouble with security, flying on their own schedule. Huge benefits. The only issue being the cost. Well, if they got some decent business, maybe it would work out financially.

She settled back in the seat and headed back to the office. The highway was busy, but not packed, and she turned on the radio as she headed for the exit, her mind going back to her scary morning experience.

No doubt it had shaken her. Shaken Dar, who had gotten into that truculent gruff mood she tended to when she'd taken a scare. Dar finally agreed that they could wait until after Kerry finished her review of security companies to engage the security group, but not before she extracted a promise from Kerry that she would be cautious and not go walking around outside without taking someone with her.

Dar would have much preferred to have stayed around, or taken Kerry with her, but they both had jobs to do and after all, it was only one day.

Yeah. Kerry sighed as she pulled into the office parking lot. Just one day. She got out of the SUV and locked it, stuffing her keys in her front jeans pocket before she started up the path heading to the door.

The door opened and Mayte trotted out to join her and walk her up the path. "Hey," Kerry said. "My afternoon appointments here?"

"The first one, yes," Mayte said. "They just arrived. I have put them in the conference room."

"Thanks."

"The police also have called," Mayte continued. "There will be one to see you here later."

"Okay." Kerry pushed the door open and paused. "Let me go get my portfolio." She started up the steps. "Is the coffee service in there?"

"Yes," Mayte said. "I will go and offer them some."

Kerry went into her office and to her desk, hoping Dar was having a much smoother afternoon herself.

Chapter Three

DAR LEANED AGAINST the counter, waiting for the flight to be called. She'd gotten through security with only a small bit of trouble, deciding to try using her charm instead of her kick ass for a change and getting a light scolding from the airport security supervisor.

Now she just wanted to get on the flight and get the trip over with.

Her phone buzzed and she stepped away from the desk. She pulled it out and glanced at it. "Hello?"

"Hello there, Dar."

"Hey, Gerry," Dar said. "I missed my flight, about to board a second."

"No worries," Gerry said. "Just wanted to give you a heads up. Heard from the boys up the road that the president wants to meet you. Tonight, after your pow wow."

Dar's eyebrow shot up. "Me?"

"Yes, lady, you." He sounded pleased. "Didn't want you to be shocked out of your knickers, don't you know. I'll let you be then, have a good flight."

"Gerry —"

"Bye, Dar. See you in a few."

Dar stared at the phone after it went dead. "I don't want to meet the president," she said. "I'm going to end up insulting his ass and they'll throw me in jail."

"Ma'am?" The check in agent behind the desk leaned toward her. "Did you need something?"

Dar sighed "No, sorry. Just talking to myself." She shifted over as the agent started announcing the boarding of the flight. She debated calling Kerry, then shrugged and dialed her number.

It rang twice, then was answered. "Hey, babe." Kerry's voice sounded wryly amused. "I made it up the sidewalk into the building. Mayte guarded me."

"Maybe she should come guard me," Dar said. "Gerry just called. Apparently the president wants to meet me."

Brief silence. "Oh." Kerry's mental track changing came across audibly. "Ew."

"Mm." Dar watched the agent step over to the ticket turnstile. "Anyway, I gotta go on the plane. Just thought I'd let you know what's waiting for me on the other side."

"Want me to have my mother show up to guard you?" Kerry asked. "Ker."

Kerry chuckled softly. "I thought you called to check up on me. We're full out nut cases, honey."

"We are." Dar smiled. "Okay, let me let you go." She shifted off the counter and got into line, handing over her boarding pass as the woman scanned it. "Thanks."

"Know something?" Kerry asked, as Dar walked down the jet way. "I really do wish I was going with you."

"I wish you were going with me," Dar said. "So let's get off the call before I run out of this airport for the second time and get gang tackled. They're not going to take my excuses twice."

"Bye, hon," Kerry said. "Call me later."

Dar put her gizmo in her pocket, entered the plane and slid into her seat in the front row after putting her backpack up into the overhead. She settled back and gazed out the window, watching the activity of the hard working people outside. She had a change of clothing in the pack, but it occurred to her that she'd be meeting the president in a pair of jeans.

Would that matter? Dar decided it probably wouldn't, and even if it did, she would convince herself she didn't care.

With that in mind, she pulled out her gizmo again and typed off a quick message to her parents in case it turned out to matter and she ended up somehow either on the news or in a tabloid paper.

You never knew. She sent the note then turned off the gizmo as the plane finished loading and the crew went to close the door. Dar glanced behind her, seeing a lot of empty seats, including the one next to her. She buckled her seatbelt, then leaned on the center console as the flight attendant came over.

"Hi. Can I get you something to drink before we take off?" The woman asked.

"Orange juice if you have it," Dar said. "Pretty empty, huh?"

The woman glanced back and shook her head. "People still don't like flying," she said, somewhat sadly. "Much as I hate working overbooked flights, this is just scary," she said. "How can they keep going, you know?"

"I think people will start traveling again," Dar said. "It'll just take some time."

The flight attendant smiled briefly. "I sure hope so." She left to get Dar's orange juice as the plane gently backed away from the jet way and the safety video started to play.

Dar settled back into her seat and removed the copy of Skymall from the pocket, leafing through it as the plane taxied. She studied the several varieties of dog beds, wondering if Chino and Mocha would like one for their garden.

Then she had to pause, and enjoy a moment of self-deprecating humor at the thought that she was sitting here shopping for pet beds and pewter giraffe toilet paper holders. What was it Alastair had said once? That she'd become a good family person?

Wacky.

Nevertheless, she kept browsing, spotting several more items she could envision invading their collective personal spaces. She paused on one page, considering, as the plane started its takeoff run. Garden gnomes. Did they need a garden gnome? What about one that recycled drinking water for a dog dish?

Her mind imagined Chino drinking from it, then the image morphed to Mocha sitting in the bowl with water pouring over his head. "Maybe not." She flipped the page, then tucked the magazine aside as the plane took off and headed skyward.

KERRY SCRIBBLED A set of notes, the last of several pages of them. "Okay, Charles, thanks," she said. "Wow, those are a lot of projects."

Charles Suarez, the man seated across from her nodded. "I know. There was a lot of pent up demand internally for these smaller projects that we don't have personnel bandwidth for and which the bigger guys had no real interest in working on." He looked apologetic. "No offense to your former employers."

"None taken." Kerry scratched her jaw with the edge of her pen. "I turned down smaller projects myself in my past role. There's a break-even point where you can recoup enough revenue to match the resources spent, and since all the groups were sized for enterprise, there wasn't much point in having them work on stuff like this." She indicated the pages. "But that's not the case here."

Charles smiled. "Exactly. My company had me contact you soon as we heard because our operations group liked working with you."

Kerry smiled back. "Thanks for that compliment," she said. "I'm glad you got to me early, though, I've had potential clients in here the last couple days with all kinds of requests. I'm a little surprised, given the economy."

"You shouldn't be," he said. "It's because of the economy. No one wants to take big risks, and everyone's looking to keep costs down. Engaging the big guys meant big costs, and engaging an unknown small firm meant big risks."

"Ah." Kerry tapped her pen on the desk. "I didn't think of that. We were always going to open our own business, it just wasn't the timing we'd anticipated. But here we are."

"Here you are," Charles said "So if you could quote all that, I'll take it to my leadership group and we can see if we can budget to get it done."

He stood up, and so did Kerry. They shook hands and Kerry stepped around her desk to walk him back over to the stairs. "I like some of the things you guys want to do with mobile communications." Kerry said. She removed her gizmo from her pocket and showed him. "I think these things are going to get popular."

"Is that the Handspring?" Charles asked, eagerly. "Can I see it?"

Kerry handed it over. "We've been testing them for the past couple of weeks. I really like it. It lets me mix text and mail with a phone, and I only have to carry one thing. I used to carry a cell phone and a PDA. This is better."

"You bet." Charles tapped on it. "Oh, I see there...are those programs?"

"Basic ones." Kerry took it back. "Dar has one on hers that tells her the tides and sea conditions."

Charles nodded. "That's what we think, too, that people are going to like having things like that. So we want some programs that let people with phones like that interact with us. We want to be able to send them notes about specials and have them text us back to hold one for them, or things like that," he said. "We're a specialty grocery, you know? It's all about local for us."

"I get it. I live out on Fisher Island," Kerry said. "We have that kind of personal relationship out there. You can call and talk to a butcher, whose name you know, and who knows you. It's sort of like recreating a small town thing."

"Exactly!" Charles said. "So these ideas, how to boost up local business, and not so much on a national level, is where our local management thinks we can take advantage of the consumer mindset right now."

Kerry saw him to the door and waved, then detoured into the conference room to get a cup of coffee. "Hey." She smiled at the cafe runner who was replenishing the cart. "Just in time."

The man smiled at her "Hey, Kerry. Heard you had a scare this morning. What a bunch of jacktards those guys are. Gary told them not to come around asking for leftovers if they were going to act like that." He offered her a small tray of neatly sliced pound cake. "Try the lemon. It's really good."

Kerry selected a slice and bit into it. "Oh." She swallowed hastily. "That is good. Really moist."

He nodded. "I don't like it when it's all dense and dried." He put the tray down and swapped out a hot thermos of coffee. "Your honey around? They sent over this chocolate chocolate chip muffin for her."

Kerry started laughing, perching on the conference room table. "Boy, it didn't take you long to zero in on her, did it? Dar's on her way to DC at the moment. She'll be back tomorrow." She took the muffin. "I'll try it for her. But yeah, this morning wasn't much fun. I have to take a lot of blame for it, though, I left the door open. Kinda dumb."

"It's a company. You had the right to," he said. "We leave ours open when we're in there. Guy had no right coming in here and messing with you. Especially that guy."

Kerry cocked her head. "Why? I heard from the police he's some kind of minister?"

The man handed her a cup of coffee. "That's what he says. From what I heard, he picked that position so he wouldn't have to get shot at but still get all the perks of being in the military." He wiped around the cart. "Anyway, gotta get back to the shop. Enjoy the muffin." He winked and took the old coffee thermos as he left her to ponder.

Kerry dropped into a seat and leaned back, breaking off a piece of the muffin and chewing it as she sipped. She checked her watch, then as if in response, her gizmo buzzed in her pocket. She put her coffee down and removed it, smiling when she saw the caller ID. "Hey."

"Hey." Dar's voice echoed softly, with the background of a busy airport behind her. "Heading to the Pentagon. How'd your meetings go?"

"Really well, and glad you got there all right," Kerry said. "Call me after you meet Dubya."

"Ah heh. Yeah," Dar said. "Later."

Kerry released the line and put the gizmo down on the table, a smile still on her face. "Hope someone takes a picture," she said. "Hey, wonder if that's going to be a publicity thing?" she asked aloud. "That would be crazy publicity."

She finished the muffin and dusted her fingers off, then picked up her coffee and returned to her office. "What a day," she said to Mayte as she crossed through the outer office. "I've got two more meetings, right?"

"Yes," Mayte said. "Florida Power and Light, and someone to see you from the Qwest."

"Ah, yes." Kerry went to her desk and circled it. "Someone who wants to sell me something rather than hire us." She checked her mail and opened one. "Ah."

Her security presenter from the previous day. She propped her chin on her fist and regarded the note, viewing it now from a slightly different perspective. There was something in her that resisted having security at the door, no matter how creepy this morning was. And, as she reminded Dar, despite what the man threatened he didn't do more than talk.

Just talk. Hot air.

Would he have done more? Kerry felt instinctively he wouldn't have, though she didn't have any solid reason why she did.

A soft knock came at the door and she looked up. "C'mon in."

It opened and Mark's head poked inside. "Hey."

Kerry motioned him forward. "Come. Did I say thank you to you for rushing in here to save me this morning?"

Mark chuckled and came inside, walking over and dropping into one of Kerry's visitor seats. "No problem about the ride in. Dar was pretty freaked out."

"I know."

"I got this guy who's a family friend," Mark said. "He's a

freelance security guard."

"Uh huh." Kerry let him talk it out, though she could plainly see where it was going.

"He's also an artist." Mark pushed his train onto an unexpected track. "He likes painting and stuff, and he does security to pay the bills. Anyway, I thought maybe you might want to bring him on for now, until we can sort out the alarm systems and monitoring and all that stuff."

Kerry leaned back. "Like a contractor?"

Mark nodded. "He's not real corporate. I wouldn't have suggested him for the old place, but he's a real good, solid guy, and he's got some buddies he can bring in to trade off."

That seemed more appealing to her than bringing in a security firm. "Okay," Kerry said. "I like that idea. I don't want uniformed guys marching around in here. I don't want us to have that kind of culture in this place."

Mark nodded and grinned. "Yeah thought so."

"So bring your guy in and let's meet him," Kerry said. "And his buddies."

"Will do." Mark stood up. "I called him earlier. He's waiting for me to call back. Okay for him to come over now?"

"Yup." Kerry leaned forward. "I would love to tell Dar we worked out security while she was in DC, Before she has to go and meet the president."

Mark stopped in mid-motion and looked at her, both dark eyebrows hiking up. "Say what?"

"Yeah. She's bummed. But maybe if they make it a photo op we'll make *The Washington Post* and get some business out of it." Kerry winked at him.

"As long as she doesn't pop him one," Mark said. "That could be more publicity than we need, y'know?"

"Oh I'm sure she won't do that," Kerry said. "She's way too smart, right?"

Mark eyed her skeptically then disappeared out the door, shaking his head.

"Right?" Kerry asked her faint reflection in the monitor... "She won't hit the president. She's way too smart for that."

"ALL RIGHT, BOYS. Now pay attention to Dar, and let's get this rolling." Gerry looked pointedly at the half dozen men sitting in the room, then nodded briskly at Dar. "Go on then. I'll go get some chow arranged." Gerry walked to the door, which was opened by his aide, and disappeared.

The men all looked at Dar, who looked back at them in a long moment of uncomfortable silence.

"Well," Dar said. "I guess we can start with hello, my name is Dar Roberts and I'm the solutions architect for your new database system."

The eyes watching her were dubious, to say the least.

Dar absorbed that wryly. "I know none of you are deaf mutes. Gerry would have warned me."

She saw the wary shift at her casual use of the General's first name. "So what is it? You don't trust civs, you don't trust women, you don't like girls who are taller than you are? I won't bite you."

The one on the far left, a brown-haired man with a scar under one eye cleared his throat. "I'm John Duggan," he said. "Senior technical officer for the Coast Guard."

Aw. Leave it to the coasties to speak up first. "Hi, John."

"We really don't know who you are, ma'am," he said. "Except some civilian woman from some civilian company we've never heard of, who we're supposed to cooperate with."

The other men looked guardedly grateful at the words but kept their eyes on Dar.

"Fair enough," Dar said. "I am some civilian woman from some civilian company you've never heard of because the company was just formed a couple weeks ago. Prior to that I was the CIO of ILS. Which is also a civilian company, but one you might possibly have heard of." Dar observed the nods. "I left there and started my own company. The very first contract I signed was the one that has me here in this room."

"You know the General," John said.

"I do. Or more to the point, the General's known me since I was born. My father is retired Navy. So though I'm some civilian woman from some civilian company, the service isn't as alien to me as you might think."

A thin, middle aged man with dark hair and glasses regarded her. "You're Andy's kid," he stated flatly. "You look like him."

Dar nodded again, and smiled. "I am, and I do."

"Ken Charles," the man said. "Head of Naval intelligence systems. So that explains why you're here, but doesn't explain what the hell we're supposed to do with you. I know all about this scheme of the Joint Chief's to get us all communicating. But what they don't know, and what I assume you do know, is it ain't that easy."

"True statement," Dar said

"Our systems aren't compatible," John said. "We all know it. We all live with it. Those goompahs up top think they can just wave their arms around and make that not the case. Well, they can't."

"We'd have to all change to new systems," a third man said, young and blond and with a ferocious crew cut. "Aside from money, which ain't coming to do that, we're at war. No time to mess around with intelligence systems." He gave Dar a truculent look. "Dan Draper. Army," he added, pointing with his thumb at a fourth man. "This is Daddy Perkins. He's my tech lead."

Daddy was a cherubic looking man of middle age, with round, astonished eyes and pink cheeks. "Hello," he said. "What he said." He pointed back at Draper. "These guys don't know what they're asking."

A little silence fell. Dar waited to see if anything else was going to be offered. She had her arms folded over her chest and she was leaning against the white board. "You all finished?" she asked, after the silence had lengthened enough to be uncomfortable.

They nodded, after glancing at each other.

"Okay." Dar turned and picked up one of the white board markers. "So let me just run down what I committed to Gerry to get done, then we can sit and argue about it."

"Gonna be a long day," Draper said.

"That's all right by me," Dar responded as she sketched. "I just need a break to go meet the president. Then I'll be back to argue all night if you want."

"What's he want from you?" John asked.

"That was my second contract."

"Holy crap."

"That's what I said."

KERRY REGARDED THE man sitting across from her with some bemusement. "So, Carlos, Mark tells me you're an artist?"

The big, square jawed man across from her, dwarfing her chair, nodded. "I paint," he said. "And I do three dimensional stuff. Like metal sculpture and carved leather."

"Really," Kerry said. "That's impressive. I'm always blown out by people who can do art. My mother-in-law's an artist."

"Yeah?" the man said. "Local?"

"She lives off South Beach. Cecilia Roberts." Kerry saw the start of recognition. "I see you've heard of her."

"Sure. Seen her stuff in the galleries down there. Nice," he said. "But y'know, unless you're mainstream it don't always pay the bills."

"That's what she says, too," Kerry said. "So you freelance as a security guard?"

He nodded. "Yeah. I lift weights and stuff and I look the part." He grinned. "But I'm always booked for late shift or mids, y'know? And I like to work on my stuff at night. Doesn't work for me during day hours for some reason."

Kerry leaned forward and rested her elbows on her desk. "Well, that would work for us, because at least right now, we're closed at night. We work pretty much eight to eight. We kinda need someone around."

"Mark told me. He was freaked."

"I was freaked, he was freaked, my partner was freaked. It was just a full on freak show here," Kerry said. "But also, we're working on some government contracts, and we think it would be a good idea to have some security around." She tapped a pencil on the desk. "You interested?"

He nodded. "I like Mark. We went to school together," he said. "I knew he was tied up with that big company and that's not my style. This is different."

Kerry's eyes twinkled. "Not most of our styles, apparently. So we can do this one of two ways. We can hire you on direct, or, if you want, if you have a company of your own, we can contract you."

He shook his head. "Don't ask me to do all that company stuff. I can't even do my paperwork for my art. I'll come work for you. I've got some buddies, if you get like you need night guards, that would love to do some hours, too, this is a nice area."

"Most of the time."

"Those vet guys—I seen them," Carlos said. "I think I can handle them."

"I think you can, too," Kerry agreed. "To be honest, I'm pretty sure Dar could have handled them, but you know we're business owners and respectable women, so I think it's better to hire some nice, big strong guys instead."

Carlos chuckled. "I've been hearing about Dar for like twenty years," he said. "Be cool to finally meet her. Mark's got all kinda stories."

"Yes he does." Kerry smiled. "She'll be back tomorrow. But for now, let's walk you down to personnel and we can get you started. Also, we can talk about what kind of money you want."

"Right on." He stood up, towering over her. "Mostly us contract guards, we get minimum wage. No one sticks around real long."

"Probably that's why." Kerry led the way toward the stairs. "I think someone with your experience should be worth more than that, don't you?"

"Oh, lady, I like you already."

DAR LEANED BACK in her chair and folded her arms, rocking her head back and forth a little to loosen the muscles on either side of her neck. "Next objection?"

The door opened and Gerry poked his head in. "Dar? Car's here from the White House for you." He looked at the scribbled full white board and the scattering of notepads with boxes and lines on them on the table. "We doing all right, boys?"

Dar stood up and pushed her chair in. "Let me go meet with them, Gerry, so these guys can answer you honestly." She winked at the group, then slipped out past Easton where an aide was waiting. "You for me?"

The aide nodded and smiled. "I've been assigned to accompany you, Ms. Roberts," he said politely. "Please follow me."

Dar amiably did. "Least I have my driver's license this time," she commented.

"Ma'am?"

"Last time I went to the White House I had no ID," Dar said. "Day or two after 9/11."

"Oh my goodness," he said. "What did they do?"

"Well, they wanted to talk to me badly enough to let me in, but they sure as hell weren't happy about it." Dar followed the man out a side door to a black sedan, whose driver opened the back door for them. The aide slid in and Dar joined him. "This is going to go a little better I suppose."

The aide eyed her. "You're pretty calm for someone being taken to meet the president."

Dar half shrugged, deciding not to admit to the stomach flutters and lump in her throat. After all, it was just another person, and one she didn't much like.

Her handspring buzzed. She pulled it out and found a message from Kerry waiting. "How does she know when to do that?" she wondered, selecting it.

```
Hey, hon!
Guess what? I hired a security guard. Here's a
picture of him! His name's Carlos and he's a friend
of Mark's.
```

Dar studied the picture, her eyes widening at the massive figure. "Holy crap."

The aide leaned forward. "Ma'am?"

"No, sorry." Dar went back to the message. "Just a note from home."

```
He's an artist who does this on the side, but I
hired him full time because he wanted to work day
hours, not night like everyone else wanted him for. I
gave him a benefit plan and brought him in on a
salary, since I want him to be in charge. He has
friends who would be interested if we needed to go
24/7 or something like that.
```

Dar looked at the big, rugged, honest face in the picture and felt a sense of relief. "Dad'll like him," she muttered under her breath, then keyed in a reply.

```
Good job! He looks like a tank. Now I feel better
about sleeping alone in Washington tonight. On my way
to meet the Prez, wish me luck.
```

She sent the note and then relaxed back in her seat.

"Was the meeting going well?" the aide asked, after a few minutes silence. "The General was wondering."

"I think it'll be fine. I was about halfway through convincing them," Dar said. "Lot of objections, but I like that."

"You do?"

She nodded. "Means people are thinking, not just going along for the ride. That's always good for everyone. The more questions, the better."

The aide eyed her. "You've never been in the military, have you?"

Dar smiled. "No. I think that's why Gerry hired me for this."

"I think you're right."

THE FIRST MEETING was with Bridges, in his office again. He had a group of four men with him and he wasn't about to let them have the kind of free for all that Dar had just experienced with the military IT staff.

"All right, people." He sat down behind his desk. "So now that I've told everyone we're doing this, let's do it." He looked across the table at Dar. "You got your plan ready?"

Dar nodded. "I have a blueprint and a starting point. I have database designers working on the framework."

Bridges grunted. "This got higher profile than I thought, faster than I thought, even though I'm the bastard who's supposed to think of all this crap," he admitted. "Laughed my ass off when I was told not to use your former company, by the way."

"So did Kerry's mother," Dar said.

Bridges chuckled dryly. "Bet she did. But because of that, this thing has to show results PDQ."

The other men in the room just listened quietly, notepads at the ready, waiting to be given directions. Dar found them annoying.

"How long will it take for that?" Bridges asked her.

Dar thought about it. "I can probably prototype it in sixty days," she said. "It'll mostly be raw and wire frame, but you'll have an idea of what it'll do."

Bridges considered that. "Might need to be sooner."

"Do you want it to work?" Dar asked, bluntly. "Or just be smoke and mirrors. I can do smoke and mirrors in two weeks but it'll do zero useful crap for you."

He chuckled again. "Let me get back to you on that one," he said. "I see you remember our last dance."

Dar smiled briefly.

"You really think you can do this?" Bridges asked. "No one wants to look like an ass. I don't want this to be paraded around *CNN* for a year and then turn out that we wasted our money and got nothing for it."

Dar steepled her fingers and rested the tips of them against her lips as she considered. Finally she exhaled. "If you're asking, can I create a system that lets you intelligently search a massive data flow, then yes. If you want to know if I can pull some magic rabbit out of my ass and prove it works by catching a bad guy? I don't know."

Bridges lips twitched. "We can fake the second," he said, with blunt honesty. "What I don't want is some smart ass to get into that system and find out it doesn't actually work."

"What I give you will work," Dar stated, then stopped talking.

Bridges waited. Then as he realized nothing more was forthcoming, he grunted. "Okay." He looked at the four men. "Your jobs, people, are to give this woman whatever it is she asks for in the way of access, data, people, authorizations, keys to the executive bathroom, you name it. She's got carte blanche to use an outdated saying that doesn't mean much anymore."

Dar, having come to the meeting expecting to have to sell her design again, was silently startled.

"Yes, sir," the oldest of the four said. "We understand."

"Do ya? If this thing works, it means there's a chance..." he looked at Dar. "A chance that some jackass somewhere in some government building sitting at a screen might find something that will prevent 9/11 from happening again. You all got that?"

They all nodded.

"The bloody idiots on Capitol Hill know about it," Bridges said. "It wasn't my idea to tell them," he added, as an aside to Dar. "In fact, the next time I'll know who not to tell. Now I've got congress-idiots calling me every ten minutes worried about privacy. Privacy!" He lifted his hands. "Idiots! They're all worried their damn affairs are going to end up in *The Washington Post!*"

Dar remained silent, her hands folded on the table.

He turned to her. "So what are you going to tell them about privacy?"

"I'm going to tell them the truth," Dar said. "If they ask me."

"Nice." He sighed. "My next career's going to be on a farm somewhere feeding chickens."

Dar shrugged slightly. "You can't search through all that data manually. It's just not possible. So either you know what questions to ask, and the system finds what you're looking for, or you trust the algorithm to make the connections and toss up something you hadn't anticipated."

Bridges frowned at her. "Are you telling me something like, this thing will have intelligence?"

"To a degree, yes."

All of them were staring at her. "Is this some kind of science fiction?" the older aide asked, hesitantly. "Because it sounds like it."

"Rockets were science fiction once," Dar said. "At some point you reach the Turing test, and the programs become so advanced it seems like there's intelligence. Once you have something that can judge and evaluate data points, and return a result based on their weighting of them, how different is that than how you, or I, decide what to have for breakfast every morning?"

Bridges pursed his lips and made a sputtering noise with them. "Think I'll just tell them I hired a voodoo practitioner and they're killing chickens in some back office of the Pentagon. It'll scare 'em less." He stood up. "C'mon, woman. Let's go get the dog and pony show over. I'm guessing you got some work to get done."

Obligingly Dar stood up and followed him out the door. They walked down the hallway of the executive office building, heading down some steps and through what appeared to be a tunnel.

"Lay off the sci-fi with him," Bridges said. "He doesn't like it."

"No problem," Dar said.

They walked down the long hall and up another flight of stairs, then through a door and they were in spaces she'd seen on television. Dar just tried to keep her mind blank and let the flashes of whitewashed walls and tall ceilings just move past her, very glad she had Bridges leading the way.

Then they were down another hallway and in front of a door, and her guide was rapping on it. "Bridges," he called out.

The answer filtered through the wood. "Come in, Mike."

"Ready? Doesn't matter." Bridges worked the latch and shoved the door open, entering the room and drawing Dar after him.

It was one of the smaller offices, Dar realized. Not the big oval one, but impressive enough. There were pictures and hangings on the wall, a plush carpet with the seal of the president on the floor, a huge desk, and behind it a somewhat scruffy looking man in a pullover with blinking eyes and a folder of papers in one hand.

"Mike, hey. Who've we got here?" the man asked, his expression brightening on seeing Dar and his posture straightening. "Hello there, ma'am."

The irony was so crunchy Dar felt like she was chewing on year old Frosted Flakes.

"This is —" Bridges turned. "What the hell is your real name?"

"Paladar Roberts. But everyone calls me Dar."

The president put his folder down and stepped around his desk, extending a hand. "Well, hello there." His grip was dry and firm. "You're the computer lady, right?"

"Right," Dar said, releasing him. "Nice to meet you, Mr. President."

"Hey, great. Thanks for coming over." He pointed to a pair of wingback chairs in the corner. "Let's sit down a minute and you can tell me what this is all about. I want to understand what we're trying to do here." He glanced at Bridges. "Tell them to send one of the photogs in,

Mike. I never like to lose a chance to get a picture of me with a good looking woman."

"Sure." Bridges gave him a droll look. "Be right back, Roberts. Remember, no sci-fi."

Dar accepted the surrealism and took a seat in one of the chairs, hiking a knee up and circling it with both hands as the president took the other chair, wishing belatedly she'd brought Kerry with her.

Without a shadow of a doubt, Kerry would know far better how to deal with this. "So."

"So." He leaned forward and rested his elbows on his knees in an oddly adolescent posture. "What did you say people called you? Dar?"

She nodded.

"Mike tells me that you're going to work up something for him that will let him find bad guys living here," the president said, in a straightforward way. "Call me George, by the way."

"All right," Dar responded. "It was explained to me that you want some way of delving into the public Internet and sifting through all that data to find things that could harm us."

The president smiled. "You got it," he said. "So you're doing that?"

Dar cleared her throat. "I'm going to try," she said, honestly. "I'm going to develop an intelligent set of automatic filters that will be programmable by the people who work for Mr. Bridges, and you, to try and do that."

Bush thought about that for a minute and Dar remained silent. Finally he looked back up at her with an unexpectedly sharp stare. "People ain't gonna like us messing with the Internet," he said. "They don't want the government sniffing all up in their business, you know what I mean?"

"I do," Dar said. "They won't like it at all. Just the idea, from an ISP, got everyone in an uproar and all they wanted to do was target advertisements."

"Yep," Bush said. "But this thing...you said it was automatic? Like machines are doing it?"

Dar nodded. "The idea was..." She found herself to her surprise laying it out for him as she hadn't for Bridges. "The programming algorithms are designed to find connections."

He nodded, but remained silent.

"And they deliver the connections to analysts, who can decide if they really are connections, or not," Dar said. "You can't have someone looking at everything, it's too much."

Bush was still nodding. "So the machines are looking, and they only kick it to a human when they find something they don't like."

"Yes."

The president smiled and gave her thumbs up. "Got it," he said. "So we can tell people—we ain't snooping on you. It's just a machine looking for patterns. No one's watching you look for porno." He winked. "See, Mike just cares about results. I care about results, too, but I'm the one who has to put their mug on television to take the blame for all of it."

"More or less, yes. The interface will look on its own for things that fall out of baseline," Dar said, smiling at him. "So if it sees a larger number of airline tickets being purchased one way, in a short period of time, it'll assemble that for review. But also," she lifted a hand. "It's to give the analysts a way to look for something in natural language."

"Like, anyone buying a lot of fertilizer components today that never did before?" Bush asked.

"Yes."

He smiled again. "You're a smart lady." He paused, watching her. "Your dad's a war hero, huh? I heard that." He glanced up as the door opened and a slim young man entered with a camera. "Hold off a minute, Josh." He put his hand up, then waited for the man to back out. "Thanks." Then he turned back to Dar. "Navy was it?"

"Yes," Dar said. "Though he probably wouldn't call what he did heroism. Just a job."

"My daddy says that, too," Bush responded. "And I always told him he'd be a hero to me if he'd done nothing but catch crabs off the coast of New England."

So odd to find a synergy in this, the most weird of places and strangest of people. "Well, that's how I feel about my dad also," Dar said. "I think we're lucky that way. Not a lot of people are."

He smiled briefly and looked away, then stood up. "C'mon in, Josh." He put his hand on the chair back. "Mike tells me you've got a lady friend, is that right?"

Dar stood as the photographer came back in. "Yes, if by that you mean I'm gay," she said mildly. "And I have a life partner."

He nodded. "Good. This'll do good for my demographics." He waved the photographer over. "And they won't think you're sleeping with half the lot of us." He grinned rakishly. "Don't tell anyone I said that. Everybody assumes I'm clueless." He pointed at the desk. "Should we take a shot there, Josh? What would look best? You're the expert."

Bridges came back as they started to get arranged and Dar had a moment to pause, shake her head, and think about the long, long message she was going to type to Kerry.

Who would not, absolutely not, believe it.

Chapter Four

DAR LAY FLAT on her back on her acceptably comfortable hotel bed, her eyes closed as she listened to the voice on the other end of the phone. "That's what I said, hon," she said as Kerry finally wound down. "I just walked in the hotel twenty minutes ago. Finally got done arguing with Gerry's boys."

"Holy crap, Dar!"

"Mm...didn't figure of the two appointments, his would be the gnarlier," Dar said. "But I finally got through it, so we can move forward with the high level design."

"Did you get dinner?"

"I got a meatball sub for late lunch," Dar said. "That's what they have at the Pentagon, apparently."

"Better than Burger King I guess." Kerry sighed. "I sent chocolate."

"So I smell and see." Dar tipped her head to one side and regarded the festive looking basket. "Thanks. Definitely better than Burger King. I think I see Kit Kat bars."

"They had that and peanut butter cups," Kerry said. "Mocha and Chino have been running me crazy all night. They finally just settled down and I'm going to have a bowl of soup or something."

"Want some of my Kit Kats?"

"I want you." Kerry's smile was audible. "Do you have to go back over there tomorrow?"

"In the morning, yes. Need to set up the delivery timeline," Dar said. "And, I guess, the ILS team there wants to get a handshake in."

"Aww."

Dar chuckled softly. "Wish you were here," she said unexpectedly. "I'm so used to having you around, it's weird when you're not."

"Funny. I was just thinking that." Kerry's tone warmed. "It's crazy isn't it? I lived by myself for a long time here before we met. Now I can't even remember what that felt like."

Dar thought about that for a minute as she listened to Kerry breathe gently in her ear. She did remember what that was like, those long years of living alone, and how quiet it was. Quiet like it was in the hotel room, just the creak of the building around her and the far off sound of street traffic.

"Dar?"

"Hm?" She dismissed the memory. "Just thinking. Been a weird day."

"Having to meet the president?" Kerry laughed softly. "You handled it really well, hon. I don't think I would have, and I'm sure you were a lot more comfortable talking about your dad than I would have been about mine."

"I did okay. Hey, you think room service would have hot dogs? I feel like a hot dog." Dar rolled up onto her feet and went over to the small desk in the room, flipping through the menu. "Why in the hell would someone want to eat the heart out of a palm, Ker? That sounds brutal."

"It's just a vegetable," Kerry said in an indulgent tone. "You'd probably like it if they dumped peanut sauce on it."'

"I like everything with peanut sauce. Especially you." Dar chuckled."Oh, here we go. Two hot dogs, a bowl of chili, and a plate of nachos. I can make my own chili cheese dogs."

"Oh, Dar."

Dar imagined her beloved's pained expression without effort. "Nah, actually they've got snapper fillet. I'll get that." She pushed the menu aside and dropped into the chair. "So we got a security guard, I sold two designs, you wrote three contracts and I met the president. All in all, a good day."

"Except how it began and the fact you're not here," Kerry said. "Aside from that, we're good. Okay, let me let you go get dinner. I'm going to get my soup and go for a walk with the kids."

"Okay. Talk to you tomorrow," Dar said. "Kiss the kids for me."

Kerry chuckled. "I will. Night, hon."

"Night." Dar hit the key to hang up and juggled the Handspring in her fingers, then let it drop to the desk. She glanced at the phone, then got up and went back to the bed, sat down and pulled her boots back on. "Let me go find a real hot dog," she said. "Better than hanging out in this boring room."

She shrugged into her jacket, slipped her key card in her back pocket, then ran her fingers through her hair before she went out the door. The hotel lobby was sparsely populated and she only glanced into the restaurant before she went outside and braced herself against the chilly wind.

She turned up her collar, stuck her hands in her pockets and strolled down the road, glancing at the store fronts as she passed. There was a scattering of other walkers on the street, and she crossed with some of them, seeing a few couples walking together hand-in-hand and talking.

Now she really did wish Kerry was there with her. She flexed her hand, almost able to feel the warmth of Kerry's as she imagined folding her fingers around hers. They had started doing that in public lately, or sometimes Kerry would ease over and slide her hand into Dar's front pocket, bumping lightly along with her in somewhat clumsy comfort.

The sudden scent of garlic distracted her and she noticed two of the couples heading toward a restaurant on the next corner. She trailed after them and found herself at the door, pulling it open and entering.

It had a typical brick and wood interior and smelled great. Dar patiently waited her turn, then followed the very busy hostess to a table near the window, passing between much bigger ones surrounded by large groups.

Busy restaurant on a weekday, good sign. Dar relaxed in her chair and opened the menu the woman left. There would be no hot dogs, but she not only recognized most of the dishes, she'd eaten a number of them before.

"Getcha something to drink?" A waitress was standing at her table, with an inquiring look.

Ah. Dar regarded her choices. She wasn't much of a drinker. Kerry could easily put her under the table. She usually indulged when they were out mostly to keep Kerry company. However. "Beer?" she ventured. "Draft?"

"Foreign or domestic?" The woman asked.

"Foreign," Dar said. "Nothing dark."

"Sure." The woman whisked off. Dar figured out what she wanted and put the menu down, then half turned in her chair to study her fellow diners.

Well, it would be better than having a hot dog. Dar leaned back and exhaled. And better than consuming the contents of her gift basket. She smiled briefly as her beer was delivered. Maybe she'd even end the night by taking a walk.

KERRY TOWELED HER hair dry. She heard a growl fest going on in the living room and stuck her head out of the bathroom. "Hey, what are you guys doing?"

Chino came trotting into the room, her tongue lolling out. "Growf!"

Mocha galloped in after her, spotting the towel Kerry had wrapped around her and seized the corner of it gleefully. He backed up and tugged the fabric with him.

Kerry made a grab for her modesty. "Hey! Cut that out! C'mon now. I ran with you guys for an hour. Aren't you tired out?"

"Yap!" Mocha stood up on all fours and peered at her, his tail wagging furiously.

"Oh my gosh." Kerry traded her towel for a pair of shorts and a t-shirt and ducked back into the bathroom to run a brush through her hair. "Give me a second, okay?"

Nearly midnight and she had to admit she was tired out. She glanced at her reflection in the mirror, then blew her damp bangs back out of her eyes. "Ugh."

She entered the bedroom and leaned against the wall, regarding the water bed pensively.

Choices. She could sleep downstairs, in what was once Dar's bedroom and was now both of theirs. The water bed was comfortable and it was where she usually slept.

However, she was never as aware of Dar's absence as when she was in that bed alone. A little silly, she knew, or probably a little crazy, but she couldn't help feeling the way she did and so, with a sigh, she abandoned the room and trotted up the steps with the dogs right behind her, moving down the upstairs hall and into the condo's master suite.

Big and with high, arched ceilings, tall glass doors that opened onto a broad, shaded patio, soft sea foam green walls, and light wood furniture she almost never used.

For a little while, when she'd first moved in with Dar, she'd put her things up here, in the plethora of drawers and cupboards, and in the walk-in closet that was half the size of her original apartment. She still had clothes hanging in that, her business suits and formal wear, but the rest of her stuff was, and had been, mingled with Dar's for a long time now downstairs.

She would occasionally spend a sunny winter afternoon on the big porch, reading for a while but more often she'd go down into the garden, or out onto the two person swing chair on the main patio where likely as not Dar would join her.

There was another guest room upstairs and the room she used as her office. Sometimes she would work up there, but never for long. It was just as easy to take her laptop and sit on the big leather couch in the living room, or in Dar's office downstairs where they would work together in companionable silence.

But tonight, here in the big room she pulled back the soft, fluffy comforter and got under it, as Chino leaped up onto one side of the big king size bed and turned in a few circles before settling down.

She reached down and picked up Mocha before he could start yelping, putting him down and giving him a kiss on the top of his head. "Chill out and go lay down by Chino, okay?"

He nibbled her chin and lay down on his back, waving his paws at her as she indulgently rubbed his belly.

"I'm glad you guys are here with me," she said. "Even if you're running me ragged." She leaned over and rubbed her nose against Mocha's and he licked her face. "It's nice to have something to distract me from missing your other mommy."

Kerry leaned over and shut off the bedside light, sliding down and pulling the covers up over her. Dar would only be gone a little over twenty-four hours and the fact that she was so occupied with thoughts of her probably was not quite sane.

A pleasant insanity, to be sure. She settled down on her pillow and then reached over to pick up her Handspring as she spotted the flashing red light that meant a message.

It was a message from Dar. Contentedly, Kerry opened it, delighted to find a picture attached. She reviewed it, turning her head slightly to one side. "What the hell is that, Dar?"

```
    I decided to go out to eat and found this Italian
place. It had these. Inside out pizzas. It's full of
stuff inside.
```

"Ah, that's what that is." Kerry went on to the next picture. "Tiramisu, nice."

```
Now I'm out riding on the subway trains.
```

Kerry sat right up. "What?"

```
I'm so stuffed if I go right back to the hotel
and go to sleep I'm going to be sick to my stomach.
```

"Y'know, Dar, much as you're the most macha woman I know, riding on the train after midnight in a strange city isn't the smartest thing I ever heard." Kerry rapidly typed out the same message.

```
Can't you just go walk around your room
```

She hit send, and waited, but not for long as thirty seconds later the phone rang. She answered it. "Hey."

"Hey." Dar's voice came through clearly, but there were street sounds behind her. "Worried about me?" She chuckled. "I'm around the corner from the hotel, so relax."

"Nutball." Kerry snuggled back down into bed, and exhaled, as Mocha curled up against her. "You said you were riding trains. I thought you got drunk at dinner."

"Can you get drunk on beer?"

"Oh yes," Kerry said. "And I have, and you've seen me."

"But you're so cute when you're drunk," Dar said. "I'm going to walk around the block twice, then go inside. It's cold here. G'wan to bed."

"I am in bed, upstairs," Kerry said. "With the kids." She put her head on the pillow. "Please be careful, okay? I don't want anything to happen to you."

Dar was quiet for a few moments. "You doing all right?" she asked in a more serious tone. "You sound bummed."

Did she? Kerry frowned briefly. "I'm fine, just been a long day."

"Sure." Dar's tone didn't alter. "Did those guys, any of them, come back near the office?"

"No." Kerry's body relaxed a little. "Mark was keeping an eye out for them and he put a webcam on the back loading dock."

Dar chuckled softly.

"He was freaked out about this morning. He said he had no real idea of what he was supposed to do once he got here except start yelling and calling the cops."

"That was enough."

"It was, but you know when I finally felt safe? When you got there," Kerry said. "Even more than the cops."

Dar chuckled again. "Here you are telling me to get off the streets of Washington at the same time as you tell me I showed up like Thor, God of the Internets, this morning."

Now Kerry had to laugh a little. "Yeah, schizo. I know. I should just shut up and go to sleep. I'm overtired."

"Sounds good," Dar said. "See you after lunch?"

"You got it. I'll be there waiting." Kerry felt an odd reluctance to hang up, but she pushed that to one side. "Talk to you later, hon."

"Bye," Dar said, then disconnected.

Kerry put the phone down on her stomach and studied the ceiling, surprised by the sudden sting of tears in her eyes. Tension gripped her chest and she sucked in a deep breath, and then released it. She glanced to the side as Mocha squiggled up between her arm and her ribs, snuffling at her. "Hey, baby boy." She allowed his cute eyes and button nose to charm her up out of her unexpected doldrums. "You going to keep me company, huh?"

The puppy had light green eyes, almost the same shade as her own. He put his small muzzle down on her arm and peered up at her. After a moment his mouth opened and his pink tongue appeared.

Chino, apparently jealous of the attention, got up and came over to sprawl over Kerry's legs, resting her chin on Kerry's knee.

Kerry sniffled a little and rubbed her eyes, clearing the moisture from them. It was hard to pin down what she felt bad about. Now that the moment was over she was a little embarrassed about it. "I think I'm overtired," she informed her attentive pets. "So let's go to bed. Right?"

Kerry pulled the covers up a little and closed her eyes.

DAR PONDERED THE phone, leaning back against the wall of the hotel as she thought about Kerry. It had been a long day, no doubt. The morning's stresses had bothered both of them. That alone was reason enough for Kerry's melancholy. Dar wished the night would go faster. And the morning would go faster. With an aggrieved sigh, she finished her stroll around the building and into the lobby. Late as it was on a weekday the space was mostly deserted, the bar with only a few single patrons sitting and watching a game she heard the echo of as she passed.

The desk clerk, busy with some papers, gave her only the briefest of glances as she crossed in front of him and angled toward the elevators. Then he straightened up. "Oh, Ms. Roberts?"

Dar stopped and turned. "Yes?"

"Sorry, ma'am, there's an envelope for you." He went to a cabinet and opened it. "It came in about thirty minutes ago." He turned and came over and handed it to her. "Here you go."

Dar regarded it. "FedEx."

"Yes, ma'am, late delivery. You can get FedEx here pretty much anytime you want."

"Thanks." Dar noted the address and tucked it under her arm before she continued on to the elevator bank and took one up to her room.

She put the packet down and changed into a pair of shorts and a t-shirt, going to the mini bar and retrieving some milk chugs she'd ordered after she checked in. Then she sat down in the leather easy chair and opened first the milk, then the package.

It was from the Herndon office. Dar opened the folder inside and paused, looking at the large, in fact oversized greeting card tucked into the covering and acknowledging the lump it brought to her throat.

Made it hard to swallow the milk. She did, then she opened the card and paused, then started reading the many handwritten messages inside.

She remembered going to that office, enjoying a rare bit of laughter in that time when Kerry had to convince the building to let her in. Her face tensed into a smile as she remembered, too, going into the control center, and having all those people there look up at her like she was some kind of celebrity.

There were messages there from the Pentagon staff, too. Dar's fingertip traced the one from Danny, who'd gotten his arm bone cracked in the attack. She remembered the handful of people they'd lost, people she hadn't known, but whose names had traced up to hers in the organizational chart.

There was a note from Nan.

Dar slowly sipped her milk and continued reading, a wistful smile appearing on her face. When she'd run through the notes twice, she got up and went to the small desk, sitting down at it and reaching for her laptop, then she paused, and took a piece of the hotel stationary out instead.

She took out a pen from her backpack and propped her head up on one hand, thinking briefly and then starting to write.

> Hello, people.
> Big surprise to get to my hotel and find a card from you all waiting. I appreciate all the time you took to put down a few words, so I thought I would take some of my own time and send a note back to you.

Dar paused and considered. Then she smiled a little and put her head back down on her hand.

> I know we only met a few times, in a bad situation. But sometimes bad situations bring out the best in people. From what I saw here, and across ILS, the best of ILS was truly extraordinary and you all were definitely a bright spot on a dark day.
> A lot of you wrote that you were honored to work for me. That's hugely flattering, but to be honest,

> it was always my view that I worked for all of you
> rather than the other way around. That'll surprise
> people to hear but if you think about it, I expected
> 110 percent from people because it's what I gave.
>
> A part of me will always live at ILS. There are
> things that are written into the DNA of the place
> that came from my blood and sweat, and those of you
> in Netops are going to run into crap with my initials
> on it for a long, long time. Likewise, a little bit
> of my head and heart will always be wondering how
> it's going, and how everyone is.

She had to stop and sit back, surprised to find herself in tears. It was a little overwhelming and uncomfortable. She waited it out, until her chest relaxed and her throat eased.

"Wow. Where did that come from? Am I that sentimental?"

Dar didn't think she had a reputation for soft-heartedness, especially among these people. She looked down at the letter again, half minding to throw it away.

Then she sighed and picked up her pen again, wiping the moisture from her eyes and continuing to write.

> At any rate, I hope you all go on being
> successful at what you do, and take the company to
> new places. Maybe we'll meet sometime down the road.
> Thanks again for the note and good luck to all of
> you.

She paused again, then smiled, and signed her name. She got up, grabbed an envelope and the FedEx pack that had the Herndon office's address and headed for the door.

"NO!" KERRY JERKED awake with a yell, sitting up and groping out with her hands to fend off the remnants of a nightmare that had her heart pounding so fast she couldn't count the beats.

"No," she uttered, covering her eyes with one hand, her entire body shaking. "Just a dream. Jesus."

After a moment she caught her breath and felt for the table light and turned it on, just as Chino started anxiously licking her ear.

"Ahh!" Kerry stifled a yelp until she realized what it was. Then she was shoved backwards by her upset pet, and Mocha climbing up into her lap. "Stop! Stop it!" she yelled, sharply. "Hey!"

Chino's ears went back as she stared in wide-eyed alarm, while Mocha cowered down flat on the bed.

"Sorry guys." She got herself upright again and leaned against the headboard, a violent headache making red flashes against the inside of her eyelids. "Shit."

She still felt short of breath from a nightmare of being trapped under the half collapsed wall with everything pressing against her and air growing short. There was no way out because she was alone and Dar wasn't with her.

Just herself and the smell of burning and being aware that she couldn't move and no one knew she was there.

No one to hear her screaming, just darkness and pressure and a terrible, terrible fear. Of dying. Of being alone.

Her hands were shaking. She tucked them under her arms and rocked forward, putting her head against Chino's. "Sorry I yelled, honey." She watched Mocha squirm closer. "I didn't mean to scare you. I was just scared myself."

Chino whined and licked her cheek.

"Thanks, Chi." Kerry closed her eyes and breathed in the scent of fur and the clean linen around her. "Oh, boy. Glad that doesn't happen often." She straightened back up and wiped the back of her hand across her eyes, blinking a little into lamplight.

Mocha made a little burbling puppy noise, snuffling at her fingers.

"Yeah." Kerry sniffled a little. "You guys want some cookies? Let's go down and have some cookies and milk, how about that?" She waited for the animals to move and then pulled the covers back, getting out of bed and heading for the steps. "I need some hot milk anyway, and some aspirin."

She glanced at the wall clock as she reached the bottom of the stairs, its luminescent face displaying three o'clock at her. "Great," she muttered, crossing the living room and entering the big cobalt blue and white kitchen. She flipped the light on as she cleared the arched entryway.

The tiles were cold against her bare feet, but she ignored that as she went to the cookie jar and opened it, removing a few of the biscuits and offering them to her attentive furballs. She watched them crunch for a minute, then went to the refrigerator and opened it.

Hot milk. She closed the door and went and got a cup, then went back and filled it from Dar's beloved milk dispenser. She drizzled some honey in it, then put it in the microwave and started it heating.

That gave her time to do something about her headache. She shook out a couple of pills from the bottle in the cupboard and swallowed them down with a mouthful of water. "Shit." She turned and leaned against the counter, folding her arms over her chest.

Aside from the headache and the still perceptible chill in her body, she was now very wide awake. The thought of going back to bed was exceptionally unappealing and when the milk was done warming she took it into the living room and turned on the TV instead.

She sat down on the couch, wincing a little as the cold leather surface hit her skin, then relaxing as it warmed up. She picked up the remote and surfed through the channels, bypassing a veritable cornucopia of infomercials and settling on a cartoon instead, turning the sound down a little as the colorful figures danced across the plasma display.

Chino jumped up onto the couch and curled up next to her. Kerry reached over and scratched behind her ears. "Chi, that really sucked," she said. "I hate nightmares. Why do I always have them when Dar's gone?" Which wasn't really true. She didn't always have them and she'd had one or two with Dar right next to her. Kerry calmed down and flexed her hands, the tension easing out of her. The thing was, when she had a bad dream and Dar was there, well, Dar was there and she'd wake up and hug her, and that chased all the shadows out fast.

Dar was very dependable that way. "Cornerstone of my life." Kerry murmured, ruffling Chino's fur. "What would I do without her, Chi?"

"Growf." Chino put her head down on Kerry's leg.

"Damned if I know." Kerry let out a breath, rubbing her temples. Then she opened her eyes and looked around. "Where's Mocha?"

Chino's eyebrows twitched.

"Mocha!" Kerry called out, then cocked her head to listen for puppy toenails. "Oh, crap." She hauled herself to her feet and started looking around. "Mocha!"

Chino hopped down and trotted after her, sniffing around in a puzzled kind of way.

"Where is he?" Kerry checked around the kitchen, then went back and stuck her head in Dar's office and then the bedroom. Nothing. "One place left to check." She went back into the kitchen and opened the back door into the garden, immediately regretting it as the brisk air hit her lightly clad body. "Mocha!"

Chino bolted down the steps and across the grass, being met halfway to the gate by a small, dark form. "Growf!"

"Yap!" Mocha galloped toward the steps, his small ears flapping.

"Get up here." Kerry patted her leg, waiting for him to patter past before she closed the door again. "You little bugger." She rubbed her arms. "It's cold out there."

"Yap!"

Well, at least it had taken her mind off her nightmare. Kerry went to the hall closet and got out a sweatshirt, pulling it on over her head and then laughing softly as it came down to her thighs and the sleeves went past her hands. She pushed the sleeves back up to her elbows, then went back to the table where she'd left her hot milk.

Only to find a white stained brown face looking at her, licking his lips.

"Mocha." Kerry put her hands on her hips.

Mocha licked his lips again and got his front paws down off the table, looking innocently up at her.

Kerry picked up the cup and took it back to the kitchen, rinsing it out and refilling it. She put the cup back in the microwave then crossed her arms, trying to figure out what to do next.

Finish the milk, she decided, then maybe catch a nap on the couch. Maybe think about the first time she'd slept there on that stormy day way back when.

She smiled, remembering how carefully she'd printed out all the material she hadn't even looked at, just to prove to Dar that she'd stuck around for legitimate reasons. What had they been? She still didn't remember, and looking back she was pretty sure neither of them were fooling themselves or each other as she pictured those blue eyes watching her as she entered that kitchen wrapped in Dar's blanket.

Nothing of business in them. That faint little smile, that knowing arch of that dark brow and Kerry knew she was lost. Even now she felt it, a rolling, sweet richness of the soul and she somberly realized she might have found the genesis of her nightmares, this understanding of what she had and was unconsciously so afraid of losing.

Kerry removed the cup of milk and brought it back into the living room. At least that was a damn good reason. She sat back down on the couch and put her bare feet up on the low table, idly watching Chino and Mocha play with a tug toy. She sipped from the cup and put her head back against the cushions, feeling the last of the twisting leave her guts.

Her mind shifted to another track. Would Dar have felt it, when she woke from the dream? Sometimes it seemed like she could, in that odd, rarely spoken of synergy between them. But surely Dar was sound asleep herself, tucked into bed up in Washington.

Surely. But Kerry wondered if she went up and retrieved her new gizmo, if there wouldn't be a note there for her. With a wry grin, she put the cup down on a higher side table this time, and got up, stepping over the tussling Labradors and walking up the steps.

She felt a tickle of anticipation in her stomach as she went into the bedroom, looked at the Handspring on the bedside table and saw the stuttering red light of a message waiting. She picked up the device and glanced at it, shaking her head a little when she saw Dar's name outlined in the back light. "Maybe it's just a coincidence."

She opened the note, saw the single word, 'nightmare?' on it, and abruptly sat down as her knees threatened to unlock and refuse to hold her. "Holy shit."

Dar knew. Without a question, no doubt at all this time, sharp as a laser point. "That's so creepy." She whispered. "But I guess in a good way." She hit reply and answered the note.

> Honey, I don't know how you know this stuff, but yeah. Freaked me a little, so me and the kids are downstairs and I'm drinking hot milk and thinking about you. I was remembering that first day I fell asleep on the couch and it made me feel a lot better. Go back to sleep!

She shook her head a little and sent the note. For someone as relentlessly logical as Dar was, to have this odd sense be a part of her — well, really, be a part of both of them did seem weird and strange. It went against everything her mind told her was rational, and edged into the sort of thing she regarded as — out there.

Dar, of course being the logical person she was, simply accepted it and said it didn't bother her since it wasn't like something she had any control over.

Kerry wasn't bothered by it either, she supposed, she was just curious about how it all worked. "I wonder," she mused. "Maybe when we go out to the Grand Canyon, around those places a lot of people are into that stuff. Maybe we could ask someone."

The Handspring sputtered red again. She chuckled and opened the response from her apparently still awake partner.

> I don't know. I just get this feeling in my gut when you're freaked out and given what time it was, and the fact you were safe at home I figured it had to be a dream.

Kerry smiled. Elementally logical.

> I remember that day. I remember watching you sleep there and wanting to crawl into the couch with you. You probably would have freaked out.

Kerry laughed silently.

> Hon, maybe, maybe not. By the time I was offering to cook for you I'd sorta figured it out.

> I probably would have freaked out. But it ended up all right anyway. You go back to sleep, too. See you tomorrow, hon. Miss ya. Love ya. DD

Kerry read the words a few times. "Cornerstone of my life," she said. "Okay well, I should get back to bed because otherwise tomorrow morning's going to be a real bitch." She got up and went back downstairs to rescue her milk, draining the cup and bringing it back into the kitchen.

Then, with a soft grunt of decision, she turned and crossed the living room again, but this time she went into their bedroom and rolled herself into the water bed. She turned up the heater a trifle before she pulled the covers over her and closed her eyes.

WAKING UP A few hours later was still a little crunchy, but a cup of coffee resolved most of that and Kerry got herself and the dogs into her car and on the road in relatively good order, though a bit later than the previous day. She settled her sunglasses on her nose for the ride, the weather being bright and sunny, with just enough winter chill that convinced South Florida it did, too, have seasons.

There were already a half dozen cars in the parking lot by the time she got to the office and as she pulled up Mayte came out to greet her. "Morning."

"Hello, Kerry. May I take one of the doggies? You have your hands so full."

"Sure." Kerry amiably handed over Mocha's leash, not in the least fooled by the excuse. "Things quiet this morning?"

"Oh yes. Much more than yesterday," Mayte said. "The new security man is here and he is very nice."

They walked into the building, which was filled with a low buzz of activity that surrounded them as they walked up the steps to Kerry's office. She spotted Mark and Carlos talking in the hall and waved at them, then crossed through Mayte's office into her own.

Chino trotted obediently after her, going over to the dog bowls in their raised platform and drinking from one.

Kerry put her messenger bag down and took her seat.

Mayte poked her head in. "Kerry, would you like some coffee? I am going to take the little one down the stairs, and I could bring some back for you."

"Sure, thanks." Kerry sat down and started up her desktop. A soft knock at the door and she looked up to find Mayte and Maria's new assistant peeking in. "Hi. Good morning."

"Pardon, ma'am, but you have a delivery. Is it okay?" the girl said in a soft voice.

"Sure." Kerry folded her arms as the woman backed up and allowed a man carrying a basket to enter. "Ah."

He came over and put it down on her desk. "Here you go, ma'am. First delivery of my day." He handed her an envelope. "Enjoy."

Kerry regarded the basket after he left. It was completely covered in multicolor cellophane and she decided to open the envelope before she risked unwrapping it.

There was a very good chance it was from Dar. But there was always a possibility it was from a prospective vendor, or even from her friend from the previous morning, in which case there could be anything including road kill inside. She'd gotten something like that more than once from business rivals, mostly full of vinegar and sour grapes.

She opened the envelope and took out the card, opening it to find a simple message that put a smile on her face.

    Thought you could use breakfast. C'ya. DD

"Aww." She put the card down and took a pair of scissors from her drawer and sliced through the cellophane.

Mayte entered with coffee. "Oh, that is so nice."

"Yeah." Kerry folded back the wrapping to expose a big package of pastelitos. "Let's pass them around. I can't eat all these. Dar decided to send breakfast in." She selected two of the treats and handed off the rest of them to Mayte.

"Dar is very sweet," Mayte said. "So thoughtful to you."

Kerry smiled in acknowledgment as she sat back down. "She is. I'm a very lucky woman, and believe me, Mayte, I know it."

Mayte grinned, but just waved as she took the tray of pastelitos out.

"I sure as hell know it." Kerry took a contented bite of her pastry and turned to her computer, only to be interrupted again by a knock. "Yes?"

"Miss Kerry?" The new girl was back. "There is a policeman to see you."

Oh well. Couldn't expect pastelitos baskets every time. "Send him in, thanks, Zoe." Kerry took a sip of her coffee as the policeman entered. She recognized one of the officers she'd spoken to the day before. "Good morning." She gestured to one of her visitor chairs. "Officer...?"

"Rudolfo Sanchez." The officer sat down and pulled out a notepad. "Good morning, Ms. Roberts. I just wanted to circle back with you on the situation we had here yesterday." He cleared his throat. "Was going to drop by here late yesterday, but I had a call I was on."

"Sure, no problem." Kerry leaned back in her chair and took a sip of coffee. "My staff said it's been quiet so far this morning."

Sanchez nodded. "Yeah, we kept Patterson—that's the guy—overnight in the holding station. Figured he could use a night under a roof anyway." He glanced at Kerry. "Joe, by the way. Joe Patterson."

"Good to have a name to put to the face," Kerry replied in a mild tone. "Roof or not, I'm sure he probably didn't appreciate the hospitality."

The officer half shrugged. He was a man of medium height and curly black hair, going gray at the temples. "He's been in before. You know these guys? They come back and they think the rules are like over there. That they can do what they want because they've got guns and a cause."

Kerry leaned on her elbows. "That's kind of what's bothering me because since my father-in-law's a retired SEAL, I'm sort of predisposed to be sympathetic to veterans. I don't want to mess with them or give them a hard time."

Sanchez scratched his chin with his pen top. "Yeah, none of us do. I tried talking to him but it's all like a permanent road rage, you know?"

Kerry studied him. "What do you think we should do?" she asked. "I don't want to escalate this, and I can see where it could get like that."

Officer Sanchez looked relieved. "Glad you see it that way," he said. "Cause I was thinking sort of the same thing. With these guys, you push them, they push back, you push harder, they push harder. Know what I'm talking about?"

Possibly better than he imagined. "My partner's very much like that, too," she said. "She absolutely does not, and will not back down, and I think that's going to end up a bad combination if we keep this up. So, what do you think we should do?"

He regarded her seriously. "You really want to press charges?" he asked. "You seem like a bright lady. I think you know he wasn't going to touch you."

Kerry thought about that in silence for a few minutes. He let her, merely sitting there across from her with his pad, waiting. "Can we use it as a bargaining chip?" she countered. "They leave us alone, I don't press charges? Or are they going to think I chickened out if I say yes."

Sanchez was thoughtful. "How about this. What if I put it like, you agree to hold off for a while and we see what happens? I don't know if they'll deal."

Kerry didn't know if they'd deal either. She changed the direction of the questioning. "What actually do they want? You said they were working at some half way house. These guys don't have a place to live, or a place to go. In the best possible case, what happens to them?"

He shook his head. "Now that, I don't know. You heard about that one guy's family moving out? These guys feel abandoned. By their family and by the service, too. It's a hard thing."

"That doesn't seem right," Kerry said. "Can you get me their names? I'd like to find out why they ended up the way they did." She saw his wary look. "Don't worry. I'm not going to publicize them on the Internet or anything like that. We do work for the Department of Defense."

"Oh," Sanchez said. "I didn't know that. What is it you people do?"

"We work with computers. But Dar was just up having a meeting at the Pentagon, so at least we know the right people to ask the questions of," Kerry said. "If we could help these guys out, I'd like to, even after the trouble we've had."

The officer closed his pad. "I heard from those guys that some military cars were here the other day. Maybe that's why they were sniffing around?" he said. "They're always looking for an angle."

"Military cars...oh, right." She nodded. "General Gerald Easton, from the Joint Chiefs, and then Michael Bridges, the president's advisor," Kerry responded with a brief smile. "They're clients."

Sanchez stared at her.

"So we'd rather not get into a tussle with some veterans," she continued. "Makes it kind of awkward, you know?"

Sanchez tapped his pen on his knee. "Okay. Let me see what that tack gets me. I'll tell them I talked you into holding off and that they'd better steer clear if they don't want their benefits chopped."

"We wouldn't do that," Kerry said. "That wasn't my point."

"No, but they don't know that." The officer stood up. "Brass? That they get. Who knows? Maybe they'll be offering to carry your briefcase to the car." He winked at her. "Don't worry, ma'am. It'll be fine." He lifted a hand. "Have a good day."

Kerry waved in response, more than a little disturbed. "That wasn't what I was going for." She sighed. "Crap." She glanced down as her Handspring buzzed. A text, from Dar. "Glad you're on your way home, hon. I think I just got us in deeper than I thought."

Her phone binged. "Yes?" She hit the speaker key.

"Hey, Kerry." Mark's voice sounded amused. "Check your email."

"I just did?" Kerry glanced down. "Oh, on my PC?" She looked over and spun her trackball, then clicked on the new mail on the screen with Mark's name on it. "What is it...oh."

"Sweet pix," Mark said. "At least she didn't whap him one."

Kerry blinked at the screen, which had a cap of a newspaper article with a picture of Dar and President Bush, the former drawing something on a pad on a desk, the latter standing by leaning on the surface and studying it. "Oh, gosh," she said after a brief pause. "That's a nice shot." She glanced at the headline. "And I guess we got our publicity."

"Sure did." He chuckled. "Barbara just called me. Someone at her office saw it. Didn't take us long, huh? Three weeks and we're famous."

No, didn't take long at all. "You got that right." Kerry had to laugh a little. "Let me forward this to her parents. They're gonna die." She scanned the article briefly but it was bland and general in tone. "Least they spelled the company name right. Mark, you probably should beef up the web server."

"On it," he said. "Top of the roller coaster...here we go!" He hung up, still laughing.

Kerry sighed as she forwarded the mail to the rest of the company, her mother, and Dar's folks. "Yep...here we go."

KERRY PASSED DAR a copy of the paper as she pulled away from the arrivals terminal at Miami International Airport. "There you go, rock star."

Dar unfolded the paper as she settled into the passenger seat. "I knew they were taking pictures but I figured...ah hell, yeah, there I am." She exhaled. "I look like a dork."

"Oh you do not," Kerry said. "Did they have you leaning over that table so you wouldn't tower over him?"

Dar studied the picture, then started laughing. "You know, maybe they did. I still think I look like a dork. Stupid-ass posed shot. I was drawing a cow on that pad."

"Were you really?"

"Yeah." Dar folded the paper and put it in the side pocket of the door. "He kept it." She looked mildly embarrassed. "He was all right."

"Bush?"

"Yeah."

"Glad I have my sunglasses on so my eyeballs can't fall out," Kerry said. "Because I would never in a million years have guessed that would come out of your mouth."

"No, me either," Dar said. "I don't know what I was expecting." She propped her elbow against the window and rested her head against her hand. "Anyway, I'm glad I'm back." She reached over the center console and curled her fingers around Kerry's arm.

Kerry moved her arm back so she could clasp her fingers around Dar's. "I'm glad you're back, too. Now maybe I can get a good night's sleep."

Dar brought their joined hands up and kissed Kerry's knuckles, waiting for her to stop at a red light and turn her head so their eyes met.

"Or maybe not." Kerry managed a wry grin.

Dar winked at her. "We should always travel together," she said. "Sorry you had a crappy night last night."

Kerry looked back at the road as the light changed and pushed her sunglasses back up on her nose. "Where you go, I go, baby. Sounds good to me." She left her right hand clasped into Dar's left and felt the squeeze as Dar's long fingers contracted gently.

"Did Mark goose up that web server?" Dar asked after a minute or two of quiet. "We'll get some traction from that dumbass picture anyway."

"Oh yes. He was already working on it before I left to get you. I can just imagine the teeth grinding going on over at the ILS boardroom, though."

"They knew that contract wasn't on the table for them," Dar said. "Bridges told me he was told in no uncertain terms that he was prohibited from giving it to any company with a multinational presence."

"I know that, but can you imagine the scene?" Kerry shook her head. "Every single one of them would have wanted to be in that picture with him."

"You know, I don't feel bad about that," Dar said. "We earned that contract, Kerry. We came to his attention because of who we are, not what ILS was."

Kerry decided not to correct her beloved, since there hadn't been any 'we' involved.

"We did an impossible task for this guy," Dar continued. "We didn't have to, but we did, and he knows that, and he trusts us because of that. ILS would have thrown Alastair to the wolves and he knows that, too. Why should he trust them?"

"That's all true, hon." Kerry pulled into the parking lot of their building. "But it won't stop them from being pissed off about it."

"Peh."

They walked toward the building, and as they did, they clasped hands again, walking up the path side-by-side, then pausing as they spotted a tall ladder blocking the way. "Oh," Kerry said in surprise. "Our sign is here. Wasn't when I left."

There were two men beneath the ladder, preparing the large wooden panel, and they looked up as the two women approached. "Be just a minute, ladies," the nearer of the two men said. "Boss just sent us over to get this ready to mount up."

Kerry kept her hand clasped around Dar's as she studied the sign. It was a honey colored wood, with the company's logo carved into it in a relief. The background of the sign was stained a dark blue, and their compass point logo was painted white and silver. "I like it."

Dar smiled. "Me too. Once it's up I'm going to take a picture and send it to Mom and Dad."

"Between that article and this, your dad's going to explode." Kerry could imagine her father-in-law's expression without much effort. There was just no prouder father anywhere, and she spared a moment remembering coming back uptown with him after they'd managed to get the stock market working.

She, half dazed and aching. Andrew sitting next to her in the limo. Both of them listening to Alastair explain what had happened to Cynthia Stuart, and ending it with the statement "I can tell you this, Senator, I seriously believe with all my heart there's nothing his kid can't do."

Andrew didn't say anything, but Kerry remembered with extraordinary clarity the glint of tears in his eyes and the paradoxical grin on his face. And despite the pain, she remembered smiling, too, if a bit wistfully.

"Or yours." Alastair gave Kerry a gentle pat on the knee. "Saved our asses."

Cracked ribs or not, it felt good.

The two workmen finished preparing the sign, then they mounted the big dual ladder and walked the panel up, positioning it on the second level ledge and clamped it in place so they could drill the bolts in.

Kerry nudged Dar. "Wave, honey. We're on candid camera."

Dar glanced up to the second level windows where there were faces watching them and waving. She lifted her hand and waved back, then made a beckoning motion to the people there. "Let's get a group picture." She draped her arm over Kerry's shoulders. "Only get a first sign once."

True. Kerry grinned as the staff emerged from around the side of the building, having gone out the back to avoid hitting the ladders. They gathered to watch, making a careful circle around their two owners.

Mark eased forward. "Hey, Dar."

"Hey," Dar responded amiably. "This our new security chief?" Dar delivered a smile to Carlos, whose head was roughly even with her own. She extended a hand. "Hi, I'm Dar."

The big man blushed a little, but took her hand. "Hi," he said. "I've heard a lot about you."

"I bet." Dar gave Mark a droll look. "Welcome. Glad you decided to give us a try."

Mayte came over. "Kerry, I have some messages for you. I left them on your desk," she said. "Welcome back," she added to Dar. "My mama also has a package for you, and some notes."

"Thanks." Dar pulled Kerry a little closer. "We just want to get a picture with everyone and the new sign." She pointed at the second level where the workmen were climbing down off the ladder after finishing with the bolts.

Mayte's eyes lit up. "Oh! That is so nice."

They cleared the ladder away and Kerry retrieved her camera from the SUV, taking a few pictures of it before everyone had come down from the office and gathered in front of the entrance. "Okay, now...." She glanced at the workers. "Could I impose on you guys to take a picture of us with this beautiful new sign?"

"Sure." One of them came over and took the camera. "Just press that to focus and then to take the picture?" he asked. "My son's got one of these. He really likes it."

"Yep." Kerry crossed over to where the group was and paused long enough to pick up Mocha, turning and coming up next to Dar who put her arm back over her shoulders. "Everyone ready?"

The workman smiled, and focused, and then it was over and everyone was swirling around again, this time coming up and asking Dar about her meeting.

Kerry took a step back and gave Mocha a hug, walking over to reclaim her camera. "You guys did a great job," she said. "It looks great."

The man nodded. "He's a good carver. Said he'd be by later to check the install and pick up the fee." He scratched Mocha's ears. "Glad he got a commission. Been a while. People don't want to pay for stuff like this in these times."

Kerry nodded. "It's tough. I was glad they referred him to us."

The man glanced around, then back at her. "I heard you had some trouble with some of those guys that hang around in the streets 'round here. That true?"

Kerry wondered if it wasn't just a little more small town like than she was comfortable with. "Yes," she said. "But I think it was more of a miscommunication than anything."

The man nodded. "Be careful with them guys. You seem like nice ladies and we heard they like to hassle women."

Kerry sighed. "I sure hope they don't," she said. "But thanks for the warning."

The man lifted his hand in farewell, then shouldered his tool kit and picked up his end of the ladder, he and his partner moving off down the street together.

Kerry went back to the crowd, who was now sorting themselves out to re-enter the building through the front door. Dar waited for her and they walked back in together and headed up the steps to their offices. "Did you get any lunch?" she asked, as they reached the top of the stairs.

"They fed us on the plane," Dar said.

"Take that as a no, then. We probably have some of those pastelitos left." Kerry bumped her with her hip.

"I've got some Kit Kats left in my backpack." Dar bumped her right back. "We can trade."

Chapter Five

THE SUN WAS setting as they gathered in the conference room, Dar and Kerry, Mark and Carlos, Maria and Mayte. Dar had a copy of the newspaper article and she put it on the table as they all sat down. She folded her hands. "We seem to have acquired some additional notoriety over the past day."

Mayte was taking notes. "It is a very nice picture," she said diplomatically.

"Well, a lot of people think so," Kerry said. Four of those five messages you left me were from people who'd seen it and want to come in and talk to us. So we have a couple issues here. One, we've become very visible very quickly."

Carlos nodded. "People might see you as a way to get in on the government."

"Exactly," Dar said. "That kind of influence is in a business sense, priceless."

"But, Dar...you always had those hooks," Mark said. "I mean, they came after you the last time, remember? Like, right out of the blue."

"That's true," Dar said. "I'm not worried about that part of it. My links to the military are what they are. I can't change that. But we need to think hard about how we're going to secure ourselves because other people might want to find out what we're doing for them."

"Cams," Mark said, then looked pointedly at their new security man.

Carlos pulled out a folder from where it had sat on his lap, and opened it. He was dressed in neatly pressed cargo pants and a blue pullover sweater that had a faint look of the military about it. "I think we should use these." He pushed a data sheet over. "They're expensive, but they're PTZ, IR, night scope, and 10X zoom."

Dar pulled the sheet over and studied it. "IP?"

He nodded. "The last place I was at, they did the wired and wireless, so if someone got some smart idea to cut the cable it would go over the radio."

"Good," Kerry said. "That's nice."

Maria folded her hands. "If you tell me the places you want these things, I will have the electrical man make the connections for them."

Dar's eyes twinkled as Carlos passed a diagram over to her. "Thanks, Maria."

Mark grinned. "Good job, buddy." Carlos grinned back.

"I like that," Dar said, passing the page off to Kerry. "Get them and get them installed. I'll write a program that takes the input from them and parse alerts."

Kerry eyed her. "We do have programmers, hon."

Pale blue eyes pinned her with ferocious intent. "When it comes to the safety of the people here, especially you, I want absolute perfection."

"Got it." Kerry muffled a smile.

"Anyway, I'd like to get the cams in before next week ends if we can. Kerry and I will be out of town this weekend. I'd like to start on the program after we get back from New Orleans."

"Business there, boss?" Mark asked.

"Valentine's Day," Dar responded without missing a beat. Her eyes twinkled a little at his blush. "Back at the old place Ker and I were pretty low key. This isn't ILS. We own this joint so I don't see any point in not being open." She glanced at Carlos. "If you have an issue with that, speak up now."

Carlos shook his head. "I'm fine with it. Mark told me."

Dar cleared her throat. "Okay, so cameras. Now we've also got to secure the data. I can write the encryption into the database schema, but what about the physical side?" She looked over at Mark. "I don't want people to be able to load up external hard drives, or thumb drives, and walk out of here."

Mark nodded. "I got a schematic to protect the server room." He pulled out his own page and pushed it over to Dar. "And it's gonna be a pain in the ass, but we're going to certify all the local storage and not allow any transfer to any device that ain't coded in."

Dar studied the page and grunted in approval.

He pointed at one of the racks. "The big data store, here? We should only allow remote access to. Work in a virtual session with sandboxing. No local transfer at all."

"So the work will actually take place on the main system?" Kerry asked.

"Yeah. I have dot1x on the net, and it'll be an encrypted session," Mark said. "They can check code in and out, it's like they're working local, but everything stays inside the big box."

"I like this," Dar said after a long silence. "Good work, Mark."

"Once we get an offsite datacenter, I'll do a real time sync over the wire to it," Mark went on, a pleased expression on his face. "That place I told you about? It's lit from three directions."

"Nice." Now Dar was smiling. "Thanks, guys. You made me feel like I can take Kerry on a month vacation in a little while and not worry about things back here."

Kerry acknowledged all the smiles with one of her own and then leaned back in her chair in a relaxed pose. "Yeah, so then I can look forward to shooting the rapids with Dar coding in her head," she said. "Someone remind me to not let them give her a paddle."

A round of easy laughter went around the table.

Dar's phone rang and she pushed back from the table a little, pulling the device out and answering it. "Dar Roberts." She paused to listen. "Hey, Dad."

Kerry chuckled and picked up the paper, pointing at the picture.

Dar rolled her eyes. "Thanks. It was all right. Got good press from it."

The group tactfully got up and busied themselves at the coffee station, giving Dar at least a facade of privacy. "Dar's mama and papa must be so proud," Mayte said, as she got herself some tea. "The last one was the paper calling, wasn't it, Kerry?"

"Yep. Business section of the *Herald*." Kerry also got some tea. "They remember us from the cruise ship debacle," she added wryly. "I blocked off a two hour session for them tomorrow morning." She glanced over at Dar. "Probably with more pictures."

"Good thing we got the sign up then," Mark said. "Boy, I tell ya this is so much damn fun."

"It is, isn't it?" Kerry said. "I mean, we've been lucky so far. Things have fallen in place in our favor."

"But even if they had not, it would still be more interesting than the other place," Maria said. "It is so in the energy, yes? To have to make everything new and not to be listening to the same things the same complaints all the time."

"You got it," Mark said. "Not have to be in the same old box all the time. This is great."

Kerry thought about that as she leaned against the wall, listening to the chatter and watching Dar from the corner of her eye. Dar had a distinct blush showing and had that look of half pleasure and half embarrassment that meant she was getting praised by her parents.

It was good. She was glad she didn't have to suffer the same routine day after day, meetings and conciliations with Marketing, and taking customer complaints about service. It was nice to have everything be new all the time, though she knew eventually that, too, would change and there would be another set of routines to get used to.

"Hey, Ker?" Dar held the phone out. "They want to talk to you." She got up and passed the phone over as she traded places with her, pulling open the small refrigerator under the coffee station and issuing a satisfied grunt as she removed a chocolate chug. "Good job, people."

"We aspire to take after our bosses." Mark grinned at her. "Your pop see the pic?"

Dar opened her milk. "Yes, he did. He's not a fan of the current administration, but he did say he was glad I learned my lesson well from him about at least pretending respect to authority."

Mark laughed so hard he almost choked.

"Yeah, that's pretty much what my mother's reaction was," Dar said. "I heard her through the phone. They're out in the BVIs right now at some tiki bar."

"They coming back any time soon?" Mark asked. "I figure if your pop shows up, we won't have to worry about those guys much after that."

"They'll be back in a couple weeks," Dar said. "They're going to stay at our place while we're gone. My mother said she painted a few canvases for our walls here."

"Oh, Dar." Maria held a finger up. "Uno momento, por favor. A person from this area came in this morning and gave me some information about a bed, and that we must get in and ride in it."

Dar blinked at her. "What?"

"Down the street, yes. All of us together, but not until September. So we have time for it."

"Oh the bed race," Carlos said. "Yeah, that's a lot of fun."

"Bed race?"

"OKAY, COL, YOU got everything you need?" Kerry finished zipping her overnight case. "Thanks for staying over."

Colleen was seated on the love seat, her own overnight bag next to her. "No problem at all, Ker." She was flipping through a *People* magazine. "It's never a hardship to stay here on Fantasy Island you know? But you'll do me a favor while you and the Mrs. are partying in Mardi Gras and see if you can find me a man who can buy me a place out here."

"Do my best," Kerry said. "What happened to that guy you were seeing...Arthur?"

"Meh." Colleen glanced up. "He's all right, but he's a bit of a bring to church on Sunday, if you catch me."

"Ah. Yeah. Kind of like Brian was for me." Kerry's eyes twinkled a little. "I've never been to Mardi Gras. Hell, I've never been to New Orleans but I'll see what I can find for you there."

"Take pictures," Colleen said. "Hey, you intending on flashing your tatas to get some of those lovely beads?"

Kerry stopped in mid-motion and looked at her. "What?"

Colleen chuckled. "What what? Haven't you seen those programs about Mardi Gras? All those tourists standing on the sidelines, lifting their shirt up to get the ladies on the floats to toss sparklies at them?"

Kerry put her hands on her hips and stared at her friend. "Colleen," she said. "It took me months to casually take my clothes off in front of Dar, alone in our bedroom. I don't see me doing it on the street for *The Travel Channel* for plastic beads and coconuts."

Colleen snickered and covered her mouth to stifle a laugh.

Dar entered from her office, carrying her own overnight bag. "What was that about plastic beads and coconuts? Are we talking about what I think we're talking about? Our hotel's on one of the parade routes, and we've got second floor balcony rooms."

"Nice," Kerry said. "That means I don't have to take my shirt off to get party favors, right?"

Dar stopped in mid-motion. "What?" She gave Kerry an incredulous look. "Babe, I'll buy you a whole damn float if you want. You don't have to take off anything, honest."

Colleen fell over on the couch, guffawing silently.

Kerry mock sighed. "Oh, good. C'mon let's get out of here before I get myself into any more trouble." She shouldered her bag. "Bye, kids. Be good for Auntie Colleen."

They escaped out the front door and got in Dar's truck, throwing their bags in the back seat. "This is going to be fun," Kerry said, as Dar started up the engine and backed out of her spot. "Especially after this week. Holy cow, Dar, we're going to be out of space for new employees in six months at this rate."

Dar waggled her eyebrows and grinned. "I figure once we get the data center going, we can move the IT people there. The support groups we're going to need, unless we can get more space around our office. To be honest I had no idea we were going to take off like that."

"Six new clients in the last two days." Kerry shook her head. "Unbelievable. Even with that press," she said. "Wait until the *Business Monday* piece runs."

"And none of them current or previous ILS customers." Dar looked satisfied. "That's a good thing, since we don't need any more hot pokers to shove up the ILS board's collective ass."

"Was that Alastair who called you before we left?" Kerry asked. "I guess they saw the story."

"Yeah, they saw the story," Dar said. "He's about tied up everything there. Figures he'll be out by the end of next week. From what I got from him, we're very persona non gratis." She pulled up to the ferry dock and put the truck in park to wait for the next ferry. "They're fuming over not getting a piece of that action."

"They wouldn't have gotten it anyway," Kerry said.

"No, I know," Dar said. "Besides, that's not the direction we'd been taking the company. They stopped doing a lot of custom software a few years back. They don't have much to be pissed about, especially since Gerry renewed those support contracts with them. Alastair said he made sure they knew why."

Kerry was quiet briefly. "How are the new guys doing?" she finally asked.

"My replacement has been busy shooting off hot air in Houston," Dar said. "Sees himself as a tech evangelist. Your replacement brought in about a half dozen of his own people and is cleaning house."

Kerry exhaled. "Damn."

"If it's any consolation," Dar said, "Alastair said Jose told him in the men's room he really misses us." Kerry smiled. "He said he thinks this guy's a bigger ass than I was."

"Oh Lord." Kerry covered her eyes with one hand.

"The test will be the first major issue they have," Dar said. "Lucky for them, we built up a lot of resilience these last few years, but problems will happen eventually. Once that happens, either they'll be able to handle it and start making things their own, or they'll lose it and the shit will hit the fan."

"Well. If they're cleaning house, chances are they'll let go the people who were closest to us," Kerry said.

"And we need people. Synergistic." Dar took the truck out of park and drove onto the ferry. "Sometimes things work out like that."

Kerry settled back in her seat. "Sometimes they do. But let's worry about it next week. After Mardi Gras."

"Sounds good to me."

"TAXI, LADIES?"

"Sure." Dar steered Kerry toward the proffered conveyance. "Royal Sonesta."

The taxi driver smiled. "You bet." He closed the door and then trotted around the front of the cab to get in the driver's seat. "Beautiful night to be flying into NOLA."

Kerry looked around at the packed airport pick up area. "It's really busy."

The driver glanced in the rear view. "You all did know you were comin' in last weekend of Mardi Gras, right?"

Dar chuckled. "We knew," she said. "We've just never been here before."

He smiled again. "First timers. Lordy, lordy."

"Got any recommendations?" Dar asked. "Hate to be a typical tourist if I don't have to be."

The driver cleared his throat. "My view is, first time you're here, be a tourist. See all the stuff, do all the stuff, 'specially if you're here for Mardi Gras. Ain't no other purpose for that than tourism, know what I mean?"

"Okay." Dar looked out the window, hearing the blare of music that fell behind them quickly. "Good point."

"Second time," he said, "then you can start being choosy."

Kerry read the plastic covered map fastened to the back of the seat. "Oh, Dar, they have a ghost tour. Can we do that?"

The driver laughed throatily. "Careful with that one if you get scared easy. There's plenty of old spirits here."

"Sure," Dar said. "Why the hell not?"

"Why do you have a lot of old spirits here?" Kerry asked. "Because the city's so old?"

The taxi driver met her eyes in the rear view. "You fooling with me? You ain't never heard of all the hoodoo and voodoo and things like that here? For real?"

Kerry looked over at Dar, who shrugged and lifted her hands in supplication. "No, I don't think I have. I don't know that much about New Orleans. Do you, hon?"

Dar remained silent for a bit, then cleared her throat. "Well, I've heard a little bit about it. My father's folks come from Alabama, remember."

"Whereabouts in Alabama?" The driver asked with interest. "Got family there."

"Small place near Ozark," Dar replied. "Nearest big town is Montgomery."

"Lordy that is deep woods Alabama." The driver chuckled. "My folks are just north of Mobile."

"Oh, yeah," Kerry said. "I remember that story he told us when he came back from his sister's wedding. You know, maybe we should have brought him and your mom here. Between his ghost tales and her being a pagan, we could have had some real fun on this tour."

"Next time," Dar said. The taxi slowed down and into a part of the city that had narrower streets and a lot more people. "Is this the French Quarter?"

"Yes, ma'am, it sure is." The driver relaxed as the pace slowed to a crawl. "Just get yourselves a good look now. We got plenty of time before we get to the hotel."

Kerry felt like a kid, her eyes taking in the scene on either side of the car. The streets were filled with revelers, dressed in everything from casual clothing to lurid masks and paint. Or just paint. "Dar...is that...?"

"Woman naked? Yes." Dar peered out her own window. "Is that legal?"

"That's what them Fleur-de-lies are there for," the driver replied with a chuckle. "You got to have the illusion of something, see what I mean?"

"Oh. Yeah. I see what you mean." Kerry put a hand on her cheek. "My Midwestern roots are curling up and screaming."

Dar patted her leg. "Breathe, babe." She heard music through the window, brassy and penetrating, a rhythm she knew only slightly, new and raw. "Here's the hotel."

Kerry's eyes lit up. "Oh wow." She studied the building, which wrapped around a corner and had old style wrought iron railings on the floors overlooking the street. "We're in one of those rooms, Dar?"

"We are." Dar opened the door as the driver got hastily out. She handed him a folded bill. "Keep the change."

"Yes, ma'am, and thank ya." He gestured to the hotel as he handed them their overnights. "You all have a good old time now, hear?"

"I'm absolutely sure we will." Dar paused as a man on stilts rambled by between them and the entrance.

"Wow." Kerry tucked her hand inside Dar's elbow and they advanced cautiously through the crowd. "Hope you packed earplugs or we're not getting any sleep."

"Didn't figure we would anyway," Dar said as they got inside the door. "I'm sure there's coffee here."

The lobby was filled with people, but it was quieter inside. Kerry kept her grip on Dar as they eased through the crowd to the check-in desk. She turned when they got there to survey the interior while Dar attended to the necessary procedures.

The space was full of old fashioned furniture and trim, heavy velvet draping and chandeliers. Everyone in the lobby seemed to be holding a drink of some kind. Some had layers and layers of beads around their necks.

Kerry turned back around as Dar put a hand on her arm and indicated the stairs to their left. "Might as well walk up," she said, regarding the crowd around the elevators.

They climbed up the old fashioned sweeping stairs and walked along the hall until Dar stopped at a set of double doors. She opened them and they went inside, presented with a suite of rooms as traditionally decorated as the lobby was.

"Wow." Kerry put her bag down and went to the French doors, which opened out onto a long balcony. "This is all ours?"

"Yep." Dar looked out to see Bourbon Street stretching out in front of them, filled with people and music and parties, along with the smell of garlic and sugar. "Hungry?"

"Hell, yeah." Kerry walked out onto the balcony and put her hands on the cold, dark wrought iron. She looked out over the crowd. "This is wild."

"Let's go to that place." Dar pointed. "I can see the sign that says shrimp and grits."

Kerry started laughing. "Okay, shrimp and grits. Then we go ghost hunting." She regarded the busy street with a relaxed and totally engaged grin. She turned, put her arms around Dar and squeezed hard. "Thanks."

Dar returned the hug with a happy grin of her own. "Let's go have fun."

Kerry added a festive burgundy silk scarf to her leather jacket and ran a brush through her hair, then followed Dar out the door of their snazzy suite and back down the steps.

The crowd was dense, the restaurant packed, but Kerry negotiated that with ease and fifteen minutes later they were seated and examining a rustic menu. "Holy pooters. I can see I'm going to be putting on ten pounds this weekend," Kerry remarked. "I want one of everything."

Dar regarded the drink menu. "Milk punch. Do I have to try that?"

"I think you do."

A waiter arrived shortly with no pad or pen, just an inquisitive eyebrow. "We'll share a large seafood plate to start," Kerry told him. "I'll have the catfish pecan, and my friend here wants the red fish on the half shell."

The waiter smiled. "Good picks," he said. "Drinks?"

"I guess I have to try the milk punch," Dar said. "Ker?"

"I'll try a Bluegrass sunset." Kerry handed the menus back to the waiting server. "And some water, please."

The waiter half bowed and disappeared.

"Do we need to make reservations for that ghost tour?" Kerry relaxed in her chair, regarding the busy restaurant contentedly. "And I thought you were going to get shrimp and grits?"

"Tomorrow." Dar took her phone out. "Let me get reservations. I'm sure they're packed tonight." She looked up the number on the gizmo, then pressed it to dial. "I like these things. Wish the Internet was faster though."

Kerry caught sight of a group of musicians outside. As the door opened to let in more diners the sounds of a saxophone blared inside, a background to the group of garishly dressed faux skeletons moving past. Way different than she'd expected, but in a good way. "This is cool."

She took a sip of Dar's milk punch when it arrived and licked her lips. "Bet these are popular."

"Yes, the ladies really like them." The waiter winked at her. "They go down easy."

"Oh yes. I can see why a lot of people end up taking their shirts off in the street in that case." Kerry settled back with her drink. "That's very good."

Dar sucked cautiously at her glass. "Hardly tastes like there's alcohol in there," she said as she hung up the phone. "We're set for ten p.m. We lucked out. They usually only go at eight."

"That's why they're dangerous." Kerry pointed at the glass. "There's a shot and a half of bourbon in that thing."

Dar eyed it. "Only one for me then." She put her gizmo away. "I don't want a picture of me showing up somewhere with my shirt off in the streets of New Orleans."

"Somehow I don't think that would hurt sales any." Kerry enjoyed the look of self deprecating exasperation on Dar's face. "Hey, I've seen you with your shirt off."

"Wench."

"Hehehe."

IF ANYTHING, IT was even busier on the street when they emerged, making their way slowly through the crowds. Kerry put her hands into her jacket pockets. "That was awesome. But I'm stuffed." She sighed. "Glad we're on a walking tour now."

"Me too," Dar agreed. "They said to meet up at Reverend Zombie's Voodoo Shop." She gazed reflectively down the street. "Two blocks from here."

"Reverend Zombie's Voodoo Shop?" Kerry said. "Seriously?"

Dar nodded. "I'm sure there'll be a shopping opportunity there. We could get a skull or something for my desk."

"We could get your mom some crystals I bet," Kerry countered.

"No skull, hon. It'll freak Maria out." She tucked her hand inside Dar's elbow again and slowed her pace, looking around at everything in the chaos they were walking through. "Do you believe in any of that magic stuff?"

"No," Dar replied.

"Even after what happened with your dad?"

"No," Dar repeated. "Do you really think the ghost of his daddy rose from the grave and was chased off by some demon?"

"Well, sweetie, he's not an oogie boogie kinda guy, you know? If he said he saw creepy things like that, I'm inclined to think something happened," Kerry said. "I can't picture him making up a story like that."

Dar sucked on the mint she'd taken from the restaurant in silence for a few minutes. "Well," she cleared her throat, "he might have done that to avoid telling us what really might have happened to those guys who disappeared."

Kerry digested that as they walked along, turning a corner and heading for where a group had already formed on the sidewalk outside a shop. "You mean maybe he did something to them?"

"He kinda makes up rules sometimes," Dar said in an almost apologetic tone. "So I think he'd rather tell us about ghosts than he would about how he maybe took those guys out."

"Oh," Kerry said. "Huh. I never thought about that. I just never could imagine him lying to us in that kind of way."

"I'm not saying he did," Dar said. "It's just possible, y'know?"

"Mm."

"Or, what the hell. Maybe he did see ghosts." Dar sighed. "I don't know. But no, I don't believe in that stuff. All that psychic mumbo jumbo just never rang true to me."

Kerry eyed her but said nothing, a brief smile appearing on her face.

Dar caught it. "Except for that stuff with us," she said. "I'll find a scientific reason for it sometime." She had to chuckle, though, shrugging a little wryly. "But that's not ghosts."

"No, it isn't." Kerry pressed her head against Dar's shoulder. "Let's go see if NOLA can cough up some ghosts for us. Here we are."

They slowed to a halt as they joined the group outside the voodoo shop, which was closed. Dar went to the window and peered inside curiously, since the guides were still getting their paperwork sorted out.

She studied the objects then gave a side glance at Kerry as she came up to join her. "Nice."

"Oh. Dear." Kerry's brows contracted. "Huh. That's some weird stuff, but hey, look. They do palm readings." She took Dar's hand in her own and turned it up most. "We could come back and get our fortunes told, right?"

"Sure," Dar answered after a brief pause. "Or maybe get our Tarot cards read." She pointed at the sign inside. "I've wondered over the years how many people have stopped in NOLA and gotten voodoo dolls for me." Her eyes flashed with sudden humor. "I always imagined Jose's inner office to have a picture of me on the back of the door filled with dart holes."

"Or BB holes." Kerry chuckled. "Didn't seem to have done you much harm."

Dar moved over to the guides to confirm their registration, leaving Kerry to peruse the window. She let her eyes run over the candles, incense, herbs, charms and trinkets. It seemed to be a veritable cornucopia of magic-inspired products including books and magazines she imagined were devoted to the practice.

A woman who was leaning against the wall turned to speak to her. "If you go in there, don't take pictures and don't ask questions about black magic. It pisses them off," she said. "I went in there today and they threw this guy out because he opened one of those books."

Kerry turned, leaned her shoulder against the window surface and folded her arms. "Not very customer centric, I guess."

The woman shrugged. "Mostly tourists, I guess, so they get tired of it. I did get my palm read though and that was amazing."

"Really? I was thinking of doing that tomorrow."

The woman nodded emphatically. "It was probably eighty percent accurate. I was blown away. So weird. But I enjoyed it and my husband did, too. It's our first time in New Orleans."

"Ours, too," Kerry said. "So far it's been a lot of fun. We just got here tonight."

"We came this morning. It's our wedding anniversary." The woman smiled. "Something different. Last year we went to Vegas."

The woman was middle aged and about Kerry's height, with curly brown hair. She was stockily built and had a knit pull-on cap on her head to ward off the night chill. "I can't wait to see the ghosts. Some people take pictures of them."

The husband came back over with Dar right behind him. "All right, Sarah, you ready?" He looked good humored about the tour. "Let's go find you some spooks."

The woman beamed at him and they moved off to get in line as the tour guides got ready to lead them off.

Dar and Kerry joined the queue and Dar put her hands behind her and rocked up and down a few times on the balls of her feet.

"Are you going to kill me?" Kerry asked, slipping one hand into Dar's front pocket.

Dar chuckled. "Only if you keep me up all night yelling about ghosts."

Kerry started forward as the group did. "You'll have to find something else to distract me with then."

KERRY FELT THAT it would likely seem far spookier on the tour if she couldn't hear people partying a street or two over. The stories behind the so called haunted places were interesting, but she didn't feel even a twinge of creepiness as they moved along from the Lalaurie Mansion to the next tale of the Octoroon Mistress.

The tour guides were dramatic and fun and everyone was having a good time, though. Kerry was standing in the front part of the circle around the guide, Dar behind her casually resting her arms on Kerry's shoulders.

"That's right ladies and gentlemen, up there on that ledge, only in the coldest nights, you can see a wispy figure of a naked woman."

Kerry fastened her eyes attentively on the spot. "You think it's cold enough?" she whispered to Dar.

"I think if we see someone it has to be a ghost," Dar said. "It's too damn cold to be up there naked. Even piss ass drunk."

"Can you just picture it?" the guide said. "As the moon rises over the building, as the mist comes up from the river..."

A gasp went up as motion was detected across the roof. For a brief moment a dark shape could be seen. Then it was gone.

"Did you see it?" the guide said, excitedly. "Anyone get a picture?" He moved over to look at one woman's digital camera. "You did!"

"Mm," Dar grumbled softly. "Did you see it?"

"I did," Kerry admitted. "I've got no idea what it was. At this distance it could have been a cat for all I know, but I saw it. Did you?"

"I saw something."

The excitement around the group was now electric. Many gathered around the woman with the camera, others shaded their eyes from the street lamps, peering up at the ceiling.

"The ghost is Julie," the guide said. "She was an octoroon. Does anyone here know what that is?" He looked around but no one answered. "It's someone who is one eighth black, seven eighths white. In the old days there were many of these women in New Orleans. Legend says they were very beautiful."

Kerry listened with interest.

"These women were much desired by the Creoles and the Frenchmen who made their home in New Orleans, but because of their social status they could never marry." The guide motioned them closer. "The Octoroon Julie fell in love with a Frenchman and very much wanted to marry him. But he refused her because of her status."

"Prick," Dar said softly, making Kerry smile.

"So one night the Frenchman thought he would put Julie's love to the test. If she met the test he would think about marrying her. He brought many friends to his house and told her if she would take all her clothes off and wait for him on the roof, he would come get her and bring her down to introduce her to society. He never thought she would take the dare."

The wind got colder all of a sudden. Dar lifted her head and her ears twitched as above the revelry she thought she heard a moan through the trees.

"But she did," the guide said. "She went up on the roof, took off her clothes and stood up there waiting for her love to come meet her."

"Ugh," Kerry muttered.

"But he never did. He finally went to bed and was surprised not to find her there warming the sheets for him. So he rushed up onto the roof and there, in the cold, was her dead, frozen body."

The crowd murmured.

"He died himself, several months later," the guide said. "Many say of a broken heart."

"Don't have much sympathy for the guy," Dar said quietly. "But it says something about how it was back then."

"If they were that hung up about one eighth of someone's blood I can only imagine how they would have felt about us," Kerry responded. "Sheesh."

"So often, today, those who work in that building say they hear Julie running around the top floor where her rooms were and hear her laughing. Also, they see the Frenchman in the garden, a sad and lonely figure," the guide continued. "Of course the fact that a palm reading and tarot company owns the building probably makes the encounters all the more interesting."

"And a good advertisement," the middle aged woman's husband commented.

"That, too," the guide agreed with a cheerful smile. "Let's move on to see the garden, shall we? Maybe we'll see the Frenchman in there." He led the way across the street toward the shadowed, gated space.

"Oh my gosh, this is so exciting!" Sarah said, reviewing her camera. "I can't believe I got a picture of it!"

Kerry glanced up at Dar. "You're not buying this, are you?"

Dar remained silent for a moment then she coughed a little. "There was something behind us back there."

Kerry almost came to a halt, so surprised was she to hear that. "What?" She looked back the way they came and saw nothing more interesting than a lamppost. "What?"

Dar put her hand on Kerry's back to keep her on the path. "There was something back there watching us. I felt it behind me."

"Something like a stray dog or a cop or..." Kerry asked, hesitantly.

"I don't know. I felt cold breath on my back," Dar said with devastating calmness. "Sort of like in the condo when you stand in that spot outside the kitchen. Under the vent?"

Kerry looked behind them again and stared up at Dar, unable to come up with a response. "Uh."

"Anyway," Dar said. "Maybe I just imagined it all. Let's go in there and see what we find." She focused her attention on the crowd, which had filtered in through the wrought iron gates into the garden. "Maybe it was just a draft from between those two buildings."

Kerry latched onto her arm and collected her scattered wits. She edged into the garden and peered around, half expecting to see a tall spectral figure watching them from between the bushes.

The guide was speaking, relating some details about the life of the Frenchman but Kerry was convinced she kept seeing whispers of motion in her peripheral vision. As she realized that her heart started to beat faster.

Dar strolled along at her side, turning her head to look between the flowers. She reached out idly with her free hand to touch the petals stained gray by the night gloom.

A frog croaked to the left and Kerry almost jumped into Dar's arms, bumping her abruptly and making her take a little hop. "Oh...sorry," she muttered. "Stupid frog."

Dar moved, shifting her hand off Kerry's back as she draped her arm over her shoulders instead. "No problem, babe." She looked up into the sky. "Was that a bat?"

"Are you trying to freak me out?" Kerry said after a pause.

"No," Dar responded. "I really did think I saw one."

Kerry looked up herself and sucked in a breath as a shadowy figure fluttered overhead, moving from one tree to another. "Oh!"

"Yeah, that's what I saw," Dar said. "That's a bat, right? Not a bird?"

Kerry let her eyes drop and she jerked as her gaze fell on a translucent form with moonlight pouring through it, staring at them. "Ah!"

Then it was gone. "Did you see that?" she whispered to Dar.

Dar was half turned, her blue eyes grayish silver in the gloom. "I just saw some fog," she said. "What did you see?"

Kerry looked back over and saw the fog, too. It was just a light mist, drifting between the bushes and she hesitated, now doubting what she herself saw. "Well."

"So sometimes people walking in the garden encounter the Frenchman," the guide said, enjoying the wide eyes of his audience. "He's always dressed in a cutaway coat and a cravat. Let's move on and see if we can find him."

Did she see something? Or was her imagination just working in overdrive? Kerry tried to recall what she thought she'd seen, but the more she looked at the fog, the less she was convinced she'd seen anything at all. After a moment she relaxed and walked along with Dar after the group, most of whom were starting to huddle together.

The sounds of music got louder and as they reached the other end of the garden, the guide almost had to shout over it. Kerry looked behind her as they moved back into the street, but the garden was quiet, empty of anything but moonbeams and some fog.

But she felt strange. She took a breath and let it out, following Dar as they caught up to the back of the tour group on their way to the next station. Despite the empty trees she had the uncanny sensation that she was being watched. No matter how quickly she glanced around she couldn't find a concrete set of eyes pointed in her direction.

"Ker?"

"Yeah." Kerry cleared her throat and tucked her hand inside Dar's elbow again. "Hon, next time just tell me to go find an ice cream parlor, okay?"

Dar chuckled.

"What in the hell was I thinking?"

Dar leaned over and gave her a kiss on the cheek. "Relax. Whatever comes out of the ether at you, I'll take care of it, promise."

Kerry was glad of the reassurance when the guide took them down a narrow lane between towering buildings. They stopped at one with a wrought iron balcony not too different from the one at their hotel. It was dark and the wind was chill. She kept hearing things being blown around behind her.

Leaves? She moved a bit closer to Dar. Sure. Leaves.

She heard a scuff and a crunch and she half turned to see a shadowy form that nearly made her guts come out of her ears before her brain sorted it out and she realized it was a dog. "Hey, looks like Chino."

Dar turned her head and smiled. "It does," she agreed. "Glad it wasn't the Hound of the Baskervilles?"

Kerry cleared her throat and focused her attention forward. "Yes."

Dar pulled her closer. "Chill, Ker, chill."

Kerry sighed, as they came up to the back of the group who had stopped on the sidewalk. "I feel kind of like a dork."

"So, we come to the tale of the Mad Butcher," the guide began. "Many cities have a legend of a Mad Butcher, but here in New Orleans it takes on a different tune because of course, it also includes sausages and a mistress. So here we go."

"Hm." Dar grunted softly.

"Back in the day there was a butcher who lived in that house with his wife, and his factory. He made the best pork sausages in town and everyone bought from him. The butcher was happy, but as the years went on and he and his wife got older, he began to tire of her."

"I don't think I want to listen to this one," Kerry said. "I can see where it's going."

"You want to duck out?" Dar asked. "It's just a short walk back to the hotel."

Kerry thought about it then nodded. "It's late. I'm tired and my mind is going in circles. Maybe we can try another tour tomorrow night."

"No problem." Dar guided her away from the back of the crowd and down the next side street. As they moved along the music got louder. They saw bright lights and something big moving. "Hey, a parade." She pointed. "That's a lot more cheerful than creeps."

Kerry was glad to leave the spooks behind as they turned at the corner of Canal Street and saw a long cavalcade of floats and marchers, all in lurid, pungent colors, brass instruments blaring. "Oh yeah, this is better." She eased in beside Dar near the edge of the street, smiling as one of the floats came even with them, full of revelers in masks. "Oh, those are pretty."

It was all very frenetic. Kerry wasn't sure who or what the float was supposed to represent, but there were people on the floats who were throwing things to the crowd with distinct enthusiasm. Strings of beads, round metal bits, cups, stuffed animals.

"Look out." Dar's reflexes saved her from being bonked by a flying disk. Then she put her hands up and found them ringed by strings of beads that wrapped around her wrists.

"Hey, babe!" one of the float members yelled, looking right at her. "Smile!"

Kerry did and was rewarded with a tossed cup. "Holy crap," she said as the float passed. "What the hell is all this?"

"They're called throws." Dar was laughing. "Hey, at least they didn't ask you to take off your shirt." She dropped the disk into Kerry's cup, took the beads from her wrists and put them around her neck. "C'mon, hot stuff. Let's see what other swag we can get."

The shadows fell away from Kerry's thoughts and she grinned, seeing rows and rows of spectators also covered in beads, necklaces, and a range of other gaudy decorations. They were also yelling at the parade. "What are they all shouting?"'

"Morpheus," Dar said. "That's the group who's doing this parade. Each parade is sponsored by a society of volunteers. They're called krewes."

Kerry studied the oncoming marchers. "They just do this for fun?"

"Yup."

"They don't get paid?"

"Nope. It's all just to party."

Kerry blinked. "Wow. I think I like New Orleans."

The band marched by, playing their hearts out, sending brassy tones up into the night air as unicycle riders wove in and out of their ranks, tossing beads and glowing necklaces as they passed.

"Jesus!" Kerry glanced down the road for the next float. "Oh, look at that. I want a stuffed animal." She pointed at two women throwing the objects randomly.

"No problem," Dar responded gallantly, starting to unbutton her shirt.

"No wait...not...Dar!" Kerry grabbed her clothing hastily. "I don't want one that bad."

"I thought you liked me with my shirt off."

"Dar!"

Dar chortled softly and put her arms around Kerry, giving her a hug. "Okay, hon." She rocked them both back and forth. "How about a beer?"

"Sure." Kerry steered her toward an outdoor cafe. "That's a lot safer than plush toys. All I need for this place is cash." She fished a bill out of her pocket and pinned the waitress with an intent stare. "I don't have to share my eye candy."

Dar started laughing out loud.

Chapter Six

IT WAS VERY late when they finally wandered back into the hotel lobby, arm in arm. Kerry felt amiably over stimulated, her ears still ringing from the music and a sense of pleasant displacement insulating her from the several mugs of beer she'd consumed.

It smelled of wood and candles in the hall and there was a sense of age and decorum about the room, historic and different and reminding her oddly of some places she'd been in the Capitol. "Shouldn't have had that last beer," she said mournfully. "Time to park my ass in bed."

"That's where we're going." Dar guided her up the steps, giving a brief smile and nod to the room service waiter on his way down.

"Evening, ladies." He returned the greeting with a smile. "Anything I can bring you lovely gals tonight?"

"Please don't say ice cream, Dar. I've got too much beer in me," Kerry muttered. "Not a good mix."

"How about some nice hot tea," Dar said, "and a couple bottles of water."

"Surely!" The waiter smiled. "Be right up with it."

"Mmm...nice hot tea." Kerry sighed. "You're the best."

Dar unlocked the door and steered them both inside. She smiled when she saw their bed turned down and chocolate truffles placed neatly awaiting them.

"Boy, that looks good." Kerry kicked off her shoes. "I don't know if I'm going to last for tea. I'm wiped." She carefully untangled the many strands of beads from her neck and put them on the desk, adding the coins to them. "That was wild and crazy."

Dar pulled something from her pocket and dropped it next to Kerry's booty. "There."

"Oh, you got one?" Kerry picked up the plush animal with a look of surprise. "I didn't see you do that."

Dar chuckled.

"Did you have to flash them for it?" Kerry peered at her from under very disheveled bangs. "Tell me the truth."

Dar obligingly came over, wrapping her arms around Kerry, gazing down into her eyes. "The truth is, I'd have stripped naked and covered myself in honey if it would made you happy." She smiled at the gentle shift in Kerry's expression. "But the truth also is that three people from the ILS New Orleans office were on that float and nearly split their pants rushing over to give me their toys."

Kerry fell against her and savored the hug that followed. "They recognized you?"

"Oh yeah." Dar laughed easily along with her. "Actually they said someone told them we were going to be here and they were on the lookout for us. You were getting beer at the time and they had to keep up with the float. They were bummed they missed you."

Kerry closed her eyes, glad the windows were sufficiently insulated that only a faint blare of horns and yells filtered through to them. She felt Dar start to peel her shirt off and merely smiled, enjoying the sensation of the room air hitting her bare skin between her shoulder blades.

Dar's fingers cradled the back of her head and their lips met.

Kerry pulled back and deftly removed Dar's shirt, then worked at the button on Dar's jeans, the well worn and broken in fabric yielding easily to her fingers. The loosened denim slid down revealing Dar's briefs, a pair Kerry had given her for Christmas that was sedately decorated with UNIX commands.

Some people shopped for lingerie at Victoria's Secrets, she shopped at *Thinkgeeks.com*, so did Dar, who gave her the Darth Vader boxer shorts she was currently in the process of losing, believing the statement—come to the dark side, we've got cookies!—seemed to fit her.

Rampant nerdism.

She had just removed the briefs from Dar's hips, and they were making a slow move toward the bed when there was a knock at the door.

"Ah, crap."

"Tea." Kerry banged her head gently against Dar's chest. "Why did we do that?"

"We're drunk." Dar nudged her over to the bed and pulled the covers back. "G'wan. I'll get it." She pulled her shirt back on and tugged it down to an almost modest length and trudged over to the door.

Kerry watched with a faint grin, and half closed eyes, as Dar opened it to accept the tray, setting it down on the credenza and walking the bill back over to the waiter and closing him out of the room once he took it. Then she went back to the tray and opened one of the bottles of water, her figure outlined by the light from the window.

"Here." Dar brought two glasses back over. "I've been told if you stay hydrated, you get less of a hangover." She sat down on the edge of the bed and offered Kerry one. "True?"

"Never tried it, no idea." Kerry drank the liquid anyway. "But it sure as hell can't hurt, right? I figured you'd find some way of making that chocolate fizzy thing if waking up tomorrow's too bad."

"Mm." Dar put her glass down, then took Kerry's and got rid of that, too. She pulled off her shirt and gave it a toss in the direction of the credenza. She licked her lips and slid under the covers. "Now. Where were we?"

"I'd just taken off your briefs and you were...ah, yeah."

She felt the straps on her bra come loose and then Dar's thigh slipped between hers. She gave herself over to the growing passion that burned its way through the alcohol and brought life into sharp, sensual focus. It brought a lightness to her thoughts and any memories of earlier shadows vaporized as Dar put her knowledge of Kerry's body to good use.

They were part of each other in this moment and this moment was the only thing she knew or cared about. Kerry felt the aching tension start to escalate and it brought a rush of adrenaline with it, making her ferociously happy.

Hangovers and ghosts be damned.

DAR OPENED HER eyes, half lifting her head off the pillow. After a moment of silence she blinked, not sure what had wakened her.

It was dark and quiet in the room, soft creaks and pops sounding at irregular intervals. It was raining outside and she heard a faint rumble of thunder, but that was it. She glanced over at her bedmate, finding Kerry curled half on her side and half on her stomach, her arm wrapped around her pillow, very sound asleep.

"Hmph." She settled back down on her side and put her arm around Kerry's waist. Without waking, Kerry seemed to sense the pressure and shifted a little, moving closer and pressing against Dar with a faint sound of contentment.

That made Dar smile. She closed her eyes, glad at least that her head seemed to be fairly clear and there were no obvious aftereffects of their fun evening. She'd had a hangover once or twice in her life and hadn't enjoyed it, but she didn't regret spending the night letting her hair down with Kerry either.

Sometimes you just had to do that. Dar exhaled and let her body relax, but halfway through that she stopped as she got the uncanny sense that something was watching her, a prickling of the shoulder blades that made her nape hairs lift.

Imagination? Dar lifted her head and turned, looking back over her shoulder at the window, fully expecting to find nothing and shocked breathless when she saw a shadowy figure on the balcony looking in.

For a long moment, she froze. Then instinct took over and she slid out from under the covers and stood up to put herself between the window and Kerry.

She straightened up to her full height and squared her shoulders, flexing her hands a little as she took a deep breath and a step toward the window. The figure was dark, tall, and indistinct, and though she couldn't see the features, she knew it was looking right at her.

It occurred to her, somewhat belatedly, that facing an unknown intruder stark naked wasn't the smartest thing she could do, but she had no intention of taking the time to put clothes on when that same intruder could burst in the doors and...

Well, it would have to go through her to get to Kerry. Expecting fear but finding only fierce determination instead, she flexed her hands again and took another step forward, spreading her arms out to present as threatening a defense as she could. Blood rushed to her skin and sent a warm flush through her muscles.

The figure moved as she did and she drew in a breath to let out a yell when thunder, followed by lightning, made her jump. It bathed her in light and she blinked from it. When it faded, the figure was gone.

Gone.

Dar walked to the double French doors and put her hands against them, looking out onto the long balcony beyond. She saw the length of it and the emptiness echoed in her senses as her heart rate started to slow back down.

"Dar?"

Dar stifled a yelp, sucking in air abruptly before she turned around to see Kerry sitting up in bed, her bare upper torso visible in the faint light. "Ah."

"What's wrong?" Kerry cleared her throat of its huskiness. "You okay?"

Dar came back over and sat on the bed. "Yeah, I'm fine. Storm out there. Woke me up." She ran a slightly shaking hand through her hair. "Whew."

Kerry touched her arm, closing her fingers around it. "That last blast woke me up, too," she said. "You sure you're okay? You look a little freaked out."

Dar turned and pulled one knee up, resting her hands on it as she studied Kerry's face. "I thought I saw someone out on the balcony."

Kerry jerked in surprise. "What?" She looked in reflex at the window. "I don't see anything out there."

"No, not now," Dar said. "When I woke up I looked over there and saw someone standing outside. Then after that big flash, it was gone."

"It." Kerry repeated, after a pensive moment of mutual silence. "What did it look like?"

Dar lay back down and pulled the covers up, the cool air of the room giving her goose bumps. "Couldn't see detail. Just something tall and dark, maybe in an overcoat or something. But it might have just been a shadow, Ker, because it wasn't there when I went to the window."

Kerry studied the glass. "Or maybe whatever it was got scared when they saw a six foot plus tall buff naked woman lunging at them." She gave her soulmate a fond look. "That'd be enough to scare off a robber, don't you think?"

Dar's dark eyebrow hiked.

"But you know," Kerry said. "I think I saw something like that in the garden we walked in. Just tall and all shadowy."

They regarded each other in silence again. "You mean, not a real thing?" Dar said, hesitantly. "As in, a ghost?"

Kerry shrugged. "It was there and then it wasn't. I don't know. I don't know what you saw, but it sounds like what I saw, and it was full of creepitude." She paused. "So what's creepier? A ghost or some guy following us around and climbing up on our balcony?"

"That puts it in perspective doesn't it?" Dar said. She gave Kerry a wry look. "I don't know, Ker. Maybe it was neither. Could have just been my imagination."

"Mm. That's what I thought in the garden, too."

Dar pondered the idea quietly. What did she see? Shadows? Her imagination? Nothing? A real intruder trying to get in their hotel room? Should she call the front desk, the cops, or a psychiatrist? "I dunno," she finally said. "I don't really want to get dressed and go out in the rain to see if whatever it was left footprints."

Kerry settled back down next to her and put her head on Dar's shoulder. "What exactly were you planning to do running out like that in your altogether, sweetie?" she asked, consciously trying to lighten the conversation. "I mean, what if it had actually been a burglar?"

"Damned if I know," Dar admitted with a faint smile. "All I was thinking about was staying between whatever it was and you."

"You're such a super hero." Kerry tickled her navel and felt the motion as Dar chuckled silently. "I'm going to get you those Superman panties I saw on the Internet the other day." She looked over to find herself being watched by those pale eyes almost glowing with affection. "And besides all that, you sure are my hero."

Dar stuck her tongue out.

"Anyway, we'll check out the floor out there when we have coffee tomorrow," Kerry said. "Hopefully this headache I've got will be gone by then. Teach me to mix bourbon and beer."

Dar tucked the covers around the both of them and shut her eyes. The rumble of thunder slowly lulled her back into some level of relaxation while she allowed her mind to ponder what had happened. She felt the warmth of Kerry's breath against the side of her neck and the gentle motion of the edge of her thumb making idle patterns against her bare skin. She knew a moment of deep echo, a wash of familiarity that seemed ancient and new all at the same time.

Weird.

What had she intended on doing? Rushing out onto the balcony and drop kicking the damn thing? Dar had to smile at herself, if only in self deprecation. What if it was a ghost? Should she have been afraid of it? She hadn't been. Or maybe it had happened so fast she hadn't had time to be scared either way.

Oh well.

New Orleans was known for odd things. They'd half jokingly gone out looking for ghosts and she was now ready to internally accept that maybe they'd seen something unexplained.

Or maybe they both just had good imaginations. Dar dismissed the events and snuggled up tighter with Kerry, content to leave any other analysis until morning when sunlight and coffee might put a completely different slant on things.

One eye opened and she regarded Kerry. Unless she had to go find an egg cream. Her eye closed again and now the silence returned, broken only by two sets of quiet breathing.

AS IT HAPPENED, no egg cream was needed. Kerry picked up her cup of coffee and sipped from it, enjoying the cool air and the completely ghost free balcony. She was dressed in a pair of ragged old jeans and a royal blue sweatshirt with the sleeves pushed up to her elbows,

There were no scuffs or footprints, but then it rained all night and she doubted there would have been any anyway. Kerry studied the long stretch of empty ground as she sipped from her cup, trying to sort out in her head what had gone on.

Dar was not an easily suggestible person. She had an imagination, certainly, but she was so logic driven, Kerry often suspected her daydreams were formed from Ethernet packet encapsulation schemes where her own mind tended to be far more flexible in that regard.

So what did Dar see? Since her imagination tended to the prosaic, Kerry was pretty sure she'd seen something. Something that was alarming enough to get her out of bed and ready to — she glanced inside the open French doors where her beloved was studiously stirring her coffee — ready to defend her from whatever it was.

Which was sort of charming. Kerry picked up her Handspring and reviewed her mails, which were refreshingly few. Most were focused on acknowledgements for pricing she'd provided, and a note from their landlord praising their new sign.

It was nice to not have a knot in her guts every time the new message alert went off. She thought about how long she'd been living with that tension. "Hey, hon?"

"Yes?" Dar came out and took the seat next to her, extending her denim covered legs with her socked feet out and crossing them at the ankles. "I went to the front desk on my way back from getting this coffee and those doughnuts."

Kerry licked her lips. "They were good."

"First time I saw carnival food presented in a French style cafe, but yes," Dar said. "Anyway, I asked about tours and stuff and said we'd had a good time last night. The desk clerk mentioned this hotel was on one of the other outfit's tours but they didn't like it."

"Because they say this place is haunted?"

"Yes," Dar said. "So I told them I saw something on the balcony last night."

"Ah hah."

"I think she was waiting to see if I was going to freak out about it and when I didn't, she coughed up the fact that maybe some other people who stayed here have mentioned that. It's why they usually rent out these rooms to big groups who want to have a party."

"I see."

"Mm." Dar sipped her coffee. "I said I didn't care."

"Do you?" Kerry watched her curiously. "You really weren't scared, were you?"

"I wasn't. Not sure why. Maybe I was still drunk. I should have been scared but I wasn't."

"Dar, you're never scared when it's go time," Kerry said in a placid tone. "I've watched you for years throwing yourself into situations starting with the night you saved my ass from being carjacked. You have more guts than sense sometimes."

Dar's dark lashes fluttered a little and she watched Kerry from the corner of her eye. "Is that a bad thing?" she asked. "I remember you doing some crazy ass stunts, too, like diving in the water after that guy."

"Well..."

Dar shrugged. "We're two of a kind. Someone once said that. Maybe Alastair." She rested her elbows on her chair arms. "So what do you want to do? Go find Madame PooPoo and get our fortunes told?"

Kerry smiled. "Absolutely. I don't think they have daytime ghost tours so let's stick to stuffed animals, tacky beads and beignets today. In fact, can you show me where you got them?"

"Sure. And I found this." Dar handed over a pamphlet.

"Boos and Booze tour?" Kerry started laughing. "Of the French Quarter. You really want to do that, hon? Ghosts more interesting now?"

Dar grinned and shrugged "Yeah, maybe. I'm kind of wondering. As in, how is that possible? Is it an energy anomaly?"

"You're looking for a logical explanation for ghosts?" Kerry watched her smile and nod. "Okay, Boos! And Booze it is." She checked the number, then dialed it on her phone. "My treat."

Dar rocked back and forth a little in contentment. Kerry had wakened without her headache and they'd enjoyed a shower together using the shower attachment in the charmingly old fashioned tub installed bathroom. "I think I want to go find a little protein with my funnel cakes," she said as Kerry hung up. "Shall we?"

"Absolutely, my little ghost busting chickadee." Kerry finished her coffee and got up, extending her hand. "Let's go find out what the future has in store for us," she said. "And get you some bacon."

THEY STROLLED ALONG the street in the sunshine toward

Jackson Square where a crowd was already gathering.

"Beautiful day," Kerry said peering along the wrought iron fence they were walking by. "Oh look, Dar. Artists."

Obligingly, Dar looked. "If we get a picture of us done by someone other than my mother, you get to explain it to her. Since we keep saying no."

Kerry put her hands behind her back and clasped them. "Good point."

Dar chuckled.

"But we can get one of New Orleans." She pointed. "See? Isn't that pretty? It's the parade."

Dar willingly followed her over to the artist, who had several examples of his art propped up against the fence. She wandered down the row as Kerry bargained for the piece, enjoying the antics of a street performer who was juggling while riding a unicycle.

That took a lot of skill and balance and she appreciated that. She'd made one abortive attempt at unicycling herself way back when in college on a long weekend down in Key West. Even now, all the years later, she winced at the twitch in her tail bone that well remembered that colossal fall.

"Hello dere, pretty lady."

Dar turned from watching the juggler to find a man at a folding table covered in a tie dye cloth straight from Haight Ashbury. He was reviewing some tarot cards and watching her with one bright, deep hazel eye, the other covered in a weathered patch.

"Hi," Dar responded after a brief pause. "Are you a fortune teller?"

"Oh my, no." The man smiled at her. He was probably in his sixties, with curly gray hair and a spare frame. "Sounds so carnival, does it not? Should I have a monkey, then, and man in the front calling people into the sideshow?"

Dar folded her arms over her chest. "Didn't mean that as an insult," she said. "What do you call yourself then?"

"I call myself Charles." The man's eye twinkled. "And you, pretty lady?"

Dar allowed herself to be charmed and drawn in. "Dar."

"Now that's a very unusual name," Charles said, sorting the cards together and putting them away. "Is this your first time here in the great N'awlins?"

"It is," Dar said. "I thought I lived in the craziest place in the US until I saw this town. Impressive." She indicated the chair across from him. "Mind if I sit down?"

Charles's nose crinkled up in a surprising grin. "Usually I have to coax people to take a seat. "Please sit, Ms. Dar." He cleared off the table in front of him and leaned his elbows on it as she sat down and they regarded each other. "What can I answer for you? Is there a question you want to ask me?"

Dar considered. "Tell me about this place." She indicated the city with a brief hand gesture. "Why is it so different? What's with all the ghost stories?"

He blinked.

"I've got some time and cash," Dar added with a twinkle of her own. "My wife's over there wrangling prices. I figure I can at least get some local information from something other than a tour pamphlet that'll be worth the price." She glanced at a passing cart. "Can I buy you a drink?"

"Ms. Dar, I don't know what our conversation will lead to, but I will surely use my professional skills to predict I will be having a very good time." Charles laughed. "And I would love a drink. It's been a thirsty morning already."

Dar pinned the cart pusher with a direct blue gaze and pointed, then raised two fingers. "Do you use those cards to tell people what's going to happen to them?" she asked as the vendor hurried over. "Or, what they want you to tell them about what's going to happen to them?"

Charles studied her while she paid for the drinks. When she turned back around he was smiling. "Ms. Dar, you are an old soul," he said. "I don't see too many of those 'round here these days."

"What does that mean?" Dar settled in to listen, curling her hands around the cup.

"What does that mean?" Charles mused. "Sometime you meet people, talk to people, and they're all on the surface. They ain't been around, see what I'm saying?"

Dar let her chin rest on her fist. "Not really...well..." She thought about the question and Charles gave her space to do that. "Hard to say. My life mostly puts me in a space with high achievers."

"Not about smarts," Charles said. "Can be the most no count, no school, depressed and raised in a trailer person, but they got a story in them. They got practice at this life thing."

"You talking about reincarnation?" Dar asked, curiously.

"Am I?" he said. "Could be. Don't cotton much to that. I more look to the old ways where earth's part of you, you're part of earth. But when I say I see an old soul, I mean there's a piece of the earth's history there in you."

That didn't make sense to Dar but she kept quiet, waiting to see what else would be forthcoming. She certainly didn't feel like she had any old knowledge in her.

"So anyway, to your question," Charles said. "Na'wlins is an old place and been a place full of hurting and bloodletting from all way back." He looked up at her. "Know what that's about?"

"My daddy's people are from east Alabama," Dar said, then paused.

Charles nodded. "See that? You got history in you. Go through places like that and the trees weep from it."

"They've been there a long time," Dar said.

He took a sip from the drink and put it down. "N'awlins is like that, too. Been a lot of heartache in these parts. Wars. Slaves. Pirates. Drowning. Magic." He waited for her to react, but the angular, intent face across from him remained still. "Black magic. Things them people being put on used to make their lives a little less hell."

"A way for them to take a piece of themselves back?"

Charles smiled. "Yes, Ms. Dar. When you ain't got no power, you make your own."

"That I get," Dar said.

"So you have all this emotion," he said. "All this misery, and so they say, it sticks. Them people who didn't have joy in their lives, they stay around after to find it." He gestured around him. "It's a pretty place, no?"

Dar smiled. "It is."

"Some people say, all them who die here stay here, 'cause Heaven ain't no better." Charles smiled back. "But it's true that you walk here, you look round a corner, behind a tree, up in a window...you see things." He laced his fingers, his single eye watching her. "Foggy mornings walking here I see things."

Dar caught sight of Kerry's distinctive little swagger heading her way. "You ever been to an old battlefield?" she asked him. "Valley Forge, or Antietam, or one of those?"

"This here square was named for Andrew Jackson," Charles said. "He and a bunch of men done beat the British not far off. War been here, but not so it's like what you mean. You been?"

"I have," Dar said. "And a lot of people say they feel an atmosphere there. But I always wondered how much of that was because they did, and how much of that was because they expected to, because they knew what happened there. My college did a psychological study of that."

He cocked his head. "And?"

Dar shrugged. "I wasn't included. I knew. I'm from a military family," she replied honestly. "But I never felt anything there."

"So, Ms. Dar, you're a skeptic," Charles said after a brief silence. "That what you're saying?"

"I live in a very rational world," Dar said, sounding even to herself slightly apologetic. "I'm an engineer in the technology space. Logic comes with the territory."

"Whose territory?" Kerry arrived at her side and gave Charles a grin. "Hello." She draped a hand on Dar's shoulder. "They're sending that picture home for us."

"Well, hello there." Charles half rose, and bowed. "Please join us, ma'am." He glanced at Dar. "Is this your lady?"

"This is Kerry." Dar looked up at her. "Charles and I were just talking about why there are so many supposed spooks here.

"Did you tell him about your ghost last night?" Kerry asked, pressing her knee up next to Dar's. "Maybe he knows about it."

Charles sat back down, looking from one of them to the other, his brows contracting. "Does Ms. Kerry live in your rational world, Ms. Dar? This is coming along to be very interesting."

Dar sighed. "There's always exceptions."

"Maybe we should ask him about our thing." Kerry's eyes twinkled. "I think that's an exception, too."

CHARLES, IT TURNED out, knew a guy. Or more to the point a woman who he said would give them their money's worth in terms of getting their fortunes told.

They were headed across Jackson Square, down one of the side streets to a small store that had a sign plastered simply with a star bisected hand and a window fully covered with dusty red drapes.

"Right this way, ladies." Charles pushed the door open and went inside, holding it for them to follow him. "Hallo, Marie!"

Kerry paused inside the door and looked around, her eyes widening. "Wow." The inside of the very small storefront was cluttered in the extreme and the ceiling was hung with what looked like bird and bat wings and bones. "Watch your head, hon."

"No kidding." Dar ducked, her eyes somewhat wider and rounder than normal.

"Hallo, Charles." A tiny woman in a purple crinoline dress came out from a back room, wiping her lips. "Who you got here, eh?"

Dar was immediately distracted by a skull mounted on a tall umbrella as a handle.

"These here nice ladies stopped and passed the time of day with me over by the square. They're interested in having their fortunes told. You busy?"

"Oh, yes. Can't you see all the people in here lined up waiting?" Marie chuckled. "Too many people at too many parties last night for sure." She turned her eyes to Kerry. "Hello there."

"Hi." Kerry edged closer. Marie had a relatively high table with a stool padded with worn denim behind it and two more on the other side. She glanced up at the ceiling. "Are those bird bones?"

Marie slipped onto her stool. She had a lined and weathered face, brown tan and silver gray hair that was pulled back in a tight bun with a pair of flying monkey chopsticks holding it in place. "They're all sorts of things," she said. "I pick things up when I walk around, you know? It's like they're looking for homes, so I bring them here."

Kerry seated herself on one of the stools. "I pick up rocks when I walk," she said. "They remind me of places and times. Is that the same kind of thing?"

Dar kept her head ducked to one side as she examined the book case that lined the side of the shop. The books were varied and old, all hardback, some with barely legible titles in a number of different languages. There was a scent of dust and aging paper that wafted out from them. They were lit by a candle sconce flickering gently nearby.

"Oh, something like that," Marie said. "Charles, there's some coffee in the back if you want some."

Charles smiled and availed himself of the offer, disappearing behind the thick bead curtain that separated the front of the shop from the area behind.

"So what's your name?" Marie asked.

"Kerry." She hooked her feet around the stool's supports and rested her arm on one knee. "Charles said you were a fortune teller."

"Oh, something like," Marie said with a brief grin. "Do you want your fortune told, Kerry? You looking for riches or gold, or a sugar daddy?"

Behind her Dar chuckled while examining a round crystal.

"None of the above," Kerry said. "I've got everything in the world I need."

The old woman studied her. "Yes, you know you seem like that," Marie said after a pause. "You're someone who has their heart's desire. But it was not always so."

Kerry felt a faint shiver. "No, that's true. Took me a while to find what I was looking for."

"Took me about thirty seconds," Dar commented from her idle browsing. "Came around the corner, stopped in the doorway, done deal."

"Dar." Kerry gave her an affectionate look. "C'mere and pay attention to my fortune."

Dar put down the rock she was examining, walked the few steps over, seated herself on the second stool and regarded Marie benignly.

"Marie, this is Dar," Kerry said. "Dar isn't into palm reading and that sort of thing. She's humoring me."

Marie studied Dar, glancing briefly into Dar's pale, intense eyes. "No, I don't figure that," she said with a smile. "You're someone who makes their own future and needs no telling from me." She wagged a finger at her. "Not often someone brings a crusader into Marie's store, that's for sure."

"I'm no crusader," Dar said.

"Of course you are," Kerry said. "We were just talking about that, Dar. A creepy ghost shows up on our balcony and what happens? Do you scream?"

Dar cleared her throat.

Marie watched them with interest. "So you've seen one of our honored guests, have you? Where is that, you said on the balcony?"

"Of our hotel. The Sonesta," Kerry said. "I woke up last night to find my modest friend here facing off against some ghoul outside, scaring him off." She put a hand on Dar's leg. "I freak out about them, Dar just wants to kick their asses."

"That true?" Marie studied Dar "You know, the departed ain't something you want to mess with."

Dar cleared her throat again. "I don't want to mess with them. Assuming they exist. But they also don't scare me and I'm not going to let them scare her."

"See, I told you, Marie." Charles had reappeared in the doorway with a steaming cup. "That's an old soul you got there." He came over and took the last stool at the table. "Most times the departed don't take much interest in the living, you know? They got other things to do. Some of them replay their ends over and over, some of them don't realize they're gone, so they keep trying to get done whatever they had to do when they died."

"That's kind of hard for me to wrap my head around," Kerry admitted. "I had a pretty conservative upbringing."

Marie smiled. "You brought up in the church, that what you mean? My daddy was a preacher here in N'awlins. Didn't stop him from consorting with the spirits. He used to hire out for exorcisms. Made some good money at it."

Kerry blinked at her. "Exorcisms?"

"Sure," Marie said. "You got people who come here and buy them a house, you see? Old houses. They like that cause they're pretty. But they find out there's creaks and bangs and stuff moving round. They hear voices, so they call up the local priest and he takes care of all that."

"Really?" Dar asked.

"Honey, I seen things," Marie said. "I done grew up in this town, and things I seen. You can believe or not believe but I don't doubt. You said yourself you saw something last night. You know what it was?"

Dar considered the question. "No, I don't. But it looked like a tall male figure wearing an old style hat and a trench coat. Couldn't see a face, just the outline." She paused. "I thought it was someone trying to break in our room at first."

"Ah huh." Marie frowned. "You sure it wasn't?"

"If it was, he jumped off the balcony after I went to the window," Dar replied. "There was a big crack of thunder and lightning. Blinded me a little, then he was gone."

Marie and Charles exchanged looks. "They got some ghosts up at that Sonesta, but the ones I heard, ain't like that one," Charles said. "They got the library ghost and the butler one, walks up and down those big stairs they have, and then the cook what done hung himself in the kitchen. They don't like to be in that kitchen after hours."

Marie nodded. "That tall one sounds new," she said.

"Is it possible it was just imagination?" Kerry asked. "We took that night ghost tour earlier in the night."

"Could be," Marie said. "You all see anything on the tour? Some of that, you know, ain't all together on the up and up." Her eyes twinkled a little. "We got a living to make, after all."

Charles chuckled. "That rooftop woman, and they do have a projection they do in the garden."

Kerry's eyes widened. "That's fake?"

Dar patted her leg and grinned. "There ya go, babe. I figured there was a logical answer."

Kerry suddenly felt like she'd been cheated. "Wow. That's a bummer. So I guess they were probably blowing cold air down your neck from that alley." She looked chagrined. "But I don't get it. You said before that ghosts were real, and that New Orleans was full of them. Why would they need to fake it?"

"Well now —" Charles put his cup down.

"Because ghosts don't perform on schedule," Dar said. "And those tours depend on people seeing them."

Marie lifted her hands and put them back down. "All those stories have a grain of truth, see. But like your crusader friend here says, you can't depend on them. Those tour companies, they need consistent visions so that people get on the Internet...you know the Internet?"

Both Dar and Kerry chuckled. "We're familiar with it," Dar said. "But I get it. People see those things and take pictures and that kind of thing, and the word spreads. Good marketing."

"Yes," Marie said. "But this thing you saw? That's new to me. You?" She looked at Charles.

"Never heard of that one," he said. "So what you say, Marie? You going to tell these ladies their fortunes?"

Marie studied them thoughtfully in silence. "I don't think I can," she said. "I think you and I could lead them to some beautiful place for lunch, but when I look to see what road these two are taking, I don't see anything at all."

Kerry felt a weird prickle go down her spine and she felt Dar's thigh twitch under her fingers. "Is that good or bad?" she finally asked.

"For me? Terrible." Marie laughed. "Honey please don't be telling everyone I said that. I got my reputation to think of." She sobered and paused briefly. "But you? I talk to people and I kind of guess where they're going, if you know what I mean. What they said, what they do, what they want. When people come to ask for their fortune, they want what they want, you know?"

Dar nodded. "Yeah."

"That's what she asked me," Charles said. "If I told people their future, or what they wanted their future to be."

"But people who go chasing off big scary ghosts? I don't know where to begin to tell you what you're going to get yourselves into," Marie said. "So what about that lunch? I got me a place you can get the best fried chicken in New Orleans. That do you?"

"Fried chicken? Always," Dar amiably agreed. "Let's go."

Kerry slid off the stool with a strong sense that the two fortune tellers were diverting their attention away from the arcane. She could tell they were both a little uneasy with her and Dar. As she followed them out the door, she also had the sense that someone inside the store was still watching them.

Or maybe it was just her imagination again.

KERRY SUCKED ON a bit of sugar candy as they walked down the sidewalk toward Jackson Square. "That was, for sure, the best fried chicken I've ever had."

"For sure," Dar agreed wholeheartedly. "And I'm willing to bet I've had more of it than you have."

"Probably true," Kerry said. "Wow, it was good." She felt pleasantly stuffed, and equally pleasantly surprised at the southern style sides that even seemed new to Dar. "I've got to try making that corn bread."

"You can try any of that on me any time you want," Dar said. "So, more shopping then back to the hotel to get ready for our Boos and Booze tour?"

"Now that I know it's all fake, I'm going to have a much better time," Kerry admitted. "That was fun, Dar. I'm glad we ran into those two. Except it was kind of weird that they just decided to go to lunch with us and left off all the fortune stuff."

"Did we freak them out?" Dar wondered. "Hey, want a cup of coffee?" She pointed. "There's a cafe, and I think there's a parade coming." She pointed down a side street, where the sounds of music were suddenly loud and present.

"Mm. I see cheap plastic beads in my future." Kerry contentedly followed her over to the cafe, mounting the steps and taking a small table off to one side. "Have I told you how much fun I'm having at our Valentine's Day celebration? I'm going to have to work my butt off to match this next year."

She sprawled in a chair, glancing around at the rapidly filling up cafe as others heard the approach of the parade and decided to get a good spot to watch it from. "I think you freaked them out," she said after the waiter left with their order. "With all that old soul stuff. What did you think about that?"

Dar leaned back in her chair and hiked one boot up onto her opposite knee. "I don't know. I'm not sure what that was about. I don't feel like an old anything right now." She rolled her head to one side and gave Kerry a grin. "Didn't make sense to me. I think they were trying to tie that into reincarnation, but I don't think I've been here before."

Kerry considered that as she watched a young couple at the next table sharing a kiss. The other onlookers watched with wry bemusement, but she wondered if that would still be the case if she and Dar were to copy them.

"I don't feel like I've been here before either," she mused. "Well, except for when I met you."

"Me?"

Kerry nodded. "Remember when we met, we were racking our brains to figure out where we knew each other from?" She reached over and curled her fingers over Dar's. "But we couldn't, because we'd never met." She watched Dar's pale eyes intently study her. "But when I met you I felt like I'd always known you."

The parade was getting closer and louder and the street was filling with watchers. Dar's gaze went internal for a few minutes until the waiter came back with their café au laits accompanied by small crunchy biscuits. She nodded absently, then returned her attention to Kerry. "Yeah, maybe," she conceded. "I definitely felt a connection to you. Always have."

Her phone rang and she pulled it out and answered it, holding her other hand over her ear. She rolled her eyes at Kerry. "Yeah, I'm here. It's loud. Sorry about that."

Kerry leaned back and watched the parade, the crowd near the street all cheering and reaching toward the floats, who were again tossing things at them with cheerful abandon. Rather than stand up and attract them, she settled for watching the street side participants as she listened with one ear to Dar's conversation.

"Alastair, they're out of their minds," Dar said after a long period of listening. "There is no way I'm going to agree with that, much less the client. Why should we? You know perfectly well how I got involved in that. Hell, Hamilton was there."

She listened again. "They did? Okay, well, then they're more brainless than I figured." She shook her head, and glanced at Kerry. "They fired Hamilton."

Kerry wasn't surprised to hear it. After the last round between the Louisiana lawyer and ILS she'd figured him for short term. "Is he coming here for Mardi Gras? Maybe we can have dinner with him."

Dar paused in mid-word and her eyes twinkled. "Good point. Is he coming to visit the family? He know we're here?" She grinned. "I'll text him. Anyway, Alastair, they need to just move on. They probably don't want any part of it anyway. It could get a little squirmy for them from a publicity standpoint."

She listened for a minute. "Because the contract involves domestic surveillance," she said. "That enough for you?"

Kerry heard the exasperated sound coming from the phone. "Didn't he know that?" She frowned. "Have him tell them from me that as the ex-VP of operations, I wouldn't touch it with a ten foot pole."

"That's what Kerry just said," Dar said into the phone. "Or better yet, have your friend the vice president explain it to them, because I saw that memo about who could or couldn't bid. Doesn't he owe you one?"

"Poor Alastair. Isn't he retired yet?" Kerry sipped the rich, fragrant coffee.

"Exactly," Dar said. "It's a contract based on delivery objectives. They're not funding anything. I just gave them a framework and brought on some programmers. I don't even know how much margin it's even going to end up having."

"You sound so sexy when you talk like that," Kerry said.

"They did?" Dar sounded surprised. She looked back at Kerry. "Mariana and Duks resigned," she told her. "That's why Alastair's still around."

"Poor Alastair." Kerry shook her head. "Maybe they'll open their own accounting and HR firm and we can outsource to them." She winked at Dar. "Hey, didn't you say Alastair was a pilot? He want to come be our private plane guy?"

"Are you listening to this?" Dar started laughing. "Kerry's got a business plan for everyone." She gave her a fond look. "I don't think Alastair wants to move to Miami, hon."

Kerry saw another float heading their way and stood up and went to the rail to see better. "Oh, wow. Look at those costumes."

Dar leaned back and admired Kerry's profile. "So anyway." She said. "I'm sorry it's such a Mongolian, Alastair. Seriously, anything I can do to help?"

"Well, Dar," Alastair said. "Call me crazy, but I did think of suggesting they contract you as a consultant."

"Oh fuck." Dar clapped her hand over her eyes. "Kill me now."

"No, listen," Alastair said. "It's really not so funny because the problem is these people just don't know what to do. They leaned for so long on you, and probably me a little, that they're striking out in panic now, Dar. If I could get you to come in and talk to them, maybe that'll help."

"How? So I can tell them what to do and they can throw their cobalt blue ceramic cups of piss and vinegar at me?" Dar asked. "Alastair, I've got my own company to run here."

"Whooo!" Kerry snagged a tangle of beads out of the air, then grinned as one of the men on the float hopped off and danced through the crowd, ducking and weaving as people thrust their hands out to him begging for the trinkets he carried.

"Well, that's the point, Dar," Alastair said placidly. "You start a company and before the paint's dry on your business card it's a success. Remember what we said about them figuring out how much of ILS's success was you?"

"Oh for Pete's sake. I'm just one person." Dar sighed. "Ker, watch out!"

Kerry had her thighs braced against the railing and was leaning over as the float runner danced over to her and leaped up, handing her a coconut as he grabbed onto the rail to hold himself in place for a moment. "Thanks!" Kerry grinned at him, pulling herself back.

"I know you're just one person, Dar, but you made a difference.

Maybe if you talk to these guys, they'll figure out how to move along instead of sitting there stewing and plotting to send lawyers after you," Alastair said. "Worth a try?"

Dar sighed. "Sure. You're the one suggesting it and in the line of fire."

"Atta girl."

"Anyway, let me go grab hold of Kerry's belt before she ends up being pulled onto a parade float," Dar said. "Whatever you want to do, Alastair, I'm good with it. Just don't promise I'll come back to work there."

"Will do, lady. Have fun." Alastair sounded pleased with himself. "Talk to you next week, and if you see Ham, buy him a bourbon on the rocks for me will ya?"

"Will do," Dar said. "Later." She closed the phone and got up, tucking her fingers into the back of Kerry's jeans waistband as she leaned over to talk to the still hanging float man. "Complications, Ker."

"They'll wait for Monday." Kerry handed her the coconut. "Say hi to the Zulu folks. They like to party."

Dar smiled and toasted the man with the coconut, getting a waggle of his eyebrows and a stuck out tongue in response. "I guess it'll wait for Monday," she agreed. "Cheers!"

Chapter Seven

SEVERAL HOURS LATER they were back in the hotel and free of beads and bangles and mostly drunken tourists that had accompanied them on their tour.

"That was way more Booze than Boos." Dar was flat on her back, regarding the slowly circling ceiling fan. "Way funnier than last night, though," she admitted. "That guide was hilarious."

"He was. My stomach still hurts from laughing," Kerry said. "That one story about the pub owner who told everyone he heard voices telling him to tap the kegs..."

Dar chuckled.

"I didn't see any ghosts. Did you?" Kerry emerged from the bathroom and joined Dar on the bed, squirming over and using her as a pillow. "Like, not even one."

"Nope." Dar stretched her body out, then relaxed again and closed her eyes. "Hungry?"

Kerry shook her head. "Oh, no. I'm still full from lunch."

"Good. Me too," Dar said. "Maybe later I'll be up for ice cream."

Kerry chuckled. "Dar, I've never heard you not be up for ice cream regardless of what we've eaten."

"But they had cappuccino mint chip hand churned on the menu and it caught my eye."

Kerry gave Dar an indulgent look. "Uh huh. Should I get an ice cream churn for the cabin?"

Dar's brows hiked up and she returned the look with interest. "We can get one that actual real people can use, not chefs?"

"Mmhmm."

"Hot damn."

"Done deal. It's healthier to use all fresh ingredients anyway." Kerry glanced up and seeing the devastatingly droll look had to laugh. "Well, that's the theory."

"The front desk said they could get us tickets to some ball somewhere. You interested?" Dar listened to the derisive snort in response and smiled. "Okay, so we've had our fortunes not told, been on two ghost tours, seen parades, have throws from at least five different krewes, eaten the best fried chicken on earth and had around a half ton of beignets. What next?"

"You forgot the picture I bought." Kerry stifled a yawn and snuggled closer, wrapping her arm around Dar's. "How about we just hang out here together and listen to the music coming from outside."

Dar began scratching Kerry's neck gently, moving along her scalp as she squirmed in pleasure. "That sounds good to me. We can chill out on our balcony, too." She smiled as she felt Kerry's breath warm the skin on her stomach through her shirt. "Or we could just lie here."

"We could do that."

Dar gave her a hug. "You're so easy."

"I love you," Kerry said simply.

Dar lifted her head a little and peered down at her. "I love you, too. And I think this is a completely appropriate discussion for Valentine's Day, don't you?"

"You bet." Kerry sighed contentedly. "You know what's cool, too? That we're both here and we don't have to worry about anything or anyone saying something because we're both here."

"Did they ever do that?" Dar mused. "Not after the first year or two, right? No one cared after that, did they?"

Kerry pondered that for a minute. "Well, I cared," she admitted. "I was always thinking about what people would think if both of us took off at the same time. Which doesn't make sense now that I'm hearing myself say that, but I think there was always a little bit of guilt there for me."

"You mean how you got the job?" Dar asked.

Kerry nodded. "Even though you told me a thousand times." She gazed up at her partner. "I'd been in that spotlight too long."

Dar nodded. "Yeah, I know. When I actually pressed all the buttons to hire you, and sent you that email, I thought about that."

"You did?"

"For about five seconds." Dar grinned sheepishly. "I knew you'd be rock star at the job, so that never bothered me. But I also knew if we ended up where I thought we would, it would be a little awkward."

Kerry smiled in response. "I remember being in a meeting one day, after we'd started sleeping with each other and I swear I was convinced everyone was staring at us because they knew. Then I realized that everyone probably did know because we were wearing each other's necklaces since we'd gotten up late that morning and just grabbed and ran."

Dar started laughing silently, shaking Kerry a little.

"And then I kinda did stop caring." Kerry mock sighed. "I said, 'what the hell, Kerrison. If they're going to think that then just thank God it's true.'"

Dar was still laughing. "I remember that day. I realized it when I went to the bathroom and I was washing my hands and looked up into the mirror. Should have seen my face. I felt like such a goofball."

Kerry enjoyed the low, musical sound of Dar's laughter. She'd remembered the day because Dar had come into her office and sprawled onto her desk pointing at her throat in eloquent silence.

Too funny. "So, I do love you." She slid Dar's shirt up and then nipped her on her navel. "Not only do I love you, but I love being in love with you. It's like Christmas every single day."

Dar folded herself around Kerry and hugged her. "My birthday everyday." She exhaled in contentment. "Do you know how nice it is to know that I don't have to worry about half the IT planet going down? I never realized what a drag that was until now."

"Were you reading my mind?" Kerry rested her cheek against the soft skin on Dar's stomach. "I was just thinking that before."

"Want to dance?" Dar asked incongruously as the music got louder outside.

"Not really." Kerry traced a light line down Dar's skin. "I'm just having fun lying here and messing with you."

"Okay."

"You could sing for me."

"I could. But I don't know the words to whatever that is they're playing and I can't compete with the volume," Dar said in a practical tone. "Want to go find a pool and swim?"

"Hm."

"Just want to lay here and mess with me?"

"Yup."

That was okay with Dar. They'd gotten up early after a long night and spent the day running around. There were some concerts on tap for the next afternoon and a carriage ride planned. It felt good to just chill out and enjoy the rich, sexy sound of the music and let her mind drift.

Kerry felt Dar's breathing even out and slow after about ten minutes of their just quietly laying there. She watched the tension in her body go slack and she hesitated, not wanting to wake Dar out of sleep when she'd just slipped into it.

Moving would. So she settled down to wait until she was sure her pillow was deeply asleep before shifting.

It was very peaceful to lie still, watching the easy rise and fall of Dar's chest as the sounds outside started to fade off a little. She heard people laughing and the clink of glass and she shifted her gaze to look out the window at their balcony.

It was empty, just the backs of the chairs visible. Beyond that she saw the splash of light from the street and the outline of leaves from the trees in front of the hotel moving in the breeze as she watched.

It was windy outside. She saw the outside shutters moving, too. Then she saw the rocking chair outside moving gently as well.

Was that the breeze? Kerry watched the chair and her heart rate picked up a trifle. The motion was regular and casual, just as if someone was sitting in the seat enjoying the view.

So maybe it was the wind. She slowly let a long held breath out and watched the motion, which remained steady, despite the variable breeze she saw in the movement of the trees.

"Hey." Dar's voice broke the silence and Kerry jumped. "What's up?"

Kerry put her head back down. "I was trying not to wake you up," she muttered. "But I saw that chair out there moving and it was giving me the creeps."

Dar lifted her head slightly. "The rocking chair?"

"Yeah."

Dar studied it. Then she hiked herself up on her elbows, waiting for Kerry to lift up off her before she swung her legs over the side of the bed and stood up. "I'll check it out." She rubbed her eyes. "I was just heading into a dream."

"I know. Sorry about that." Kerry patted her hip. "I saw you twitching a little." She got out of bed and followed her across the floor to the balcony. She put her hand on Dar's back as she opened one of the French doors and looked out.

The chair stopped rocking.

Kerry eased her head around Dar's shoulder and looked at her.

Dar regarded the piece of furniture pensively. She walked out and circled the chair. She gave it a tentative push. It rocked back and forth two or three times and then settled down to a mild creaking. Dar paused and then she half shrugged and sat down in it, putting her hands on the chair arms.

Kerry sat down in the regular chair next to her. "I was expecting that chair to squeal when you sat on it."

"So was I," Dar said. "But this is our porch for the time being and I'm not going to surrender it to a moving chair." She leaned back, hiking one knee up and folding her hands around it. "So now that I'm wide awake again, how about some ice cream?"

"Absolutely." Kerry leaned over and kissed her shoulder. Then she got up and went back inside and picked up the room service menu to study the possibilities.

THE NEXT EVENING, after a long day of parade and concert watching, Dar and Kerry were seated at a table on the outside deck of a Mississippi River paddle wheel steamer cruising slowly past the dockside festivities as they waited for dinner.

"This is nice." Kerry leaned back and regarded the scene with a smile. "Beautiful way to end up our Valentine's Day celebration."

"It is." Dar sipped at a glass cautiously. "Holy crap." She put the drink down. "You could take the paint off the hood of my new truck with that."

Kerry chuckled. It was a bit chilly on the water, but she had a pair of heavy jeans on and a thick woven pullover. Dar had a newly bought hoodie encasing her tall form and neither of them fit into the more formally dressed couples around them.

Her mother would have been completely scandalized and she couldn't care less. The seating hostess didn't bat an eye either and she was glad they'd opted for the cruise rather than one or the other of the balls the concierge had tried to entice them with.

Tomorrow morning they would fly home and probably go into the office in the afternoon. She took a sip of her own drink and luxuriated in the sense of freedom. She hadn't scheduled anything for Monday, so if they were in the mood when they landed, they could just go home and stay there if they wanted.

"Too bad Hamilton's up in Boston," Dar said. "Since it's snowing there. But I'm glad he suggested this." She indicated the cruise. "I could picture him on this, in his tux, with a mint julep."

"I'm kind of surprised they fired him, but kinda not," Kerry said. She smiled at their waitress as she put down two bowls of golden colored gumbo in front of them. "Those guys are in a place where they don't want to be told what to do."

Dar munched thoughtfully on a spoonful of the gumbo. She swallowed and took a sip of her drink. "Hope so. Then they'll tell Alastair to get lost when he suggests I talk to them and he can finally get loose of the place."

"Oh." Kerry wiped her lips. "I've got to figure out how to make this. It's awesome." She poked around in the bowl. "Are those shrimp?"

"Crawdads," Dar said. "Also known as mud bugs." She watched Kerry's eyes lift and pin her. "Or crayfish." Her eyes twinkled.

"Ah." Kerry then recognized the animals. "Same as we had at the Zydeco festival last year?"

"Right, but just the tails."

They cruised along the river, passing a wooded section that came right down into the water, giving the impression that the trees were marching down the bank and under the surface. They were outlined in the moonlight and as Kerry looked at them she thought she saw something moving.

Then she was sure she did, a human shaped figure appearing at the water's edge between the trees, going into the river up to their knees. "Dar..."

"I see him."

Kerry continued spooning her gumbo into her mouth as she watched the shadowy form. He appeared to be a black man of middle height, dressed in pants, rubber boots, a collarless shirt and a ragged denim jacket. She saw the appearance of suspenders under it all. He leaned against a long walking stick propped in the water in front of him.

There were no features to his face, but his dark skin and the night illumination could be obscuring them. Then she recalled what river she was on and smiled faintly. "Could be Jim from Huckleberry Finn, huh?"

"Could be," Dar said. "Probably some guy they pay to dress up like that and give the tourists a thrill. Coincidence he shows up right when the boat gets there."

"Cynical."

"Realistic." Dar's blue eyes twinkled at her as she looked up across the table. "C'mon, Ker, you heard those guys."

True. Kerry sat back as she finished her gumbo and watched the bank, the figure on it turning his head to follow the boat as it went past. So Dar was probably right that he was a bit of window dressing. She lifted her hand and waved at him and the figure tilted his head and looked back at her.

There were eyes there, she was sure of it. But they seemed too large and too luminous. She felt a shiver go down her back and then the trees were between them. "Maybe fake, but sorta creepy." She folded her hands as the waitress removed the bowls and set down their main courses.

"That could sort of describe Mardi Gras." Dar investigated her plate. "You still seeing ghosts, Ker?"

Kerry wrinkled up her nose in reaction.

"I think the whole idea of ghosts is pretty sad," Dar said, carefully separating her shrimp from her grits.

"Sad?"

"Yeah," Dar said. "The whole idea is, if you subscribe to an existence after death that you go on to some other place. Do something else, whatever. But ghosts, if you agree with the idea, are stuck here."

"Yes, like those stories they told us the other night," Kerry said. "They're looking for something, or whatever." She thought about that as she slowly detached forkfuls of her blackened catfish. "Just left behind." She paused. "You're right. That is sad."

"Not something I'd ever want to have happen to me, you know?" Dar said. "I'd rather have anything happen than that."

Kerry stopped chewing and merely sat there for a moment, staring slightly past Dar's shoulder. She thought for a moment what it would be like to be separated for eternity from Dar and the food lost all its taste and appeal.

She put her fork down and sat back. "Boy so would I," she said after a long pause. "I think I'm going to go throw up now."

Dar swallowed hastily and set her utensils down. She reached across the table to clasp Kerry's hand. "Sorry, hon. I didn't mean to get you crazy."

No, of course she didn't. Kerry sniffled a little and lifted her free hand to wipe her eyes and rub the bridge of her nose. "I just imagined what it would be like to be without you."

Dar got up and came around the table, crouching down at Kerry's side, putting her hand on her leg. "Totally dumbass of me, Ker." She watched Kerry give her head a little shake. "Don't worry. There's nothing that's ever going to keep us apart, no matter where we are."

Kerry peeked down at her.

"I won't let that happen." Dar gave her a wry smile. "Ghosts or angels or dust, you won't ever be without me."

At the words, the sounds around them rushed back in and the music struck up. Kerry's body relaxed as some part of her understood the truth being spoken that had nothing to do with what was said. She glanced around, feeling a little foolish as she saw the other diner's eyes quickly go elsewhere. "Thanks, sweetie." She managed a grin, patting Dar's hand. "Go finish your grits before they solidify into plaster."

Dar waited for a moment. "You okay?" she asked, head cocked slightly to one side.

"Yes." Kerry offered her a bit of catfish on her fork, which Dar accepted. "You knew just what to say."

"For once." Dar got up and went back to her chair, settling into it and returning her napkin to her lap. She looked up and past Kerry to find the people at the next table staring at her. "Is there a problem?"

"Only that people like you should keep their unnatural behavior behind doors," the man answered. "Not ruin other people's dinners with it."

Kerry took a breath to turn and answer, but Dar lazily lifted one finger and wagged it slightly at her and she subsided.

"Buddy," Dar said in a tolerantly amused voice. "If you thought that was unnatural, you've got a lot to learn about life. Better get started on that before you try breeding." She shook her head and went back to her shrimp and grits, ignoring the continued stare.

The waitress came back. "How is everything, ladies?" She stood with apparent randomness between their table and the next. "Can I get you a glass of bubbly to wash that down?"

"Sure," Dar said. "Got any Cristal?"

The waitress's smile went from indulgent to dazzling in a flicker of an eye. "We do. A flute each?"

"Bring a bottle," Dar countered. "And two nice big glasses."

Kerry chuckled under her breath.

"Yes, ma'am." The waitress left with a cheerful wave, moving past the other table without a glance.

They passed a brightly lit area that drew the other people's attention and they were left in peace in their corner. Dar quickly consumed her grits, which had in fact started to stiffen in the cool night air. She'd already dismissed the jerk at the next table, but she could tell by the furrow in Kerry's brow that she hadn't.

Jerks were jerks. Dar didn't waste her time on them. "Chew, hon. It's too good to waste."

Kerry paused then smiled and went back to her plate. After a minute, though, she picked up her gizmo and tapped on it briefly, reviewed the results, then texted Dar a message.

Dar fished her device out and regarded it, then looked at Kerry, her brows hiking. She watched Kerry shrug and reviewed the note again before answering.

What are the odds we'd end up sitting next to one

```
of the heads of Aryan Nation?
```

Kerry put her fork down and typed back.

```
    About the same as him ending up sitting next to
Roger Stuart's kid and a descendant of the American
revolutionaries.
```

Dar laughed. Could be worse. Could have been Pat Robertson.

And that was also true. Kerry put her phone down and finished off her catfish just in time to smile at the waitress who returned with a gently off gassing bottle and glasses. "Can we get a couple of pieces of the strawberry shortcake too?"

"Absolutely." The waitress finished pouring their bubbly, and then tucked the bottle into an ice filled holder against the wall of the ship. "Be right back."

Dar lifted her glass and they touched rims. "Happy Valentine's day, sweetheart," she said, slightly louder than needed for Kerry to hear her.

"Same to you, my love," Kerry responded with a wry grin before taking a sip. "But boy, am I ever going to have to bust my ass to beat this the next time."

"GOOD MORNING, KERRY" Mayte said as Kerry entered. "Did you have a good time in New Orleans?" She put down what she was working on and focused on her boss.

Kerry grinned, walking over and depositing a handful of beads and trinkets. "I had the best time. I've got some pictures I'll show you. It was a riot. What a party that is. Between the music and the parades and everything. Nonstop craziness."

"I was watching the news on television last night. They had some video and it looked amazing," Mayte replied. "I was hoping maybe we would see you but we didn't."

"Oh, we might have been in the crowd." Kerry's eyes twinkled. "We got to see some parades, went on ghost tours, and did a riverboat dinner on the Mississippi. We had a great time. We got home just after lunch yesterday. The flight was late, but that was the only issue we had."

"My mama said it looked like a crazy place," Mayte said. "But papa said he'd like to go there sometime, only maybe not so close to the carnival. But I think he wants to go because there are all those pretty ladies with no clothing."

Kerry chortled under her breath. "Well, there were those there for sure. Some of them take their clothing off so that the people on the parade floats will throw favors at them. Dar threatened to take her shirt off to get me a stuffed monkey but I made her stop."

Mayte clapped her hand over her mouth to stifle a laugh.

Kerry removed the monkey from her pocket and waggled it. "She managed anyway."

Dar entered, carrying her jacket over her shoulder. "Am I being made fun of? You were the one hankering after that coconut."

"I would never make fun of you, hon." Kerry bumped her affectionately as she passed. "I was just telling Mayte how you got me my monkey."

Dar paused at the entrance to her office, looked over her shoulder, smiled and lifted one eyebrow in silent, yet sexy eloquence. Then she shook her head and chuckled, disappearing from view as she headed for her desk.

Kerry muffled a halfway embarrassed grin and moved along into her own space, tossing the monkey up and down. She went over to the built-in shelves and plopped the memento onto one of them next to a stuffed pig she'd won in a baseball toss at a street carnival a few months past.

She studied it then went to her desk and set her briefcase down, aware of Dar's low tones next door. She sat down and started up her desktop, pulling out the laptop and setting it down on the desk. While she waited, she brought up her calendar on her gizmo, reviewing her appointments as the machines booted.

Busy day.

She was glad they'd decided to go straight home instead of coming in the previous day, though. It was nice to settle back into their space, play with Chino and Mocha, and deliver to Colleen the presents they'd bought for her. Even nicer to take a late night swim and relax in the quiet of their home.

No loud bands, no drunken people, and no weird visions of potential ghosts around anywhere, not even around the Vanderbilt mansion they'd passed on the way back to the condo.

She'd had no bad dreams, no spooky visitations. In fact she'd managed to mostly forget completely about any of the odd things they'd seen as she'd curled up in their water bed wrapped up in Dar's long arms.

So it was all good.

She put her gizmo down and stretched her body out, feeling the mild ache of well used muscles from their session at the gym that morning. A little longer than their usual but a natural reaction to having spent the preceding three days in nonstop indulgence.

Worth it though.

Kerry smiled, and opened her mail, then she removed the contents of her inbox and began to sort through them. Four contracts to review, three new hires, and a report from their real estate agent on possible expansion options in the area. She set aside the report and pulled the contracts over, picking up a two ended pen and focusing her attention on the text.

DAR WRAPPED HER legs around the base of her chair and leaned on the small worktable in the programmer's area. Two of the database coders were across from her and they had a structure diagram spread out between them.

"We started with the base platform but you said you wanted it to be flexible," Fidel, a clean cut and dark haired Latino with broad shoulders and power lifter arms, said. "So we want to use relational, but we're going to need a big box, maybe one of the IBM pSeries to run it."

"Here's the problem with that, Fidel," Dar said. "We know the customer's good for the cash, but this is a step-by-step delivery project. We'd have to shell out for the hardware, then hope they'll accept it."

"Why wouldn't they?" the other coder asked. "It's not like we're getting it second hand from North Korea. It's IBM."

"True," Dar agreed "But those guys always have tech lists. We need to see what's on theirs, or get their buy-in on the box before I sign the check for it." She studied the diagram. "You always have to pre-buy to some extent, but you try to limit it wherever possible. It's a gamble otherwise."

Fidel propped his chin on his fist. He was restless and aggressive and reminded Dar a little of herself back in the day. "Maybe we can get IBM to give us one for a POC?" he said, "so the deal would be, if it goes, then we buy it and they get paid."

Dar suppressed a smile. "Why would they do that?"

"We tell them we're going to buy a box from someone else. Like HP," Fidel said. "I bet they'd do it. They did on my last gig."

Dar tapped her thumbs on the table. "If I'm going to play that game with them, might as well up the stakes," she said. "Let me see if I can get them to use us as a platform for whatever experimental they've got on tap. No sense in going for a mid range."

Fidel looked surprised. "Experimental?"

Mike, the second programmer spoke up. "Like that Big Blue thing that beat the chess guy? That would be cool."

"Something like that," Dar said. "I like the idea of leveraging them. But I'll bring the guys from Cray in, too. See if we can get a high level pissing match going."

"Cray? Wow," Mike said. "You think they'll play ball with us?"

Dar smiled briefly. "We'll find out. It's worth asking at any rate. Good ideas, people."

Both men looked pleased at the acknowledgment. "Okay, so." Fidel put his finger on the grid. "Then I can work out some three dimensional dynamics for the database structure. I'm going to need a crapload of table space."

"And a bigger SAN," Mike said. "We're going to run out of LUNs."

Dar sighed. "Yeah, Kerry's already looking for more space for us." She shook her head. "Mark's working on bringing up a datacenter. I can't put in any bigger systems until we get that done. Won't fit in that server room."

"No way," Mike said. "This all going faster than you thought?" He asked Dar.

It was strange, yet refreshing, to have these people treat her so casually. Regardless of how long she'd worked with people at ILS, they'd never regarded her the way these men were. "It shouldn't have," she admitted straightforwardly. "But yeah, I was expecting a little more runway."

"Well, we can work out the structure on paper anyway," Fidel said. "We could use that new coder they interviewed yesterday."

"Kerry's working on it," Dar said. "Okay, thanks for the recap. I'll go give the big boys a call." She pushed herself to her feet. "Onto the next group."

"Thanks, Dar." Fidel collected the printouts. "Check back with you later."

Dar headed across the programming bull pen over to the other side where she heard a spirited argument about search metrics. The overhead lights were out, flashes of neon impacted her eyes as she went past desks covered in wall hangings. Over in one corner she saw the outline of a bean bag chair. It all made her smile.

"Hey, Dar?"

She paused and looked around a cube wall. "Yes?"

"Can you check this code progression?"

Even more so. "Sure." Dar pulled up a rolling stool and cracked her knuckles. "Lemme see."

KERRY SIGNED OFF on the contracts and dropped them into her out bin, then paused. "Well, since you made your admin a manager, who are you expecting to come pick that up, Kerrison?" She asked herself wryly. "Get out of that big company mentality, get off your ass and take them down instead."

She got up and retrieved the contracts, then made her way out through Mayte's space to the main corridor. She waved at Maria through her open door, then continued on to the suite of offices taken up by the accounting group. "Hey, Col."

"Hey, girl." Colleen was supervising the installation of a set of file cabinets that lined the walls of the good sized storage area assigned to her department.

Kerry came over to where she was standing. "Wasn't technology supposed to get rid of all this paper?"

Colleen laughed. "Oh, sure." She held her hand out. "When you bits and bytes types are one hundred percent sure you can't lose them in the ether, we'll stop printing."

"Point made." Kerry handed her the contracts. "Can you execute these, please? I'll stop by HR with the personnel requests for them."

Colleen studied the contracts, whistling softly under her breath.

"Good gracious." She glanced up at Kerry, who returned the look with a wry, slightly sheepish grin. "I told my brother about this place. He thinks it's that you and the tall dark and dauntless one have the touch."

Kerry cocked her head to one side. "What touch?"

Colleen rubbed her thumb against her first two fingers. "The money touch, or really, success. Most people would have been out there pounding the pavement handing out fliers looking for work. Not you guys."

Kerry shook her head. "That won't keep up. We caught a break because of the government projects."

Colleen held up the contracts. "And these?"

"Well, we're lucky in that we've got a history in this industry." Kerry put her hands behind her back and rocked up and down a few times. "And we've got a history of success. If we didn't we probably would be out there pounding pavement."

"Lucky for the rest of us." Colleen winked at her. "Let me get these squared away and filed in these bonny new cabinets of mine. Half a drawer already with documentation." She indicated one set with carefully labeled drawers.

"We should talk about offsite storage," Kerry said. "Set up an account with Iron Mountain, at least."

"Already did that, m'dear," Colleen said. "But it would be better if we could transfer it all digitally. The tapes...I never did trust them."

"Me either," Kerry said. "Let me see what I can come up with, okay? I'm going to go grab a cup of coffee."

"Surely." Colleen went into the office with the folder.

Kerry headed for the stairs, dropping down them in an easy rhythm. The receptionist answered the phone, as she got down to that level.

"Roberts Automation. Yes? Oh, yes, let me put you through to our accounting department." The receptionist gave Kerry a little wave. "I'm sure they're interested in a new stationary vendor."

Kerry rolled her eyes and chuckled as she ducked into the downstairs break room, newly finished and equipped with tables and microwaves and two big refrigerators. The coffee service had been moved inside and off its cart and she nodded in approval at the newly plumbed drink machines and the box with its selection of teas.

The refrigerator was already full of lunch boxes and jars of various condiments in the door pockets as well.

They had a smaller kitchen upstairs, but Kerry had decided to keep things on the lower level to encourage people to get up and move around, not get stuck in their chairs all day long. She opened one of the cabinets and spotted lines of neatly logoed mugs inside, in their blue, gray and buff colors.

"Nice." She took one down and examined it, then put it down and selected a green tea bag rather than the coffee she'd intended on making. She added some honey to the beverage then took her cup and strolled around the lower level. She heard carpenters and other workmen nearby and stuck her head inside one of the nearly finished staff work areas.

The room was empty and looked large, but Kerry knew once they got the modular furniture inside it would rapidly shrink. She counted in her head how many cubes it would hold. "Sheesh."

This would be the room for the support group the HR firm was busy hiring. They would report to Mark. She studied the space and made a mental note to set aside the back section—which had a little angle to it and windows that overlooked the garden—for a supervisor.

Yet another person they'd have to hire.

Wow. Kerry moved along the corridor and headed around to the back side of the building where the HR group had moved, having expanded to require more space. She entered their new office, finding six people there, all busy on the phone.

She looked around, but the supervisor spotted her and hurried over. "Busy in here."

"Boy is it," the woman said. "Let me tell you something, Ms. Roberts. I've been doing this for fifteen years and I've never seen a company come off the blocks like this one has."

Kerry smiled. "I'll take that as a compliment. But I've got another set of requests for employees. We're going to need four more web developers and two mobile specialists."

"My goodness."

"And next week the support area's going to be ready, so we need to fill it," Kerry said, almost apologetically. "Six tech support people and a supervisor. That's all for us."

The woman seemed slightly overwhelmed. "I'm going to have to call up some other agencies. Our pools are almost empty." She grinned, though. "But that's the kind of problem I like to have."

Kerry remembered something. "Let me send you a list of possibles. I heard of some layoffs in the recent past that could end up working in our favor." She patted the woman on the arm. "See what I can do."

She left the HR people in a buzz of activity and went along the back side hallway heading for the other set of steps leading back up to the second floor. She paused when she heard voices outside. She went to the big rolling dock door and stuck her head out. Carlos was there with their persistent antagonist, Wheels. "Hey."

Carlos was standing on the dock, his big, muscular arms crossed over his chest, regarding the disabled man at street level. "Hello there, ma'am. Was just having a discussion with this guy." He indicated Wheels. "He doesn't like that I had Waste Management put a locked hatch on the garbage dumpsters."

Kerry didn't realize their new security manager had done such a thing. "Well, it's a shame that people can't abide by our wishes, but there ya go. Good job." She returned Wheel's dour glare with a mild expression. "I'm not sure what your problem is."

"It's just garbage," Wheels said. "Why do you care if someone roots in it?"

"Cause it makes a mess we gotta clean up," Carlos said. "I saw what you did yesterday. That's why I had them come out today and lock it. Guy had to spend two hours cleaning up after you."

"There ya go." Kerry started to pull her head in.

"Hey, chick!"

Kerry debated on responding. Then she leaned against the door frame. "Hey, jackass," she called back.

But Wheels held up a hand. "I'm not trying to be an ass, that's what we call women."

"I'm not trying to be an ass either, that's what I call men who call women chicks," Kerry responded. "So now if we've got that clear, I've got work to do."

Carlos chuckled and started to follow her inside.

"Hey wait," Wheels yelled after them. "I want to ask you a question."

Kerry paused just inside the door, exchanging a look with Carlos, who filled the opening. "I'm going to regret going back out there, aren't I?"

"Not with me around," he said with a faint grin.

Kerry sighed and eased around him and out the opening, emerging on the loading dock with Carlos at her heels. She walked over to the edge of the concrete and sat down, dangling her legs and leaning her elbows on her thighs. "Yes?" Her eyebrows lifted in question.

Carlos leaned against the building wall, watching them closely.

Wheels stared at her for a minute, apparently surprised that she'd come back. He looked embarrassed and he checked around him carefully before he looked back at her. "I seen new people around here all week."

"Yes. We're growing." She studied his scared face. "Why do you ask?"

He looked away furtively. "Just wondered," he muttered. "Stupid queer who owns the place said you were hiring. Just wondered why we never get a piece of that."

Kerry felt warmth between her shoulder blades and knew if she looked behind her, she'd find Dar there watching them. Either from the dock door or the windows above. She knew it as surely as she knew going down the road this disabled vet was heading on would likely bring them nothing but trouble.

But that had never stopped either of them. "Piece of that," she repeated slowly. "As in, why we wouldn't consider hiring you?"

"Us. Any of us." He waved a hand in a vague circle. "All I heard was crap about bringing jobs in here. But not for us." He refused to look at her.

Kerry regarded him in silence for a moment until he looked up. "The jobs are open for anyone who's qualified for them," she said. "We didn't tell the agency not to look around the neighborhood."

He stared truculently at her.

"We're an information technology company," Kerry said in the same mild tone. "So if anyone around here is interested in that kind of job, they're free to apply. I can give you a list of the openings we have and you can show people."

"You're just saying that," he accused.

Kerry sighed. "You want to see them or not? Honestly, I wouldn't bother just saying that. I've got enough to do as it is, but we're expanding and we need people. If there's someone around here who's qualified and wants a job, better for me."

There was a long silence and then Wheels finally lifted his hands off the arms of his wheelchair and put them back down. "Yeah, okay. I'll look at them. You're probably way too snooty for the likes of anyone here, but what the hell."

Kerry started to get up but heard steps behind her and looked over her shoulder to see Mayte trotting out with a folder in her hands. She took the time to tip her head up, finding the windows overhead empty but the swinging plastic curtain of the main entry swayed enough to give her a glimpse of a tall figure inside.

"Thanks, Mayte." She took the folder and then hopped off the dock, walking over to offer him the papers. "There you go."

He grabbed them from her and shoved the folder between his body and the side of his chair. "Yeah, okay thanks," he muttered. "Sorry about the mess. We didn't think anyone cared."

Kerry crossed her arms over her chest and leaned back against the dock wall. She heard the scuff of footsteps behind her and a moment later Dar stood next to her, hands planted firmly on her hips. "Hey, sweetie."

"Hey," Dar responded. "Was that a good idea?"

Kerry shrugged. "We do need people and you never know, hon. Maybe one of those guys has tech experience."

"Maybe," Dar said. "But do they have a bank account we can drop an ACH into, and will they pass the security review?" She took the cup Kerry still had and drank a sip of her tea. "At any rate, that was a lot better outcome than last time and we don't need to call the cops."

"True."

Dar handed the cup back. "Think I'll go get some java and apologize to my coders. I hauled ass out of their crib like the schizoid overprotective nut case I am and knocked some sodas over."

Kerry eyed her. "You didn't really."

Dar made a face. "Maria came hauling past me saying you were out here and she was going to get security. I didn't have super secret psychic powers this time."

Kerry smiled. "I think it was a good choice, Dar," she said in a sober tone. "Halfway through escalating a bitch fest with him it occurred to me that we weren't going anywhere with that attitude. Then he took a step in. I took one, too."

"Trust your judgment one hundred percent." Dar offered her hand. "Let's go back to work."

"You got it."

Chapter Eight

KERRY WHISTLED SOFTLY under her breath as she folded another pair of underwear, bopping gently to the song playing in her ear buds as she worked. Chino and Mocha were sleeping in Chino's bed nearby, after being run to exhaustion by Dar earlier in the evening.

Now Dar was diligently upgrading the wireless in the condo while she got two washes done, just a typical weeknight at the condo taking care of chores.

Dar poked her head in the bedroom a few minutes later. "Hey." She entered, removing one of the ear buds. "Dinner's ready."

Kerry finished folding the pair of fire engine red panties in her hands and removed the other bud. "What are we having?" She turned off the digital player clipped to the waistband of her shorts. Dar had offered to cook, or actually, had offered to obtain a meal for them. That could pretty much be anything from corn dogs to filet mignon from the island's restaurant.

Never was the same thing twice.

"Chicken and rice."

Kerry put the ear buds down on the dresser. "You haven't had time to cook that so did it come from the Italian place?"

Dar smiled. "Haven't had time and have no idea how to," she said. "Would you believe the Cuban place across the channel delivers here by boat?"

"I do now." Kerry followed her to the kitchen where there were aluminum foil wrapped packages on the counter top. "I don't even want to know what the delivery charge is." She unwrapped the items as the clatter of toenails sounded on the tile. "Ah, our children heard the crinkling."

They moved to the living room with plates of fragrant chicken and rice and sprawled on the couch. Dar flipped on the television.

Kerry forked up a bit of the tender chicken. "This is good," she said. "You get the Wi-Fi all worked out?"

"Yep." Dar slung one long leg over the couch arm and studiously ignored the two pairs of Labrador eyes watching her every move. A nearby handset rang and she set the plate on the side table and reached over to answer the house phone. "Don't know who the hell this might be. Hello?"

"Hey, Dar," Mark's voice echoed through the handset. "Just heard from one of our old workmates so I thought I'd give you a buzz. I figured you could use a laugh."

"Sure." Dar put the handset on speaker. "Kerry's listening too. What's up?"

"Remember you said eventually they'd have a fuck up and then we'd know how screwed up they were?" Mark sounded amused. "Happened sooner than later. Pete, the guy who took over my spot? He just called me. Total cluster. They did some change that the new ops VP told them to do and everything's cocked up."

"Oh. Damn." Dar mentally pictured it. "What kind of change?"

"Pete was in too much of a flop sweat to tell me. He was just praying to cheezus I could tell him what to do, because everyone's screaming at him."

"Did you?"

Mark hesitated a trifle then cleared his throat. "No. Not...I mean, if I could have given him a quick ten word answer, I might have, you know? But I don't know what they changed."

"Sounds like a mess," Kerry said, fishing out a small bit of chicken breast for each of her two furry acolytes.

"Yeah, it is," Mark said. "So besides thinking you'd think it was kinda funny, I thought I should warn ya because Pete knows, and probably everyone else knows there's only one person they could call who maybe could help them."

Dar sighed.

"Would you?" Kerry asked, curiously.

"I would tell them just revert their damn change," Dar said. "Shouldn't take me to do that, though. It's common sense, Mark."

"Hundred percent, boss," Mark said. "That's what I told Pete. Problem is, so many cooks were in the kitchen and making changes to try to fix it, they never recorded the start state and they don't know what to do to put it back."

Dar frowned. "Pull the configs from the repository and push them."

"They tried that," Mark said. "Something went wrong with it. Pete's kinda freaked."

Dar paused thoughtfully and took a forkful of her dinner. "Someone making things worse on purpose?" she asked after she swallowed. "Big coincidence the repository going down in the mix."

"I kinda thought about that but the guys left there want their jobs. I don't think they'd do that. Bigger gain for them if they run smooth and get in good with the new dude," Mark said. "So anyway, like I said, just thought I'd let ya know because you never know. They might swallow the pill and pick up the phone."

"I doubt it, but thanks, Mark," Dar said. "Let us know if you hear any more tidbits. Pays to be in the know."

"You got it, boss." Mark sounded satisfied. "See ya tomorrow."

"Later." Dar hung up the phone and for a long few moments they simply ate together in silence, deep in thought.

"It's so weird," Kerry finally said. "Knowing that's going on and not getting any calls for it."

"Uh huh," Dar agreed. "They won't call me. Too much loss of face. They'll bring in specialists or someone from the vendors to sort it out."

"I think you're right."

Dar handed over a bite of chicken to the patiently waiting Chino, then provided a smaller piece to Mocha who stood up on his hind legs and pattered on her knee with his front paws. "When they get through this, maybe they'll start forgetting about us and move on."

"I sure hope so." Kerry wiped her lips and got up, putting her plate down. "Watch that for me will you? Want some ice tea?"

"Sure."

Kerry went into the kitchen and got a couple of glasses out, pausing a moment to think about how she felt about ILS being in trouble.

Part of her felt a little gleeful and she wasn't sure if she was altogether happy about that since she'd spent so much time on the other side of the coin. But there was resentment there, too, of how ILS had treated her and Dar, and it would be folly to pretend that didn't exist.

And if they did call Dar?

Hm.

She opened the refrigerator and poured the beverage, the tea itself having been made using the sun method. It had tea, of course, but also raspberries and blackberries. It was murky and weird looking but tasted fine.

She brought the tea back into the living room where Dar had found a special on penguins to watch. "Oh, cute." She settled back on the couch, this time with her shoulder right up against Dar so she could let her head rest there, too.

Dar shifted and touched her head to Kerry's. "I was just thinking about what I was going to do if they do decide to call me," she said.

"I was in the kitchen wondering the same thing," Kerry said. "Hon, tempting as it is to be the knight in shining armor that saves them, I think those bastards will just use that as leverage to say you deliberately crippled the company by leaving."

Dar smiled. "Now who's being psychic?"

"Seriously. I think the reason they fired Hamilton is because they want to come after you no matter what our agreement was. They'll take any excuse."

"They're businessmen," Dar said. "I hope that would mean they'll do things just to continue the company's success. Coming after me doesn't do anything for anyone."

"I think some of them don't care."

Dar shrugged. "Could be. Anyway, it's a moot point unless they call." She paused thoughtfully. "I don't think they will. I think it'll kill them to have to. But if they're desperate enough to do that, if I do help, I get one up on them."

"I don't know, Dar."

"Wait 'til it happens. Or not," Dar said. "They don't have idiots there. I'm sure they can figure it out."

Kerry snorted, but remained silent, finishing up her chicken.

"KERRISITA?"

Kerry looked up from her desk to find Maria in the doorway. "Hey, Maria. What's up?"

"The receptionist has someone downstairs who wished to speak with you," Maria said. "I think it might be one of those terrible men."

Kerry tapped her pen on her desk. "Can you ask Carlos to bring him up?"

"Surely," Maria said and ducked out.

"This might be interesting." Kerry cocked her head to one side to listen for Dar in the next room. Silence greeted her, but she figured if Carlos was bringing the guy, it should be all right.

A couple of minutes later Carlos knocked softly at the door frame, then stood back to let his charge enter, following him inside.

Kerry was waiting, her desk cleared, the folder she had of the job openings off to one side. Not to her surprise, the man who came in was the guy who had stalked her. She remained neutrally silent while he crossed over and sat down in one of her visitor's chairs.

Carlos went over and stood on the other side of him, hands clasped in front of him. "You be polite to this lady or you're going out the window, bud."

The man looked at him then back at Kerry without commenting.

"What can I do for you?" Kerry finally broke the silence. "Mr. Patterson, is it?"

"Yeah." He cleared his throat. "Wheels told me you gave him a list of open positions."

"I did," Kerry said. "He asked me why none of the jobs were offered to you and your friends. The reason is that none of you are registered with a technical placement agency. But I gave him a list of openings in case he was qualified for one of them."

"Seems like he can talk just fine," Carlos commented. "Not sure why you're all in his business."

Patterson turned and looked at him. "Why don't you get out of here?"

"'Cause I don't have to. I work here," Carlos replied in a mild tone. "And my job is to make sure that this lady doesn't have to deal with jackasses. So don't be one."

Kerry really liked Carlos. He stayed relaxed, maintaining a benignly friendly expression that was at complete odds with his words. He didn't see any need to bluster, there was just a calm confidence about him that reminded her a little of Andrew.

"Whatever." Patterson turned back to Kerry. "So here's the deal," he said. "All of us come in together."

Kerry folded her hands. "Do all of you have IT experience?"

"Wheels knows that stuff, and Doug, too. But it's all or nothing. We're a team."

Kerry cleared her throat. "Mr. Patterson, I don't hire gangs." She paused. "If any of you have experience I'd be more than happy to have you apply. If you qualify for a position, I'll hire you. But no one gets to work here on someone else's back."

"That's not how it works," he said.

"That's how it works here," Kerry said. "I get to make the rules. I own the company." She had to stifle a smile as she said it because it was impossible to suppress the shiver of pride that went through her. "So if you, or any of your friends, individually, are interested in a position, c'mon in and fill out an application."

Behind him Kerry caught sight of Dar standing quietly in the doorway between their offices, arms crossed, watching Patterson like a hawk.

"So what's it going to be?" Kerry asked, since Patterson was just glaring at her. "I don't have time to debate with you about it."

"Okay look," he grudgingly responded. "All of us been friends since grade school. If we could do civ stuff we woulda. But we ended up going into the service and had each other's backs there. Same thing here. We want to stay together and we can all do useful stuff. Just not all that tech crap."

"I get that," Kerry said. "But it's not how we do things. We're a small company and every person has to be here to help us go forward. I can't just hire people with useful skills, because they might not be useful to me."

"Yeah well I figured you'd say that." Patterson stood up. "Screw it. We'll go find someone else who appreciates veterans who served their country." He turned his back and started out, pausing when he saw Dar watching him. "Too many queers around here anyway."

Dar looked him up and down. "Takes one to know one," she said with a smile. "Carlos, see the gentleman out, please."

"Yes, ma'am." Carlos caught up to Patterson at the door and followed him out.

"That was icky," Kerry said as Dar sauntered over and parked herself on the windowsill behind her desk. "Was he serious, Dar? Did he really think we'd just hire a bunch of guys like that?"

"Should have offered to take all of them but only pay for the guys who were qualified. Let them share that," Dar said, muffling a smile when Kerry turned all the way around and stared at her. "Just kidding."

"Jesus."

Dar folded her arms. "I think those guys are in a place where it's them against everyone. You let someone get ahead, like Wheels maybe, and the group breaks down. I can see why they'd want to stick together."

Kerry eyed her thoughtfully. "Isn't that sort of a fantasy land?"

"I think they're looking at it like that's all the family they have," Dar said. "They don't have anything else. I don't agree with the request. I think they're a box of assholes in a pink paper wrapper, but I remember what my dad used to say about his teammates and it is what it is."

Kerry sighed. "Wish Dad was here. Maybe he could talk to them since he's been there."

"I think we should talk to Wheels on the side," Dar said. "If he's the one with tech skills, it's not fair to him to hold him back. Maybe we can force a split there. Might be a good thing for all of them." She pushed herself up off the sill. "But I wouldn't hire the guy who was here even if he was Charles Babbage himself."

"Booyah," Kerry agreed, giving her a wry grin as she retreated back to her office. "Okay, next." She picked up the phone and dialed a number. "Charles? Hey, it's Kerry. Just wanted to make sure you got those quotes."

DAR DROPPED INTO her chair and leaned back, glancing over her shoulder at the darkening sky. Mark had just settled in her visitor chair and they both had bottled drinks they were sucking on. "Hear from your buddy?"

Mark rolled his eyes. "Six times," he said. "I'm feeling it for the guy. They're roasting him. They got like three contractors and half the tech staff from two vendors and they're still in the weeds."

Dar frowned. "What in the hell could they have done to screw things up that badly? Network was stable for two god damned years before I left."

Mark muffled a smile. "He told me that new guy — the one who took Kerry's spot — said we'd been doing it wrong, you know? So he had them switch all the routing protocols because it would make everything faster."

Dar covered her eyes in eloquent silence.

"Boss, it's a mess. They literally had to static route stuff in the main office just to keep systems up."

"Oh my fucking god," Dar muttered. "Are you kidding me?"

"Pete's sure it's gonna get out he was talking to me and he's gonna get fired, but he said today, he's probably gonna get fired anyway because the new guy's got Teflon boxers and he's throwing them all under the bus."

Dar lowered her hand and stared at him. "What?"

"He told the big cheeses that Pete and his team screwed up the change and he's doing his best to fix it." Dar's face changed from exasperated bemusement to a dark, cold anger in the flash of an eye. "I felt bad for Pete. He was kinda losing it. Said he never thought his boss would do that."

"No," Dar said, in a clipped tone.

"We never had to worry about that," Mark added gingerly. He saw Dar was totally pissed off, her body was getting restless and she was breathing a little faster. "Sorry, boss, didn't mean to tick you off."

Dar took a deep breath and released it. "What an asshole."

Mark grinned wryly at her. "I kinda hope they call you," he admitted. "I want to be there when you finish fixing that crap and tell that guy, David Willerson, what he's going to die of."

Kerry came in, sorting through a handful of papers. "Charles signed the letter of intent. He got funding for about ninety five percent of the quotes we gave him." She glanced up at Dar and saw the storm clouds. "What's up?"

"Just filling Big D in on stuff at the old place," Mark said. "Anyway if I hear any more, I'll clue you." He got up. "Time to go get on the bike and ride." He lifted a hand and waved, then left.

Kerry put her papers down and went around behind Dar to start massaging her neck and shoulders. "What's got you so torked? They still screwed up?"

Dar exhaled again. "The new guy told them to make that change, then when it went south he blamed them."

Kerry winced. "They would never see that coming."

Dar braced her elbow on the arm of her chair and rested her head against it. "Yeah, that's what Mark said."

Kerry leaned over and gave her a kiss, along with a compassionate hug. "Aw, hon." Dar reached up and took hold of her hand. "Hey, maybe those guys will figure out how to fix it and turn the tables."

Dar shifted and looked up at her, eyebrows hiking.

"You never know."

DAR TAPPED HER boxing gloves together and studied the big hanging bag, determining what to pound the crap out of next. She'd spent forty five minutes whaling at the bag.

Kerry was wisely across the gym, doing sit-ups. They'd been together long enough for her to know when to leave Dar alone for a little while. She knew Dar would come over to join her at some machine once she felt better.

She was almost at that point.

Dar switched bags, going from the big body bag over to the speed bag and starting a slow rhythm on it. As she sped up the routine the stress finally released out of her and she was able to focus on the exercise and not wish it was a human being taking the punishment.

She spent ten minutes on a rapid patter battering of the bag, then slowed it down and finished, feeling a pleasant ache in her arms. With an exhale of satisfaction, she turned and left the boxing area, working the gloves off her hands.

The island gym was mostly empty at this hour and she was

unimpeded as she crossed the floor and zeroed in on Kerry, who was taking a break from her routine. "Hey."

"Hey." Kerry wiped sweat from her eyes. "Feel better?"

Dar smiled. "Yeah." She shadowboxed at Kerry. "When you're done, want to take a swim?"

"Sure." Kerry stretched her body out, one way and then the other. "Let me just do the leg press and we can go splash." She got off the incline board and moved to the next machine while Dar took her place and hooked her feet under the holders and started a set of sit-ups herself.

Kerry settled on the leg press and unlocked it, adjusting the weight and slowly starting the exercise. She saw Dar's profile and was glad to see the furrow gone from between her brows and a relaxed expression on her face. Much better. "Guess what I have when we get back?"

Dar eyed her. "Does it start with ice cream?"

"It does."

"Mm." Dar looked contented. "Y'know, something you said before gave me an idea."

Kerry paused at the top of her extension. "Yeah?"

"Yeah."

"Is that good or bad?"

Dar smiled, and boxed a little with her hands as she continued her sit ups. "We'll just have to find out."

THE SUN WAS just thinking about peeking over the horizon as Dar closed the door to her truck, clicking the lock on the door before she shouldered her backpack and started for the building.

Hers was the first car in the lot, as she'd expected it would be, and she paused at the front of the walk just to look up and regard the sign on the wall for a moment.

Her face scrunched up into an unapologetic grin. Then she shook herself a little and continued up the path toward the door. She reached into her jeans pocket for the hard key as she walked. A bird started warbling in one of the olive trees on either side of the walk and she pursed her lips and warbled back, the sound fading off as she came around the last bend and saw the figure crouched on the front porch.

"Ah. Nice way to start the day," Dar muttered under her breath as the figure heard her boots on the path and straightened up a little in his wheelchair. "Morning," she said as she climbed the few steps up to where he was seated.

He blinked at her, bruises evident on his face, one hand wrapped in a makeshift bandage. "That other lady coming?"

Dar put her backpack down on the small wrought iron table and sat on one of the little chairs next to him. "If you mean my partner, Kerry, she's taking our puppy for his checkup at the vets. Something I can do for you?"

He avoided meeting her eyes. "I'll wait."

Dar rested her elbows on the chair arms, glad she had a hoodie on when the chill of the metal transferred even through the cloth. She laced her fingers together and studied him from the corner of her eyes, knowing a moment of unexpected compassion for him. "Your buddy came to see us last night. He was trying to sell all of you as a package."

"Yeah, I know."

"That your idea?" Dar kept her voice light and mild. "That's not how civ works."

He peeked up at her briefly, then looked away. "Wasn't my idea. I showed Joe the jobs. He thought maybe it would be good for all of us." He shrugged. "Told him you all'd say no way."

"We did," Dar said. "He told us it was all or nothing. He change his mind or did you?"

Wheels stared dourly at his hands for a long moment. "Told him I was going to come back anyhow. No one else round here will even talk to any of us."

"He hit you for saying that?"

He looked up again, more sharply. "Nah, we just scrapped." He kept eye contact with her. "Not on your fucking sidewalk either."

Dar smiled. "Thanks. I do appreciate that."

He looked away again, a flush rising up his neck up to his ears.

"You here on the porch waiting to ask us for something in particular?" Dar said after a moment of silence. "Whatever it is you're going to ask Kerry for, she'll tell me before she answers anyway."

The man studied her in silence. Dar sat there waiting, returning his gaze in mild neutrality.

He shifted in his wheelchair, his face old before it's time, lines of pain etched across it. He pulled out a folded piece of paper and offered it over to her. "Wanted to ask about this here."

Dar unfolded the paper and studied it. "One of our tech support positions. This something you do? You do that in the service?"

He shook his head. "Infantry. I did that before I went in. In high school I was the guy who messed with all the computers in the lab and all." He shifted again. "I used to set up the machines from scratch, reload them after all the classes, you know?"

"Yes, I do know," Dar said. "You fix printers and that sort of thing, too?"

He nodded. "I can take apart and fix a laser fuser," he said. "And solder components, that stuff."

Dar's eyebrows lifted a bit. "Why didn't you stick with that instead of the Army? You can make a living with that. Or why not specialize in it? Army uses tech."

He looked at her. "Went with my buddies. They all wanted to go into the Army and I went, too. Stayed with them when we all got picked for grunts." He scowled a little. "Guess you think that's stupid."

Dar folded the paper and ran her fingers over the edges. "Not really, no. I was a signature away from the Navy myself, mostly because my dad was in and I grew up on a base." She cleared her throat. "So no, I don't think that's stupid. But I bet you think so now."

He flushed again. "Didn't think about coming back like this." He indicated his lower body, one leg missing mid thigh and the other below the knee. His pants legs were drawn closed with twine, dirty and ragged. "Dead's one thing. This?"

"No you don't think of that when you're going in. I saw people coming back with half their guts missing. I saw my dad hurt and still didn't think about it. When you're that young you think you're invincible."

She saw his neck muscles relax and he straightened up, looking at her. "Yeah." He studied her briefly. "What made ya back out?"

Dar smiled briefly. "They wouldn't let me get a berth where I wanted it and I wasn't going to settle for anything else," she said. "I'm a hardass that way. Always have been, even back then."

He considered that. "Ballsy," he said. "You want intel or something?"

"Special forces." Her eyes twinkled a little at his reaction. "So I ended up doing technology instead. Worked out better for me in the long run."

He snorted a little. "Fuck."

Dar pulled her Handspring out, studied it, then tapped out a message. She glanced up at him. "Are your friends going to be pissed off by you coming here to talk to us?"

"Yeah."

"That going to be a problem for you?"

For a very long moment he didn't answer, his gaze going past her and unfocused. Then he looked back up at her with his most straightforward, honest expression yet. "Don't care."

She glanced down at the phone as its message light stuttered red. "We'll try to make it worth the hassle then." She looked back up at him. "Let's go inside." She stood up and went to the door, keying in the alarm code and opening the door with her hard key.

"For what?"

Dar's brows lifted and she held up the folded paper. "You want a job? I'll give you a try at one."

He looked around with a stunned expression. "Don't you have to talk to that other lady?"

"I did." Dar held up the Handspring as she pushed the door open and held it. "C'mon, let's get the ground rules settled before everyone comes in and freaks out."

He stared at her for a very long moment. "Sorry I was such a jackass," he said. He swiveled the chair and rolled in the door.

Dar smiled. "Takes one to know one." She closed the door after them and indicated the right hand turn down the hallway. "Let's go to the HR office. You can start filling out paperwork."

"You're really going to hire me?"

"Yup."

"Somebitch."

KERRY TUCKED MOCHA under her arm and opened the door to her SUV. She put him on the seat and hopped inside, getting the door closed before Mocha could get any clever ideas in terms of jumping out. "C'mon, Mochie. Let's go to work and see what trouble mommy Dar's gotten into."

"Yap." Mocha sat down on the passenger seat, his tongue hanging out.

It didn't surprise her that Dar hired their crippled veteran troublemaker. She'd sensed a sympathy in Dar for the guy. She was a little surprised, though, that he'd showed up after the grandstanding play by his buddy last night.

She navigated the busy city streets carefully, not wanting to spill Mocha on the car floor with a sharp stop. They'd been the first ones at the vet, and Mocha passed his exam with flying colors. He was happy to be the center of attention even when that center meant various things being stuck in him and in unpleasant places.

So now this new employee. Her mind started to count up the issues she figured they'd need to face which would start with, did this guy actually have a place to live?

Did he have a place to shower? Did he have clothes to wear to work? If he stayed around with his buddies, would he be reliable?

Was she being a little too WASP-y about it?

Kerry pulled into the office lot and parked. She stuck her sunglasses up in the visor and opened the door. "You hang on there, Mocha. I'll come get you." She got out and shut the door, walking around to the passenger side as the puppy raced around inside, barking excitedly.

"Relax!" She chuckled as she got the other door open and collected the bouncing fur ball.

"Hey, Kerry." Mark appeared at her side, two cups of coffee in his hands. "Crazy morning already, huh?"

Kerry put Mocha down and looped his leash around her wrist. "You mean our new employee?" She grinned. "Hey, I never argue with Dar's hiring."

Mark chuckled too as he walked alongside her up the path. "He kinda surprised me. He's got some skills," he admitted. "I thought Dar was just being...like she was humoring him. But he knows what end of a cable to plug in stuff."

"Dar sees things in people," Kerry said. "Sometimes she sees things other people don't and sometimes she sees things the people she sees them in don't."

Mark grinned as he pushed the door open for her with his elbow and stood aside to let her enter. "I had you pegged the second I saw your file."

Kerry eyed him. "You did, did you?"

"Yup." He winked and headed up the steps to his office.

"Good morning, ma'am," the receptionist said. "Only one dog today?"

"Only one. Chino was very upset I left her behind. If she'd known we were going to the vet I bet she would have laughed." Kerry headed up the steps, carrying Mocha since his legs were still a little short to handle the stairs well. She got to the top and waved hello to Maria, then ducked through Mayte's office toward her and Dar's. "Hey, Mayte."

"Good morning, Kerry." Mayte grinned at her. "I have some messages for you on your desk."

"Thank you." Kerry went in and put Mocha down in the puppy playpen Dar had constructed. It had a plethora of toys and bones and a dish of water and one for kibble. "There you go, little man. Chill out for a while so I can get my phone calls done."

"Hey."

Kerry paused in the middle of sitting down to look up and find Dar in the inner doorway. "Hey, hon."

"Hey, beautiful," Dar responded amiably. She came over to the play pen and leaned over to give Mocha a pat. "Our new employee is going through the typical orientation routine," she said. "His name's Scott Brewer, by the way."

Kerry leaned back. "So how did that all come about?" she asked. "Did you know he was going to come back here?"

Dar stepped inside the playpen at Mocha's urgent paw scrabbling request and sat down with him. "He was on the porch when I got here." She glanced up at Kerry. "Had one of your job requests on him. I wasn't expecting to see him there, but I wasn't surprised either."

"Isn't that going to piss off his obnoxious friend, Joe?"

Dar nodded. "He said it was, but he didn't care. That's why I hired him. That and the fact he actually was his high school's nerd and knows how to disassemble and reassemble a laser printer." She grinned briefly. "Naturally he also brings complications."

"Of course," Kerry said. "At least the tech support office is going to be on the first floor, though he can use the freight elevator."

"He wants to use the stairs."

Both of Kerry's brows shot up. "Our liability insurance is going to skyrocket."

Dar chuckled. "No kidding. If he loses his grip halfway up he's going to take out our reception desk on the way back down. I said I'd see what we could work out." She gave Mocha one last scrubble then got up and stepped over the fencing. "Sorry, buddy, gotta go back to my programming."

"Does he live at the halfway house, or under our hedges?" Kerry asked. "He kinda does need to come in with relatively clean clothes and all that, Dar. Not fair to the rest of them otherwise."

"He has a room at the church house, but he doesn't like going there." Dar came over and sat down on the bench behind Kerry. "He says maybe after some paychecks he can get his own place, but I had an idea."

"Of course you did." Kerry reached out and gently ruffled her dark hair.

"I threw in a membership for that little gym around the corner," Dar said. "It's got showers and all that. Told him until he got everything sorted out, he could go there in the morning and get ready for work."

Kerry thought about that, honestly impressed by the suggestion. "So it's not like charity," she said. "You could have offered to get him a place."

Dar shook her head decisively. "He's tired of begging for handouts and getting the government runaround. He wants to try and make it himself."

"You like him."

Dar smiled briefly. "I could have ended up just like him."

"No, never. Your parents would never have left you to live on the streets, Paladar Katherine Roberts." Kerry put her fingertip on Dar's nose. "There's nothing in the world you can say that would make me believe that."

"When you met me I could've been living on the streets and they would have never known. Don't color my childhood in rainbow snow cones, hon. There was a time, after we thought Dad was gone, that I was just as alone as this guy is, even more so since at least he thinks he has friends."

Kerry didn't refute that because she knew it was true.

"So anyway," Dar went on. "We'll have to put up with his ratty clothes until he gets his first paycheck. Mark checked him out and says he'll be okay on the tech side."

"Good enough for me."

Dar nodded and glanced around before lowering her voice. "Now on another subject."

"Uh oh."

A soft knock interrupted them. Kerry projected her voice toward the door. "Yes?"

Zoe poked her head in. "Miss Kerry, your ten o'clock appointment is here."

Kerry sighed. "Rats. Yeah. Can you get them a cup of coffee and give me five minutes?"

Zoe nodded and backed out, closing the door behind her.

Kerry turned in her chair and scooted closer to Dar. "So."

"Mark talked to his buddy today. They're on the verge of doing something idiotic," Dar said, quietly. "I don't think they're going to call me."

"Good," Kerry said.

Dar nodded. "But I feel for those guys. I don't think it would be a good idea to contact them."

"Good," Kerry said again with a faint smile. "So far we're in one hundred percent agreement."

"Here's the deal. You know that network forum I mess around in sometimes?" Dar asked. "The one where people post questions and all that crap?"

Kerry frowned. "No, I...oh." Then she nodded. "Yeah, you showed me that once. Nerdfest."

"Nerdfest," Dar agreed. "Everyone posts there — engineers, nerds, wannabe nerds, trolls and interested onlookers. I don't post often, and not under my real name, but every once in a while I throw a hat in."

"Ah. I'm beginning to see the light."

"So I told Mark if his buddy wanted to post a few questions in that forum, if I can answer them, I will. He doesn't have to give his name. He can make the questions general enough not to identify ILS."

Kerry was silent for a moment. "Will it stay anonymous, though? Dar, I think they'll use any excuse they can find, no matter what it is, to make you responsible for whatever bad's going on there."

Now it was Dar's turn to be quiet for a bit. "I don't know," she finally said. "But it's the only way I can think of to give them help without causing a riot. I don't necessarily know who this guy is, and I do occasionally give answers on there."

Kerry watched the planes of Dar's face shift as she looked briefly away, then back at Kerry. "You really are a crusader, you know that?" She smiled and leaned forward to touch her head to Dar's. "Be careful, Dar."

"I will. And anyway, the guy might not want to go that route. It's a risk for him, too. Maybe he just wants to wait it out and see what happens."

That was true. "Okay." Kerry patted Dar's knee. "But you might want to —"

"Go through a proxy so they can't track the IP back here?" Dar's eyes twinkled. "Good idea."

They both laughed then Dar got up and sauntered back to her office, turning to give Kerry a wink before she disappeared.

Kerry pressed the intercom button. "Zoe, please bring my visitor in." She released the button and shook her head. "Crusader Dar. Boy did that woman nail her."

"ALL RIGHT, ROBERTS." Bridges voice sounded bemused. "Remember that conversation we had about smoke and mirrors?"

Dar leaned back in her chair. "I do."

"Senate Intelligence Committee wants to see this thing before we go any further with it," he said. "Now, understand this doesn't change anything between us and you. It's going forward regardless."

"Uh huh."

"But we have to show these mental midgets something so they'll shut their yaps and go mess with something else, like voting themselves a raise."

Dar pondered that. "When?"

"Soon as you can."

She sighed. "I can mock up a prototype by next week. That soon enough?"

There was a brief silence then Bridges chuckled. "That'll do. Will it show them what they expect to see?"

"Will they understand what I show them?" Dar countered. "I'll lay out for them how it's going to work and what the agents on the other end will see when they make a query."

"No Internet snooping?" Bridges said. "By the way, you nailed that with George."

"It'll be rough," Dar warned. "Just command line. But it should be enough to give them an idea."

"Good," he said. "Now, a completely different subject. Your old friends are screwing things up."

Dar looked at her phone with a puzzled expression. "What? Are they still making waves about the contract?"

"Hell, no. Something's screwed up over there. Things aren't working, according to what I hear from the Pentagon. Got a bunch of pissed off medal pushers out there yelling about it."

"Ah."

"Know anything?"

Dar drummed her fingers. "I heard some rumors there was some kind of incident," she answered carefully. "But I don't know any details about it."

"They haven't called you?"

"No," Dar said. "I don't expect them to."

"Idiots."

She smiled in reflex. "Last thing they want is to have to call me in to fix something," she said. "Embarrassing all the way around."

Bridges cleared his throat. "Might not have a choice. If you catch my drift."

Dar grimaced. "Don't do that. Not good for them, and not for me."

"No offense, Roberts, but we don't care if it's good for you, or for them. It's screwing up stuff for us," Bridges said bluntly. "Know what I mean?"

Dar sighed again. "Yeah."

"Anyway, if you grudgingly hear from them, it might be because someone here told them to get their heads out of their asses and get some real help. Or, alternatively, you might get a call from someone at that rock pile wanting you to take over the contracts."

"We're not set up for that."

"Well then put on your big girl panties and get a move on getting set up," he said. "This is serious stuff, Roberts. We don't have the time, or people, to be running around doing things the hard way because their crap isn't working. Got me?"

"Yeah, I get it. But I hope they can straighten themselves out without my interference," Dar said. "I don't want to get back into that arena."

Bridges grunted. "My gal will set up a time next week for your cat and donkey show. Stay by the phone. Answer it if it rings. Later."

Dar released the line and exhaled. "Well, shit." She half turned and looked out the window, where the sunset was splashing a deep gold light along the window. "This is going to be a huge pain in the ass."

"What's that, hon?" Kerry came in with Mocha in her arms. "You ready to go home?"

Dar told her the latest.

"You think Bridges will actually force them to call you?" Kerry already had her messenger bag over one shoulder. "Holy crap, you think they'd make them give us those contracts? Dar we can't handle that."

Dar got up and put her laptop into her backpack. "I know." Dar slung the pack onto her back. "I'm sure they won't end up doing that. It's far too intrusive and probably illegal. I'm going to concentrate on doing the mock up. ILS is going to have to let their chips fall as they may."

She shut her desk lamp off and bumped Kerry toward the door. "C'mon. I need to chill out. Mark said there's no sign of his buddy posting."

They walked down the stairs and waved at the people still left working. Mark stood in the lower hall, his helmet in his hand and he waited for them to reach the bottom.

"Hey." Kerry shifted Mocha to her other arm. "How's our new guy doing?" she asked as they headed out the front door. "I think I got the HR people to stop freaking out about him."

"Not bad," Mark said. "He's still back there reading manuals." He looked and sounded surprised. "Left field pick, boss. How'd you see any cells under all the grunge?"

"Just a hunch," Dar said. "His fast pass come through all right? Since we left him in that room?"

"Oh, yeah sure," Mark said. "Just waiting for his military records to come back, but his civilian stuff's okay, what there is of it. He went into the Army at like eighteen." Mark tossed his helmet up and caught it. "Know what he told me? Said he was digging in that garbage container for manuals and crap, thought we would toss them with the boxes."

"You think that's true?" Kerry asked.

Mark shrugged. "He's in there reading manuals. He said he knew we were a tech company when he saw the deliveries."

"Well, that could be true enough," Kerry admitted. "But I told Carlos to keep an eye on things because I don't want him bothering people."

"Yeah, he told me," Mark said. "My other guys are going in and talking to him, too. I told them to give him some room, but make sure he knew the rules."

Mark's cycle was parked next to Dar's truck, and Kerry's SUV was right behind that. They stood a moment and watched the sun go down as the cool breeze rustled the leaves over their head.

"Pretty night," Mark commented.

Kerry got Mocha into her SUV and tossed her messenger bag in after him. "It is," she said. She turned around and leaned on the car door. "Mark, the problems at our old place are starting to affect customers we have in common."

Mark paused, taking a seat on his bike sideways and regarding her. "Yeah?"

Dar opened her truck door and hopped up onto the seat. "Yeah. Apparently the Pentagon isn't happy with whatever's going on."

"Wow." Mark put his helmet on his lap and rested his arms on it. "I tried to call Pete twice but he's not answering his personal cell. Maybe because it's me. Didn't want to get in any deeper."

Dar sighed. "Wonder if I should call Alastair."

"I'm kind of surprised he hasn't called you," Kerry said. "Unless, like we suspect, he wants to keep you as far out of it as he can."

Dar exhaled. "Damn it, I don't want to get in the middle of this. At first it was just dumbass on their part. Now it's getting serious."

"Crazy they haven't gotten it fixed yet," Mark said. "I just can't figure out what the hell they did, you know? If the repositories tanked we had hard copy of the configs in the files. Even if they restored a thirty day out copy, it would bring everything back."

"Unless he's determined to make it work his way," Kerry said. "The new guy, I mean."

They all stood there thoughtfully for a minute or two. Then Dar cleared her throat. "It won't work any other way," she said. "The metrics...they're all balanced based on the mesh of those routing protocols."

Mark and Kerry stared at her.

"Convergence, hop count—it's all predicated on using the protocol metrics I designed." Dar folded her arms. "It's in the architectural diagrams and overview."

"And that thing you put in," Kerry said. "When we were getting hacked."

Dar nodded. "It's a crude kind of artificial intelligence. Something like what I'm going to use for Bridges."

"Shit. I should tell Pete that," Mark said. "They probably have no clue what all that is. Hell, I had no real clue of what all that was."

"I documented it," Dar said.

"Sure, big D," Mark said. "You put all the words in there but how many people could understand them if they read them? You're like a little rocket scientist y'know?"

"That's all proprietary," Kerry said, "and you're probably the only one who can fix it, aren't you?"

Dar spread her hands out. "They're ILS's patents." she said. "They have all the paperwork on it."

"Yes, hon, but it's your name on those patents. I saw them. Actually, I kept a copy of them so you could look back at them sometime and chuckle."

"I'm not chuckling now," Dar responded dourly.

"Me either." Kerry sighed. "You know, that's probably what happened. That jackass decided he wanted to put his stamp on the system and wanted your stuff taken out." She gave Mark a shrewd look. "You think?"

Mark scrunched his face up. "Crap."

"We're not going to solve it here in the parking lot," Dar said. "Let's go home, Ker. Maybe I'll get a brainwave on the ferry." She slid around in the seat and closed the door. "Maybe I will give Alastair a call. I'm surprised he hasn't given me one. Maybe he walked out and doesn't know what's going on."

Kerry got in her SUV with Mocha, who was scrambling all over putting tongue prints on everything.

"Is it okay for me to tell Pete about that custom stuff?" Mark asked as he straddled his bike. "I'll text him."

"Sure." Dar started the engine. "But if they really did take all that out, it probably won't help."

"Ugh." Kerry put the SUV in reverse and started backing out of her spot. She caught motion in the corner of her eye and turned to see a group of figures watching them. "Double ugh." She glanced forward at Dar's pickup and realized she saw them, too.

Mocha sat down on the passenger seat. "Yap."

"Yap," Kerry repeated and shook her head. "Not going to be a good night, Mocha. I can just feel it."

Chapter Nine

DAR WATCHED THE screen refresh on her computer as she pondered again what to do. There'd been no answer on Alastair's cell and her message hadn't been returned yet. Mark didn't get a response from his buddy either, so she was left to drum her fingers on the desk and listen to Kerry's stir frying from the kitchen nearby.

She got up and circled the desk, going out into the living room and passing the big, new, double-sized dog bed with its snoozing occupants. "Ker?"

"Yes?" Kerry half turned, briefly shifting her attention from her wok to Dar. "Nothing yet?"

Dar shook her head and joined Kerry, peering over her shoulder at the stove. "Yum."

"Well, maybe they did figure it out." Kerry went back to stir frying. "I sure hope so."

"Mm." Dar moved her hair aside and kissed the back of her neck. "Me too." She went to the cupboard and removed a pair of plates, setting them down on the counter. "What I don't want is them turning this around and blaming their screw-up on my design."

Kerry glanced at her, then back at the stove. "Could they do that?"

Dar added two glasses to the plates. "It's unconventional," she admitted, "but that was the whole point. I wanted to make something that set us apart from the rest of the pack."

"Hon, you did document all that," Kerry said. She added a pile of cooked rice noodles into the wok and tossed them with the rest of the ingredients. "It was part of the sales portfolio. I think if they want to bitch about it, they also have to go back and discount all the money they made selling your design."

"Yeah, I know." Dar got a bottle of sparkling cranberry apple juice from the refrigerator and poured both glasses full. "But it can make for some really bad press right when I'm up on Capitol Hill showing off another unconventional design."

Kerry sorted the stir fry out and divided it across both plates. "We've survived bad press. We survived your vice president of global operations being exposed as your lover who threw her father to the wolves. On national television."

Dar paused, then chuckled wryly. "Good point."

"C'mon, Dixiecup." Kerry picked up the plates and carried them into the dining area. "Just let it roll."

Dar put the glasses down and took her seat on the short end of the table, while Kerry took the chair to her right. "Not much choice in the matter. Ball's in their court." She picked up her chopsticks and maneuvered them into the stir fry, which seemed to have shrimp and scallops in it, along with sauce covered vegetables of some kind.

Baby corns and bamboo shoots, Dar decided, munching on them. They both tasted more or less the same with the sweet and spicy sauce on them. "This is good."

Kerry smiled. "I'm glad you like it. I threw some different things in this time. They had fresh scallops at the market."

"Yum."

"Yap."

Dar looked down to find Mocha standing on his hind legs, his front paws scrabbling at her leg. "Excuse me, buddy. You got dinner already." She tapped him on the top of his little dome shaped skull. "Get down."

Chino came over, tail wagging. "Neither of you get any of this," Dar said. "You'll be sick all over the tiles."

"How about a walk down the beach after dinner?" Kerry suggested. "It's nice out."

"Sure."

And so they did, getting Mocha's little puppy harness on him, but letting Chino free as they walked across the garden and out the back gate.

It was a nice night. Dar looped the leash over her wrist and slowed her pace, gazing out at the dark Atlantic ahead of them. There were lights on the horizon—a cargo ship, maybe—and the sky overhead was brilliant with stars. They strolled along the beach front in companionable silence, only the snuffling of the dogs and the soft hiss of the waves to be heard.

After a while Kerry cleared her throat. "So, you saw those guys in the lot before we left?"

"Yeah," Dar said. "I don't think they made any trouble or we'd have heard."

"Mm."

"They're so angry," Kerry said in a thoughtful tone. "Isn't there anything the government can do for them?"

Dar exhaled and walked along for a few paces. "The problem is they don't like to showcase the fact that people who go into the military can come back in pieces. Either physically, or in their heads. Screws up recruitment."

Kerry peered at her in astonishment.

"They want their funding to go to great new weapons and sexy hardware," Dar continued. "Not paying medical bills. That's why it's so hard to get them to admit to being responsible for things like PTSD. It's also why they don't like to admit stuff like that happens, because watching a soldier break down in tears and not be able to shoot is embarrassing to them and bad for morale."

"That's—"

"Crappy. Sure," Dar said. "But it's universal. Look at New York. All those people, those workers and first responders having health issues and absolutely no one wants to say it's because they were down there breathing asbestos and ground glass for months."

Kerry thought about that for a few steps. "Your dad was so insistent we wear those masks."

"He knows."

Kerry sighed. "Humanity sucks sometimes."

"I think they could and probably are doing some things to help those guys," Dar said. "But I think maybe it's not what they want to have done for them. Or not what they expect," she clarified. "I think they want what they see everyone else has, a home, a car, a job. But there's no way to get them from where they are to there." Long speech, for Dar. "So they come from having this job—I mean, the military is like a job, right? You get paid and you're valued for what you're doing. They feed you and house you, then you come back here and..." She lifted a hand and let it fall. "It doesn't translate."

"Wow," Kerry said. "I never thought about that."

"I saw that when I was growing up," Dar admitted. "Me, I always had skills. I knew that. I had a technical aptitude and I was smart. For me, coming back wouldn't have been that much of a problem. I could find a job."

"You started working when you were what...fourteen?" Kerry said. "So I get that. I was talking to my mother once about you and going into the Navy. She was puzzled as to why you wanted to, since you were so smart." She looped her arm with Dar's. "But maybe these guys didn't have any other options but either go into the military, or flip burgers?"

"Maybe," Dar said. "But if you're skilled like I am, the military can be a good career. It's not a dead end, not for everyone."

"Like Gerry."

"Like Gerry. Or even my dad."

Dar's Handspring rang and she fished it out of her pocket. "Hey," she said after glancing at the caller ID. "What's up, Mark."

"I'm here at Dave and Buster's with Pete," Mark said. "I ducked outside to call you so the noise wouldn't kill the reception."

"If you're at Dave and Busters, is he celebrating? Everything squared away?"

Mark sighed. "I wish. What a fucking mess. So, he met me here because he was afraid to even text me. The maniac over there told everyone if anyone leaked what went on they'd be fired and then arrested."

"Not really possible on being arrested," Dar said.

"No, I know, but you know?"

"I know."

"Anyway, so, of the two hundred people in ops IT, a hundred and fifty quit."

Dar's eyes popped wide open. "What?"

"That's who's here at Dave and Busters. They all just walked out," Mark said. "It's like old home week here. They saw me and went nuts."

"Holy shit." Dar covered her eyes, then glanced at Kerry. "Most of the IT department at ILS Miami walked out."

Kerry sucked in an audible breath. "Jesus!"

"Not only that," Mark said. "The dipshit told everyone that this whole mess was your fault."

"That was expected," Dar said.

"That's why people walked out," Mark said, a smile evident in his voice. "My whole old gang just said fuck you and wrapped their creds around David Willerson's neck and left."

"Wow." Dar wasn't sure what to say to that.

"And, they booted out the big cheese."

"Alastair?"

"Yep. Told him to take a hike and he said he was more than happy to. That's why, I guess, he hasn't called ya."

"Holy shit," Dar repeated. "What the hell are they going to do?"

"Beats me. Beats Pete. He's the only one who stuck it out and he only did it because he's got this hard on to prove that jackass wrong and make the thing right."

"Uh huh." Dar thought a moment. "Does he want me to help?"

Mark muffled the call. "Yeah, I'm here. Hang on I'll be right back in there." He uncovered the mouthpiece. "Sure he does, but he's scared."

"Understandable."

"He's got a wife who's nine months preggers and about to pop. They're living on his salary. He said that was the only reason he agreed to do my gig, it gave him a bump."

"Mark. If something happens to this guy because of something we did together, I'll take care of him," Dar said.

"I know. I told him that," Mark said. "But he's scared they're going to see that online forum thing. He wants to talk to you in person, see if there's something you can tell him to do."

"Sure," Dar said. "You want to bring him by the office tomorrow morning, early? I don't seriously think there's surveillance watching us."

"Can I bring him by your place tonight?"

Dar glanced at Kerry, who was plastered to her chest listening, watching the blonde head nod. "Sure. I'll leave your name at the ferry."

"Great. See ya soon," Mark said. "All right! I hear ya! I'm coming back!" He closed the line and Dar hit the release button on her end.

"Holy crap," Kerry said. "This is nuts."

"Total nuts." Dar shook her head. "Let's just hope I can give him some useful advice."

"Ugh."

DAR WAS BACK in her office with Kerry perched on one end of the desk, and Mark and Pete sitting on the couch. She leaned on her elbows, mostly just listening as the young, tow-haired man in jeans and a hoodie talked.

"So." Peter took a sip from the glass he held in both hands. "That's how it happened. Nobody really...I mean, we looked at what he wanted us to do but no one realized what it would...I mean, do."

"Uh," Dar grunted softly.

"So then," Peter continued. "He made us reload all the routers from scratch. So we didn't have anything left to roll back to. He said he wanted to make this work, so he dumped the repository so we couldn't reload from backup."

Kerry leaned forward a little. "That is criminally idiotic."

Peter nodded. "Yes, ma'am. I tried to argue with him."

"What you shoulda done is copy the repository off to an offline storage before you dumped it," Mark said. "What a fucking moron this guy is."

Dar spoke up for the first time in a while. "If what he thought was that the configs were so proprietary he couldn't wrap his head around them, it would make sense to do it from scratch so he knew everything."

The other three in the room stared at her.

Dar folded her hands. "I'm guessing he thought he could put his own configuration in and it would work."

"Uh...I suppose, ma'am," Peter said, meekly.

"I might have done the same thing."

"Yeah, but the difference is your stuff would work," Mark said. "Because you actually know how to do this."

"That's true. But I'm guessing he thought he did, too. Even though I think he's an idiot in terms of management, no one is stupid enough to take down their whole company and put all their clients at risk a couple weeks into a new job."

Peter nodded. "What pissed everyone off is he tried to blame us first, then you. He refused to man up and say it was him that caused the problem."

Dar pondered that. "What does he want to do now? He want this fixed, or he want to sit there and have his ass on fire until he ends up having to redo everything, which is going to take probably a month?"

"Up 'til today I'd have said he wanted to rig it," Peter said, promptly. "But after everybody walked out I saw him in ops and he was really freaked out. He told me I wasn't supposed to tell anyone but he needed to get this stuff working because some big customer was yelling."

"Okay, that's good," Dar said. "Because if he was going to stick to his original plan it would never have worked. The layout's not designed for anything but the metrics we had."

Peter nodded. "I sorta thought maybe that was it. Willerson

thinks you did something."

"I did," Dar said with a brief smile. "But everything I did is written down in the design documents. He didn't erase those, too, did he?"

Peter shook his head. "No. He said he read those and that's why he wanted to make that change, said it would make things better."

Dar studied his face then she sighed. "All right. Ker's on the money. He's a moron."

Kerry gave her a puzzled look. "Were you really trying to give him the benefit of the doubt?"

"Yes." Dar leaned back in her chair. "If he had half a brain then I could call him up and we could maybe get this taken care of. But that kind of idiot doesn't back down. At this point, he can't. He has to go all the way with it or he's done."

"Yeah," Peter agreed. "But at this point he's freaking. I think he'll let me get in there and try to fix stuff if you can tell me how."

"Should you?" Kerry asked, half turning to face Dar. "I know there's the issue with the military contracts, Dar, but honestly, should you go in there and make this right? Considering that they already are trying to blame you?"

Dar hitched her knee up and circled it with both hands, pondering in silence as the rest of them waited. "It's a valid question," she finally said. "I don't feel like I owe them anything at this point." She took a breath and released it. "But I'll be damned if my legacy at that place is going to be a colossal fuck up they're trying to paint my name on."

Everyone nodded in agreement, even Kerry. "I get it, hon. Let's figure out how to get it done."

"That's the hard part. I don't have any copies of the configs," Dar said. "I left everything in the repository so we'll have to depend on my memory to rebuild them."

"Sorry about that, ma'am." Peter looked glum. "Mark's right. I should have copied everything off before I deleted it."

"You guys made those changes without copying the config on a notepad at least?" Mark sounded incredulous. "What the hell, man?"

"Notepad," Dar muttered, her eyes shifting off to one side. "What did that remind me of?"

"Let me go make some coffee," Kerry said. "I'm guessing we're gonna need it." She got up off the desk and headed for the kitchen with Chino trotting behind her.

"You know, all of us probably did," Peter said mournfully. "But with all the crazy making, stuff was moving and systems got rebooted, and you know."

Mark got up. "Let me get my lappie. Maybe I did something illegal and crazy like left some copies on my personal external."

Dar made a clucking noise with her tongue.

"Hey, boss, I know where that code repository came from." He gave Dar a wry look. "Even if it was all yours." He ducked out and that left Dar and Peter alone in the office.

Peter looked profoundly uncomfortable.

Dar leaned forward again and rested her chin on her hand. "Weird, huh?"

He made a face. "Yes, ma'am. Too much strange for me."

"Yeah, I can imagine," she responded, though she really couldn't. "Listen, let's start off by you calling me by my name, okay? I never was much for the ma'am stuff."

Peter smiled uncertainly. "I sort of feel like I'm stuck between that rock and a hard place. I don't want to be a troublemaker, you know? I just want to go in and work and go home and enjoy my family."

Dar nodded. "I get that. You were in the wrong place at the wrong time."

He nodded.

"You could get nailed here, doing this," Dar went on. "But you don't have much of a choice. At least not until things start working again."

Peter relaxed visibly. "You get it."

Dar smiled at him. "Sorry, Peter," she said. "One way or another I'll make this right for you. Promise." She watched his expression become more open. "I made things there the way I did so it would give the company an advantage. Not to be a jackass."

Now he smiled. "Yes, ma...I mean, yes. We all knew that. Even Mr. Jose said that in the big meeting we had yesterday. He said no matter what David Willerson's said, or what he thought, you did the right things."

Ah, Jose. Dar felt a little tickled. "He should know, because no matter how much he and I disagreed he did the right things, too, for the company."

Peter nodded. "The guy said Mr. Jose was stupid, then everyone started yelling and we all just left."

That, unfortunately, Dar could easily imagine. She'd been in enough of those meetings. With a sigh she leaned back and her knee bumped the desk drawer, nudging it open. She reached over to shut it then paused when she saw the edge of something inside and pulled it all the way open.

"Huh." She took out the old Palm and examined it, then fished around in the drawer for the charger. "I wonder?" She plugged it in and waited for it to start up. "Wonder if I left any notes in there from last year."

Kerry came back in with a thermos and some cups, setting them down on Dar's desk. "Whatcha got there, hon?"

"My old PDA," Dar said. "I might have saved some of my notes from when I was doing the rig at the Rock."

Mark came back in with his laptop and a small case hung around his neck. "I think I've got the mesh diagram." He sat down and opened the laptop. "I was gonna have it printed out and laminated."

Dar looked up at him and frowned. "What?"

Kerry nudged her. "Keep surfing."

Peter got up and timidly fixed himself a cup of coffee. "Been a long day," he said, by way of explanation. "It's nice of you all to let us come over here. It's a pretty place."

"No problem. Dar would tell you that she prefers our cabin down south," Kerry said, handing over a small ceramic jug of creamer. "And, actually, so do I."

Dar focused past the conversation and started to root through the PDA as it finished booting. She took out the stylus and tapped around, calling up a note program she remembered using. There were several folders randomly named and she clicked on one.

After a moment she closed it. She shook her head and opened a second, tilting the screen so she could read the text. She closed that and clicked on the next. "I keep the weirdest crap," she muttered. "Ah." She sat back and regarded the PDA. "I think this might be...yeah. The config for the two big routers in Miami."

"Cool." Mark came over and looked over her shoulder. "Yeah, that's them."

"Mm. I saved a copy before I did the changes to make the reroute at the Rock work." Dar gave him a droll look. "So at least I can't feel hypocritical about it."

"Those were a lot of changes."

"They were." Dar sent the note to her private email from the PDA and waited for her desktop to pick it up. Then she regarded it and sent it to the printer. "Okay, let's see what this gets us."

KERRY WAS LYING on the couch, her head resting on the arm and her legs extended out and crossed at the ankles. Mocha was sleeping on her chest and Chino was curled up just past her feet. She listened idly to Dar give Mark and Peter some last instructions at the door.

Then the door closed. She turned her head and opened one eye to see Dar heading her way. "Think it'll work?"

"Probably not." Kerry sat up and Dar slid into the empty place on the couch then pulled her back down on top of her. "If they let him make the changes, there's probably even more changes in there that I haven't seen that'll screw things up."

"Ugh."

"I need to just go in there and do it," Dar acknowledged mournfully.

"You need to concentrate on making that demo for Congress," Kerry said. "Dar, I know you want to make this right, but there's only so much you can do."

Dar sighed. She put her arms around Kerry and hugged her. "We'll see what happens. Maybe he'll work it out, He's a bright kid."

Kerry patted her leg. "Then let's go to bed. It's two a.m. Tomorrow's going to suck."

Dar remained in place. "You pissed off that I'm doing this?" she asked. "You seem like it."

"I'm not. I mean I'm not pissed off at you," Kerry clarified. "I'm just pissed that ILS can't seem to let go of us. I want out of it. I don't want to worry about them sending lawyers after us and blaming us for stuff and...you know."

"Mm. Sorry."

"It frustrates me," Kerry said. "I just want that part of our life to be over and it seems like all they want to do is suck us back into it." She looked up at Dar's profile. "But I get it, Dar. I know you spent a good part of your life there and you can't let it go so easily."

Dar smiled at her with open and sweet affection. "I love you," she said. "I'm glad you get that because I don't want us to fight over it."

"I don't want us to fight over anything," Kerry responded.

"Yeah, that's no fun."

They untangled themselves and got up, Kerry carefully letting the sleepy eyed Mocha down on the ground. "There you go, little man. You want a piddle stop before we go to bed?"

Chino jumped down and yawned, stretching her paws out. Then she trotted over to the dog door and through it, with Mocha galloping behind her.

Kerry wandered into the kitchen and leaned on the counter, watching the dogs in the garden as the motion sensitive lights came on. She turned her head as Dar entered, coming over to stand next to her, gazing outside with her arms folded over her chest.

Kerry edged over and let her head rest against Dar's shoulder, pausing to give the skin there a kiss. "Can I come with you to Washington?"

"Want to come with me to DC?" Dar asked at the same time. They looked at each other then started chuckling.

"We're sappy, useless poster children for bad romance novels, you know that?" Kerry sighed. "I sometimes feel like our lives are set to Disney princess music."

"Aw."

"Though, I'll keep you company right up to the door to the senate chambers. I don't think my presence will win you any points in there." Kerry leaned on the counter with her elbows. "I'd like to talk to Bridges's team about implementation."

"Sure," Dar agreed. "Let's get the pooches and sack out. Maria can make the arrangements tomorrow."

Back in the bedroom Kerry wiped Mocha's dew drenched feet and watched him march over into Chino's bed and curl up.

It was late and Kerry was tired. She got under the covers and smiled as she listened to Dar humming in the bathroom. Dar came back in and joined her, making the water bed rock a little. Kerry waited for her to settle then eased over and curled up against Dar's right side. "Hey."

"Hey," Dar replied, her resonant tones making Kerry's ears tickle just a trifle.

"Can we be late to work tomorrow?"

"Sure."

"We own the company."

"We do," Dar said. "Once you teach Mayte how to handle your stuff, you can spend the day with your feet up on your desk writing poetry and no one's gonna say word one to you."

Kerry had to stop and think about that for a minute. "Except that someone I know taught me one of the golden rules is to lead by example." She felt Dar chuckle silently. "So I can't do that unless you're going to use those poems as the basis of a new client offering."

"True, but we can still go to work late tomorrow," Dar said. "It's not always a bad thing to let the staff work things out on their own, y'know."

Kerry lifted her head and gave her a wry look.

"Yeah, okay, let's wait to see how we feel when the sun rises."

AS IT TURNED out, the morning wasn't nearly as painful as Kerry had feared. They woke only a half hour later than the alarm would have normally sounded. With mutual shrugs, they got up and got about their usual routine.

"C'mon, kids." Kerry zipped up her light jacket, waiting for Mocha and Chino to come trotting over. "Let's go for a ride to the office. You ready?"

Chino twirled around in a circle and barked, while Mocha eyed her warily.

Dar got her backpack on her shoulder and joined them, her head bent as she texted a message on her Handspring. "Asking Mark if he heard anything." She picked up Mocha and followed Kerry out the door.

They were taking Kerry's car and she hopped up into the driver's seat after letting Chino into the back seat where she curled up on the fuzzy dog blanket attached to the leather that conveniently kept her from sliding around.

"It's fun taking these guys with us," Dar commented as Mocha stood up on her knee and looked out the window. "You know what I was thinking? For the demo I think I'd like to tie in to a simulated Internet node back here."

"Like fake traffic?" Kerry asked.

"Yeah. We don't have any way of tying in for real yet."

"I have a call in to AT&T and Level Three," Kerry said. "They aren't happy, but they knew this was coming. Do we know yet where they're going to want the private circuits dropped and who's paying for them?"

Dar let her head rest against the seat. "They're paying for them, but that's a good question. I have to find out who's supposed to order them and make sure they're the right size." She glanced at Kerry. "Good thing you're going with me."

Kerry grinned.

"Same thing for Gerry's project, but that will be a mesh. We already talked about it. They're going to house the central database in the Pentagon."

"Good." Kerry headed west on the causeway. "I'll work with them in a remote support circuit for you."

Dar grunted in contentment, then glanced down as her Handspring buzzed. "Ah."

```
Hey, boss. Pete's in with the big dude now. He's
going to text me when he gets out. He told him he
found an old config saved to a switch NVRAM.
```

She reached around Mocha and typed a response.

```
If the dickwad kicks him out, have him come over.

You got it.
```

Dar thumbed through her messages and frowned. In the light of day she realized her attitude toward the problem had changed a little. Maybe Kerry's uncertainty had affected her, but she had to acknowledge a sense of irritation in her when she thought about having to dedicate her personal resources to a company that now held very little affection in her heart.

It felt fickle. She wasn't entirely happy with her motivations. She felt caught between guilt and outrage and it was giving her a stomach ache. "Hey, Ker?"

"Yes, o love of my life?"

"What do you think about us getting a datacenter for test systems? Not ever hosting clients there? I don't know that I want to be in the services side of the house."

Kerry considered that as she turned into Coconut Grove and headed for the office. "You mean just do what our web site claims— custom systems and solutions? Deliver it and the only support we do is for the software itself?"

"Uh huh."

"Hm. Let me think about it."

"If we did that, there's no way ILS could ever come back at us because we're not doing anything they do," Dar said. "Matter of fact, I don't want to do any of the stuff they do because I'm kinda tired of being on the hook for everyone's bottom line."

"You're just deciding this now?"

"This router thing is pissing me off," Dar admitted. "I've been thinking about it since we got up. I just get madder and madder when I think about that warthog trying to weenie waggle to make his bones and then becoming a neuter when it comes to taking responsibility for it."

Kerry pulled into one of the parking spots. "Colorful," she said. "Let's just get past the next seven days, then we can talk about it, okay?" She patted Dar's leg. "I'm going to call Richard, though, and let him know what's going on."

Dar got out and put Mocha down, then retrieved her backpack and got it settled. "Maybe we'll get lucky and it'll all go away."

"Really think that's going to happen?"

"Meh."

DAR ROLLED HER trackball a little, moving the wire frame diagram across the screen and observing the results. She switched over to a command line session and pecked out a few commands, then switched back, issuing an approving grunt and rerunning the process.

It wouldn't be an elegant demonstration. Dar looked at the plain screen, which was a simple black background with fields in magenta, green and yellow. It used very straightforward instructional text and the boxes and outlines around it were only there to make it look relatively functional.

She typed in a query and ran it against the test repository in the server room. The screen chewed over it for a minute then spit out a response.

"Hm." Dar went back into the command line screen, revised some of the lines, recompiled it and tried the query again. This time the results were more acceptable and she moved on to her next task.

She heard Kerry talking with someone next door and recognized the other voice as Colleen's. Their relaxed tones and the crinkle of paper meant that lunch was probably going to be delivered to her any minute now.

"Hey, hon." Kerry entered, carrying a bag. "Tacos."

"Yum."

"Making progress?"

"Yep." Dar slid her chair sideways and moved over to the open area of her desk. "I've got the query engine working at least. I still have to figure out how to demonstrate the autonomic parser."

"Oh. Sexy." Kerry sorted out her tacos and put her drink down. "That small business conference called back. They already have a keynote speaker. I think this guy must have seen that *Miami Herald* piece because he told me he'd like you to do a half hour presentation on anything you want—if you want."

Dar chuckled.

"Do you want?"

"I want," Dar said. "Tell them I'll do..." She pondered a minute as she unwrapped a taco. "Thirty minutes on using B to B networking to boost business between small business owners."

Kerry eyed her. "Really?"

"Sure." Dar licked a bit of sauce off her fingers. "C'mon, Ker. It's a small business convention. I can't go in there and start talking about routing tables or database structures."

"No, that's true," Kerry said. "But I think that's more a speech I would give."

Dar's eyebrows twitched. "So then you give it? Think up a topic for me and just let me know what it is." She swallowed then chased the mouthful down with a sip of ice coffee. "I can do one that's IT related, but I think general's better."

"Let me think of one." Kerry reached over and ruffled her hair. "It's next Monday and Tuesday, then Maria has our flights booked on Wednesday for DC."

"Cool."

"I've got a project management meeting with two clients this afternoon. I'm going to have Mayte sit in with me and see if I can let her run with them."

Dar lifted one hand with her thumb pointed up. "You should see if we can get her PMO certified, and then get her some baby PMs to work with her."

Kerry smiled, then waggled her fingers goodbye and went back to her own office.

Dar finished her tacos and sucked the last of her coffee down, disposing of the wrappers in her cobalt blue garbage can before she turned back to her screen and started up her program again.

White on black or black on white? Dar pondered the difference, calling up an image in her head of doing a presentation. For the military guys, white on black. For the politicians? "Hey, Ker?"

"Yes?" Kerry stuck her head in the door opening.

"What's your mother's favorite color?"

"What?"

DAR SET HER backpack down near the receptionist's desk and diverted around the hall, walking to the side corridor and passing the closed door to the HR department. She went a little farther and slowed, pausing at the door to the tech support office and sticking her head inside.

Scott was at his desk. He was still the only support person on staff so the other cubes were empty, but there were a few things on the shelves of his, a cup, a little canteen, and a rock. He didn't hear her stop, his head was bent over an open PC case and he was carefully assembling the parts inside.

Mark was reasonably satisfied with his new guy. Scott had performed the several maintenance tasks he'd been given with competence and he'd been on time every morning.

More than on time, actually. Mark said he'd been on the front porch waiting when the first person had gotten there, freshly showered and ready to work.

Dar leaned against the door frame watching him work. She sensed a contentment in him she couldn't have imagined seeing before.

Not wanting to disturb that, she silently pushed off the frame and headed back to the empty receptionist's desk where she spotted Kerry and their kids waiting for her. "Hey."

"Potty break?" Kerry asked.

"No...wanted to see how our new tech was doing." Dar picked up her backpack and slung it on her shoulder then took Mocha from Kerry's arms. "Seems okay."

"Col said he doesn't talk much." Kerry opened the door for her. "Just comes in and sits there and fiddles with things."

"Exactly what you want a tech support guy to do." Dar closed the door behind her. "Mark said he was working on something, that he'd close up."

"Any word from Peter?"

"Nope." Dar opened the back door of the SUV for Chino and then got in the passenger seat with Mocha. "He knows how to get in touch if he needs to. I don't want to push it."

"Wise woman." Kerry opened the driver's door and paused as she caught motion from the corner of her eye. She turned, half closing the door against her legs. "Dar."

"I see." Dar put Mocha in the back seat and opened her own door, sliding out and coming around the front of the SUV to stand between Kerry's door and the oncoming figures.

"Who said chivalry was dead?" Kerry leaned her arms on the door frame.

Dar cleared her throat. "What can we do for you, folks?" She addressed the group of veterans, who had come just close enough for her latent defensive instincts to prick, making her hands flex.

"Got the cops on the speed dial," Kerry said. "So don't get too spunky."

"Look," Joe, the group leader aka pastor said. "We're not gonna hurt you."

"No, you're not," Dar agreed readily. "I'm not in the mood for you. You're standing between me and a romantic dinner with my spouse and

I'm going to kick you in the head if you don't clear out."

The pastor put his hands on his hips. "Look, lady, cut the crap, okay? I just got a question for you."

Kerry saw it start to happen and debated closing her eyes. She heard Chino bark in outrage just as Dar moved. The next moment the Labrador squirmed past her and out the door, racing over to get in front of Dar with a growl.

Joe jumped back and held his hands up and Dar made a grab for their unexpectedly ferocious pet. "Chino!"

"Growf!" The large dog bared her teeth and the thick fur along her spine lifted up.

The other men just blinked at her. "Holy shit you weren't kidding," the one who'd been fighting in front of the office said. "Keep that dog away from us."

"I'm not kidding," Dar said. She warily watched them. "I'm tired of you all messing with us. Leave us the hell alone."

"You're the one who keeps screwing with us!" the man said, edging in front of Joe. "What did you do with Wheels, huh?"

"His name is Scott," Kerry said.

"What?"

"His name is Scott," she repeated. "And what we did with him is we hired him."

"That little son of a bitch...he crossed us," the man said to Joe. "You said he was going to hold out."

Dar got her hand on Chino's collar and backed up until she hit the front of the SUV with her butt. "He didn't. No reason for him to. This is a right to work state. I can hire whoever I want."

"He said—" Joe started, then stopped. "We ain't seen him for a few days."

Dar shrugged. "Not my problem."

The other man eyed her. "You hired, Wheels?"

Joe stepped up and got in front of him. "Never mind that, Cliff. If he screwed us, he did. Just let him know not to come back around looking for us, lady. He won't get any more help."

"Great," Kerry said. "I bet that'll make all of us happy. But in answer to your question, Cliff, we really did hire him to do tech support for us and so far he's done a good job."

"Let's go." Joe turned and shoved him and pointed back the way they'd come. "We found out what we come to."

Dar stayed where she was until they disappeared, then she turned and regarded Kerry. "They made our dog growl." She looked down at Chino, who had seated herself on the tarmac, tongue lolling. "I never heard her do that before."

Chino looked up with innocent brown eyes.

"They did," Kerry said. "And you know, I think we might have done some good this time. Maybe these guys'll leave him alone now."

"Mm." Dar didn't sound convinced, but she opened the back door again. "Get in there, madam ferocious."

Chino jumped up and sat down, wagging her tail and sniffing at Mocha who scrambled back to join her.

Dar went around and got in the passenger seat, her head bent as she texted. "Just want Mark to know what happened so he can tell his newbie to watch his back."

"You think they'll do anything? I think they're all talk." Kerry started up the engine. "Just like that guy was when he broke into our office. All bullshit."

"That could be," Dar said. "Let's get out of here before something else happens."

"You got it."

"Ker, they made our dog growl."

Chapter Ten

DAR WALKED TO the bow of the boat, using the freshwater hose to rinse off the fiberglass as the early morning sun bathed her. She whistled softly under her breath, glancing around at the crowded marina as she continued to work. Dar was glad she'd gotten out early before everyone started moving about.

Seas looked good offshore and after she finished cleaning and stocking the boat she and Kerry planned on a reef trip off Key Biscayne and a picnic lunch on the water.

Their gear was already out on the bench seats and there was a basket of grapes and apples sitting on the waterproof table awaiting her attention.

She worked a grape off its stem and popped it into her mouth, enjoying the crisp coolness of it as she bit into it. She paused to take a second, then stood quietly as she noted a man walking down the dock with a purposeful stride coming in her direction.

Wasn't someone she knew. He had a pair of dark blue sweatpants and a white sweatshirt on and he came right up to the slip and put his hand on one of the piers, leaning in toward her. "You, Roberts?"

A number of answers occurred to Dar, who didn't feel like she wanted her Saturday morning to start with an asshole. She sighed inwardly, though. "Yes."

He nodded. "My name's Roger Post. I know you've got no idea who I am, but a friend of mine who works for AT&T said he knows you and said I should talk to you," he said. "And coincidentally, I was in the market and heard you call in for supplies so I asked them where I could find you."

"C'mon aboard," Dar said in a genial tone, indicating the two chairs on the deck. "I'm going to head out in a while, but I've got a few minutes to talk."

The man nodded and stepped over onto the transom, then onto the deck with the skill and ease of someone well used to boats. "Thanks." He held a hand out. "Sorry to just barge in here. Thanks for being decent about it."

Dar took a seat and he did also. "What can I do for you?"

"Here's the thing," Post said. "I won't waste your time, or mine. But I'm bankrolling a startup who's going to offer private networking and Internet surfing to high end clients."

"For what purpose?"

"Avoid the snoopers," Post said promptly. "You've seen the headlines, people wanting to be able to watch where people are going, snoop into their business. I want to make systems that let people go where they want on the Internet and not be afraid of someone watching them."

The irony made Dar smile. "I can see there would be a market," she said. "Why hunt me down? In case you missed the story in the *Herald*, the government's one of my clients."

"I know," he said. "That's why I wanted to talk to you. I want to hire you to tell me how to get around things."

Dar studied him. "Around what things?"

"Come on," he smiled at her. "We all know they're tapping the Internet. My buddy at AT&T told me they've got those big black boxes looking at everything."

Dar was almost shocked until she remembered who had suggested that to the government. "Well." She laced her fingers. "If they have big black boxes in line at the ISP level, you can't get around it."

Post gazed at her. "Can't?"

Dar shook her head. "Can't. If the data stream goes through those boxes you can't avoid your traffic going through them. The only way to get around that is buy point-to-point circuits between your clients and whatever they want to connect to."

"That's expensive."

"Yup," Dar said. "And not very practical if you want to surf the Internet."

"Damn. That's what Chuck said."

"Even if you encrypted the channel," Dar said. "A good hardware based decrypt encrypt card with spoofed certificates could get around it. My advice to you and your clients? If you want something to stay private, don't let it out of your control. Don't use the Internet to send it."

He frowned.

Dar studied him for a moment. "Or have their porn or pirated stuff delivered on a hard drive. I mean seriously," she said with a smile. "Just don't do it."

"They're not doing illegal things," he said. "They just don't want anyone to see what they're doing. They think that's a right, you know?"

"I do," Dar said. "Why not talk to my former employers? They can set up a private net if they're serious about that and can pay for it. With a proxy out to the Internet on their own backbone."

"Yeah?"

"ILS," Dar said. "They absolutely can do that."

The man thought about that for a minute. "Would they want to do that?"

Dar lifted her hands and then let them fall. "Depends on what the project scope was. There's nothing illegal in setting up a private Internet. They would want common carrier protection, though. They wouldn't want to know what you were running over it."

He paused and thought again. "Can't we just do...what do you call them, a virtual private thing?"

Dar's eyebrows twitched a little. "Sure. You can make a VPN to a specific end point. That encrypts the traffic from you to that endpoint, but then you still need to go out onto the Internet."

"Huh."

"Mm." Dar's eyes twinkled a little bit. "Most of the time people we...I mean, that I used to deal with when doing projects for ILS, were more concerned about not letting their people surf things on the Internet than protecting them while they were doing it."

He nodded. "There's just not a lot of trust out there these days," he said. "People want their privacy and they don't want anyone in their business."

They both heard footsteps and the patter of dog toenails approaching. Dar looked over to see Kerry heading their way. "I'm not sure you can have it both ways," she said. "All the freedom of the public Internet and privacy, too."

Post sighed. "There has to be a way," he said. "Some way to make just looking around anonymous." He got up as Kerry neared the boat. "But I know you've got things to do. Thanks for the chat at any rate." He offered his hand, which Dar took and pressed. "Have a good morning."

"You too," Dar said as he hopped off the boat onto the dock. He gave Kerry a brief smile as he passed her.

"C'mon, Chi." Dar got up and walked over as the dog gathered herself and hopped on board. "Glad you showed up," she said to Kerry.

"What was that all about?" Kerry stepped over onto the deck and put Mocha down to go sniff. "New neighbor?"

"Something like that." Dar opened the door to the cabin, stepping back as Chino bustled inside ahead of her. "Guy was looking for someone to build him something that lets people Internet surf without being eavesdropped on."

Kerry stopped and regarded her in surprise. "Really?"

"Mm."

"Interesting coincidence?"

Dar shrugged. "I'm going to get the hamsters going. Untie us?" She headed up the ladder onto the flying bridge and got herself settled behind the controls. She started up the engines and checked the gauges, listening to the sound as they rumbled to life.

"Okay, we're clear." Kerry climbed up and sat next to her as she gently applied power. "I locked the dogs inside in case they get any funny ideas about jumping overboard."

"So I hear." Dar swung the bow out as she got clear of the dock and started out of the packed marina. "Here we go."

Kerry put her feet up on the lower shelf of the console and leaned back as the breeze picked up around them. "So that was an interesting visit."

"It was. Not sure if it was a legit question, or something someone's floating out because of the press we just got, or someone fishing me from inside the CIA."

"CIA?"

Dar smiled. "You never know. I told him to go talk to ILS about building his clients a private network."

Kerry started laughing. "You didn't."

"I did. Why not? They do that. I figured regardless of the reason for the question, that won't get me in too much trouble. He said someone from AT&T sent him. Think that was your buddy?"

"I think I should ask him," Kerry said. "I don't like the timing of that, Dar. Maybe it was someone from ILS wanting to cause us trouble."

"Ker."

"You never know, right?" Kerry said. "Frankly I'd rather have it be the CIA testing us to see if we were going to spill some details on the project. That, at least, would make sense to me."

"This guy said he knew about the black box they've got tapping everything," Dar said after a brief pause. "I told him there's no way to get around that."

Kerry frowned. "Is that true?"

"The box being there, or not being able to get around it?"

"Yes."

Dar nudged the throttles forward as they cleared the entrance to the marina. "I think the first one's true since you told them to go do that." She eyed Kerry, who made a face. "Yeah, I know. As to the second? From a technical perspective, given that it would be an in line tap, there is no physical way to avoid it."

"But?"

Dar remained silent for a moment as she adjusted the engines. "Should I be looking for a way around it?"

Kerry merely looked at her.

"Good point."

IT WAS LONG past dark as Dar piloted the boat back into the harbor, the engines rumbling softly as she made her way between the lines of yachts to either side.

There were a few people still out on the piers, some coiling up hoses, others moving boxes of supplies from the land onto the boats. There was a cascade of curiously musical clanking of the riggings as the boats moved slightly on the tide.

Their slip was one of the outer ones and Dar had no problem maneuvering the boat into it, cutting the engines and sliding in a little sideways as they eased against the bumpers and Kerry hopped off to tie them up.

It was quiet once she shut power down, the soft creak of the wooden pilings and the scuff of Kerry's footsteps sounding loud and distinct. Dar relaxed a moment, flexing her hands out and letting them rest on her thighs before she got up from the console and turned to head down the ladder.

She paused when she heard her pocketed cell phone start to ring. She pulled it out and answered. "Hello?"

"Hello, Dar?"

She hesitated. "Yes...Jacques?"

There was a faint sigh on the other end. "Yes, it is me. May we speak for a moment?"

Dar went back over to the console and sat down. "Sure. So long as you're not calling to threaten me with a lawsuit—in which case I'll give you my lawyer's number—or call me an asshole."

Jacques chuckled briefly. "No, it is neither. Though I am sure you know my colleagues wish nothing better than to try and throw some legal trouble your way."

"Nice, thanks for a job well done," Dar said dryly. "Hope they all step off a cliff and croak."

He sighed again. "Let us put that aside for a time as at this moment there are other things occupying their attention. I suppose you know what is going on?"

Dar leaned back and considered. "Yes," she said. "I know what's going on. But if you're wondering if I had anything to do with it, the answer is no."

"No, we know that," Jacques responded surprisingly. "If that was the case, so much as I respect you there would already be legal filings in process. You understand?"

"Sure."

"So there has been an investigation, yes? In no way was it found out that you had any part in this massive failure," he said. "You did not participate. That is what is understood."

Kerry climbed up onto the flying bridge and paused, looking questioningly at her. "Trouble?"

Dar shrugged. "Jacques." She mouthed silently.

Kerry rolled her eyes. "Going to take the dogs in, see you back at the house." She patted Dar's leg and retreated down the steps again.

"Okay, so why the phone call then?" Dar asked. "Jacques, honestly, I'm sorry someone screwed things up so colossally. No one wanted that."

"Yes, I knew you would think so," Jacques said. "The mistake that was made was underestimating your influence. So let me ask you a few questions if I may do so?"

"Sure."

"This thing that went wrong, do you think it was a thing done on purpose?"

Dar's brows contracted a little. "Not sure what you mean," she said. "If someone went in and made changes, sure that was on purpose. It's very hard to accidentally log yourself into a device and type things into it."

"No, no," Jacques said. "I understand that the action was purposeful. But do you think that the intent, the changes being made, were done on purpose to cause us harm?"

Oh. Completely different question. "Ah. You mean, was the change done to screw things up on purpose?"

"Yes."

"Have no clue," Dar said honestly. "From what I heard it was done to put someone's mark up. You know what that means?"

"Not so much."

Dar considered. "There's a lot of me in those systems," she said. "Seemed to me like someone wanted to take that out and put their own stamp on it."

"Ah."

"So, was it done on purpose? Sure. But was it done maliciously?" Dar shrugged. "I don't know the guy and I don't want to guess at his motives. Seems like a stupid and very public screw up though."

Jacques was silence for a moment. "The investigation, it was just finished earlier and the report I was given said there was bad intent in the action."

Dar folded her arms and leaned back against the console. "Making the change I could believe was honest desire to take my rep down," she said. "But making it impossible to go back? Either that was ego way larger than mine, Jacques, or...yeah, maybe there was something behind it."

Jacques grunted softly.

He was one of the few board members Dar liked. She had developed a respect for his practicality and what she'd felt was an honest desire to simply attend to business, caring more about share value and making money than any politics behind it.

"What are you going to do, Jacques?" Dar asked after a long silence.

"I have taken the chairman's slot, yes," he said. "After some contention."

Dar could only imagine that. Jacques was one of Alastair's biggest allies on the board. "Would have liked to have seen that dogfight."

He chuckled dryly again. "I believe you can fix this problem, yes?"

"Probably. But I'm not going to," Dar said, a little surprised to hear herself say the words. "That would be bad for both of us."

"Yes, exactly so," he agreed in a mild tone. "I had no intention of asking you to do so. Which I would think maybe surprises you?"

"Depends on how desperate I think you are." Now it was Dar's turn to chuckle a little. "C'mon, Jacques. You didn't call me just to pass the time of day."

He cleared his throat. "To be sure, I did call just to advise you of my new position," he said in a careful tone. "And also to see if you would speak with me and not just hang up the telephone."

"I would never do that, Jacques. You were always fair with me," Dar said. "I'm glad you took charge. You've got an even hand and you've been in the mix a long time." She pushed off the console and went to the rail, looking out over the harbor.

"You were very close with Alastair," Jacques said. "He continually defended you and that's what was the reason for his leaving."

"And Hamilton's I'm guessing," Dar said.

"Now that is an interesting story. Hamilton was let go yes, because he refused to follow the board's directions. But..." Jacques paused. "He is also a large stockholder and threatened to bring suit against the board if they brought suit against you."

Dar was charmed. "Good for him."

"So this brings me to the real reason for this conversation," Jacques said. "I would like to ask you for your opinion. I would like you tell me, Dar, what you would do if you were in my position, to resolve all these difficulties."

"Huh."

"We have many people who have left. We have systems that are not doing well. We have customers who are very upset and contracts at risk. What would you do to resolve that?"

Dar was silent for a few minutes, thinking. "You need those people who left more than you need anyone's egos, or to save face," she said. "You'll never get them back if you keep your new guys. Get rid of them and call the people who walked out and ask them to come back. Including Hamilton."

"It would be very difficult for me to get the backing enough to do that." Jacques sounded regretful. "There is quite a lot of pride involved."

"Money trumps pride," Dar said bluntly. "They want to lose money? They keep going down this route you'll lose everything. One of your customers has already called me and said they were thinking of terminating your contracts."

"Do they want to offer them to you?"

"Yes, but I don't want them. It's not the direction I want my new company to go," Dar told him honestly. "I would rather you repair that relationship and keep them."

Jacques sighed. "Your opinion walks side by side with mine. I just do not know that I can make this collection of people on the board go along with it," he said. "Dar, I thank you for taking your time on this Saturday night to speak with me. I wish you good luck with your new enterprise, though it seems to me you don't need it as you are doing quite well."

"We are," Dar said. "At the rate we're going we'll be able to hire all the people who walked out on you, so if you're smart, get those board asses turned around before you lose the chance to make things right."

He chuckled softly. "Do you need an investor?"

"When we're ready for that, I know who to call," Dar replied. "Gotta go. I just parked my boat and it's getting nippy out here."

"Thank you, Dar. I can't say I will be able to follow your advice, but it's good to have it," Jacques said. "Good night to you, and please give my regards to your housemate."

Housemate. Dar pinched the bridge of her nose. "Well, I've heard her called worse. I will. Good night, Jacques. Good luck."

She hung up the phone and stuck it in her pocket, before she closed the weather proofing around the console and retreated back down onto the main deck. She checked the door to make sure it was locked, then hopped off the boat and onto the dock, walking along the wooden pier past the rows of gently bobbing yachts.

As she came up onto the marina side, she started to take the path leading back to the condo but went into the little island store instead.

"Good evening, ma'am," the cashier greeted her as she entered. "We have fresh stone crabs and hand churned chocolate ice cream today."

Dar paused and eyed her. "You sure have us pegged," she said with a smile. "Give me a pound of each."

"Yes'm." The cashier smiled back, a fresh faced young girl with dark streaked blonde hair pulled back into a neat pony tail. "We like to keep track of our nicer residents."

Dar brought the box of dog biscuits up to the counter and put it down, waiting as the cashier put together a goodie bag for her. "Are there residents who aren't nice?"

"Oh sure." The girl put the bag on the counter and took Dar's resident's card, sliding it into her system. "I mean, there are all kinds of people everywhere, you know what I mean?"

"Sure." Dar took her card back. "I've run into some idiots here. But most everyone minds their own business."

"Most people do, but some people act like because they live here, it gives them carte blanche to treat everyone who works on the island like servants. We're not."

Dar blinked. "Do they?"

"They do. A man was in here about twenty minutes ago," the girl said, obviously remembering with irritation. "He got all ticked off at me because we didn't have fresh goat's milk." She handed over Dar's package. "He actually took a bottle of the stuff we had and threw it against the wall. Can you believe it?"

Dar took her items and shook her head. "There are jerks in the world," she said. "That seems like a crazy thing to get mad about though."

The girl shrugged. "He's rich. His family owns like ten properties and they go from one to the other. He's got a big sailboat and a personal assistant. His name's Grossner. Do you know him?"

"Nope," Dar said. "I don't think we travel in the same circles." She smiled. "I actually work for a living."

"Right?" The girl waved. "Good night, ma'am. Have a nice weekend."

"Thanks." Dar pushed the door open and started down the path with a thoughtful expression. The gravel crunched under her sandals and she hooked the bag by one finger and slung it over her shoulder.

How narrow a life did you need to have to worry about goat's milk? She pondered that as she passed between the ring of trees and started to cut across the golf course toward their home. Or was that a different perspective you got when you had so much that worrying about the basics of life never happened so you focused on the sharp points of tiny details.

Was that part of what was wrong with the board members? Dar began to whistle softly under her breath. Had they become so used to constant success and plenty that being faced with what amounted to corporate mutiny left them unable to figure out what to do? So what they did was flail around and fire bullets in a circle hoping to hit something that would make them feel better?

Hm.

She heard the soft chatter of the sprinklers on the course and glanced ahead to see if they were going to douse her. The path ahead was clear of water, but there were two tall figures moving in her direction and she shifted to one side of the gravel to make space for them to pass.

"I'm telling you, Tom, that kid was asking for it," one of the men said as they came even with her. He glanced briefly up at Dar, then lifted a hand. "Evening."

"Evening," Dar responded cordially.

"Yeah, she might have been, but you should keep in check, Billy," the other man said as they moved away. "This is a small place. Word gets around."

"Like I could care? We'll just pay off whoever's in charge. I'm going to go get what was coming to me." The voices echoed softly, trickling back to Dar's ears from where she'd come to a halt on the path.

Coincidence? Or was that goat's milk boy on his way to bring more trouble to the kid in the store.

Dar regarded the sky overhead with a somber look then smiled a little, acknowledging that old crusader label maybe wasn't so far off after all. With a sigh, she turned around and started after the men, pulling out her Handspring and typing in a brief message as she walked.

SHE GOT TO the door and pushed through it just as the shorter man reached across the counter and grabbed the cashier's blouse. He twisted his fingers into the fabric and yanked her close to him.

"Hey!" she barked. Both men turned at the sound and a moment later the man released the girl and stepped back. "What the hell are you doing, buddy?"

The taller man stepped back uncertainly, looked at the door and edged toward it. "Just a misunderstanding," he said. "No problem here, lady."

"Fuck that." The shorter man came at her. "None of your fucking business, you bitch. Get the fuck out of my way." He reached to shove her and Dar reacted instinctively, swinging her arm around to block him, forgetting what she had in her grasp.

The ice cream and crab smacked him in the side of the head and he reeled backwards, stumbling to one side and crashing into the counter.

The other man took off, bolting out the door.

Dar dropped the bag, got over her center of balance and brought her hands up into a defensive position. The other man shoved off from the counter, sending bags of potato chips flying all over the floor.

He pulled his hand back and curled it into a fist and then paused, taking in the balanced posture and unafraid expression of the woman opposite him.

"I'm calling security, Ms. Roberts," the cashier called out.

"Get out of my way." The man came at her and swung. Dar ducked out of his way and he walked rapidly away and yanked the door open, nearly smashing full into Kerry who was coming in with some speed.

Dar felt every hair on her arms lift up as he reached out to push Kerry. The next thing she knew she was hauling him down from behind, turning with his arm in her grasp, yanking him backwards and pulling him over to the ground. "Don't you touch her."

He twisted in her grasp but Dar's temper snapped and she sent a knee hard into his groin, then slammed her elbow into his chin and knocked his head backwards.

He stumbled and went down. She almost went after him, but backed off as Kerry got in next to her, breathing hard.

"What in the hell is going on here?" Kerry asked.

The cashier came out from behind the counter. "Security's coming. Thanks a bunch, Ms. Roberts. That dumbass said he was going to take me into the cooler and teach me a lesson."

The door opened and two uniformed security guards came in. "What's the deal here?" the nearer one asked, giving Dar and Kerry a glance. "Ladies."

"Hello, Charles," Kerry responded. "It seems this guy was causing a problem in here."

The man got to his knees. "Everyone here is gonna pay out the ass for this," he said. "I'll sue every single one of you." He glared at the cashier. "Especially you, little cunt. I didn't do anything to you. I was just talking to you."

Kerry looked at him, then at Dar. "I don't think you hit him hard enough, hon," she said mildly. "I don't know who you are, mister, but my partner doesn't smack people around for no reason."

He stared at both of them. "Oh, that's right. You're the queers my brother was talking about. That'll make an even better lawsuit."

"Okay," the security supervisor said. "Let's just settle down and we'll do a report."

"Screw that." The man got up and stomped to the door. "You can't hold me here you rent-a-cops. You want anything from me call my office." He walked out the door still a little hunched. "You'll be hearing from my lawyer in the morning."

Charles sighed. "Can I get some info from you ladies?"

"Sure." Dar sat down on one of the stools near the small lunch counter, pausing to pick up the bag and putting it down on the counter surface. "Wasn't the way I was looking for this night to go."

"I'll put these in the cooler," the counter girl said. "And, thanks, Ms. Roberts. I mean that. He scared the crap out of me. I didn't even have a chance to grab a radio."

Kerry leaned her elbow on Dar's shoulder. "Crusader Dar."

"I knew you were going to say that," Dar muttered. "Listen, Charles, if he's going to call a lawyer we probably better get Metro-Dade over here."

Charles sighed. "Do we have to?" he asked. "Listen, Ms. Roberts, Billy's nothing but a jerk. He's already sued Mrs. Christoff for her dog barking and Doctor Ed for washing his car too early in the morning. He's a pain in the ass, but it's usually a bullshit pain in the ass, if you know what I mean."

"You saying he's just a spoiled white rich boy?" Kerry asked with a wry twinkle in her eyes. "As in, someone my father would have wanted me to marry?"

Charles shrugged sheepishly.

"He's a jerk," Kristie said, having put the bag in the freezer. "He was in here before making trouble about some milk. I told Ms. Roberts about it."

The security guard nodded, making some notes. "So then he left?"

"He did."

"He and his buddy were coming across the golf course path," Dar said. "I heard him saying to his buddy he was going to come here and make trouble, so I followed him."

Charles eyed her. "You coulda called us."

"I could have," Dar agreed. "In fact, I should have. But I didn't. When I came in here he had Kristie by the neck and was about to pull her over the counter."

Both security guards looked over at the cashier, who nodded in confirmation.

"Wasn't going to stand there and let them," Dar said. "I yelled and told them to stop and then that jackass came at me."

"Was he drunk?" Charles asked. "Guy gets caught doing something like that he should just beat it."

"Well, he didn't. He swung at me and I went to block him and smacked him in the head with the bag I was carrying," Dar said. "So he got clocked with a pound of stone crabs and a lump of chocolate ice cream."

Kerry eyed her. "Was that dinner, Dardar?"

"Ouch," Charles commiserated. "I've been hit with lobster tails. Hurts." He scribbled a note. "So then?"

"Then I let him pass me and he hit the door."

"And hit me," Kerry said. "And Dar hauled him back like he was a sack of wheat and kicked him in the nuts for that." She gave Dar an affectionate look.

"Ah," Charles said. "Well, Ms. Roberts, chances are he's gonna file charges against you and Kristie, and probably me, because he's got more money than sense. But Kristie here...you'll step up and testify?"

"Sure," Kristie agreed at once. "Listen, my dad's not going to like hearing about this guy, and if he knows what's good for him he'll just keep out of here. He doesn't want to mess with my father." She glanced at Dar and Kerry. "He owns this place."

"The store?" Kerry asked.

"The island." Kristie smiled. "He owns the development company. We live here. He just never believed in raising us kids to be rich feckless brats."

Kerry smiled at her. "You going to college?"

Kristie shook her head. "Not my thing. I like to do graphic artistry. Dad says he'll maybe hire me to design our ad copy."

"You like computers?"

"Want a job?" Dar and Kerry said at the same time and then exchanged looks.

"Okay folks, can I just finish here before we start something else?" Charles begged. "So that's all that happened? Then we came in?"

"Yes," Dar said. "Sorry to ruin your night, fellas."

Charles grinned briefly at her. "I've seen you in the gym, Ms. Roberts. Sorry we missed the dust up. Kristie's right. That guy's nothing but stupid bad news."

"So are we going to call the police?" Kerry asked. "We have a lawyer but I'd rather not have to use him for this."

"Let me have my boss go talk to Billy," Charles said. "I'm thinking he's pretty new around here. Been here only three months. He probably doesn't know who Kristie is." He gave the girl a smile. "She's right. He don't want her daddy to get involved. He's got a temper."

"Okay by me," Dar said. "You guys handle it. I've got stone crab and ice cream to get home."

The guards left, talking in low tones together and looking at the pad of notes. The door closed behind them and the three women were momentarily silent.

Kerry finally cleared her throat. "Sorry that had to go down. It was a really cool Saturday before that."

"That was really cool," Kristie said. "Don't worry about that guy. My dad'll take care of him," she added, confidently. "He knows about you."

Dar's brows lifted. "We're computer nerds."

She nodded. "Yeah, he knows that, but I also heard him telling someone...I guess someone had a problem with your dog? Or something? The gym maybe? Anyway he told them to shut up and leave you alone."

Dar still looked surprised.

"You have some contacts with the government?" Kristie prompted.

Kerry smiled. "Yes, we do have some contacts with the government. So anyway, Kristie, you interested in a career in computers? We run a consulting company and we sure could use some help in the media department."

Kristie made a face. "It's kind of gross for me to say this, but I don't think my dad would let me."

Kerry's eyebrows shot right up.

"He doesn't like gay people," she said in a matter of fact tone. "So like I said, he knows about you guys. He'd go apeshit if I said I was going to work for you. I think he'd think you were recruiting me, you know?"

Dar blinked a few times then shrugged. "His loss," she said, "and maybe yours."

"Are you mad?" Kristie looked wistfully at them. "I don't want you to be, I just don't want to lie about it."

"We appreciate that," Kerry said. "But tell your dad to do himself a favor and never say anything like that to her dad." She indicated Dar. "He won't care if he owns this place."

Kristie cocked her head to one side. "Is that the tall guy, Andy?"

"That's my dad," Dar said. "He's a retired Navy SEAL and I'm his only kid." She glanced at Kerry. "Well, his only blood kid."

Kerry smiled at her. "Anyway, no hard feelings, Kristie. My father felt the same way about gay people. He went to his grave hating me for it." She leaned on Dar's shoulder. "That's why I'm glad I found Dar and her family."

Kristie nodded. "He just is like that," she said. "It's not a religious thing. He just thinks a family should be a man, a woman and kids." She glanced at the clock. "It's time for me to close this place up before any more weird stuff happens."

They got up and Kerry retrieved their bag, then tucked her arm inside Dar's as they headed for the door. "Night." She glanced back at

Kristie. "Hope Billy doesn't give you any more trouble."

Kristie looked troubled but she waved. "Night."

They made their way out of the store and headed once more along the path toward their home.

"That didn't end the way I figured it would," Dar said.

Kerry shrugged. "People are like that. It's just getting more evident I think."

"Yuk," Dar said. "My conversation with Jacques was more interesting. He took charge of the board. Seems like there's a big fight going on there."

"Big surprise," Kerry said. "You give him any advice?"

"Yes. But I doubt he'll be able to take it." Dar sighed. "It's not our issue anymore. Let's go have some crabs and chill out."

Kerry accepted the change of subject and remained quiet for the rest of the short walk, pondering the stars visible over the tops of the buildings as she thought about the evening's surprises.

Yuk, about covered it.

THE NEXT DAY it rained. Kerry was content to watch the heavy clouds disburse their contents across the seawall as she stood at the kitchen window enjoying an early morning cup of coffee.

The kitchen floor had towels on it, mopping up from the wet dog footprints and she carefully stepped over them as she went back into the main part of the house.

Dar sat on the floor, legs sprawled out with a knotted towel in her hands being tugged at by both Labradors.

It was adorable. She put her cup down and grabbed her camera, focusing quickly and snapping a few shots of the action. "You guys are hilarious."

"I'm not sure who Mocha's helping more." Dar watched the puppy get in Chino's way, then grab the end hanging from the bigger Lab's mouth and hang off it.

Chino let go and barked at him in outrage.

Kerry laughed and perched on the back of the love seat. "You all set for the conference?"

"Yup." Dar rolled onto her back and let the dogs clamber all over her. "Got the demo done too. Going to spend the rest of today just relaxing."

"I'm up for that," Kerry said. "It's going to rain all day and I'm going to enjoy it now that I sent an email to Richard warning him about little Billy Jacktard."

"Peh."

Kerry put the camera down and joined them on the floor. She grabbed the towel and waited for Mocha to latch onto it. "What are you doing there, little man?"

Mocha tugged fiercely at the fabric.

Chino plopped down next to Dar and put her head on Dar's shoulder, exhaling and stirring the dark hair on the side of her face.

"Hey, Chi." Dar curled an arm around the dog. "What are you up to, huh?"

Chino licked her ear, making Dar chuckle.

Kerry played with Mocha for a minute then glanced at Dar. "I was thinking of making a big pot of barley soup. You up for that?"

Dar peered past Chino's furry body at her. "Whatever you make I'm up for," she said. "You have yet to produce something out of that kitchen that I haven't liked."

"Is that true?" Kerry pondered. "I've made some kooky things in there."

"It's true. I grew up on a Navy base," Dar said, "and you know how my mother cooks."

Kerry edged over so she could lie down and put her head on Dar's stomach. "Dar, can I tell you something?"

"That stuff last night is still bothering you," Dar responded.

Kerry looked at her.

"The part about us being gay," Dar clarified. "I don't usually care about that but it bothered me, too. I've lived here for years. You've lived here for years. Finding out people don't like our lifestyle is like sandpaper on the ass."

"No, it's not that," Kerry said. "I always assumed there were people who didn't like it. But that everyone now feels so comfortable saying it does kind of bothers me. It's become okay to diss our relationship in public."

"Ker, it always was," Dar said. "C'mon. It's been a damn short time where anyone's accepted it."

"Mm. It still feels weird," Kerry said. "It's like we've become a target, lately."

Dar studied her briefly. "Does it make you uncomfortable living here?"

Kerry was silent for a bit. "You mean because the guy who owns the place doesn't like us?"

Dar nodded.

"I don't know. Maybe I'm just in a mood today." Kerry said. "Why should it matter? We've never even met the guy. It makes me feel a little weird about Kristie though."

"Mm."

"Do people really think we recruit?" Kerry asked. "Like we're some creepy vampire club or something?"

"Sure. Didn't your dad think I turned you gay?" Dar asked in a reasonable tone. "People believe what they want to believe and it's easier to think someone is making your loved one change than it is to believe they were born that way."

Kerry frowned.

Dar ruffled her hair gently. "Go make your soup, Ker. It is what it is."

Kerry rolled onto her side and then got up onto her hands and knees. She leaned forward and gave Dar a kiss on the lips. Then she yelped as Mocha bit her toe and then grabbed the tail of her old t-shirt and started pulling it.

Hopefully it would be a nice and quiet, rainy Sunday.

DAR WAS IN her office messing around with her demo when the doorbell rang. She glanced up to see Kerry cross the living room to answer it. She wondered who the hell was calling on them this late on a Sunday evening.

"Oh, hi," she heard Kerry say, then heard the sound of footsteps and the door closing. Dar looked up to see Kerry and their two security friends from the previous night. "Hey, Charles."

"Hi, Ms. Roberts."

Dar leaned back and propped her knee up against the desk. "C'mon in. What can we do for you?"

The two men came in and stood awkwardly until Kerry guided them to the sofa then went back behind Dar's desk and leaned on the credenza behind it.

Charles exhaled. "Sorry to bother you ladies so late. We just finished all the paperwork and I wanted to come over so we could tell you the low down."

Kerry extended her legs and crossed them at the ankles. Her reading of body language made her think the message wasn't going to be all bad and she produced a faint smile. "Would you guys like some cold apple cider? I was just about to bring some in here for Dar."

"Sure," Charles said. "We just walked all the way across the island. Gets you thirsty."

Kerry eased past the desk and headed for the kitchen.

Charles cleared his throat. "That guy, Billy, he kicked up a big fuss. He went to the island admin offices and wanted to get them to throw you ladies right on out of here."

Dar blinked at him. "He wanted to get us evicted? For me defending myself with shellfish?"

"Not so much," Charles said. "He said it was a moral thing, you know?"

Dar rolled her eyes as Kerry came back in with a tray. "I'd like to know — in a graphic way — what breeders think we do with each other that's so different than what they do."

Kerry put the tray down and handed glasses out. "I'm not even going to comment." She took her cup and went back to leaning against the credenza. "So what were they told? I know evicting us wouldn't be legal."

Charles nodded. "That's what the association secretary said. That you ladies mind your own business and don't hardly cause no trouble. So then he went in to talk to Kristie's dad, only he didn't know he was."

"Oh, I can see this coming." Dar covered her eyes with one hand.

"So Big Jim broke his arm." The other guard nodded. "They took him off in an ambulance."

"That's right," Charles said. "Broke his arm and his nose, too. He shoulda stuck with you ladies. All he got from that was a bump on the noggin."

"Wow," Kerry said. "Is he going to sue Kristie's father now?"

"I'm thinking he's gonna be evicted himself," Charles said. "But I heard Big Jim say he was going to come talk to you ladies so I thought I should let you know that." He paused, looking a touch uncomfortable. "He's an old fashioned kind of guy."

"Here we go again," Kerry said. "You know, it's not against the law to be homosexual."

Dar cleared her throat. "Not so much with our variety, no. But I think sodomy is still illegal in Broward County."

Kerry covered her eyes and the two guards blushed in embarrassment.

"Anyway, he can come talk to us all he wants. But this place is paid off and we own it. There's not a damn thing he can do about it," Dar said. "Thanks for the heads up though, guys. We appreciate it."

The guards finished their cider and got up. "You ladies have a nice night," Charles said. "And keep out of trouble."

Kerry saw them to the door then returned, dropping onto the couch with a frown. "I'm not sure I liked that conversation."

"He can't do anything to us."

"No, I don't think so either, but it's just not cool, Dar."

"No, it's not. It's not even cool that he'd try it with that butt load. Guy has a right to live where he wants to live. Most he should do is file charges for him grabbing Kristie."

"You're defending him?"

"I'm saying he needs to be dealt with via the legal system. Kicking him off the island for what he did is the same as kicking us off for being gay," Dar said. "I'm not saying I wouldn't cheer if he got tossed into Government Cut."

Kerry sighed. "Yeah."

"Let's wait to see what he says to us," Dar said. "I can hold my own in any verbal ass kicking contest."

That brought a smile to Kerry's face. "And most other kinds." She got up and collected the cider cups. "I'm going to get in the hot tub. Interested?"

Dar got up and flipped off the monitor, leaving it behind without a second glance. "Go baby go."

THE COCONUT GROVE convention center was small but stylish and Kerry liked it a lot more than the Miami Beach facility, which was huge and echoing and gritty. She picked up a cup of hot tea at the café and wandered over to the presentation area where Dar was getting ready to speak.

It was all small companies. No one probably knew who they were. Kerry liked the idea of that and exchanged smiles with another woman about her age in a business suit nearby.

There were a lot of booths set up representing a lot of small companies. Kerry had already earmarked three or four she wanted to talk to and she was planning a route through the hall after she listened to Dar's presentation.

Quite a few people were gathering and Kerry imagined she felt Dar's nervousness building up, seeing the restless motion of her tall frame up behind the podium.

Dar wasn't fond of public speaking. Kerry actually didn't mind it and of the two of them, she was the more skilled. They both knew that. But Dar volunteered for the event and if there was one thing that overwhelmed any nerves, it was her standing tall in defense of her own ego.

Kind of adorable, actually. Kerry gave her a thumbs up and saw the rakish, wry grin that told her Dar knew perfectly well what she was thinking. Adorable, because Dar was.

They were both dressed relatively casually. Slacks and collared shirts. In Dar's case an embroidered vest and in Kerry's a long sleeved sweater she had draped around her shoulders at the moment.

The morning was half over and they'd just come out of the keynote speech. Kerry was of the opinion that Dar would have done a far better job at it, but she'd clapped with the rest as the owner of the local television station went on about innovation and the American dream.

Now the crowd was settling down and Kerry carried her cup of juice into the auditorium, taking a seat in the back row, which was a little elevated, and gave her a view of her partner. Dar had stepped up to the podium and was standing there quietly, waiting for everyone to focus on her.

Just as they did Kerry's Handspring started to buzz. She quickly removed it and got up, ducking out of the room to answer it. "Hey, Maria."

"Ah, Kerrisita." Maria's voice came over the wire. "I am so sorry to disturb you at your meeting but there is a person here who is insisting on speaking with you. It is a customer. Mayte has told me she thinks they are interested in doing a program."

"Sure, put them on." Kerry positioned herself in the doorway so she could keep an eye on Dar, finding another smile appearing as Dar's rich and slightly melodic voice emerged from the microphone. "I didn't think information technology was that sort of spur of the moment on demand thing, but you never know."

"Si, you never do know," Maria said. "Please wait one moment."

Kerry watched Dar put her hands on the podium. She knew how much self control it took for her to leave them there and not fidget with them. Dar did that when she was nervous. She would flex her hands and crack her knuckles, stick her mitts in her pockets and tap her thumbs on any flat surface.

She gave Dar a thumbs up for her discipline and got a smile back in return, along with the slightest cock of the head that made her realize Dar was wondering what she was doing on the phone.

Ah well. "Yes, this is Kerry," she said into the phone as a voice came on. "Sorry, it's a little loud here. I'm at the small business conf — what?"

"Yes, hello? Kerry? Did you hear me?" the voice said. "This is Evelyn Chambers, from Dade County public schools?"

Kerry paused and frowned, then shook her head a little. "Yes...um...oh, right," she said. "We met at the gym a while back."

"Right. My sister's son works for you there. He was talking about your company. We want to hire you. I mean the school system does. We were given a lot of money to upgrade all the computers and we can't think of a better person to do it than you."

Kerry pulled the Handspring away from her face and stared at it. Then she put it back to her ear. "Okay, Evelyn — sure. I'd be glad to talk to you about that...but you know we're not hardware vendors."

"But your new company is about computers, right?"

"Well, sure. All the things we do generally involve computers but we don't...I mean, let's talk about it," Kerry said. "I'll be in the office tomorrow morning and we can sit down and look at what you need, okay?"

"Could it be early?" Evelyn said. "We've got a meeting about the budget at nine. Can I see you before then? I want to have you ladies do this because I am so freaking tired of the men in the office telling me only guys can buy computers. They are driving me out of my cotton picking mind!"

Ah. The light bulb went off over Kerry's head with an almost audible bing. "Gotcha. No problem, Evelyn, I'd be glad to meet you at seven or eight. Or if you want, we'll be back in the office this afternoon after Dar's speech so — "

"Oh perfect! I'll go get some lunch and come back." Evelyn sounded utterly relieved. "See you in a little while, Kerry! Thanks!"

"Uh...no problem. Bye." Kerry removed the Handspring from her ear and peered at it then put it back in her pocket. She started back into the auditorium only to halt when she spotted Peter and Mark entering the building from the other direction and looking around.

"Oh, bet that's not good." Kerry backpedaled and waved. Sure enough the two men looked relieved on seeing her and headed in her direction. "Poor, Dar."

MARK STEERED THEM all over to the snack area where there were high top tables he put his laptop down on. "Pete, you want to start?"

"Not really." Peter looked glum. "Mark said I should come over if they booted me, and they did. There was some big huge blow up again today and that big jerk came in and told me to clear out."

"No problem, Peter," Kerry said. "We said we'd take care of you and we will."

"Thank you, ma'am." He looked a little more confident. "My wife about gave birth prematurely when I told her. She gave up her job when she got pregnant and this whole thing's been near killing her." He stuck his hands in his pockets. "I don't even know what I did to tip the scales. I didn't make any changes, you know? I just gave them the configs and said what I thought we should do."

"The man you worked for is an absolute moron," Kerry said. "They had one chance to turn it around. Dar even told the board of directors' new head what to do. I guess they didn't do it."

Peter's ears visibly perked. "Whoa, maybe there was something going on with that because David was totally torked off. He said something like if they think they can just throw us out they're mistaken, or something like that."

"Hm." Kerry glanced up as she sensed Dar's presence, to find her emerging from the room, heading their way. "Save the story for Dar," she said. "Let me get her some milk. Looks like she's going to need it."

"I could get a complex." Dar looked from Mark to Peter. "What's going on?" She glanced behind her. "I have to go back to finish a question and answer session."

"Pete got booted, boss," Mark said. "You put a cat in the chicken coop? Sounds like they freaked out this morning."

Dar cleared her throat. "I had a conversation with Jacques Despin," she said. "He just took over the chairman's position. Wanted to let me know about that." She put her hands on the high top as Kerry came back with two large cups. "What happened?"

"Here." Kerry handed over the milk.

Dar's eyes grew round and alarmed. "How bad is this that you got me a quart of milk?"

"Well, David was pissed off," Peter said. "It was like a tomb in there this morning. There were only like five of us there and they threw us all out."

Dar put her hands on her hips. "That leaves no one there to run the place."

"Except the dorks," Mark said. "Maybe we'll be getting a bunch more customers along with more employees."

They all looked at each other for a moment, then Kerry sighed.

"I've got a bad feeling about this."

Dar took a long swallow of milk. "Let me go do ten minutes of Q and A, then we'll get back to the office.

"Just in case?"

"Just in case."

Chapter Eleven

BUT THE AFTERNOON was almost preternaturally quiet. Kerry munched her spicy chicken sandwich at her desk, glancing at her email as she listened to Mayte talking to their phone vendor in the outer office.

Or really, her own office. Kerry thought about the open spaces they still had, pondering whether or not to move Mayte out and into her own space. She was working on three projects now and it was probably time for her to get her and Dar an actual admin since they'd promoted theirs.

Mark came in the door with a fistful of papers. "Hey, Kerry. I got Pete through his paperwork. You mind if I make him my assistant?"

Kerry swallowed hastily and wiped her lips. "Not at all. You're a director. Make him a manager if you want to. We've got more than enough projects to need one."

"Yeah, no kidding." He sat down. "You think they're doing funky stuff back at the old place? Or maybe they're just bringing in a whole new crew?"

"I find it hard to believe that they'd be doing something malicious," Kerry said. "It's a business, Mark. They probably promised they'd turn everything around and they wanted to clear out anyone who could tell them any different."

Mark nodded. "That's what I figure, too. Pete was the one who was pushing back on them. He's pretty sharp. I think he'll be okay for us."

"And now that they've done that, I'm fine with putting the word out to anyone who left there to come talk to us," Kerry said. "We can't hire everyone, but with these four new contracts, and the Dade County schools thing, we need bodies."

"Will do." He got up and handed over the papers. "Maria said you and the boss are going up to the Hill Wednesday."

"We've got to demo the database for the feds," Kerry said. "Not the real thing, a mock up. Politics."

"Kinda creepy."

"Kinda. But worse comes to worse, Dar will tell them to kiss her ass and we can't worry about it. With this new business we don't really need it." Kerry looked at the folders on her desk. "It's a lot of prestige, but yeah. Creepy."

Mayte poked her head in. "Kerry? There is a reporter here to speak to you? It's from the paper."

"Speaking of creepy," Kerry muttered. "That didn't work out so well last time." She drummed her fingers. "Okay, give me ten minutes to finish this and I'll see them."

Mark made a face and mimed tiptoeing out of the room, almost bumping into Dar as she appeared in the doorway between their offices. "Whoops"

"Got a reporter outside." Kerry had her head propped against her fist as she chewed.

"Got *CNN* on the phone wanting an interview," Dar responded. "Trade?"

"Nope."

"Wench."

DAR HAD HER boots up on her desk, her eyes closed and her hands folded over her stomach. It was dark outside and the building was almost empty. "Ker?"

Kerry poked her head in from her office. "We got another fifteen minutes to wait for *CNN*. Want some coffee?"

"Ungh."

"I'll take that as a yes. Be right back."

Dar remained where she was, letting her mind go blank as she waited. *The Herald* request was innocuous. The small business editor was at the conference and saw her speak, then did a Google search and decided they might make an interesting blurb.

Kerry had handled it.

But *CNN* wanted to know about the government project and that was far more dicey an interview. It involved a film crew and one of the high profile talking heads. She would rather dive into a vat of peanut butter than go through it.

Dar heard Mayte still rattling around in the outer office and there were creaks and footsteps that indicated to her that others were still hanging around as well. The lure of television cameras and quasi-famous people irresistible.

Peh.

Her desk phone rang. She reached over and keyed it, still keeping her eyes closed. "Dar Roberts."

"Hello, Dar, Gerry Easton here."

"Hey, Gerry," Dar responded. "We'll be out there tomorrow night. Got a meeting with Bridges on Wednesday. You free for dinner?"

"Well, sure. Be happy to and I bet the missus will be happy to also. But that's not why I'm calling. We got some big problems here, Dar, and I need your help."

Dar's eyes slid open and she regarded the ceiling. "What kind of problems, Gerry? We're not actually doing anything for you yet."

"It's that other thing." he said. "The connections."

"Ah." Dar slowly shifted her feet of the desk and sat up. "You mean the stuff ILS is doing for you?"

"That's right. It's all screwed up," he said. "I know you don't work for them anymore, Dar, but we're in a pickle and I mean a real dill pickle, if you catch my drift. Been trying to call them all afternoon, no one's answering the phone."

"Oh boy," Dar muttered.

"Anything you can do to help us out?" Gerry asked. "I got people chewing me up and down over it. Stuff's not working. We can't get reports, they can't send files. Dar they're driving me crazy. It's been off and on, but just around lunchtime it went down the tubes, y'know?"

Kerry entered with some coffee and spotted Dar's expression. "What's up?" she mouthed.

"Gerry." Dar mouthed back. "Network problems."

"Oh boy." Kerry put the coffee down on the desk and took a seat on the windowsill.

"Gerry, I don't know if there's anything I can do but let me make some calls," Dar sad. "All the people I knew there are gone."

"Eh? What?"

"Long story," Dar said. "Let me see what I can do. I'll call you back."

"All right. Anything at all you can come up with, huh, Dar? This is serious."

Dar sighed. "I know it is, Gerry. I'll get back to you. Bye for now." She hung up and swiveled to look at Kerry. "They must have really screwed it," she said. "Right around the time Peter showed up here it all went to hell."

Kerry folded her arms. "Won't be long until that hits the news," she said. "Not necessarily the Pentagon, but everything else."

"Surprised it hasn't already." Dar got up. "Let me call Jacques. He's the only one I can think of that might be able to...well, hell. I have no idea what he's going to do but he should know his customers are calling me."

Mayte appeared in the entrance to Dar's office. "The news people are here," she said. "Where do you want to speak with them? I think the conference room?"

Dar and Kerry exchanged glances. "That'll be fine, Mayte. Let them set up in there. We've got to discuss something then we'll be right down."

Mayte nodded and disappeared.

"I'll go keep them occupied," Kerry said. "Are you going to offer to go fix it?"

Dar shook her head.

"Hope we can swing that." Kerry patted her on the arm then headed for the door, shaking her own head as she disappeared.

"Yeah." Dar sat down on the edge of her desk and pulled her phone out again, keying through the memory. She found the number she was looking for and hit dial, holding it to her ear as she waited. It rang six times then voice mail picked up. "Great."

She waited for it to finish and beep. "Jacques, this is Dar. I just got a call from a mutual customer of ours saying his services with you were down and he wasn't able to get a hold of anyone to talk about it. He's in a big non-square office building in DC. Just letting you know in case you want to do something about it. Later."

She released the line then studied the phone. Was there anyone else she could call?

Anything else she could do? Dar stood up and shoved the phone into her pocket. Was there anything she really wanted to do?

She trotted down the steps and heard voices in the conference room. She paused for a moment to riffle her hair into some kind of fluffiness, then forged ahead into the conference room. "Evening."

There was a man there with a thin, angular face that Dar thought she sort of recognized. On one side of the room she saw two women who had over the shoulder messenger bags, with pens and pads and stopwatches hanging from them. On the other side of the room were two men with cameras and gear.

The man half waved. "Ah, Ms. Roberts. You probably don't remember me."

"I do." Dar produced a smile. "You interviewed me in New York." She did remember that in a hazy surreal kind of way that most of the events were enfolded in. "We talked about cupcakes."

The man grinned. "We did," he said. "So we're a galaxy away from that moment, huh? You're not with ILS anymore."

"Nope." Dar took a seat at the head of the table. "Hung up my own shingle." She indicated the building around her.

"Okay, Pete," one of the women interrupted. "Why don't you sit down here and we can shoot from that angle across the table."

"Sure." Pete amiably came around the table and sat down. He was wearing a pair of jeans and a leather jacket. "To be honest, Ms. Roberts, that interview with you got me interested in the technology biz. So now I do in-depth stuff for *CNN* about it. Nice change."

Kerry came over and sat on the other side of Dar. "This has been a nice change for us, too," she said. "Getting to start everything from scratch and all that."

The cameramen busied themselves getting a tripod arranged behind Pete's shoulder and settled a camera on top of it, flicking on the battery packs that powered up with a soft, faint whine. "We got sync to the truck?" one of them asked.

"Eyup...got a signal back to base," the other responded. "Cheryl, we're good."

"Thanks." The producer put her pad down, with notes. "Let me just make sure I've got everything accurate here, ladies, then we can get this and let you get on your way. I know it's late." She glanced up at Dar and Kerry. "Thanks for hanging out and waiting for us."

"We were glad to," Kerry said. "I suppose you tracked us down from that picture in the paper?" She smiled briefly. "Dar enjoyed her visit to the White House."

Pete cleared his throat. "Actually, we did pick that up on research, but really you popped up on my radar because I'm local here and I was home on vacation when my brother-in-law's scatterbrained son got hired to write games and I wanted to see who'd be crazy enough to hire him."

Dar chuckled. "Ah, I see." She leaned back. "He's got good programming skills. I always look everywhere for talent. Your nephew, once removed, might turn out to be the Bill Gates of the family."

"He loves this place. He was at dinner at our house a week ago talking nine to the minute about some program you did with a hamster in it."

"That would be a gopher," Kerry corrected. "Gopher Dar, in fact. It's an animated program Dar writes on sometimes."

They all chuckled "So then I ran a scan on headlines and found the picture of you with the president and figured, hey, it's time for me to get back in touch with Dar Roberts," Pete said with a smile. "I guess you just recently left ILS?"

"About a month or so ago, yes," Dar said. "After the time we spent in New York, Kerry and I decided we wanted to retire and go do our own thing."

"Get out of the spotlight?" Pete said, his eyes twinkling. "Didn't work out so well for you on that front I guess."

Dar shrugged.

"Okay, we're ready," the blonder of the two women said. "Pete, you're on."

He folded his hands on the table and paused, clearing his throat. "We're rolling to archive, Dar, not live to the channel."

"Now that's a good idea," Dar said. "Especially if you remember what I said the last time about not asking me anything you don't want to hear the answer to."

One of the producers pulled a phone from her pocket and held a hand up, moving to the door and slipping outside.

"We're speaking here today with Dar Roberts, who is a well known business person in the technology field," Pete said. "Ms. Roberts, you recently left the big corporate world and opened up your own IT-related business. Tell me about that."

Kerry quietly got up and eased back, glad to give Dar her moment in the spotlight. She ducked outside the door and went across to the small kitchen, pausing when she almost bumped into Scott in his wheelchair. "Hello."

"Hi." He was removing a small container from the refrigerator. "What's up with *CNN*?" He rolled out of Kerry's way and put the container on the table, opening it up and revealing what looked like a fruit salad.

Surprising. Kerry got one of the cold ice teas and opened it. "Their technology desk saw Dar's picture in the paper and wanted an interview," she said. "How's it going with you? Mark says you do good work."

"I like it," he responded. "It's good to do stuff that's just normal."

Kerry sat down at the table. "I remember when I got back from New York after 9/11, it was a relief to just be able to sit down and have a boring staff meeting."

He glanced briefly at her. "You were in there when that went down? I was in the hospital in Frankfurt."

"No, I was at my family's home in Michigan. But I went there the next day," Kerry said. "The company we worked for had people in the Pentagon and also in downtown New York."

He ate several pieces of the fruit with a spoon, chewing it thoughtfully. "I saw pictures. That was a mess."

"It was," Kerry agreed. "We did some work down by the stock exchange. The destruction down there was incredible."

"Yeah. Only thing I was glad I got half blowed up because I knew I wasn't going to have to go back there," he said. "We're going to go back there and beat the shit out of them for that. Everybody knows it."

"Mm." Kerry sipped her tea thoughtfully. Their new tech had gotten himself some polo shirts and work style chinos, she noted, remembering they'd been paid the previous Friday. "Everything working out for you?"

He was silent for a long moment, then nodded. "Glad I came and asked for that paper."

Kerry smiled. "I think we're glad, too," she said. "Sometimes you just have to take a chance, you know?"

He looked up at her expressionless. Then he smiled.

Kerry started to speak again, then paused as the *CNN* producer stuck her head in the door. "Hi."

"Hi." The woman looked harried. "Listen, I'm really sorry. And I mean, really really sorry, but we've got to pull out of here. There's some big issue in the banking industry and they need us on it."

"Wow sorry to hear that." Kerry got up. "A technical issue?"

"Something to do with how they talk to each other. Something's gone wrong," the woman said. "Hell, you want to come with us? You probably understand more of it than we will."

Uh oh. Kerry managed an apologetic smile. "Sorry, we've got plans," she said. "But I'll be watching tonight to see what it was."

"We'll get back to you," she said. "Let me go get my guys packed up." She bustled out and left them in contemplative silence for a moment.

"Hm." Kerry leaned against the wall. "Wonder if I should start ordering pizza." A moment later Dar came into the room, leaning one long arm against the door frame. "Hi."

"Interbank's down," Dar said.

"Yeah, I figured."

"Should we just stay here?"

"I was just considering ordering some dinner in," Kerry said. "Let me go tell Mark what's going on."

Dar exhaled, went to the refrigerator, removed a chocolate milk chug and opened it. She turned and leaned against the appliance, eying Scott.

He watched her in silence in return, chewing his fruit salad.

"Your buddies still giving you a hard time?" Dar asked, after a bit.

He nodded. "I keep clear of 'em," he said. "Stay around that gym a lot. They let me work in there too a little, at night."

"Make friends with guys in there," Dar suggested. "I've seen some of the dudes that go in there. They look like ass kickers."

He nodded again. "They got a pool in there. I like that." He paused. "There some kind of problem here?" he asked, bluntly. "With them press people and then everyone running out?"

Dar sat down and rested her elbows on the table. "No, there's no problem here. There's a problem where we used to work." She took a sip of her milk and looked up as Mark skidded around the corner and came barreling into the room. "Hey."

"Hey," Mark said, glancing at Scott then back at Dar. "Kerry told me and I got a call from our old guy at the NAP. Crap's coming down"

Dar nodded agreement. "It is."

"You think they're gonna call you?"

"I think they're going to have to," Dar said. "I'm just sitting here trying to figure out how to tell them no."

"Why?" Mark said. "At this point, it's all in the crapper, Dar. They can't blame you for any of it. You could go in there and show them all up."

"I know that, but where does it get us? I don't want to go back in there. I want them to figure out their own problems and leave us the hell alone." Dar got up. "I fix this, they'll never let go of me in the short term and I've got better things to do." She drained the chug and tossed it in the recycle bin. "I'll be in my office."

"K, boss." Mark shook his head. "Man, I remember the days when I was glad to just be a tech yonk. End of the day, you just go home."

Scott finished his fruit salad and put the container carefully back in the plain, dark blue holder. "Gonna finish that printer," he said. "Someone bent the frame, that's why it keeps jamming."

"We've only had it two weeks. Who had a chance to do that?" Mark said.

"Probably the delivery company." Scott put the container in his lap and prepared to roll out. "Might need some tools."

Mark opened the door for him. "Give me a list," he said. "I'll get 'em ordered."

They emerged into the hallway. "We'll be here a while so take your time with the printer," Mark added. "Let you know when chow gets here."

Scott nodded and headed off down the hall to the support office.

Mark watched him go and then turned toward the stairs, pausing when Kerry came around the corner to join him. "This gonna be a long night?"

Kerry lifted her hands and let them drop. "I've got no idea. Maybe those guys will find a way around having to call for help. I sure would if I were them."

"Kerry." Mark eyed her. "Trust me. I lived in that place for long as she did. If it's this fucked up, no one's gonna be able to fix it but her."

Kerry sighed.

"Pizza?"

"Chinese buffet."

"Whoof."

"ARE WE KIDDING ourselves and no one's calling us, or considering calling us?" Kerry was seated on the windowsill, manipulating a shrimp with her chopsticks. "How long are we going to hang out here?"

Dar was chewing a very red spare rib. She paused and licked her lips. "We just saw them go over the Interbank outage on *CNN* and they said they were searching for a senior spokesperson from ILS. Either they're crapping their pants and trying to find my phone number right now, or they're going to blow them off."

"They can't be that stupid."

"They can. So either they call me in the next fifteen minutes or we'll just go home." Dar took another bite of her rib. "They can't afford to have all their customers start calling *CNN*."

"Maybe they'll figure it out themselves," Kerry said philosophically. "I don't want to end up with my ass parked in that mausoleum lobby tonight anyway."

"I hope they do." Dar picked up her bottle of green ice tea and took a swallow. "Then we can finally leave them behind."

Kerry leaned against the windowsill and hiked one boot up on the wooden surface. She fished out another shrimp and bit it in half, swinging her other leg a little to the soft new age music playing in the built-in nearby.

Everyone else had gone home, in some cases at their insistence. They were alone in the building, doors locked with the security system in place. The street outside was quiet, befitting the middle of the weekday night she heard the faint sounds of a softball game going on at the field down the street.

"We could form a company softball team," Kerry commented after a moment. "That would be fun. Want me to see if there's a league around here?"

"Sure."

"I'd like that. I thought the league we started to be part of before 9/11 was going to be fun, but it would be more fun if we had our own team. We can get uniforms in our colors."

"Sounds good." Dar munched thoughtfully. "You look adorable in those baseball pants."

Kerry rolled her head around and gave her a droll look.

"You do," Dar insisted. "You've got a really cute butt, hon. Those pants show it off."

Kerry actually blushed. "Dar."

Dar opened her eyes wide in mock hurt. "What?"

Kerry stuck her tongue out.

"Same to you." Dar finished up her ribs and put them in the silver lined bag they'd come in. "Let's go home. Screw it." She got up and shut her laptop down. "I'm out of patience. With any luck they've solved everything themselves and I won't get shanghaied when I walk into the Pentagon tomorrow."

Kerry was more than ready enough to leave. She wrapped up the remains of her meal and Dar's and took them downstairs to store them in the refrigerator. She glanced around, nodding in approval at the neatness from the cleaning service then went back in the hallway just in time to see Dar trotting down the steps with both their bags.

She took hers, then waited as Dar triggered the exit allowance for the alarm system. She opened the door and they walked quickly out, Dar locking the door behind them as they heard the alarm reset softly inside.

It was a nice night. Kerry drew in a breath of cool air, savoring it since they were on the long downhill slide into summer. In a month or so, any chance of outdoor comfort while fully dressed would be gone.

So she enjoyed the crispness and the smell of the leaves in the trees around the building. She waited for Dar to join her and then they walked down the sidewalk together toward the parking lot. "Glad we left the pups home today," she said. "Would have made a late night for them."

"Mm," Dar agreed. "I think they like it though, being with us." She beeped open the doors to the truck. "Everyone pays attention to them in the office."

Kerry opened the passenger side door and put her bag inside, then hoisted herself up after it. "We should have gotten a running board for this thing. I feel like I'm doing a vault."

Dar chuckled. "I'll call the dealership tomorrow," she said then paused, looking out over the steering wheel through the front window. "Oh crap."

Kerry looked up quickly and spotted the group near the trees on the side of their building. "Is that—oh, yeah. It is." She recognized their rowdy antagonists, and in the middle, the shorter outline of Scott in his chair. "Well, poots, Dar."

Dar opened the door and slid out. "He's one of us now," she said as she hitched up the sleeves on her shirt and started toward the gang.

"Wouldn't have stopped you in any case, Crusader Dar." Kerry reconciled herself to some after hours conflict and got out on her side, shutting the door and trotting quickly after Dar.

The group was clustered around Scott and it was obvious they were pissed. Kerry caught up to Dar just as they came up next to the group and she got her balance set and squared her shoulders.

Not that either activity would come off as imposing. Not nearly as much as Dar's did when her six foot plus partner stood up straight and glared at the men.

"What the hell's going on here?"

The men turned abruptly, one of them letting loose of Scott's chair arms. He looked up in surprise and saw them. Kerry saw a brief moment of relief that almost put a smile on her face.

So yeah, he'd crossed that line, too.

"What the hell is it your business?" the closest man responded, turning and revealing himself to be Joe, the group troublemaker.

"You're messing with an employee of mine," Dar responded. "In front of my office. I thought I made it clear to you people I wasn't going to put up with that." She stood square on to him, her hands in her pockets.

"You don't own him, you bitch," Joe said. "Get out of here."

"No." Dar took a step closer. "I don't own anyone. But I value people, which is a lot more than you do. You want to get away from me? You leave. It's his choice to leave with you, or stay."

"I'm not going to take that from you, lady." Joe hauled back and swung on Dar and in a second they were grappling as she blocked his punch and put an elbow into his chin.

Kerry watched the gang carefully as she looked around for something to use as a weapon, not nearly as confident in her martial skills as Dar was.

Joe backed off and touched his jaw, watching Dar's tense figure and flexing hands. "You know how to fight." He sounded surprised.

"I do," Dar answered shortly. "I don't want to, and I don't like to, but if you push me I will."

Joe studied her for a minute. "I want to, and I like to, but I don't like fighting with women," he answered. "My daddy didn't raise me to hit girls."

A voice came out of the darkness with more than a hint of amusement in it. "Y'all are out of luck then, boy, cause I didn't raise her to care about what was in the pants she was kicking."

Dar relaxed and smiled. "Hey, Dad," she said. "Didn't know you guys were back."

Andrew Roberts sauntered into the lamplight, hands in the front pocket of his hoodie. The hood was pushed back to reveal his scarred and rugged face. "Hey there, Dardar. We done just tied the boat up at that there marina down there," he said. "We gave your other place a call and didn't get no answer so we thought we'd try this here one."

He observed the men, who were all now watching him with extreme wariness. "What all's going on here?" he asked after a moment of silence.

"Hi, Dad," Kerry chimed in, moving past Dar to put her arms around him. "Glad to see you. Is Mom around?"

He returned the hug. "On her way up here. She done passed one of them little knicky shops on the way and stopped to look," Andrew allowed. "You boys standing around here for some reason?"

"Scott here works for us." Kerry indicated the man in the wheelchair. "These other people are some friends of his."

Andrew observed them closely. "Ain't that nice," he said in a flat tone.

"We'll be going." Joe lifted a hand and started walking off. "Night."

Andrew caught him by the back of his jacket and hauled him backwards. "Now." He looked him in the eye. "Do not be here hanging around no more bothering my children," he said clearly. "You find yourselves some other place to do nothin'."

Joe looked at him. "That some kind of threat?" he asked.

"Yes," Andrew answered, then he stopped talking and went very still.

"Okay." Joe held his hands up. "I got it. We're leaving."

Andrew released him and stared at the rest of them until they all backed off, leaving Scott to sit there quietly in his chair watching them go.

"Peh." Dar's father shook his head. "What the hell they teaching kids these days."

"Thanks, Dad," Dar said. "I wasn't looking forward to soaking a sore hand tonight." She looked down at Scott. "Sorry if we embarrassed you."

Scott was sitting there with an expression of mixed amusement and thoughtfulness on his face. "I'm all right," he said. "They were just being assholes. I'm used to it." He put his hands on his chair wheel rims. "Maybe they'll clear out of back behind there. Easier to bunk there than the church."

"In the bushes, behind the office?" Kerry asked. "I thought there was an opening in there."

Scott nodded. "Little house back in there, in the other property, but you can't get at it from that side. Just was a..." He shrugged. "Maybe a kid's place? Has some bunks and stuff."

"Y'all living in there?" Andrew asked.

Scott nodded again. "Sometimes. When the rest of them are

someplace else." He started around them. "Night."

"Night," Dar responded.

"Night, Scott," Kerry echoed.

They watched him turn up the small path that went between the buildings, then Andrew folded his arms across his chest and regarded the two of them. "Y'all gonna show me this new place?" His eyes twinkled. "S'got my name all over it?"

Dar grinned back at him. "Sure. Glad you caught us before we left." She started to lead the way toward the door. "We stayed late because...well, it's a long story."

"Figure it can wait for your mom."

"Yeah, it can. I'd hate to have to go through it twice," Kerry said. "I'm so glad to see you. I wasn't looking forward to how that was looking to end either." She put her hand on Dar's back. "Not that I had any doubt in what the result was going to be, still."

"Jerks," Dar muttered.

"What's up with them boys?" Andrew asked as they came around the corner and paused, looking at the sign and the small front porch.

"They're a bunch of veterans who are out of work and homeless," Dar said. She put her hands on her hips. "Like the sign?"

"Ah surely do," Andrew said with immense satisfaction. "Looks better than it did in them pitchers." He glanced at Dar. "So you done hired one of them fellers?"

"Part of the long story. Let's go inside and sit down." Dar led the way to the door and opened it, then ducked inside quickly to silence the alarm. "C'mon in," she said as she flipped on the recently doused lights.

Kerry was the last in and then she turned as she heard light footsteps behind her. "Hey!" She waved at Ceci, who had stopped to admire the sign in her own turn.

"Well, hello yourself," Ceci said and waved back. "What a trip across the gulf stream." She caught up to Kerry and scooted inside the door. "How are you?"

Kerry gave her a quick hug. "Where do I start?"

"Uh oh."

"So many things have happened since the last time we saw you...holy cow," Kerry said. They followed Dar and Andrew inside, Dar giving a running commentary of their space. "We were late here tonight because we were pretty sure Dar was going to get a call from the people running ILS now."

"Oh?" Ceci seemed surprised. "Are they different people from the ones that were doing that before we left?"

"Oh yeah. Most of the company, at least our part of it, quit," Kerry said. "Anyway, they did something to screw things up there and we started hearing about it in public earlier on."

"Really."

"Yes. The *CNN* crew that was here had to go run and find out about it." Kerry cleared her throat. "Where was I?"

"*CNN?*"

"They were interviewing Dar." Kerry pinched the bridge of her nose. "And we knew things were going south because Gerry Easton called from the Pentagon saying they were having problems. So we figured they'd finally cave in and call Dar, but they didn't."

Ceci whistled softly under her breath.

"So I guess maybe they sorted things out," Kerry said. "I'm glad if they did, because I don't want to have to deal with that when we go to Washington tomorrow."

"Washington?"

"Dar has to go explain advanced heuristics to Congress."

Ceci stopped and burst into slightly hysterical laughter, falling back against the wall and holding her stomach.

"Yeah, I know." Kerry smiled and waited. "I'm going to bring a camcorder," she said. "So we don't want the government all of a sudden to stop in the middle of it and ask us to fix what is not our computer problem."

Ceci let her laughter peter off. "You're probably screwed in that case."

Kerry sighed.

"There isn't a problem on the planet that doesn't end up on your platter, kid." Ceci patted her arm. "C'mon. Let's go finish the tour and find a beer."

THEY ENDED UP at a café a short walk down the road, seated outside as Kerry ran through the whole catalog of recent events.

Dar contented herself with her spiked coffee, listening to Kerry and watching the expressions on her parents' faces react.

"They did what?" Ceci leaned forward. "You mean this guy deliberately screwed everything up?"

Kerry lifted her hand off the table and turned it palm up, then put it back down. "Depends what you consider deliberate. Like Dar said to someone, the fact that they did something was deliberate but she doesn't think the intent was to screw everything up."

"Had me some Navy jobs like that," Andrew said.

"Unintended consequences," Ceci said. "Frankly, I think you two should go hike the Himalayas for a couple months and stay as far away from this thing as you can."

Andrew nodded.

"We think so, too," Kerry said. "That's what we've been trying to do but because we've got customers in common, and not just the guys down the street kind of customers, it's tough."

"Gov'mint."

Dar gave her father a wry grin at the dour comment. "Maybe we should start our vacation early," she said. "I don't reall..." She paused as her cell phone range. She fished it out of her pocket and looked at the caller ID. "Mark."

"This could be good, or bad," Kerry said. She watched Dar answer the phone. "Hopefully, it's good."

Dar sat listening, her elbow propped against the table, brows twitching a little.

The other three fell silent, watching her and waiting.

"Okay, so, David Willerson's called you?" Dar said after a long while. "What does he want you to do?" She paused again. "Oh. He wanted you to call me. What a little smarmy chickenshit."

Kerry sighed.

"That doesn't sound promising," Ceci said.

"He said what?" Dar's voice rose.

"Uh oh." Kerry pulled out her Handspring "Let me get a note off to our lawyer."

"Rich Edgerton?" Ceci asked.

Kerry nodded.

"He must be having the time of his life. He once said going into investment management was almost as boring as being a library card sorter."

"Well, well, what do we have here?" A new voice interrupted them. "I do believe I know you people."

Kerry looked up in surprise. "Hi, Hamilton." She indicated a seat. "Join us. I'm sure you want front row center at this circus."

Dar looked up and smiled. "Never guess who just showed up here," she said into the phone. "Hamilton Baird."

Hamilton took the chair, raising his finger at the waitress and pointing to the beer mug in front of Kerry. "I just dropped by your new place and was told I might find you here by a man in a wheelchair on your front porch. Never is boring around you ladies. I will say that."

"They collect personalities," Ceci remarked, in a dry tone.

"Mark, we're at the café down the road from the office. C'mon over." Dar said. "Bye." She disconnected the call. "Smarmy little jacktard said he 'found' Mark's number on a sticky note." She took a sip of her Irish coffee. "Said he was willing to pay him to contact me and get some technical information."

"Million dollars a word, maestro." Hamilton smiled. "Want me to negotiate that for you?"

Dar sat back and hiked one knee up. "Hello, Hamilton," she said. "What brings you to Miami?"

"You," Hamilton said. "I'm now representing a consortium of ILS investors who want to stage an unfriendly takeover since they've seen their shares plummet in the last month."

The waitress arrived and put a cold mug down in front of Hamilton. "You folks like anything else?" she asked. "We've got a bar snack platter special tonight."

"Sure," Kerry said. "Bring enough for everyone."

The waitress smiled at her and vanished.

"I want no part of it, Hamilton," Dar said. "Not that I don't sympathize with the investors. I do."

"Hear me out, maestro." He leaned back and took a sip of his beer. "These are the smart people who tossed money at ILS, not the dumb people. I would not be bothering with the dumb people. I had enough to do with them when I was still drawing a paycheck."

Andrew chuckled under his breath.

"Why do I get the feeling there isn't enough liquor in that bar to cover this," Ceci said.

Dar sighed again. "Let's wait for Mark to get here," she said. "It'll hold another ten minutes." She caught the waitress's eye and pointed at her mug, now empty. "If I have enough of these I can use it as an excuse not to put my hands on a keyboard."

"Darlin', even drunk off your ass you're more competent than those idiots in there right now," Hamilton drawled. "I just got off the phone with Jacques on the way here. He's ready to do whatever."

"Whatever?" Kerry eyed him.

"Whatever. As in, whatever it takes to get the wolves' teeth out of his buttocks," Hamilton clarified. "Where they are verily implanted."

"I don't get it," Ceci said after a moment. "They're the ones who decided they wanted to get rid of these kids here. So why now is everyone losing their minds and wanting action? They did it."

"Yes, they did," Hamilton said. "And they were told what fools they were. But that, for some reason, does not spur in them a desire to get down on their knees and apologize to the world and God for it."

Dar pondered that in silence for a moment. "Doesn't spur in me a desire to help them regardless of the scheme you're going to pitch me."

"Now Dar—"

"I'm not kidding, Hamilton," Dar said. "My first advice would be—put everything back the way it was before you broke it. There were safeguards in place that stored copies of everything so that could be done. This person, this moron they hired, deliberately circumvented and deleted them. They should be arresting him."

Ceci nodded. "What she said."

Hamilton steepled his long fingers together and tapped his lips with the tips of them. "You sure about that, maestro?"

"Am I sure? I'm sure that when I left there was a configuration repository to save a device's configuration every time a change was made, yes," Dar said. "And I'm sure that the operations directives for infrastructure had that requirement in writing."

"It did," Kerry confirmed.

"So if that fella said there wasn't no record of how things were set up before he got there, he's not telling the truth?"

"No," Dar and Kerry answered at the same time. "He's lying," Kerry added.

Hamilton made a little face. "I don't suppose you kept a copy of that stuff somewhere?"

Dar took a breath to respond.

"Like your head?" Hamilton gently interrupted her.

Dar exhaled. "The only old copy of configs I had I already turned over to one of the guys who was trying to help, but they never let him use it. They fired him."

"Moron upon moron upon idiot." Hamilton sighed. "Okay, cut to the chase, Dar. If you had to, could you go in there and go into those things and make them right?"

They paused as the waitress returned with a big, round platter full of exceptionally unhealthy things. She put it down in the middle of the table and handed around long handled forks and napkins. "Go for it, folks."

"Thanks," Andrew said. "Get me another of these?" He held up his mug and the waitress scooted off.

Then all eyes went back to Dar.

After a moment she shrugged. "Sure," she said. "I designed it. It would take me a while to undo whatever it is they did, but I could."

"What's your price?"

Dar shook her head. "Hamilton, I won't do it. Not can't, won't."

"Why not?" he asked. "Dar, these men are literally willing to give you whatever in the world you want to save their shorts. How many times do you get that kind of opportunity?"

"What I seen, every other month," Andrew said. "They done got her saving some damn thing or other thing cause some dumbass made some bad choice."

"Hamilton, I appreciate that," Dar said. "There's just nothing I want that they could give me." She glanced briefly at Kerry. "I've got everything I need pretty much right here at this table."

Her parents smiled. Kerry smiled. Hamilton looked wryly exasperated.

"There's nothing and no one left there for me to even feel like I'd want to do it to make their lives better," Dar said. "Even Jacques, whom I like and respect, was ready to throw me down the river a few times. Hell." She half shrugged. "Even you and Alastair were. I had no friends there."

Hamilton's face shifted into a quiet, serious expression. "That's not one hundred percent true, Dar. But I get it."

"Ah remember being in that big old place," Andrew said. "Listening to them fellas want to fire her that last time. She's right. Ain't no one was on her side in that place."

"I remember when I started working there," Kerry chimed in.

"How many times people there tried to throw Dar under the bus. I remember hearing what they said. I remember seeing what they did. ILS didn't deserve her."

Dar looked from one to the other. "Sometimes I was driving the bus," she said.

"No, Dar, that's not true. Every time you made a decision, no matter who got hurt or in the way, it was the right decision for the company. For all of us," Kerry said firmly. "You don't owe anyone there, especially the stockholders, a goddamned thing."

The sound of a motorbike ended the conversation briefly as Mark arrived, parking his bike in the front of the café and stashing his helmet before joining them. "Hey." He sat down next to Kerry, who handed him a fork and a napkin. "Um...thanks."

"No, darlin', you don't owe them anything," Hamilton said. "You produced value for the company for a good long time. That's not the issue here. No one's saying you should do this. No one's saying you have an obligation."

Mark retrieved a mozzarella stick. "That guy says he's going to tell everyone you broke in and sabotaged the company unless you make things work." He chewed thoughtfully, watching Dar's face. "I told him to fuck off on your behalf."

Hamilton sighed and covered his eyes.

"That's why I'm not going to do anything," Dar said. "Because if I do, no matter what anyone says, or does, or infers, everyone on the planet will believe I screwed it up."

"Glad I sent that note to Richard," Kerry muttered. "If that asshole ever comes near us he better hope I'm not driving Dar's truck because I will — so help me god — run him over with it."

"I told Jacques he needed to fire those guys," Dar said.

"They have contracts," Hamilton responded. "Very expensive ones to buy out. It will be, as you don't need me to tell you, a publicity nightmare."

Dar lifted her hands up. "*CNN* took off to go cover the Interbank outage. I'm surprised they haven't called me back for commentary on it."

Her cell phone rang and she glanced at it then held it up before holding it to her ear. "Hello, Dar Roberts."

Ceci scooped up a bit of ranch dressing with a celery stick and munched on it. "This is one big fat mess."

Andrew shook his head. "This is a squad with the trots and one outhouse kinda mess."

"I told 'em Dar wouldn't do it," Mark said "Matter of fact, since I had him on the phone, I told him exactly what kind of no brain ears out the sides of his asshole jerkwad he was."

Dar had one hand over her ear and the phone pressed to the other. "Yes, I hear you. No, I don't have anything to comment on about that since it's not my problem anymore." She took a sip of her coffee. "I'm sorry they're having issues, but I suggest they direct their questions to the management at ILS. I don't know what's going on."

"Lord," Andrew said. "This ain't never gonna end good."

"You got that right, daddy Roberts," Hamilton said. "Let me go call those poor idiots who sent me and tell them they should go off and buy some banana plantations in Curacao and get out of this damn technology business."

Kerry reached over and put her hand on Dar's thigh, feeling the tension under the fabric of her jeans and the slight vibration as she jiggled her foot restlessly. She met Ceci's eyes across the table, exchanging a faint shake of the head with her as she tried to reason a way through the problem.

There was no reason, though. That was the problem. She could only consider the actions of their replacements as some kind of ego driven insanity and she agreed with Dar one hundred percent that she should stay the hell out of it.

"Yes, I agree it seems odd that a system that was working well stopped working, but again, you would need to ask the current management," Dar said in a firm tone. "I don't want to speculate on what would have caused it." She listened then glanced at Kerry and rolled her eyes. "Do I think it's a cyber attack? I have no idea. I have no data at all to base any theory on."

"You're actually being extraordinarily kind to those people," Ceci said. "They're lucky it's you they're talking to not me."

"Willerson was an ass," Mark said to Kerry, lowering his voice. "I mean, like really. Just all snide and creepy. He made it out like he knew we'd planned this all out, and when I called him on the whole change thing he did, he said he'd sue me if I told anyone else that."

"Wait. He called you for help and then said he was going to sue you? Really? He must be nuts," Kerry said. "What in the world is wrong with these guys? They think this is some kind of stupid game?"

Mark shook his head. "I felt so slimy after talking to him I took a shower."

"Well, yes, I could do that," Dar said into the phone. "If it's a general interview on how that type of technology works, sure." She glanced at her watch. "I'm at a café down the road from our offices. If you want to come back over, I'll give you a few minutes."

"Lord."

"C'mon, Dad, don't you want to be on *CNN*?" Kerry smiled at him.

"No, I do not."

"Okay see you in a little while." Dar released the line and let her head drop back against the back of the chair. "Son of a bitch."

"Wouldn't take no for an answer?" Ceci guessed. "Well, I've seen you on television, kid. You draw eyeballs." She regarded her tall offspring and smiled at the droll expression directed back at her. "Make sure you get a nice plug in for the new company."

"Kill me now," Dar said. "Mark, where did you leave it with this jackass?"

"Told him he needed to clean up his own shit," Mark said. "Sorry, Dar. I wasn't going to let him talk smack to me, especially when he was calling me to beg for help."

"Didn't have the guts to call me directly?" Dar smiled briefly. "I know my home number's in the records there. Hasn't changed in years. He wouldn't have even had to search for a sticky note."

"The angle he took was, he was doing this as like a favor to me, sort of letting me come back in and help you help him so you didn't have to get dragged in the mud," Mark said. "He said if he went public, you could kiss your new business goodbye."

Hamilton turned his head toward Andrew. "What do you say we go visit this gentleman? He's from the North, y'know."

Andrew looked thoughtful. "If that there feller is making threats at my kids, I do believe I should go talk with him."

"Let's wait until after *CNN* interviews Dar for that." Ceci took a sip of her wine. "Because that would be too much excitement for them to handle and I want to put a deposit down first on that little cottage in St. John's for us to escape to."

Dar leaned forward and put her elbows on the table. "Hamilton," she said. "Can you get me the number of Higgs, the jackass who replaced me?"

"He didn't," Hamilton said, straightforwardly. "But I can get you his phone number, sure."

Dar made a come hither gesture at him. "Let me make one stab at giving him some advice. Jacques wouldn't take it, maybe he will."

Hamilton started fishing in his cell phone, shaking his head all the while. "More chance of getting a pig to sing," he lamented. "But what the hidey hell. Let's give it a whirl."

Chapter Twelve

THE *CNN* LADY producer turned her ball cap around and settled it back on her head. "So just for some prelim, we went over and tried to get some information about this outage that's apparently affecting a good portion of the banking business."

"Interbank," Dar said. She was seated behind her office desk, leaned back in her comfortable chair and had her hands wrapped around one hiked knee. "It's a central clearinghouse, a meet point for a lot of the large banks where they exchange information."

"Right."

"Lets you use some other bank's ATM from your own," Dar said.

"Exactly," the producer said. "So ILS runs it." Dar shook her head. "No?"

"No. Interbank runs itself. It happens to have contracted a third party to carry the connections instead of building their own network. Lot of companies do that. Building and maintaining a wide area network is hellish expensive and complicated."

"Ah." The woman took a seat across from Dar. "How does that work?"

"Same way as you buy telephone service for your house," Dar's said. "Or to be more familiar to you, it's how you buy satellite transponder space from Intelsat to send your signals to and from Atlanta."

"Ah!" The woman nodded. "So they buy transport."

"Yes. Transport and the management services that goes with it. Making sure there's enough bandwidth, tracking outages, rerouting, all the things that go with keeping the data going from point a to point b," Dar said.

"So what'd they screw up, Dar?" the woman asked. "I know you know. I heard them talking in the background in a different room than we were in. Didn't know we were listening."

They were alone in the office. Kerry and the rest of the gang were entertaining the camera team and the on screen talent downstairs, serving them gratefully received strong coffee. Hamilton had driven off to go have a meeting with someone. Dar hoped as soon as they were finished talking she could take Kerry home and fall into bed. Long ass day.

"I can't discuss that on the record," she said candidly.

"Why?" the woman asked. "You don't work there anymore. It's a cock up. We know about it. Why not give me a scoop?"

Dar shook her head. "Sorry, Cheryl," she said. "If they decide to go public, I'll comment on it, but I'm not going to talk about someone else's problems."

"That's an interesting bit of integrity," Cheryl responded. "Because I'm pretty sure if you'd been the one who caused the problem they would have outed you in a heartbeat." She smiled. "I tried to make them."

Dar smiled back. "It's always better to stick to the truth or nothing at all."

They studied each other in silence for a bit. "So no, huh?" Cheryl finally said. "It's frustrating for us because we know there's news here. You get a sense for that after you do what I do for a while."

"There is," Dar said straightforwardly. "Unfortunately, it's not my news to discuss. It's their issue, it's their customers."

Cheryl eyed her thoughtfully. "We could make this off the record. I could make you an anonymous source. They don't have to know."

"I'd know."

Cheryl lifted her hand up and let it drop down. "Okay, fair enough. Mind if I ask you one more question?"

"Nope." Dar glanced at her Handspring, hoping Higgs wouldn't pick now to call her back.

"How did ILS deal with you being gay?" Cheryl asked. "I assume they knew."

"They knew," Dar responded. "There were people who probably cared and were disgusted, but as a corporation ILS didn't care. Even when Kerry and I became an item, they didn't care. They put an exception in our employment records and we carried on."

"Because you were important."

Dar nodded after a brief pause. "If I was working in the mailroom, probably would have been a different reaction. I was useful to them. They needed my skill set, and, in fact, they appreciated Kerry's."

"Practical."

Dar stood up and stretched. "We did a good job for them. We ready to do this interview? My day's about to end." She pondered taking the following morning off before the flight to Washington, the idea becoming rapidly very appealing.

"Sure," Cheryl said. "The reason I asked about that is the guy we talked to over there inferred that you left because you felt you were being pressured to leave due to your lifestyle."

Dar laughed.

"No, huh?"

Dar took a step back and leaned against the windowsill, folding her arms over her chest. "I've been out of the closet for a lot longer than I was being strategic for ILS," she said. "The only pressure I was feeling in terms of getting out of there was the pressure to be my own boss."

"Hon?" Kerry poked her head in the office. "Can we get this show on the road? The kids are waiting for dinner."

"We're heading down." Dar pushed off the sill and waved Cheryl ahead of her. "I was just being grilled on the nerve wracking consequences of our bedroom."

Kerry stopped in mid-motion and looked from Cheryl to Dar. "Uh what?"

Cheryl went with the flow. "You have kids?"

"Dogs." Kerry held the door open. "Two Labrador Retrievers. Now what was that about our bedroom?"

"THINK HE'S GOING to call you back?" Kerry had the car seat pitched back and she was sprawled across it, eyes closed as the ferry rumbled its way across the channel. "At this point I sure hope not."

"Don't care," Dar responded, eyes also closed. "We're taking tomorrow off."

"I love you."

Dar smiled into the darkness of the interior of the truck. "Did I do okay with that interview?" She turned her head and looked at Kerry. "I felt kind of dorky."

"Actually, you came off as reserved yet mysterious." Kerry rubbed her nose, pinching the bridge of it. "I liked when you started talking about BGP routing metrics after he kept asking you about what could cause stuff like that to go down."

"Mm. Well, that is one reason it might stop working. Wrong metrics," Dar said, stifling a yawn. "Maybe that's what that monkey did. Skewed the metrics. That would fit the symptoms."

"Well great, Dardar. When Willerson sees the *CNN* report, maybe it'll give him a brainwave and he'll fix his problem." Kerry patted her leg. "Tell you what, though, I'm glad Mom and Dad are back."

"Me too."

Kerry smiled at the prompt and immediate response. "I hope we get this contract all settled out in the next couple days. I don't want that hanging over us when we head out to the Grand Canyon," she said. "This is going to be so much fun, Dar."

"I think I'm going to wear those new hiking boots to the gym tomorrow. Break them in a little," Dar said as the ferry pulled up the dock and she moved her seat upright. "I don't want to mess with blisters on the trip."

"We can hike around the island, too," Kerry said, straightening up her own seat as they got ready to drive off the deck. "That's a good idea."

Dar put the truck in gear and drove up the ramp, giving the man directing traffic a casual wave. They got up to the top of the slope and she was about to turn left onto the perimeter road when a figure in a security uniform trotted toward her, waving his arm. "Ah."

"Oh, please no drama," Kerry moaned. "It's too damn late, Dar."

Dar pulled the truck to a halt and opened the window. "Hey, Charles."

"Ms. Roberts!" He leaned on the side of the vehicle. "Glad I caught you. Listen, have you heard from Billy, since the other night?"

Dar shook her head. "Not a word. Why? He suing?"

"We don't know," Charles said. "We haven't heard a peep from him and Clemente went over to do his cleaning service and there's no sign of the guy. We were just wondering if you'd seen him, or if he'd contacted you."

Dar looked at Kerry, who was leaning on the console. "Maybe he took off for a while?" she said. "Figured he'd let things cool off?"

"Maybe," Charles said. "But we don't have record of him going off island and he didn't have a boat."

"Could have gone on someone else's," Kerry said. "Or he could have been in someone else's car going off the island. You all don't check everyone in the back seat, do you?"

"That's true enough, ma'am, but it just seems strange, you know? He was around and about the island for weeks before that, kinda bothering everyone, now poof. He's gone."

"Well, in a week or so we'll be gone so if we see him before that, we'll let you know," Dar said. "Ker and I and the dogs are going on vacation."

Charles smiled. "We'll keep an eye on the place for you, ma'am. Don't worry." He tapped the door and stepped back, giving them a wave as Dar rolled up the window and they proceeded on.

"That was weird," Kerry said. They pulled into the lower level parking and Dar tucked the truck into the spot next to her SUV. "Dar, did it sound to you like they thought we might know if something happened to that guy?"

Dar rested her hands on the wheel and considered. "No," she said after a moment. "I think they were just asking everyone they knew was involved with him." She opened the door to the truck and slid out, shutting the door and heading for the steps up to their home. As she reached the door her Handspring started ringing and she pulled it out. "You know what?"

Kerry reached around her to key the door open. "What?" She pushed the door inward and stepped in quickly to greet Chino and Mocha's excited wiggling.

"Fuck him." Dar hit the ignore button and shoved the phone back in her front pocket, sending the call to voice mail. "I gave him a chance. I'm done." She followed Kerry inside and shut the door, reaching down to pick up the frantic Mocha puppy. "C'mere, squiglet."

"Are you glad to see us, kids?" Kerry knelt and gave Chino a hug. "Did you take care of the little man today, Chi?"

"Growf." Chino wagged her tail gently.

"Time for dinner." Kerry stood up and moved toward the kitchen, picking up the mail on the dining room table and sorting through it as she walked. She put the stack down and went to the cupboard, taking out two portions of dog food and retrieving a mixture of chopped beef and chicken from the refrigerator.

Mocha hopped up and down at her feet, his front paws scrabbling at her kneecap. "Yap!"

"Yes, I can see you're hungry." Kerry assembled the meal and put it down, getting hastily out of the way as the dogs hoovered the contents as though they were being chased down by wolves threatening to take it away from them. "Take it easy, guys."

Dar wandered in behind her and draped her arms over Kerry's shoulders. "I turned off my phone. I think we should just move on. Let's go to DC tomorrow and just leave ILS behind."

"I'm all for that, hon. I just hope ILS doesn't chase after us, given our mutual customers." Kerry enjoyed the warmth surrounding her. "You want some tea?"

"Sure," Dar said. "I'm going to go change and chill out." She gave Kerry a squeeze, then released her and stepped over the dogs, busy licking their dishes clean. "Like little vacuum cleaners."

Chino left her empty dish and went to the dog door, bustling through. Mocha first made sure she didn't leave any food behind, then chased after her, yelping as the door flap swung back and nearly knocked him over.

Kerry chuckled and went to the door. "I'm going to stretch out a little." She opened the door and went out onto the landing and watched the dogs bolt down the steps into the cozily lit garden. "Nice night."

It was clear overhead and the stars were vivid against the darkness. Kerry went down the steps and walked over to the seating area, going into the work space and putting water on to heat.

She could have done it inside, of course, but there was something sweet in the air that made her want to savor the night and she got out the small tea set she kept in the outdoor cupboard as she hummed softly under her breath.

Kerry glanced over her shoulder, giving the dogs an indulgent smile as they chased each other in a circle. She set the pot on the burner and stepped to one side, reaching up and grasping the chinning bar Dar had installed there and letting her back stretch out.

It felt good, easing muscles that were cramped from too much sitting around during the whole of the long day. She slowly let her knees unlock and relax, taking her weight on her firmly gripped hands and feeling her shoulders rotate and pop into place. "Ah."

Chino spotted her and paused, then picked up a sadly bedraggled stuffed lamb and raced over.

Kerry pulled herself up, getting her feet under her as she was nearly knocked off them. "Hey!"

Chino pushed the sodden toy into her thigh.

"Yuk." Kerry took it and tossed it across the garden, then retreated back to the little outdoor stove to measure out some dried green tea leaves and added a handful of mint leaves along with it into the ceramic teapot.

"C'mere." Dar's voice echoed softly over the garden, along with the rasp and scuff as she trotted down the steps. "Give me that."

Kerry smiled as she poured the heated water over the leaves, then set the top on to let the herbs steep. There was something charming and old fashioned about the beverage and she enjoyed mixing the tea leaves with other things to mix it up a little.

"Got orange peel in there this time?" Dar cocked her arm and tossed the ragged lamb. "I brought out the cookies."

"Mint this time." Kerry left the pot alone and went over to the bar again, gripping it and steeling herself for the effort of doing a chin up. She paused a moment then lifted herself off the ground, letting her legs relax.

"Nice." Dar sprawled in the canvas bucket chair, watching her. She took the lamb Chino tossed onto her stomach and threw it again. "You're getting better at that."

Kerry managed a grin as she got through a couple more of the exercises, feeling the burn in her arms. "Thanks, honey."

"And you look sexy doing it."

"Dar, no one looks sexy doing pull ups." Kerry let herself down and released the bar, shaking out her hands. "At best, you don't look like a wuss."

Dar chuckled. "When I was in school they always tried to make me use the girls' bars," she said. "Idiotic."

"Cause you were too butch?" Kerry leaned over the chair and gave her a kiss on the head.

"No. I was nearly six feet tall at the time. The bar was only a foot over my head. I could hop and get my chin over it. I finally just started using the guys' high bar."

"And your gym instructors didn't realize this? Where did they park their guide dogs?" Kerry asked. "Or were they just oblivious?"

"I was a smart ass. They didn't like me."

"That's my favorite part of you." Kerry grabbed the lamb and sent it flying. "Their loss." She went over to the table, retrieved the teapot and poured out two cups, adding honey to them. Then she came back over to where Dar was sitting and set the tray down. "I never got the chance to try that in high school. We did do the uneven bars when I messed with gymnastics, though."

"Bet you were cute." Dar picked up her tea and blew cautiously on it, then sipped.

"Bet I was a complete dork and I have pictures to prove it," Kerry said. "I think I hold my school record for falling flat on my butt, or worse on my head." She handed Dar a cookie and took one, then sat down and leaned back as the dogs came trotting over. "Ah, the cookie monsters heard us chewing."

Dar broke off a bit of her cookie and offered it to Chino. "Want to turn on the news?"

"Nope."

"Me either. Turned off the phone and I'm just going to enjoy the rest of our night."

Kerry lifted her tea cup and they touched edges with a soft clash of crockery. "Sounds good to me."

KERRY TAPPED HER boxing gloves together then edged around and started punching the heavy hanging bag in front of her.

It was midmorning and she was thoroughly soaked in sweat, but satisfied with her efforts so far. She felt a deep burn in her shoulders as she pounded the bag's surface.

Dar was doing bench presses nearby, flat on her back on the pressing bench, steadily lifting a bar in an easy rhythm up from her chest.

Kerry moved around to get a better look and amused herself by watching the play of the light on Dar's nearly bare body, admiring the sculpted shape as she studiously exercised.

A moment later the swinging bag swung a little further than she'd expected and whomped her backward. She rocked back off her feet and landed on her butt, arms flailing. "Whoa!" she yelped. "Ouch!"

Dar racked her weight bar and got up, scooting over to where Kerry was now flat on her back, knees hiked up and one arm over her eyes as she laughed silently. "You okay?" Dar went down to one knee and put her hand on Kerry's stomach. "Ker?"

Kerry chortled softly. "Yeah, I'm fine." She wiped the sweat from her eyes. "Serves me right for lusting after you in public."

"Huh?" Dar sat down next to her. "When were you doing that?" She glanced around, but the gym was empty save the two of them. She reached over and smoothed the sweat dampened hair from Kerry's eyes and watched them close briefly, then open again.

"Just now." Kerry extended her legs out on the padded surface and folded her hands over her stomach. "I was so busy watching you I didn't realize the bag was swinging at me and it smacked me in the head."

Dar leaned over and kissed her on the lips. "You really give my ego a boost." She smiled. "But try not to do that, hon. You'll end up with a bruise."

Kerry contentedly absorbed the look of affection in Dar's eyes as she regarded her. "My ego raises your ego one." She exhaled. "What a couple of goofy saps we are."

"We are," Dar said. "Want to go for a swim?"

"Yes." Kerry sat up and tugged on the glove strings with her teeth. "That would feel absolutely awesome right now. I'm soaked."

Dar gently removed the strings from her incisors and untied the gloves for her, both of them sitting there on the padded ground splashed in warm sunlight from the windows. "Indoor pool, then hydro, then shower."

Kerry got up and collected her gear. "Then lunch." She followed Dar through the gym toward the changing area. "I'm so damn glad we took today off. It's so nice to chill out and spend some time just doing stuff."

"Uh huh."

"Just during the week when it's quiet here instead of on the weekend, when it's packed." Kerry exchanged her boxing outfit for a swimsuit. "Not having to be at the office."

Dar came over and leaned on the teak wood locker. "Tired of our new one?"

Kerry thought about that as she got her towel out and wrapped it around her neck. "I like our new place."

"I do, too," Dar said after a long silence.

They walked toward the gym's indoor pool and passed through the door into a humid, chemical scented space with thick plastic panels surrounding a placidly lapping concrete lake.

Kerry put her towel on a ring hung on the wall. "I just like spending time like this not working," she admitted with a wry grin. "Maybe after our vacation I'll get it out of my system. I think I got the idea of not working in my head after we got let go, so that minute of 'oh cool!' is still in there."

Dar nodded in a thoughtful sort of way. She hung her own towel and stretched her arms out, flexing her hands and then putting them on her hips. "Yeah," she eventually responded. "Is what it is I guess." She walked over to the side of the pool and dove in.

Kerry folded her arms over her chest and thought about that for a long moment, long enough for Dar to surface and stroke across to the other side of the pool with an easy motion. Then she shrugged and went to the side of the pool, preparing to dive in herself.

Her attention was drawn by the sound of the door to the pool room opening and closing and she glanced over to see a tall, heavily built man entering. "Good morning," she said, vaguely remembering the man's face but not entirely sure of from where.

He paused, and regarded her. "Morning." He changed direction and headed her way. "Been wanting to speak to you two people."

Kerry wasn't surprised to hear the motion of water and a splash as Dar came up out of the pool, sensing the compression of the air as Dar arrived at her back.

The man's voice was gruff but not threatening, but it was nice to have that presence behind her anyway. "Sure," Kerry said. "What can we do for you?" She remembered who the man was just as he closed on them.

"Hello, Jim," Dar said. "What's up?"

He nodded at Dar. "My daughter told me all about what happened at the store. I appreciate your getting involved, Roberts, because I don't like people being jerks to anyone on this island, much less my kid."

"He was a jerk," Dar said. "I didn't appreciate that either."

Jim nodded again. "So thanks for that. But now we come to this. I don't like the way you people live, and I don't want my kid exposed to it."

He stopped speaking and regarded them.

"Too fucking bad," Dar responded promptly. "Grow up and come into the twenty first century. Kerry and I don't bother anyone." She put her hand on Kerry's back and felt the tension under her fingertips.

"I know that," he said. "Or I'd have already had you kicked out of here. I'm not into bullshit and I don't think you are either. But my daughter means everything to me."

Kerry put her hands on her hips. "What exactly do you think we're going to do to her?" she asked. "She told us you didn't like gay people. Okay. I get it. My father didn't either. But you think we're going to sell her tickets to a Melissa Etheridge concert and turn her gay or something?"

He paused and looked at her.

"I was gay before I met Dar," Kerry said. "And I was brought up in a very conservative family, went to Sunday school, went to Christian high school, you name it. Didn't stop me from being gay."

"We don't recruit." Dar looked and sounded faintly amused. "Jim, I grew up on a Navy base. If proximity to testicular overload could have kept me straight, it would have. Trust me. I saw more well hung naked men before I was ten than you probably have in your life."

Kerry pinched the bridge of her nose. "That was a mental image I didn't need," she muttered.

"That's not the point," Jim said. "I don't want her getting any ideas."

"Well, all I can tell you is, any ideas she might get won't be from us. We're in a closed relationship." Kerry said. "I've never talked to your daughter about anything other than artisanal cheese and French bread."

Dar leaned closer. "I get the protective father thing, Jim. I've got one, too. Lucky for me he's not a closed minded bigot like you are."

"I'm not a bigot," he said. "I just don't like gay people. I don't want them around my family." He didn't seem angry, just resolute. "So my advice to you is find some other place to live, because I've got ways to make it very uncomfortable for you here. Don't push me to that."

Kerry felt Dar's whole body stiffen and she put her hand out to stop her forward motion. "Not worth it, hon."

Dar stopped and went still and took a few breaths. "No, you're right," she said in a flat tone. "Jim, you better find yourself a new place to live. Because if it's the last thing I do on earth I will ruin you and you will truly regret ever saying that to me."

The ice in Dar's voice put a chill down Kerry's spine. She stayed still and watched Jim and Dar lock eyes, keeping her jaw locked shut on the torrent of angry words piling up behind her tongue.

Jim's eyes narrowed. "I don't take threats well, Roberts."

"Neither do I," Dar responded instantly, a rasp on the edge of her voice. "Especially not a slimy, pointless threat like yours is. I've lived here a decade and paid your resident's fees. You took them and you knew damn well what my lifestyle was. So now I save your damn daughter from being raped and you threaten to have me evicted? Fuck you. Fuck you and everyone like you."

Dar was furious. Kerry had never actually seen her this angry and she was at a loss to know what to do to defuse it. Or if she should, because that anger felt clean and right to her.

It was at that point where dangerous things could happen and for a moment she was sure they would. Dar's body was vibrating with tension and Kerry knew there was a potent, actual threat in the tall frame next to her.

Maybe Jim realized it. Or maybe he was smarter than he appeared, because he took a step back and lifted one hand up in a holding gesture. "I can see this has the potential of getting very unpleasant for both of us."

"Are you used to having people just run away or cave in when you threaten them?" Kerry asked with a note of curiousness in her voice. "Please don't expect that from us."

He turned his eyes to her. "I am used to that and people usually do back off. I've got a lot of power on this island and most people who live here want to."

Kerry felt Dar shift next to her. "I appreciate that. It's a very nice place to live. But the business Dar and I are in? You don't want to get in that kind of fight with us."

He exhaled and put his fists on his hips, shifting his attention from Kerry to Dar's set, cold expression. "Know what? You're right," he said. "You did me a big favor. I'm just scared and my wife is scared, that you're going to influence our daughter. Especially that she told us you offered her a job. I get crazy."

Kerry felt Dar slowly relax next to her. "That was my screw-up," she said. "She said she wasn't going to college and we just started a new business. She's a bright kid. I had no idea you were a homophobe until after I asked her."

He shook his head. "She's going to work for me," he said, "but I'm..." He lifted a hand again and then let it fall. "Apologies. Just stay away from her." He turned and walked hurriedly out of the pool area, letting the door swing shut behind him.

Dar let out a long, shaking breath. "Mother fucking son of a bitch."

Kerry nodded. "What you said."

"I think I'm going to throw up." Dar folded her arms over her stomach, hunching her shoulders and blinking. "Holy crap."

"We absolutely are going to move," Kerry said after a moment. She put her hand on Dar's arm. "But at our time and when we feel like it, not his."

"Yeah." Dar went over and sat on one of the high top chairs scattered around, leaning back and covering her eyes with one hand.

"You okay, hon?" Kerry went over and took hold of her free hand, chafing the cold fingers between her own. "I thought for a minute I was going to be a witness to murder there."

"Close. I was seeing blood red," Dar admitted. "What an idiot."

Kerry saw the pulse point fluttering against the skin of Dar's neck and she shifted her hands, moving them to her shoulders and gently massaging them. "Easy, babe," she murmured. "Just breathe, huh?"

"Ungh." Dar grunted. "What a jerk."

"Maybe we should have gone into work instead," Kerry said. "This wasn't what I was expecting to get out of our pool session." She continued to knead the skin across Dar's shoulders and felt the tension slowly ease.

"Holy crap he pissed me off."

"Yeah. I know." Kerry leaned over and kissed the damp skin behind Dar's right ear. "Really not worth you getting so worked up, my love. There are always idiots in the world, you know?"

"I know. I just didn't expect..." Dar leaned to one side, resting her elbow on the chair arm and letting her head lay on Kerry's shoulder. "Didn't expect to get that kind of reaction for doing something I thought was right."

No. Kerry sighed, and draped her arm over Dar's shoulders. She remembered with somber vividness the moment in her own life when she had to face that hatred and she knew in her gut what Dar meant.

"Why the hell do people have to be so damned stupid?" Dar asked. "At what point is humanity going to grow the fuck up and stop inventing reasons to hate?"

"C'mon. Let's go back home and play with our kids," Kerry said. "I've about lost my taste for the facilities here today."

Dar got up off the chair and took Kerry's hand in hers as they walked across the concrete deck back toward the gym. "You know what we could do?"

Kerry cleared her throat a little. "Find a place in the Grove?"

"Mind reader."

KERRY FINISHED PACKING their overnight bags and set them down near the door. She glanced over her shoulder at the couch where Dar was curled up with both dogs draped over her as she studied a small notebook.

She was wearing a pair of dark cargo pants, a rugby shirt and looked quite adorable to Kerry's appreciative eyes. Especially with Mocha curled up behind her left knee, resting his small head on it.

It was quiet and peaceful and the stress of the morning had slowly dissipated, though the feeling of disappointment didn't. Looking around at this place she'd called home for the last few years now made her a little sad.

Ah well. Kerry sighed and leaned against the door, dismissing the thoughts as unproductive. It was late afternoon. They had about a half hour before they would have to leave for the airport and she'd just received a call from the marina letting her know that Andrew and Ceci were pulling into a guest slip and tying up.

"Hon?" Kerry went over and perched on the arm of the couch. "We going to tell your folks about Jim?"

"Yes," Dar said without looking up. "In case he decides to try something stupid while we're gone I want them to know what's up."

"You think he will?"

Dar shrugged. "Depends. Did he really back off or did he just not want to end up in a boxing match with me?"

Kerry got up and went to her briefcase and Dar's somewhat retro looking messenger bag and started putting the folders full of presentation material into them. "Are we letting your dad drive us to the airport?"

"Nah, I'll just park the truck there."

Dar got up and set Mocha down on the floor, then walked over to the dining room table and handed over her notebook. "I'm glad we're going out of town tonight."

"Me too. I still feel kinda slimy after what happened this morning." Kerry tucked the notebook into Dar's bag along with a sack of hard candies. She fastened the flap and stood back, resting her hands on a chair and considering if she'd remembered everything.

"Thanks." Dar nibbled her ear, sending her thoughts rapidly off track. "For taking care of all the details so I don't show up there with half my gear forgotten."

Kerry smiled. "My pleasure." She lifted Dar's hand and kissed the knuckles, then ducked past her as the front door bell rang. "I'd get some beer ready. I think they're gonna need it."

"Mm." Dar detoured to the kitchen, listening to Kerry's voice as she greeted Andrew and Ceci. She opened the refrigerator and studied the contents. "Beer or milk?" she mused. "Maybe a beer for Mom, and chocolate milk for Dad?"

"Dar?" Kerry's voice echoed softly from the dining room.

"On the way." Dar plunked a choice of beverages on a round wooden tray and headed out into the living room where Andrew and Ceci were now occupying the love seat, having gained the rapt attention of the two dogs. "Hi."

"Hi." Ceci eyed her. "What exactly are we going to hear about that you're bringing everything from seltzer water to vodka out?"

"Vodka's for me," Dar said, putting the tray down. "It was that kind of morning."

"Lord." Andrew sat up and stared at her. "What in the hell happened? You get drafted? By the Army?"

"Don't give them any ideas, Andrew"

DAR WATCHED THE lights go past through the window of the hotel room, idly listening to Kerry talking to her mother in the background. It was dark and they'd landed a half hour prior. It seemed that a sushi dinner was in her future with a senator and probably some aides.

That was all right. She didn't mind spending some time with Kerry's mother. At least it would keep her mind off the stresses of the day and keep her from thinking about their morning presentation tomorrow.

"Okay, we'll meet you there in twenty minutes." Kerry said. "Bye, Mother." She hung up and came over to where Dar was sprawled, perching on the arm of the chair she was sitting in. "We're going to that little Japanese place I told you I went to with her the last time I was here."

Dar amiably nodded. "Sure. Round of Saki and a platter to share is just about what I'm in the mood for right now." She let her head bump against Kerry's hip. "Don't even mind that it's with your mother."

Kerry chuckled. "Yeah, the world sure has changed."

"You going to tell her your name has?" Dar asked.

"Oh, hmm...you know I sort of forgot about that," Kerry said. "What do you think her reaction's going to be?"

Dar thought about that for a minute. "Damned if I know. On one hand, she's pretty up on the whole family thing, but on the other hand..."

"She was married to my father and changed her name to his," Kerry said. "So yeah, she shouldn't have much to say about that, but sometimes my mother is oblivious to hypocrisy."

"Up to you, babe. I'll go along with whatever you tell her." Dar half closed her eyes as Kerry gently ran her fingers through her hair. "Today sucked my brain out. Hope it soaks back in overnight."

"C'mon." Kerry got up and plucked Dar's sleeve. "It's only a couple blocks from here. Let's walk over."

So they did. Dar zipped up her leather jacket and stuck her hands in her pockets, following Kerry out the front door of their hotel and out onto the sidewalk.

It was cold and windy, but as Kerry had promised the walk wasn't long. In under ten minutes they were turning into the entrance of the restaurant, Dar pulling the door open and standing aside to let Kerry precede her inside.

"Thank you," Kerry said. She hooked a finger into one of Dar's pockets and pulled her along as they entered the small restaurant and stopped at the seating station. "Hello," Kerry greeted the young woman standing there. "I'm expecting at least one more person, so maybe a table for four?"

"Yes." The woman picked up some menus and gestured to them to follow her. She led the way through the mostly empty restaurant to a lacquered table in the center. "Okay?"

"Fine." Kerry took a seat and picked up the menu as Dar went around the table and sat down to her right. "Can we get two glasses of white wine to start?"

"Yes, sure." The waitress whisked off to the bar.

Dar leaned back in her chair and looked around. The restaurant had booths around the edges and a square sushi bar where five or six patrons were seated with plates in front of them. It looked like a thousand other sushi joints she'd been in but the customers here were a touch more conservatively dressed and there was no big fish tank.

The restaurant door opened and Kerry's mother entered with an aide at her side. Dar lifted a hand in greeting, gently nudging Kerry's knee under the table.

Cynthia Stuart brightened, then evaded the hostess and came over to the table. She slipped her fur lined jacket off and settled it on the back of the chair. The aide remained behind, slipping past them and taking a seat at the end of the sushi bar. "Hello there, Kerrison, Dar, how nice it is to see you."

Kerry felt the slightly squirmy discomfort of not knowing exactly how to respond, but she stood and took her mother's outstretched hands, giving them a squeeze. "Hello, Mother. Thanks for agreeing to subject yourself to sushi again for our sakes."

"Oh, but it's no sacrifice." Cynthia released her and sat down, settling the small white napkin on her lap. "I have been coming here quite often since your last visit. I do quite enjoy it now."

"That's cool," Kerry responded. "I'm glad I introduced you to it then."

Dar cleared her throat and kept quiet, feeling more than just a little zoned after the long day. She listened to Kerry and her mother exchange pleasantries, content to sip her wine and ponder the menu.

"The intelligence committee is so looking forward to hearing you speak tomorrow, Dar." Cynthia caught her attention away from the unagi. "There has been quite a lot of debate about this new program of the administration's."

"I can imagine," Dar said. "Hope they feel the same way after I stop talking. I tend to get pretty technical."

"Oh I'm sure it will be fine," Cynthia said and then paused, seeing the wry look on Kerry's face. "Won't it?"

"There's no doubt, Dar does get technical," Kerry said. "But it's a technical subject so I think you'll all have to muddle along. I'll be there to translate for you though if you want, Mother."

"Oh." Cynthia blinked a little. "Yes I'm sure it'll work out just fine then," she said in a determined tone. "It's quite amusing you know. Some of my colleagues were fit to be tied about the whole thing until the president showed his support."

"They probably swallowed so much bile they turned the color of a salamander," Kerry said. She looked up as the waitress returned for their order. "What's it going to be, Dardar?"

"Mm...spicy tuna roll and a chef's choice," Dar said after a pause. "And some hot green tea, please."

"Same," Kerry said. She stacked her menu on Dar's and leaned back a little as her mother ordered and the waitress zipped off. "How's Angie doing? I got an email from her the other day sounds like she's having some fun with the kids."

"It's been quite active," Cynthia said. "She and Brian have just finished some house hunting. I think they're going to make a decision soon. Though I have enjoyed having the children around the house, it's right for them to want to start their own I think."

"Given Kerry's tendency to smash your furniture, I'm sure it's probably safer that way in the long run," Dar said, ignoring the droll look she got from Kerry. "I think that was the only comic relief to be had that night."

Cynthia looked uncertain then she smiled, apparently deciding Dar was making a joke. "Yes, that was a terrible, long, and stress-filled day. I hope I never see another like it."

"Oh, me either," Kerry agreed at once. "Never want to go through that again. I think that's one of the reasons Dar and I decided to participate in this new program. Maybe something we can do can prevent that."

"That's exactly what the administration said in the proposal," Cynthia said. "That we had to find a way to make the technology work for us to give us a way to stop this sort of thing before it happens."

"Well, that's the idea," Dar said.

"You can do that then?" Cynthia asked.

"Dar can do pretty much anything when it comes to technology, Mother." Kerry took a sip of her wine. "I've gotten a whole new appreciation for that after the last month of us starting up our own business."

Dar produced a charming smile at that. "Flatterer."

"Not really," Kerry said. "All these people are calling us, wanting all these different things and Dar is just like, 'yeah, I can code that, no problem.'" She flicked her fingers in a throwaway gesture. "Want an accounting system? I got that, no problem. Do we need a customer database? Give me a minute, I have that on a hard drive here somewhere."

Dar started laughing. "Ker."

"Sweetheart, it's true." Kerry mock sighed. "Somehow ILS had you so busy being management they forgot to take shameless advantage of you as a programmer."

"Well, isn't that nice?" Cynthia rallied gamely. "If that's so, then I think this project will be successful. It would be nice to have a political scene become something useful for a change."

"We'll do our best," Dar said.

Cynthia nodded. "And how has it been going with your new business?" she asked. "It must be strange after working for that other company for so long, Dar?"

"A little. We'd already tendered our resignation though," Dar said. "So in the end it was just annoying with all the garbage going on." She leaned back as the waitress returned to deliver their sushi. "After all that time, it would have been nice to have a graceful exit."

"Many of my colleagues feel the same," Cynthia said. "And very often end up being chased out of their offices by newcomers with very little ceremony."

"Wonder what that's like at the White House?" Kerry mused. "That must be weird."

Dar wielded her chopsticks, tapping the tips together. "Wonder if they do things like leave an old fish in a garbage can in the Oval Office."

Kerry snickered.

Cynthia frowned. "I'm sure they don't. After all, these are professional people." She paused in thought.

"Thinking twice about that?" Kerry's eyes twinkled a little. "But seriously, I think in the past even though there was a lot of head bashing and competition, there was a sense of...um..."

"Decorum," Dar supplied.

Kerry nodded. "Yes. That you didn't always get to hear exactly what everyone was thinking. That's faded."

"But anyway..." Dar paused as her phone rang. She pulled it out and glanced at it and then gave Kerry an apologetic look as she stood and pushed her chair in. "Be right back."

"Oh, boy." Kerry watched her step outside. "I'm sure that's not good."

Her mother eyed her warily. "Is something the matter?" she asked in a diffident tone.

Kerry used a piece of sushi to give herself a moment to think about answering. Then she swallowed. "Where do I start?" she answered wryly. "So much has happened in the last month. But what Dar's worried about right now, and me too, is that our former company is kind of in the crapper."

Cynthia's eyebrows lifted. "Kerrison."

Kerry chewed another piece of sushi and swallowed it. "Actually I was going to say it was a Technicolor clusterfuck but I thought you'd freak out."

Cynthia stared at her, chopsticks half lifted in one hand.

Kerry winked at her, then went back to her plate. "Want to hear the details?"

DAR WAITED FOR the door to swing shut behind her before she answered the call. "Dar Roberts." She leaned against the wall of the restaurant, watching the cars go by.

"Hey, Dar, it's Mark."

"Hey."

"So listen, I know you guys are up in DC, but that skanky guy called me again," Mark said. "Only this time he wasn't slimy, you know? He was scared shitless."

"Well, that's better than slimy, I guess." Dar hitched one knee up. "So what'd he want now?"

"What he said was, okay, so, no bull, he'd be very grateful for any information me, or you, would be willing to give him to get this fixed."

"That is better than slimy. It's borderline honest," Dar said. "So, I assume you told him the obvious—put things back?"

"Sure. He didn't go so far as to say he'd tanked the repository, but he said it was down and far as he knew, unrecoverable."

"Idiot."

"Yeah."

Dar studied the road in front of her. "Shit."

"You came to the same conclusion I did, then," Mark said. "Hey, you're pretty close to Herndon, right? That's got both sides, you can get to everything."

Dar considered walking...no, being walked into the control room and seeing all those people again and it made her stomach churn. "I don't want to go to Herndon," she said. "I don't want to put my hands on a keyboard, matter of fact."

"Dar, they're not going to be able to fix that shit," Mark said. "We both know it."

"No, I know."

"So?" he said. "Like, no offense, Big D, but I want to get this crap to bed. I don't want it hanging out over you, or me, you know? I'm done with them."

"Okay," Dar said. "You can call him back and tell him if he'll send me the current configurations of all the master routers, I'll look at them and make whatever changes seem reasonable to me and send them back. See what he says to that."

"Unless his brain's migrated back to his ass, I bet he'll cry like a baby," Mark said. "Okay, send you what I get if he even knows how to pull them."

Dar nodded to herself. "Okay. Talk to you later, Mark. I'm having some dinner with Kerry and her mom."

"Ah...have fun?"

"Yeah. Bye." Dar closed the phone and folded her arms, trying to decide how she felt about the new development. On one hand, it seemed like some sense was returning to the situation, but on the other hand she thought there was still an opportunity for her to get screwed in the process of trying to help.

After all, trying to help on the island didn't end well, did it?

Dar sighed and pushed off the wall, heading back into the restaurant. Maybe she could get away with providing the minimum of help. She wondered if she could just look at the configs and send them back saying they were hopeless and she couldn't fix them.

Dar paused with her hand on the door and watched her own eyes reflect back from the outside surface. She gave herself a wry, knowing smile, then opened the door and went back inside.

Chapter Thirteen

"AH AM SOME pissed." Andrew sat squarely in the chair on the porch, arms folded. "Ceci, ah know no good deed done go unpunished but Jesus P Fish."

"Yeah." Ceci was in the other chair and a tray with rum punch sat between them. "Dar didn't deserve that. She did the right thing helping out that kid." She had one knee hiked up and her arms wrapped around it. "I'd have done it. You would have, too."

"Jackass."

"He would probably have invited us for dinner," Ceci said. "Instead of being so stupid as to wave a red flag in front of us and threaten to evict us from his preciously pretentious rock pile."

"Kids should go live on down in that little place in the keys." Andrew said. "Ain't a right place for Dar here anyhow."

Ceci smiled. "It fits them better. But that's one hell of a commute, you know? Especially in weather."

"Mmph," Andrew grunted softly. He reached down and picked up Mocha, who had taken a seat on one of his boots, and set the puppy on his lap. "Cute little thing."

Mocha seemed to enjoy his new perch, his small pink tongue emerging as he looked around.

Ceci accepted the subject change. "He is cute. I wonder what made Dar decide to get another one?" She gingerly patted Chino on the head. "To keep this one company?"

"Could be," Andy said. "Social critters."

Chino wagged her tail. Then she got up and walked over to where Andy was seated, putting her nose up against Mocha's nose and giving him a lick. She moved to the edge of the porch, standing up and putting her paws on the rail, peering out over the ocean.

Ceci regarded the animal, watching her upright but folded ears twitch as she sniffed the ocean air. She'd never considered dogs to be interesting, but now, having minded Chino so many times she'd come to the conclusion that there was some kind of intelligence in the beast that surprised her.

When the big dog looked at her, there was definitely something going on behind those soft, brown eyes. Thoughts, though not human kinds of thoughts, but thoughts nonetheless. "Hey there, Chino." Ceci waved at her.

"Growf!"

"Dar said they'd been bringing these two into the office with them," Ceci remarked. "Must be cozy."

"Think it's good," Andy said. "Dogs love those kids and no politics about it." He held his hand out and Mocha put his paw in it, then turned his head and looked at Andy. "Crazy things that happen to them, that's all right."

"Yeah." Ceci leaned her arms on the chair and regarded the horizon. "We going to go talk to that guy, Andy?"

Andrew pondered that in silence. "Ah am not sure talking will do much for the situation."

"You could be right, sailor boy, but I'm not in the mood to be put in jail tonight and we promised to watch the dogs until Dar and Kerry get back. So maybe we could try talking first and then, after the kids get back, find other ways."

"All right," He agreed. "We can go have us some pizza pie anyhow."

Ceci warmed to the plan. "We can take these dogs for a walk over there and sit outside. We'll look like a total set of snoots."

Andrew gave her a droll look that reminded Ceci of Dar and she grinned. "Okay well, a pretend pair of snoots." She got up. "Let me go get the leashes."

Chino's ears perked. She went to the sliding door and stood waiting, her tail lashing back and forth.

"That dog understood what I just said."

"Yeap."

"Is that normal?"

KERRY STOOD WITH her hands on Dar's shoulders as Dar studied a series of printed pages in front of her. "Is it a mess?"

Dar settled back and folded her arms. "It's a mess."

"Ah huh."

"They all have to be rebuilt," Dar said. "It's a lot of work."

"You don't want to do it?" Kerry leaned forward a little and pressed her body against Dar's. "Let me rephrase the question. Of course you don't want to waste your time fixing someone else's screw up. But you don't want to do it just because you don't want to do it."

"I don't," Dar admitted. "I keep looking at these and knowing what effort was put into designing them and the thought some moron just screwed them up is making me nuts."

"Well, hon..."

"Yes, I know. I offered. We should make it a rule that you stand next to me when I'm on the phone with a roll of duct tape ready." Dar pushed the sheets aside and pulled over her laptop. "Let me get started on this."

Kerry kept up her massage, reasoning that no words were appropriate. She glanced over Dar's shoulder as she started to setup a work session on the large, crisp screen, her body relaxing after a few minutes as she pecked at the keyboard.

Dar was a fast typist. She seemed to not need a connection between her eyeballs and what she was typing and it was a little odd to Kerry to watch those flying fingers and not hear the rattling smack of their older style keyboards. "These laptops are a lot quieter."

"They sure are. Softer on your fingertips, too." Dar nudged one of the sheets over with her elbow. "I could probably work on this all night and not keep you up."

"Like I would let you?"

Dar glanced up over her shoulder and smiled, got a kiss on the top of her head, then went back to typing.

"Can I help you with the setup?" Kerry asked after a few minutes of quiet. "I can see what you're doing there. Send me the rest of those files and I'll get them ready for you."

Dar opened up her mail program without even a grunt of protest and Kerry went over to get her own laptop, settling in the round, almost comfortable, hotel chair next to the desk and flexed her hands. "Glad we picked a hotel with Wi-Fi."

"Maria put it in our travel profile," Dar said absently. "Wi-Fi, room service, and big, fluffy king size beds."

Kerry looked up over the screen of her laptop, one eyebrow lifting. But it seemed Dar was serious so she just chuckled and shook her head.

She retrieved the files from her mail and opened them, placing them onto her desktop while she prepared to work with them.

Plain text files. There was nothing complicated about the configuration in that sense. It was just something edited in a text editor, full of lines of cryptic commands that made the routing system work.

But they were exact and unforgiving. Kerry sighed. "Are you commenting these?"

"No. Fuck them," Dar said, in a cranky tone. "If they want to know why I do things the way I do them they can read the design archives. Unless they deleted those, too."

"Want some hot tea?'

"Meh."

"How about some ice cream?" Kerry tapped at her keys. "Or a milkshake?"

"That has possibilities."

CECI AND ANDREW were tucked into an outside table at the Italian restaurant on the island, both dogs sitting patiently nearby. "Do you suppose that fellow is going to come out and meet with us?" Ceci nibbled on a bread stick, looking forward to a vegetable lasagna and some minestrone soup.

Andy shrugged. "Knows what's good for him he won't." He picked up a frosty mug of root beer and took a swallow. "What the hell's he going to say about it, Cec?"

"Maybe he'll reconsider how unwise it was for him to threaten the kids," Ceci said. "I mean, you can say a lot you don't mean in the heat of the moment."

Andy was quiet for a moment then nodded. "True thing."

"If he doesn't we can take a walk around the golf course and enjoy the weather," Ceci said as their dinner was delivered. She took her first spoon of soup when the door to the restaurant opened and a man came out and approached them. "Ah."

"You people want to talk to me?" the man said, stopping at the table. "Jim Beakman."

"Have a seat." Ceci indicated one of the empty ones. "Thanks for taking the time to chat. I'm Cecelia Roberts and this is my husband, Andrew." She waited for him to warily take a seat. "We're Dar's parents."

Andrew sat chewing a bite of his pizza, content to let Ceci do the talking for the moment. He knew the man vaguely from seeing him around the island, usually on a gas powered golf cart.

Looked like a construction type of man. He was heavily built and had dark hair, with hard, intent eyes and big, squarely made hands. Acted like a fellow who'd been in charge of things with no contesting it for a good long time.

Andy had known men like that — long timers — in the service. Fellas who had gotten used to command and had carved themselves out a patch where their word was law.

He smiled a little. None of them had much liked him and he didn't figure this feller was going to end up liking him either.

"You must be real proud then," Jim said.

"We are," Ceci said, aware of the sarcasm but answering at face value. "You always hope for the best for your kids but to have Dar become the very successful and stand-up person she is makes me very gratified as a parent."

Beakman regarded her. "So you don't care she's gay?"

Right to the point. Ceci rather liked that. "No. Why would I? I don't want to sleep with her. She's my daughter. That would be horrific and probably immoral and perhaps even illegal in Broward County."

Andrew chuckled.

"You don't care?" He turned his attention to Andrew. "Bet you'd care if she was a boy."

Andrew chewed his pizza thoughtfully. "No point in wondering, cause she ain't," he said. "But ah probably woulda gotten into a half ton more fights over it if Dar'd been a boy. Ain't so bad the way it turned out."

Jim shrugged. "So what did you want to talk to me about? She ready to back down on the threat she made against me?"

Now it was Ceci's turn to dryly chuckle and she did. "Dar never backs down. My reason for wanting to talk to you is to ask you what the hell you thought you were doing threatening her and Kerry with eviction."

He studied her warily.

"Because while my husband here is not a legally inclined man, I come from a family with a very long history of litigation, who holds very long grudges." Ceci leaned on one elbow and regarded him with a cold eye. "And I know just how illegal what you said to her was, even here."

"I don't care what's legal or not," he responded frankly. "I just care about protecting my family."

Andrew put down the bit of crust he'd been chewing and dusted his hands off. "Now that there's something you and I can see eye-to-eye on." He focused his attention on the man. "Cause Dar's my child. There ain't nothing at all in the world I won't do to keep her safe and defend her from jackasses making threats at her." He paused. "Buddy."

They stared at each other in silence.

Ceci cleared her throat. "Let me part the machismo for a moment," she said. "This is an idiotic conversation. It's idiotic that you want to evict my kid because she's gay, and it's idiotic that my husband is having to state the fact that he's ready to shoot you in the head if you keep on doing that."

Beakman sat up straight and looked over at her. "What?"

"That's what he just said," Ceci advised him. "We do not play games in this family and we're more nuts than otherwise. Really. So look." She leaned toward him again. "I don't know what you think that either my daughter, or the daughter of the late Roger Stuart, is going to do to your kid, but just stop it. It won't happen."

Andrew looked at her, then back at Beakman. "That what you all think?" His voice lifted in surprise. "Dar didn't say that."

"I read between the lines," Ceci muttered.

Andrew snorted. "Boy, let me tell you, Dar ain't got eyes for nobody else but who she's married to. She ain't made that way." He shook his head. "If that was what this here thing was about, nothing but a big old waste of evr'body's time."

He got up. "Let's go take these here dogs walking." With another shake of his head he collected both leashes and headed off down the patio, both animals trotting eagerly after him.

Ceci finished her soup and set it aside. "So," she said to the silently watching Beakman. "What's your real problem? Since Dar's been living here for a bunch of years and she hasn't molested anyone yet and you apparently didn't care about her lifestyle all that time."

"That's right I didn't," he said, after a long pause. "Kept to herself, didn't make much trouble. But now she's got my daughter all interested in things she has no business being interested in."

"Huh?"

"Since that other night, now she's some kind of hero. I don't want my kid thinking no pervert is a hero," he said. "It's got my wife upset and we're not going to risk her running off and getting herself into trouble."

Ceci blinked at him for a long moment. "Oh," she finally said. "So the problem isn't Dar, it's your daughter."

"This is my patch," Beakman said. "You get that? She belongs here."

"I get it," Ceci said. "So the fact that Dar saved your kid from being raped, or worse, doesn't matter."

He shook his head. "You can call me a shithead for that and I probably am," he admitted. "But I'm not having her think something like that should make her turn into a freak." He got up. "I'm not afraid of you people. I'm not going to have my family chased off my patch. You understand?"

"Better than you could possibly imagine," Ceci responded. "Had a great-great-great-grand-something who fought with Washington at Valley Forge, and Andy's great-great-grand something was a Confederate general in a place that war hasn't quite ended yet. I get it."

He paused and regarded her somberly.

"That's what Dar's heritage is," Ceci said. "So while I do get it, and on some level as a parent myself I have a sympathy for wanting to protect your family, think about evils and the lesser of them before you do anything."

They looked at each other in silence.

"We're better friends than enemies," Ceci concluded, lifting her glass of wine and raising it in his direction.

He nodded briefly, then turned and walked away.

Ceci sighed. "Well, mother goddess, I tried." She shook her head and went back to her plate. "Complete and utter waste of my time, and a pizza I think."

"IS THAT ALL of them?" Kerry was lying on her stomach on the bed, her head resting on her arms. "It's almost five a.m., Dar."

"Couple more pecks." Dar glanced at a page on the desk, then back at her screen. "I think I'm getting too old for this all night crap anymore."

Kerry opened one eye and regarded her drolly. "Let me go order you a bowl of prunes, grandma."

Dar chuckled and finished her amendments, running her eyes over the scripts one last time. "What a pain in the ass this has been." She saved the last changes and lifted her hands off the keyboard, flexing them and then cracking her knuckles.

"Done?"

Dar assembled the group of new files into an archive and then opened up her email program. "Let me just send these to Mark." She attached the archive and sent it on its way. "That is, I hope, the end of that."

Kerry snorted softly.

The light in the room altered as Dar shut off the lamp and got up from the desk, moving over to join Kerry on the bed. "Ugh."

"Alarm set?" Kerry mumbled indistinctly.

"Yeah." Dar got the covers over them and wrapped Kerry up in her arms, all in the same unlikely motion. "Let's hope the presentation is short and easy."

"Like me?" Kerry started chuckling silently as she felt Dar do the same. "Let's get through your demo and come back here and take a nap."

"Sounds good to me."

DAR TOWELED HER hair dry and regarded her reflection. She made a face at herself and stuck her tongue out after a moment. "I'm not a morning person today."

Kerry edged in next to her, dressed in only a towel. "I'm never a morning person." She leaned both hands on the sink basin and eyed Dar through damp, disheveled pale hair. "I definitely am too old for this all night crap."

"Funny," Dar drawled. "You kept me up all night just the other mphf—"

Kerry removed her hastily clapped hand from Dar's mouth. "That's different."

"It sure was a hell of a lot more fun than editing router configs." Dar ran a brush through her hair and pondered if using a dryer was in the cards. She felt a nibble on her arm and looked down to find Kerry leaning against her, eyes half closed. "You are tanked."

"I need some stronger coffee," Kerry said. She straightened up and pulled over her toiletry bag. "I think it's mostly that I keep thinking about having to sit in the room and listen to two dozen people like my father deliberately misunderstand every single word you say."

"Just think," Dar said. "Next week at this time we'll be picking up the RV and heading out on the road."

Kerry visibly perked up. "Boy I can't wait for that. I'm looking forward to that rafting trip. I just want to flush the world out of my head for a while and see new stuff."

"Me too." Dar decided against the blow dryer. "Let me go get my duds on and I'll call down for some double shot espressos."

"That sounds wonderful." Kerry brushed her hair out and started to put on the light makeup she now very seldom used. She listened to Dar ramble around in the outer room, hearing the low whistling.

She got into fresh underthings and went out into the other room, going over to their joint suitcase and taking out the conservatively cut business suit that had been in the back of her closet for at least a month.

Dar buttoned the sleeves on her silk shirt. "Know what I forgot to throw in? Hose. Oh well. Guess they'll just have to deal with my tan."

"I've never seen you wear hose. You have some?" Kerry adjusted the belt on her skirt. "Oh wait, I remember seeing a pair stuck in the back of your sock drawer. I thought they were just a token."

Dar chuckled. "They are." She tucked in the shirt. "I like that teal color on you." She studied Kerry. "You want to do this demo? You look better than I do."

Kerry glanced at her reflection in the mirror. "I don't think so. You look good in burgundy and I really like that shirt."

They both fell silent as they finished fastening and buckling then Dar looked up. "We done being girly now?"

"Hehe." Kerry pulled on her jacket and tugged the sleeves straight. "Hey we are girls." She walked over and straightened the collar on Dar's shirt. "Are you going to wear your microchip pin?" she asked. "We can stop in the coffee shop downstairs. We don't need them to bring something up."

"Sounds good." Dar removed her jacket from its hanger. "I didn't bring the pin with me. But let me get my earrings."

Kerry went over and made sure Dar's messenger bag had all her notes in it, then buckled it shut as the windows took on a pink glow from the rising sun. They had the presentation scheduled at the White House, then the grilling from Congress, hopefully a break in the afternoon, then dinner at Gerry Easton's.

Then an early morning flight the next day back home. Kerry got her sunglasses and tucked them into the belt on her skirt. She draped the messenger bag over her shoulder as Dar finished fastening her earrings. "Ready?"

"Let's go." Dar put the key to the hotel room in her pocket and went to the door, opening it and stepping back to let Kerry go through. "Mark should be sending off those files right about now," she said. "Glad that's behind us."

Kerry headed down the hall to the elevator stack. "You think that's enough information for them to fix the problem? Is there anyone even left there to fix it?"

Dar shrugged. "Any competent engineer could apply those configs and would understand them. I'm sure if they offer enough money they can get some hot shot in there to do it."

They offered their valet ticket up on the curb and waited. Kerry opened the back door and put the bag inside, then went around to the driver's seat and slid behind the wheel. She got her sunglasses settled as the valet closed the door and spent a moment adjusting her position.

Dar eyed her. "Sorry about that. Should have adjusted the seat when I got out."

"No problem, hon." Kerry got the car into drive and started off, pulling out and turning right onto reasonably well-remembered streets. "Better for me than you anyway. You always end up cracking your chin on your knees,"

"There's a Starbucks." Dar pointed. "And it has a drive through."

"Awesome." Kerry turned in the driveway and rolled down her window as she pulled up to the ordering station.

Dar settled back and took out her Handspring, thumbing through the messages. She saw a new one from Mark and opened it, reading through it and making a noise of disgusted irritation. "Doesn't it just figure?" she said. "I stay up all night fixing that crap and they boot the guy."

"Huh?" Kerry turned and looked at her.

"Mail bounced back as nonexistent." Dar held the phone up. "They deleted his inbox. Can you believe it?"

"Augh."

Dar shook her head and started typing. "I'm going to tell Mark to find someone—I don't care if it's the goddamned cleaning supervisor—and get them those files."

"Jesus." Kerry set the cups down in the console between them and paid for the coffee, then rolled the window back up and pulled back onto the street. "That's ridiculous, Dar. How could that have happened between last night and this morning?"

"We got fired between a Saturday morning and afternoon, Ker." Dar finished her note and sent it. "Actually, that's kind of a relief because this guy was no good news for anyone." She picked up her coffee and took a sip.

Kerry headed down the road that eventually led to the White House. "Yeah, but who knows how long it's going to take to get it fixed now."

"Do we care?"

Kerry glanced at her. "Dar, don't pull that on me. We both know you care."

Dar sighed.

"Of course you care. You built that whole system byte by byte." Kerry softened her voice, seeing the sudden tension in Dar's face. "C'mon, hon. You put a lot of blood and sweat into it. You were damn proud of that design and so was everyone else."

"I just keep getting the feeling you think I'm an idiot."

"What?"

"I think you want me to keep way clear of them. That it was a mistake to work those files."

Kerry was silent for a few minutes as she turned into the administrative gate to the executive building. "Yeah, maybe I do," she admitted. She rolled down the windows and took Dar's and her own identifications into her hand. "Maybe I'm so pissed off at them because of how they dissed you. I hope they all go down in flames no matter if some of our customers suffer."

"Morning, ma'ams." The guard took their ID respectfully. "Be right back."

Dar relaxed back into her seat. "Sorry Ker. You're probably right." She rested her elbow against the arm rest and her head against her fist. "It's like a knee jerk."

"I know." Kerry reached over and patted her knee. "Let's wait until later to fight. We've got enough on our plate right now."

"Go right through there, ladies." The guard handed them their IDs. "You're expected. Park in that first lot and it's the second gate, right hand side."

"Thanks." Kerry smiled at him then rolled on when the barrier lifted. "Let's get this show on the road." She drove inside and found a parking spot and then they got out and gathered their things.

It was cool and overcast and she was glad she had her suit jacket on. Kerry followed Dar up the path to the gate that was opened readily to admit them. "Good morning."

"Morning, ladies," the guard at the gate said. "Can I direct you somewhere?"

"No, we're okay," Dar said. "Thanks."

They entered the building and Dar led the way down the hall to the briefing room she was becoming familiar with. The administrator sitting at the entry desk glanced up, then focused attention on them. "Good morning."

Dar fished out one of her new cards and handed it over. "I think I'm expected."

The woman took it and looked at it, then consulted a book on her desk. "Yes, Ms. Roberts, you are. You can go on in and set up. Mr. Bridges is in a briefing right now, but he'll be back down in a minute." She glanced past Dar to where Kerry was patiently waiting. "Are you—"

"With her? Yes," Kerry said in a deadpan voice. She gave the woman a smile and followed Dar to the big conference room, which was empty and quiet.

Dar put her messenger bag down and pulled her laptop out. She sat down near the front of the table and opened the hatch in it where the connections to the overhead projector were.

Kerry took a seat next to her and simply sat waiting, knowing enough about Dar's prep methods not to bug her with inconsequential talk.

The admin came in and opened up a roll up cabinet in the back, exposing urns of coffee and other liquids. "Please help yourself," the woman said. "The technical committee is on its way down and if I were you, I'd get a cookie first before they get here." She gave them both a smile and left.

"I don't think I can get down any more coffee," Kerry said. "My kidneys are going to come out my ears."

"That's an attractive thought," Dar murmured, obsessing over her keyboard.

"I love you, too, honey." Kerry got up and went over to the credenza, selecting a glass and a bottle of fizzy water and bringing them back over to set next to Dar's elbow. Then she resumed her seat and half turned as the door opened and people started to file in.

Mostly men, but two were women. They all had the slightly harassed and impatient look of people who had too much to do and were being asked to stop doing what they had to do in order to listen to someone they didn't know about something they didn't care about.

Kerry was used to the look. She'd seen it enough times in conference rooms at ILS. She gave them all a brief smile as they settled into chairs, some detouring over to the credenza with low, muttered words to each other.

One of the men had sat down next to her. "You the people doing the new system?" he asked.

"Yes," Kerry said, extending a hand. "I'm Kerry."

"Paul." He took it and gripped firmly. "So is this going to work?"

"It'll work."

"Not like everything else lately?" Another man took the seat next to him and was leaning against the table. "Our whole reporting database's been down for three days. Last thing we need is some new complicated thing that craps out."

Dar looked up from her keyboard and peered at him. "The statistical analysis collator? That's down?"

"Uh oh," Kerry muttered under her breath as she swung around to face Dar. "I don't think we're supposed to know about that." She mouthed silently.

Dar lifted both hands in a shrug and put them back down. "Is it?"

"Yeah...you know something about that?" Paul asked. "I didn't know you people were involved in that. Hell, I'm surprised they don't have you in a little padded room upstairs getting your kneecaps whacked."

Dar sighed. "Actually we're not involved in it. We just know about it." She went back to her keyboard. "And that's all I'm going to say about that or I'll get my kneecaps whacked by my partner here."

Kerry looked mildly abashed. "We used to work for the company who handles that system for you. That's how we know."

"Oh." Paul leaned back in his chair. "So why'd you leave?"

"They pissed us off," Dar said. "Okay, I've got this set now." She stood up, twitching her jacket straight and flexing her hands. "We just waiting for Bridges?"

"He's getting a briefing on all the outages," Paul said. "He's in a bad mood."

Kerry folded her hands on the table. "Well, hope we can show him something that makes him feel better."

"Mm." Dar made a low noise in her throat. "Is it too late for us to find some coveralls and cross dress? Pretend we're someone else?"

"You're the one who said we knew about it," Kerry said.

The door opened and Bridges came in with two aides. He did, as promised, look like he was in a very bad mood. "Roberts!" he barked, as he came around the table. "What in the hell's going on?"

Dar put her hands in the pockets of her skirt. "We're about to do a demonstration for you," she answered calmly. "Want to sit down so I can start?"

Bridges paused, put his hands on the back of the chair at the head of the table and regarded her.

"It's not my problem anymore," Dar said. "I know it's a complete cock up there, but I don't even have any way of thinking about trying to help."

"Don't want you to help. I want you to take it over." Bridges tossed a folder on the table and slid it over to her. "Now. Sign."

Kerry pulled the folder over and opened it.

"We don't have the infrastructure to do it," Dar said. "You'd be in the same state until we could spool up. Find someone else — I'll give you some names."

The others in the room watched them, heads turning back and forth like those at a tennis tournament.

"I don't want any goddamned names," Bridges said. "I've already talked to half a dozen half-assed, nit-brained, nerd heads and you know what every single one of them told me?"

"They said they can't do it," Kerry said, still leafing through the folder's contents. "And probably some of them told you to call Dar." She closed the folder and pushed it back across the table. "Unfortunately we honestly — no bullshit — can't do it either. You need time and a ton of facility and we don't have either one."

Bridges sat down in the big chair and glared at her.

"Really." Kerry said. "I'm not making that up. If I thought we could pull it off and yank it out of ILS's hands, I'd do it in a heartbeat."

Dar turned and looked at her, both eyebrows hiking up.

Kerry saw the look and suppressed a smile. "I would. They've been absolute morons over the last month. I'd take that contract like this." She snapped her fingers. "But we can't do it."

He steepled his fingers, tapping the ends of them against his lips. Everyone else in the room was dead silent, very still, just waiting.

Even Dar stayed quiet, her hands still in her pockets, eyes slightly unfocused.

"What do you mean they were morons?" Bridges finally asked. "They do this on purpose?"

Kerry folded her hands on the table, the light briefly catching her wedding ring and reflecting off it. "A lot of people have asked us that.

No, I don't think they did this on purpose in the sense that they were trying to sabotage anything."

"It's worse," Dar said. "Someone trying to make their mark made some changes and it went very south."

"That so?" Bridges mused. "So it was stupid rather than treason?"

"Far as we know, yes," Kerry said in a quiet voice.

He got up. "Go on and give your talk, Roberts. I'll be back shortly. Everyone take notes." He waved a hand at the room. "There'll be a test later on."

He motioned the two aides, who had stayed standing near the door, out ahead of him like he was shooing chickens and followed them out, slamming the door behind him.

Kerry let out an audible sigh.

"Who in the hell are you people?" Paul finally asked with a touch of awe in his voice. "Do you know who that guy is? He could have you sent to Mars."

Dar switched the screen to her output. "Who are we?" she said. "Well, I'm Thor, God of the Internets and this is She-Ra. So I guess Mars doesn't scare us much." She got her remote out and moved to one side. "And on that note, let's get this started. "

Kerry was busy typing a message into her Handspring, shaking her head repeatedly.

"THAT'S HOW THE algorithm works." Dar clicked to a new screen. "What we did was try to write the front end to the enterprise service bus so that it was a more natural way for people to interact with the data."

One of the women in the back spoke up. "What does that mean? Do they talk to it?"

Dar brought up the very basic, simple input screen. "I can write a plug in that'll take voice commands. But right now it's just keyboard." She pointed at the woman. "C'mon up here and ask it something."

The woman hopped right up and came forward. She put her hands on the keyboard as Dar took a step back. "Ask it...what do I ask it?" She looked up at Dar.

"If you were an analyst and your job was to find something wrong, what would you ask?" Dar had one hand on the back of Kerry's chair. "Don't look at me. I don't know what to ask. I'm a systems architect."

The woman thought for a moment then started typing. "Tell me about anyone who wants to shoot the president."

She hit enter and straightened, looking first at Dar, then at the screen.

A spinning star took over the middle of it and twinkled for about thirty seconds. Then typing started to fill the screen, plain white on black, san serif font.

Email: Parsed header returns "He makes me so mad I want to kill him." Content contains keywords: hate, revenge, under the radar, politician, POTUS. Return extended header?

The people in the room stared at it. "Is that real?" Paul asked.

"It's real in the sense that I created a database that had random records in it with different source types," Dar said. "It's not real in the sense that the thing you're looking at is a real threat to the president."

"But...that's the kind of thing it would come back with?" the woman asked. "Really?"

"Really." Dar smiled a little at the reaction. "The information I used to make this test database is a dump from the actual Internet, scrubbed to remove personal information and then mixed to provide you with some hits to questions."

"So it wouldn't say whose email that was?"

"It would come back with a fictitious name," Dar confirmed. "But since it's a fictitious email, that would be appropriate. It could have originally been an email from someone who was pissed off at their SO, and the keywords could be from six different other emails."

The woman stepped back to the keyboard. "Tell me about anything threatening Yankee Stadium." She hit enter and they all looked at the screen expectantly.

The machine chewed over that for a bit and then started spewing out listings.

```
     1.) Invoice: Industrial: Phosphorous, Deliver to
Yankee Stadium, volume plus 1,000 lbs.
     2.) Legal: Resident: Lawsuit filed against
Yankee Stadium over parking fees.
     3.) Email: Parsed. Text includes 'going to make
a killing at Yankee Stadium.'
     Enter item to retrieve additional data.
```

There was a moment of silence. Then they all exhaled at once. "Holy shit," the oldest man, who was standing in the back of the room, spoke up. "So that thing can just read all that stuff on the Internet and it'll know all this?"

Dar seemed pleased. "It will," she said. "This is, of course, a test database. It's only half a terabyte in size and this demo program is a very simple model. The real system will be a lot bigger, a lot more powerful, distributed, and it'll probably take longer to return a response because it will be looking at a hell of a lot more raw data."

She regarded the screen. "But that's the idea. It also will employ a flexible heuristic framework that will learn over time to know what to look for. So eventually it will start suggesting things rather than wait to be asked."

Dead silence. "W...what?" Paul stuttered. "You mean it has artificial intelligence?"

Dar nodded, "It continually parses data, so it will start looking for connections," she said, her voice getting a touch more animated. "So if it sees, for instance, a pattern of telephone calls between places that also show deliveries of gunpowder, that's something it will bring up as part of a generated briefing. Could mean something, might not mean anything, but the operators will have the choice to follow up or not."

"Humans have to make the real connections," Kerry said after being silent for a very long time. "But they can't look at all this data. It's like a firehose. But a computer can and it just tries to find patterns and that's what it returns to us."

"Oh my god," the woman sat down. "I thought this was just an intelligence budget scam. You actually made this."

"In two weeks," Paul said. "You really are Thor, God of the Internet."

"Have at it." Dar sat down next to Kerry and waved them toward the laptop. "But remember, it's just a demo system. I just wanted to give you all an idea of where we were going with it."

She slid backwards out of the way and watched in contentment as they all gathered around her machine and started peppering it with questions, the woman finally ending up being the typist.

Kerry smiled. "Rock star."

"It's just a test system with a lot of spaghetti code and duct tape in there. They ask it the wrong thing it'll probably croak."

"Dar, stuff a sock in it. I know how long you worked on that." Kerry poked her in the ribs. "You're a rock star."

Dar shrugged modestly, but smiled.

The door opened and Bridges came back in, pausing as he saw the crowd at the head of the table.

Paul turned and spotted him. "Sir! You should come see this! It's boss!"

"Whoop de fucking hoo," Bridges said. He pointed at Dar and Kerry. "You and you, come with me. The rest of you stay in nerdgasm." He turned and headed back out, waving them after him. "Let's go people."

"Why do I suddenly wish I was an actual rock star?" Dar said as she and Kerry followed him out and the door shut behind them. "And all I had to worry about was tuning my guitar?"

"What?" Bridges glanced at her. "Nevermind. You two are going to help me solve this problem here and then we can go back to talking about whatever the hell it is that has those goops so excited."

"This doesn't sound good," Kerry muttered.

"No," Dar agreed.

Bridges led them through two hallways and up a staircase, then through a padded door and down another hallway, stiff arming everything out of his way until he got to a pair of double doors that he grabbed the knobs to and shoved them open.

Beyond him they heard angry voices. When they cleared the door and saw the interior of the room, Kerry heard Dar make a low, grunting noise that she knew meant nothing but trouble.

It wasn't really a curse, but it might as well have been one.

"I don't know what you're talking about but we've got our best— what the hell is she doing here?" a tall, crewcut yelled.

"She's here to help us figure this out," Bridges said. "Now sit your ass down."

"Help us? She caused this!" The main pointed at Dar.

"Is that..." Kerry muttered.

"Yes."

"Let me start texting."

Bridges turned to look at Dar. "You cause this, Roberts?"

"No," Dar responded in a flatly calm voice. "Moronic male ego caused this. I had nothing to do with it. Assuming what you're talking about is the fact that a company I used to work for maliciously and deliberately disrupted your systems."

"Now, Dar." Jacques stepped out from behind a block of angry bodies. "That's not true."

"Fuck you, it is," Dar said. "I told you what to do and you didn't do it. All of you put pride in front of your customer. From my perspective, that makes you all useless sacks of shit who frankly deserve to be taken into some green painted cell somewhere in the basement of this place and beaten to death."

She stopped talking and sat down, resting her elbows on the big conference table. "Please get this over with. I have a demonstration to do in a half hour."

There were very few times that Kerry was prouder of Dar than she was at this moment. She quietly sat down next to Dar and folded her hands on her lap.

"Dar," Jacques regrouped. "I was just—"

"Shut up. You're a goat bag. I have no respect for you," Dar said in a clipped tone. "I have no respect for any of you. Be men. You fucked up. Own it."

Bridges sat down with a grunt.

A tall, dark haired man, dressed in a green linen suit, put his hands on the back of the chair directly across from where Dar was sitting. "Can I ask who you are?"

"My name is Dar Roberts. Can I ask who you are?"

The man sat down. "You're Dar Roberts? Funny. From what I was hearing I expected you to have a horn and a long red tail," he said. "I'm Steve Booker."

"Ah. We've spoken," Kerry said. "He's the governmental systems technical coordinator, Dar."

He peered at her. "I know that voice. Kerry Stuart?"

Kerry drew a breath, then just merely nodded.

"You going to sit down?" Bridges stared pointedly at Jacques and the man with the crew cut. "Or do you want me to call the goons to have you dragged down to the not nearly as fictitious little green room downstairs?"

Reluctantly they sat.

"All right." Bridges leaned back in his chair and folded his hands over his stomach. "I don't have time to screw around with you people anymore," he said. "Shut up and don't speak until I tell you to," he said, as Jacques drew breath.

Bridges looked at Dar. "What is the actual fucking problem, Roberts, since I know deep in my complete lack of a heart that you know."

Kerry put her hand on Dar's arm, applying gentle pressure. Then she cleared her throat. "We don't know specifically what happened," she said, "because only the people who actually did it know what they did."

Bridges rolled his eyes.

"But what I believe happened is that the people ILS hired to replace Dar, and I, decided to put their imprint on the systems that were in place there. They made changes to them that caused a pretty serious degradation in performance."

Higgs took an angry breath. "That's a—"

"Don't," Kerry said sharply. "Stop playing games. This is the government of the United States you're messing up. The consequences of that are a lot more important than you understand."

"You are liable for this," Dar said, in the small silence that followed. "What you did will take ILS down. You'll lose the company." She looked directly at Jacques. "And you will deserve to lose it. I am so disgusted by you and what you allowed to happen here that I'm about to throw up on this table."

Jacques's face twisted into a grimace. "Dar—".

"We risked our lives for this customer." Dar cut him off, but in a very quiet, gentle voice. "And you allowed this moron to knowingly and deliberately put them in jeopardy."

Higgs stood up. "You made that system so impenetrable you caused this! Don't blame this on anybody but you, you fucking immoral piece of shit!"

"So you did make some changes?" Bridges asked.

"To make things better. Sure," Higgs said.

Bridges sniffed reflectively. "John, get the MPs up here," he said. "I want this guy put in lock up." He turned to Dar, leaning on his chair arm. "Can you fix this, Roberts?"

"She's not touching anything!" Higgs said. "I've got our lawyer coming over here and he's going to serve the damn papers we've been trying to serve to this bitch for two weeks. Then we'll see who's going to jail."

"Brook, sit down," Jacques said, quietly.

"The hell! I'm not going to sit down, and I'm not going to stand by while my reputation and yours gets tossed in the garbage!" Higgs started around the table toward Dar. "Wait 'til I get my hands on you."

The door opened in front of him and he stopped abruptly, taking a step back as a man walked in with rolled up sleeves and a casual pair of slacks on. "What's all going on in here?" he asked, looking around. "Oh, there you are."

"Hello, Mr. President," Bridges said. "Just having a meeting."

"With all that yelling?" Bush seemed surprised. "Hello there, ladies." He gave Dar and Kerry a smile. "Hey, is this your lady friend?" he asked Dar.

"It is," Dar said. "My partner, Kerry."

"Hi, there. Call me George." The president extended a hand, which Kerry took. "I just heard from someone down the hall that your new thing's really something."

"Looking forward to demonstrating it to you shortly," Dar said. "So far, so good."

"Well now that's great. So what's all the yelling about?" Bush asked, a touch more sharply. "Something wrong?"

"Just getting some issues ironed out," Bridges said. "Nothing too tough."

"Uh huh." Bush nodded. "Well, you all try not to keep Ms. Roberts too long. We've got an appointment." He eyed them, then slipped out the door and closed it behind him.

Higgs went back to his seat and sat down, looking like he was trying to pass a gallstone. Jacques leaned back and half hid his eyes with one hand.

Bridges ignored both of them. "Okay, now where were we. Roberts? Can you fix this thing or not?"

"In point of fact, she's been trying to," Kerry said. "Except these bimbos keep firing the people she was trying to help."

Bridges tapped his lips. "Roberts?"

"I won't do it to help them," Dar finally said. "But I will do it for you. Pull their contracts. After that you get me access and I'll fix it."

"What?" Higgs yelped.

"Dar, please don't be so hasty."

"Done," Bridges said with a brief smile. "Steve, call the GAO and make it happen. Cut the new contracts to Roberts's company and mandate the gizmos, gears and whatnot that makes it all up goes to them, too."

Kerry grimaced. "Oh lord. That honestly won't work."

"Then go with him and figure out how to make it work," Bridges told her. "You've got a shitload of your father in you. Go prove it." He nudged her with his elbow. "Go on."

Dar leaned closer to him. "You keep insulting Kerry and I'll tell you to fuck off, too."

"No, it's okay." Kerry was surprised to find that it actually was.

"He meant it in a good way." She stood up and patted Dar's back, then circled the table and pointed at Steve. "C'mon."

"Let's clear the room," Bridges said. "Except you, and you, and me." He pointed at Jacques and Dar. "John, keep that bozo entertained." He indicated Higgs. "Move, people."

Five minutes later they were alone in the room.

"So," Bridges said. "Explain to me why you turned into such an idiot?" he asked Jacques.

Jacques merely shook his head. "There comes a point," he said after a pause, "when all the bad decisions are made of so much weight, you cannot push them off."

"You could have," Dar said. "I told you what you needed to do."

"You did," he said. "But I am only one man and there were so many on the board who refused to go along with that, because it meant to the world a total failure."

Bridges brows hiked. "And this is?"

"Now? It is in fact a total failure," Jacques said. "We will all be cast out."

"You should be," Dar said. "You butchered that company."

"Dar."

"Jacques, that's why they pay you the big bucks," Dar said. "The buck stops with you. Just like when I was there, the buck stopped with Alastair."

"We were very sure we knew what to do," Jacques said. "We were absolutely sure we had picked well to replace you."

Dar regarded him. "You are a moron," she said. "Higgs could no more replace me than I could flap my arms and fly to Mars."

"That is the problem isn't it? You made yourself un-replaceable," Jacques said. "I think you knew that. You arranged things so that anyone who followed you would be lost."

Dar regarded him thoughtfully. "I did," she said, surprising everyone. "Not on purpose," she added. "It's just who I am. I'm a leader. An Alpha if you want. I did things my way. But you all knew that and you let me. If that wasn't what you wanted, then you should have stopped me a long time ago."

Bridges nodded in turn.

"So yes, I knew I was impossible to replace. I just wasn't going to sacrifice my life because of that. I was hoping you'd find someone who would study what I did and then make a plan to make it their own. Not do something as mind-bendingly stupid as make some random change then make it impossible to recover from it."

"So now you will wreck us," Jacques said.

"Yes. I can't let you wreck both the company's reputation and mine," Dar said. "So I will take you down and force a replacement of the board. If the company's very lucky, Alastair will agree to take over again until things can be made right."

Jacques shook his head "They will not stand still for that."

"They won't have a choice," Bridges said. "Considering how much of the operations of the government you goat heads are disrupting, I could have all of you held as suspected terrorists. You do realize that, right?"

Jacques looked at him, startled.

"You do realize where you are, right?" He pointed at the desk. "You do realize the guy who walked in here a while back in the chinos and button down was George Bush, right? Leader of the free world and all that crap?"

Dar sighed.

"She gets it." Bridges pointed at Dar. "If I were you, I'd start catching up before the best thing that will happen to you and all your Wall Street buddies is they'll end up in Guantanamo." He leaned forward and lowered his voice. "And I don't even need a warrant. Your families will never see you again. You'll never get a lawyer. You get me?"

Jacques was silent for a moment. "Yes," he said then. "I understand you."

"Good." Bridges looked satisfied. "Today might end up all right after all." He leaned back and twiddled his thumbs, humming softly under his breath.

Dar waited a moment to see if anything else was going to happen, then she pulled out her Handspring and started to type.

Chapter Fourteen

KERRY FOUND HERSELF in a rectangular office, with desks against the walls and old fashioned drapes over the windows above them. There were two men behind one of the desks, with big ledgers open in front of them, and her new friend Steve on the phone next to her.

"We can't," she answered Steve's question. "We don't have anything close to the space, people, systems, all that, to be able to actually manage the contracts."

"But Ms. Roberts said—"

"Yes, I know what Dar said." Kerry sighed. "I'm totally with her on getting that board out of there and getting people into position not to mess everything up again, but there is just no way for us to take over the service like that." She snapped her fingers.

"So what do we do?"

That was a good question. Kerry leaned against the desk behind her. "What are the...wait, why am I asking you that? I wrote the damn contract." She rubbed the bridge of her nose. "It's a three year and it was renewed about eighteen months ago, wasn't it?"

"Yup."

"Got a penalty clause," one of the accountants said.

"Yes, it would. But it also has SLAs in it. Can you pull them?" Kerry said. "And the monitors that prove they were broken?"

Steve scratched his head. "Do we do that?"

"You should."

"I think they depended on ILS to tell us," he responded with a grimace. "But all that doesn't matter. Bridges said to just make it happen, so that's what we need to do, you know?"

"I know but it's not that easy. The stuff that's running your stuff is on pieces of gear that other people's stuff is running on."

"That's not right," Steve said. "You can't mix top secret stuff like that."

"I can if the other stuff is just as top secret," Kerry said. "There's an awful lot of government stuff on the..." She paused and pondered the options. "Okay wait. The government nodes in the area are segregated..."

"We should take over everything. It wasn't right to have some company doing it," Steve said. "I told everyone that."

"That's it." Kerry straightened up. "We can't do it because we don't have the people."

"Well, we sure don't have the people. That's why we hired ILS," the accountant said in a practical tone.

"But you could," Kerry said. "You could put your own people into all the places where the connections are and you monitor them."

Steve's eyes literally lit up. "Yeah!"

"We don't have those people," the accountant repeated. "Where do we get them?"

"You hire the people who are already there." Kerry's pale green eyes twinkled, just a little. "The ones that work for ILS. They would be out of a job if you took away the contracts."

The accountant smiled, thinly. "I see."

"That way they're not cutting the contracts to another company, you're in sourcing," Kerry said. "You just terminate the contracts for non-performance and conscript the equipment due to national security reasons."

"You bet..." He paused. "Can we do that?"

"Sure why not?" Kerry smiled. "They all have government security clearances," she said. "And they know what to do with your stuff."

One of the other accountants looked up at the words. "Wait, we're hiring people?"

"That's a super idea," Steve said. "Kerry, you are the bomb."

"Don't say that." The other accountant said. "You know they don't like it."

The first accountant started shuffling through papers. "We better get someone to rubber stamp a budget then...let me get the forms." He shook his head a little and went over to a filing cabinet. "Bridges will sign this, right?"

"Right," Steve said. "He said whatever it takes."

The accountant rolled his eyes. "Yeah, that's what they all say when it involves taxpayer dollars."

"So now what?" Steve turned to Kerry. "Should we go over to the place where all our stuff is?"

Kerry drew in a breath then released it. "Let's get all the paperwork in line, then yeah. I'll go over there with you. I know the people there." She was hard pressed to know whether to be relieved or apprehensive about it. She knew there were a lot of long timers in the Herndon office.

Loyal people. Competent people who had welcomed her leadership with open arms in very tense times. How would they feel about this?

Would it be a betrayal?

A rescue?

"Should we tell them we're coming, or just go over there?" Steve asked. "They could screw things up worse if they get pissed off, right?"

Kerry was briefly silent. "We'll just go," she said. "I don't think they'd do anything but there's no saying ILS won't."

Steve clapped her on the shoulder. "Right on," he said. "Let's get some coffee. I'm thinking it's gonna be a long day."

DAR OPENED THE message on her Handspring, ignoring Jacques's staring eyes. "Well, crap," she said. "There's not one single solitary person left in IT in the Miami office." She looked up and across the table. "Mark is there. He said there's not one person he can give a new set of configs to, to maybe, maybe solve this."

Bridges spun around in his chair. "Tell him to go fix it himself," he said. "Can he?"

Dar dialed Mark's number. "Let me talk to him."

"You'll get him inside whatever that is, right?" Bridges looked pointedly at Jacques.

"Yes, of course," Jacques answered instantly. "Dar, is that Mark Polenti?"

Dar nodded. "I spent last night revising your fucking router configs because your brainless idiot called him and begged him for help."

Bridges chuckled under his breath. "You should have gone into the service, Roberts. You've got the mindset for it."

"I would have ended up court-martialed for insubordination before I left basic," Dar responded crisply. "Mark?"

"Yea, boss," Mark said, somewhat indistinctly. "They just brought me a tray of pastelitos. Hang on." He swallowed. "Okay, so, here's the deal—ain't no one for me to give this stuff to. Like, no one."

"I know. They want you to go in and put them in yourself. You up for that?"

Long silence. "Are you shitting me?"

Dar sighed. "I'm sitting in the briefing room at The White House with White Fang here crouched over me and Jacques with a gun to his head. No. I'm not shitting you."

Bridges chuckled dryly. "That was my favorite book as a kid," he said. "That and some Zane Gray Indian stories."

"They won't let me in there, boss," Mark said. "They pulled my creds as fast as I pulled yours."

"They will if Jacques tells them to." Dar said. "You willing to do it? It's up to you."

There was a long silence, and Dar endured it, keeping her eyes on the table and refusing to meet either man's.

"I don't think I should, Dar," Mark finally said. "I think they're just looking for a scapegoat. I'll end up being sued. I don't have the bankroll you do to stand up to that."

Dar nodded. "Okay. I get it," she said. "Leave the files in an envelope with security."

"Hey!" Bridges sat up. "What?"'

"Wait...I said I would get them to let him do this!" Jacques said at the same time.

"Shh." Dar held up a hand. "Hear that Mark? Make sure you write on it what the contents are."

"Will do." Mark sounded profoundly relieved. "I'm gonna head back to the office. Call me if you need me for anything but this."

"You got it." Dar hung up and looked at Jacques. "He won't do it and I won't make him," she said. "He's afraid, with good reason, that you'll turn around and sue him."

"Dar!" Jacques threw up his hands. "Please!"

"You have no trust," Dar said. "I am not going to stand proxy for you and tell him you won't do that because you know what, Jacques? I don't know you won't."

"Jackasses." Bridges rolled his eyes. "You people make me nuts."

"Yes, sometimes I am and do," Dar agreed. "But that man on the phone trusts me. That means more to me than your contracts, or threats, or your little padded green room." She rested her elbows on the table. "So if he won't do it then I guess I'll have to."

"What?" Jacques put his hands on the table. "Now this?"

Dar pushed herself to her feet just as Kerry pushed the door open and stuck her head inside. "Hey," she greeted her.

"Hey," Kerry said. "I need to go to Herndon. I'm going to have the government hire all those people and take over the systems."

Even Bridges blinked. "Hey, what?"

Kerry eyed him. "You said to solve it. Careful what you ask for."

"Good, because I have to go there, too, so I can fix the damn thing so when the government takes it over it works," Dar said. "Did you say there was a Wendy's around here?"

"Yeah."

"Great. I need a cheeseburger."

"Wait." Jacques stood up. "You cannot just do this."

"Sure they can." Bridges apparently decided to roll with it. "I like that, Stuart. So we're buying out the contracts and bringing it in-house? Security group'll be very pleased. Intelligence jackass committee will, too."

"Taxpayer's won't," Kerry said.

Bridges smiled. "Oh, they will," he said. "When George finishes telling them how much safer they'll be. Good press for him." He got up. "Get going, people. I'll tell him you'll be back later to show him your new whoo hah."

Jacques stood up. "I think I should —"

Bridges turned serious. "No, you shouldn't. Sit your ass down and don't move. In fact, give me that cell phone." He held out his hand. "I don't trust you either."

Kerry had it in her to feel sorry for Jacques, in that moment. She could read desperation, fear, and an overwhelming anxiety in his face, and she knew here was a man in a very bad spot who hadn't either expected or prepared for that.

But then in the next moment she remembered that he and his henchman were here trying to throw them under the federal bus and she didn't feel sorry for him at all. "C'mon, Dar." She held a hand out. "Let's go make things right."

Dar handed a piece of cardboard to Bridges. "Call this guy," she said. "Tell him to take over ILS. Tell him what we're doing. If anyone can pull their corporate head out of their corporate ass, it's him. And tell him to call Hamilton the lawyer, who's got a whole crapload of investors ready to back him."

Bridges took it. "Will do, Roberts. Now go get this crap done. I've got a headache from all the bitching and I don't want to hear it anymore." He waved them out. "Take Steve with you, he's got credentials and shiny badges and things that'll keep you out of trouble."

Dar was glad enough to escape the room and she willingly followed Kerry to where Steve and two Federal Marshals were waiting. "Okay...oh crap I need my laptop." She turned and started back down toward the briefing room. "Be right back."

"I could have..." Steve started after her.

"Kerry pulled him to a halt. "Let her go. She's going with us to try and fix what's wrong."

"Oh, really? Will we have to do all this then?" Steve asked. "I want to do it anyway. No offense to you, since you used to be in charge of all that, but I don't trust private companies when it comes to this stuff."

Kerry folded her arms. "I understand what you mean, but honestly? Before this last truly Technicolor clusterfuck, ILS was very good at what it did and kept the government on the top list of its priorities."

"If you say so," Steve said in a dubious tone.

"I say so, since it was my job to make it that way," Kerry responded with more than a slight edge to her tone. "And I don't appreciate being accused of incompetence while I'm on my way to save your ass."

He lifted his hands and took a step back. "Okay, okay! Sorry!"

"And don't bring that attitude with you to Herndon," Kerry warned. "What happened here wasn't their fault. The idiot you had in that room did it, or at least was responsible for it."

"Okay, I get it. I'll shut up," Steve said. "Let's go meet her coming back. The car's outside that middle door anyway." He pointed. "C'mon, guys."

They walked down the hall and had almost reached the door when Dar came around the corner of the hallway and headed back toward them, her messenger bag slung over her shoulder. She had her Handspring in one hand typing on it, dodging people in the hall by some sort of nerdic radar.

Kerry pulled out her own as she felt it buzz, glanced at it, then hit the answer button. "Hey, Maria." She took a step back and half turned away from Steve and his goons. "What's up?"

"Have you finished the demonstration to the government? I was just hoping it went so well, and also, that you and Dar have enjoyed the hotel."

"Where do I start?" Kerry sighed. "Let me get back to you, Maria. I think the demo went fine but everything else just went to Hell."

"Ay yi yi."

IT WAS A long ride and traffic was atrocious. "Last time we went here no one was on the road," Kerry commented as she studied the buildings going past.

"Yeah, people got back to normal. Whatever that is," Steve said.

Dar remained silent. She was wedged against the other window, her sunglasses on and her eyes closed behind them.

Kerry suspected Dar was asleep and she spared a moment of affectionate envy for her ability to shut out the world that way. Her own eyes felt tired and sore. She was looking forward to the day being over in the worst way.

Maybe this, maybe now, they'd get some closure.

Or something.

"So, we're going to hire everyone and then she's going to fix stuff, right?" Steve asked, after being quiet for a long time.

"We'll probably have to play that a little by ear," Kerry admitted. "I don't know how they're all going to react to us showing up like this. Everything's been pretty chaotic. Matter of fact, I hope they let us in."

"They'll let us in," Steve said confidently. "Nobody says no to the GAO and Federal Marshals."

That probably was true. Kerry suddenly wondered if this mixture of anticipation and dread was what Dar felt when she'd been the one to go in and give the news of never wanted change.

She remembered vividly being that person in that place, looking up and facing that change, all unaware of how much more personal it would be for her than she'd ever anticipated.

They slowed to turn in at the gate and Kerry reached over to gently touch Dar's leg, watching her as Dar's eyes opened and turned her way. "We're here."

"So I see." Dar flexed her hands and straightened up and looked out the window. "Wonder how this is going to go?"

Steve rolled down his window and was talking to the guard. He handed out his business card and indicated the back of the stretch sedan they were riding in. The two Federal Marshals were in the back of the car. The Marshals hung their credentials around their necks and checked their side arms.

The guard at the gate bent down and looked in the window. His eyes met Dar's and the look of relief on his face made her feel sad. She lifted a hand and waved and he backed away and gestured the way forward, pulling the gate aside rapidly.

"Think he recognized you, hon," Kerry said.

"Yeah." Dar pushed her sunglasses up on her nose and folded her arms.

"That was easy," Steve said, glancing behind him. "Just mentioned your name."

Dar got her messenger bag strap over her shoulder as they pulled up in front of the building. She opened the door and got out, stepping back to let Kerry slide out after her.

They walked to the door and pushed it open, coming into the public entrance where two people were at the desk, already straightening up as they entered.

The receptionist let out a gasp of recognition and her eyes widened. "Oh my gosh!"

After a hesitant moment, Kerry took charge. "Hi, Stacy." She walked forward and held her hand out. "Wish this was under better circumstances." She took a breath. "Can you ask Paul to come out here please? We need to speak with him."

"Yes, ma'am, right away." Stacy turned to the other woman standing there. "Go get Paul. He's in the break room. Hurry!"

The girl looked confused, but left, badging through the door and disappearing.

"I know he'll be glad to see you," Stacy said. "It's been horrific here this week. A dozen people walked out. It was just too much. All those screaming phone calls."

"Yeah, I know it's been tough," Kerry said quietly. "Shouldn't have fallen on you all, though. None of this was your fault."

"That's just it." Stacy said. "It wasn't the customers yelling. That's part of the job. It was those people who took over from you. They were so nasty."

Dar removed her sunglasses and tucked them into her bag. "So I heard."

Stacy looked from one of them to the other. "So did you come back?" she asked, hopefully. "We heard they fired that one guy and we haven't heard from that man who replaced you, Ms. Roberts, for a while."

Dar was spared from answering by the door abruptly opening to reveal a harassed looking man in chinos and a long sleeved buttoned shirt. "Hello, Paul."

He stared at them. "Oh lord it is you." He looked about to collapse. "What's happening?"

Kerry moved toward him. "Let's go into the conference room, Paul. We'll explain what's going on." She saw the apprehension come into his face and internally winced, remembering what that felt like.

He came around the desk though and preceded them into the public conference room, taking a seat at the table as the rest of them entered and Dar closed the door behind them.

Kerry went over and sat next to him. "So, okay, I know things are rough right now."

Steve sat down across from them and the two accountants they'd brought also took a seat to either side. The two Marshals went to opposite corners of the room and stood there, not quite at attention.

Dar dropped into the seat at the head of the table, content to let Kerry handle the meeting.

"Rough." Paul sighed. "Yeah." He rested his hands on the table. "So what's going to happen now? We all getting fired?" He looked at her. "Are you guys back with us or what?"

"No," Kerry said. "Here's the deal. We know something got horribly screwed up. That affected a lot of customers."

Paul nodded. "All of them have been chewing my ass for days," he said. "I ran out of things to say to them and when I called exec ops, all they told me was to shut up."

Dar made a low, grunting sound.

Paul glanced her way. "They told me it was my job to handle the customers. I didn't know what to do."

"Well, one of the customers was the government, as you well know," Kerry said. "To make a long story short and get this on the table, the government ordered the General Accounting Office, which these gentlemen represent," she indicated Steve and the others, "to terminate the contracts and take control of the systems."

"I guess I can't blame them for that reaction," Paul said, glumly. "They bringing in a team? I'm too tired to even feel bad about it. I guess I'll get my deferred vacation now anyway."

Kerry rested her head on her hand. "I've got some bad news, and some good news. Which do you want first?" She didn't wait for him to answer. "They have no team to take over, Paul. What they do here is very specialized and it would take months to replace the people."

He eyed her warily, but remained silent.

"So what I told the government was, they should just hire all of you and let you keep doing what you're doing."

"But what we're doing isn't the screwed up part!" Paul burst out. "Ms. Stuart, it doesn't mean anything about what's in here, it's the whole system!"

"We know," Kerry said. "That's why Dar's here."

Paul swung around to face the figure at the head of the table. "They're going to let you make this right?" he asked. "Because we were told under no circumstances to even talk to you."

"They have no choice," Kerry said. "The government stepped in. They asked us to help get this straightened out."

Dar cleared her throat. "It's not a matter of them letting me do anything, it's a matter of you letting me."

"Pohsh." Paul made a spluttering noise and stood up. "Let's go," he said. "We can talk about becoming civil servants later. If you can make this right we're wasting time here."

He headed for the door as Dar stood up and followed. A moment later the rest of them did as well. They crossed the lobby and Paul slid his badge into the reader, hauling the door open as it clicked and standing back. "After you, ma'ams."

"Paul," Stacy stood up. "Don't they need to sign in?"

"No." Paul waited and followed the last of the Marshals. "Fuck it. There are no rules today."

IT WAS STRANGE and somewhat uncomfortable to enter the ops room where tired, frustrated people were clustered around one of the consoles, arguing.

"Just do it, Bill! What the hell are they going to do, fire you?" He looked up as the door opened then closed. "Oh shit..."

Everyone swung around to see what he was looking at and then everything went still and quiet for a long minute.

Kerry broke the silence with wry irony. "Hi. Everyone want to sit down and chill out for a minute?"

The group slowly dispersed and went back to their stations. "Someone clear space on the government side please," Paul said. "Our clients took matters into their own hands it seems and sent some help."

Bill stood up and stepped back. "My station here's on net," he said. "Boy they sure knew who to call, huh?"

Dar walked around the Marshals and went to the console, setting her bag down and regarding both the console and its operator. "Hi, Bill."

"Hello, ma'am," he answered quietly. "I'm sorry about everything."

"Me too." Dar responded. "So here's the thing. You have two choices. If you're a level fifteen or above, you can create me a login to make some changes. Or I can use yours. Pick."

Bill smiled briefly. "You can use mine, ma'am. No problem." He hesitated. "Is it okay if I watch you?"

Dar sat down. "Sure. Pull a chair over." She regarded the green and black screen. "What were you about to do that they were yelling about?"

He cleared his throat nervously and pulled another chair over. "Well..."

Kerry went over to the supervisor's desk and motioned Paul over. "Steve, why not have your folks sit down. This will probably take a while."

The two Marshals found convenient corners to stand in and the rest of them sat down at the round conference table in one corner. Kerry waited for them to get settled then she turned back to Paul. "So."

He had sat down behind the desk and let his elbows rest on his knees. "How did this happen?" he asked softly. "How did it get so bad so fast?"

Kerry leaned against the desk, her back to the room, her arms folded over her chest. "Good question. I hope you know this wasn't anything Dar and I wanted."

He shook his head. "They told us she did something." He glanced at the console where Dar and Bill had their heads together in low conversation. "We didn't believe it. No one here did. Anyhow we heard about all those people leaving. It was like 9/11 all over again but this time we failed."

"Yeah, I know," Kerry said. "It was hard for us to believe with everything going on. But I think maybe things will turn around now. I hope so. We want to move on."

"I guess we'll all end up doing that, too," Paul said after a pause. "I thought I was going to retire with them. You know?"

"I think Dar did, too, at one point." Kerry glanced around. "Any chance of some coffee? I'd like a chance to go over the options with you without an audience."

Paul managed a smile. "Sure." He pushed himself to his feet with an obvious effort. "Let me get our ops team in there, too. Might as well save your voice and not say it more than once." He motioned her to follow and went to an inside door she remembered leading to the ops center break room.

Might as well get it over with.

"OKAY." DAR STUDIED the screen. "That wouldn't have done anything but it wouldn't have hurt anything either." She opened up her laptop and waited for the screen to come on, then clicked on the folder she'd put the files in. "So let me show you what they did."

She felt motion at her back and glanced around to find most of the operators out of their chairs and leaning over their workspaces to watch. "C'mon over here. Maybe if I let you all in on what happened it won't happen again."

The entire team came trotting over, making a solid circle at her back. "We knew they did something," one of them said. "They said it was you, Ms. Roberts, but I've been working here for ten years and I know what your stuff looks like." He shook his head. "Your changes are scary sometimes but they work."

Dar suppressed a smile. "Thanks," she said. "I think."

"So what did they do?" Bill asked. "We were going along like normal one day and then all of a sudden it all just gummed up."

Dar brought up the configuration of their local router and the file on the screen that mirrored it. "This." She touched one line with her index finger and drew it down the screen. "The idiot who did this didn't have any understanding of situational routing."

"What is that?" Bill asked. "Is that how all the traffic knows how to go?"

"Yes." Dar indicated the file on her screen. "You see all this? That's the configuration that used to be in this router that would tell it how to know where to send things and would flexibly reroute if it saw congestion or an issue."

"That's custom scripting," one of the other operators said.

"Yes," Dar said. "I wrote it."

"But...that's actually calling the firmware," the man said.

Dar nodded. "We worked in conjunction with the firmware vendor to make it work that way. It's in the architecture workbook."

"They took that offline," Bill said. "Same time as the repository. They said it was for security."

"So, all we have to do is put that all back in and it'll start working again?" the first tech said. "It's just typing? Holy crap, Ms. Roberts, we can type. Give each of us one of those and we'll get this knocked out and go get a damn beer with a clean conscience. I'm buying your first one."

Dar smiled just a little. "That's all. I rewrote these last night." She rubbed the bridge of her nose. "We tried to give them back to the stupid bastard who did this but they fired him before we could give them over."

"Holy crap."

"Holy crap!"

"Someone grab some thumb drives!" Bill turned around and yelled out. "Hurry!"

KERRY HAD SAT at many tables like this one, facing many faces like these and she understood the heavy sense of fear and dismay in the room. "I know it's crazy."

Charlese Harrington lifted one hand up. "Look, Kerry, I know you got dragged into this. But it is crazy. Someone somewhere else makes a huge screw up and we have to pay the price?"

Kerry sighed. "That does happen," she said. "None of this was anyone here's fault, but the fact is, it impacted some people who aren't very forgiving. What was worse, they weren't being given good information."

"That's not our fault," Paul said. "We weren't getting *any* information from exec ops. Just bullshit. All they kept doing was either blaming you, or telling us to suck it up."

"And, like, don't even mention Ms. Roberts's name," Charlese added. "They sent an email out that said they were fixing years of screw-ups and we'd just have to sit tight until they were done. Figure out something to tell the customers."

"And what's happening now? I know they let you all in here," Paul said. "But that broke security regs, and we should be getting a call from the PTB any minute screaming."

"You won't," Kerry said. "Jacques is under guard at The White

House and they put Dar's replacement into a holding cell."

Silence. "Wh...what?" Paul stuttered. "Are you kidding me?"

"I'm telling you they screwed around with the wrong customers," Kerry said. "The president's advisor is the one who sent us over here. Dar and I were there demonstrating a new project for them. We didn't intend on any of this. I just..." She glanced around. "They wanted us to take over this contract."

The reaction surprised her. Everyone sat up and their eyes brightened. "That means we'd work for you?" Paul asked. "Hot damn."

"Guys," Kerry said. "Thank you, that's a big compliment, but the company Dar and I started can't handle this. At least, not yet. We're fifty...no...wait. Seventy people in Coconut Grove doing database design."

"Who are at The White House demonstrating programs for the president?" Charlese eyed her. "I saw that picture of Ms. Roberts and Dubya."

"But still, we're small," Kerry said. "ILS is a quarter of a million people. It's not our scale for this. So when they started talking like that, like maybe they'd bring in a squad of Marines in here, I thought a better route would be to get them to hire you all and let you keep doing what you do."

"Weren't you the one fending them off from us the last time? The government, I mean?" Charlese asked. "I don't mean to be rude."

"Situations change," Kerry said. "If you'd rather not accept the offer, that's okay, too. My aim was to get a working solution in place for as many people as I could."

"If Ms. Roberts fixes that stuff, can't we just go back to being normal?" Paul asked, plaintively. "I mean, it'll work again and everyone will stop yelling at us."

"I don't think they'll let that happen," Kerry said, then paused as the receptionist opened the door and stuck her head in. "But hell. You never know. I've seen stranger things."

"Oh, good. Ms. Stuart, there's a phone call for you. They say it's urgent."

Everyone looked at Kerry, who stood up and sighed. "I'm not supposed to be here. I don't work here anymore. What the hell." She went to the door and followed Stacy out, shaking her head as she heard voices rise in agitation behind her.

"OKAY, GO AHEAD." Dar folded her arms and watched as the techs got to work, eyes flicking from the notepad files to their consoles as they confidently typed in commands.

It was insane, really. The level of change control they were violating would have dropped internal audit at two paces and there was no doubt that all the concurrent changes would be skewing already faltering services across the wide network.

Couldn't be helped. Dar flexed her hands, resisting the urge to take over one of the consoles to make the work go faster. It was right that the techs be the ones to do this and not her. She had no business touching a keyboard.

"Wow." One of the supervisors was watching the big board that showed mostly reds and yellows flashing luridly overhead. "I don't think that's making things better."

"It won't until they're finished," Dar said. "Classic case of busting eggs to make pancakes."

The man glanced at her. "Isn't that omelets?"

"I like pancakes better."

"I'd call ops but there's no one there but this one guy who's just answering the phone and taking messages," the man said. "I heard they got some temp company to send some people in, but that won't happen until tomorrow I think."

Dar just folded her arms and leaned against one of the consoles.

"There goes my phone," the supervisor said mournfully.

"Want me to answer it?" Dar asked with a wry smile. "That'll confuse everyone." She pushed off from the console and went to the desk. She settled behind it and picked up the receiver. "ILS Mid Atlantic ops. How can I help you?"

She listened for a moment. "Yes, matter of fact I do know. There's a recovery operation going on to try and restore performance to the network. Your service will be down until that's finished."

She listened again. "I understand. But when it's done you'll have the same service level as you did several weeks ago before the problem started." She glanced up to find everyone not typing, watching her in fascination. "About twenty minutes."

"Can you tell them that?" the supervisor mouthed. "Holy cow, they'd fire me for saying that!"

"Who'd fire you?" Dar mouthed back. "Me? No I wouldn't. There's no one left to fire you and the government's going to hire you anyway. Chill out."

She went back to the phone. "Absolutely. I'm sure the service is going to get a lot better. I promise you that." She paused. "Roberts. First name's Paladar. Yep, with a P. Thanks. Goodbye." She put the receiver down, then punched the button and picked it up again. "ILS Mid Atlantic ops, how can I help you?"

"Someone should record this," the supervisor said. "No one's gonna believe it."

KERRY STOOD AT the receptionists' counter, leaning against it with the phone pressed to her ear. "Alastair you're not making any sense," she repeated. "Listen, I realize that was probably a shock getting the phone call but..."

She paused to listen. "What were we supposed to do?" Her eyes lifted and met the receptionists. She shook her head. "Okay, put yourself in my place. You're in The White House, you have the Senate Intelligence Committee breathing down your neck, Bridges hauling you into a room with Jacques and that jacktard, telling you to fix it. What do you do?"

She paused. "No, I'll tell you what you would do, goddamn it, you'd have picked up the phone and called Dar. That's exactly what you would have done. We just shortened the process. So now Dar's in there doing what we all agreed was the last thing on Earth she should do because we ran out of goddamned options."

She heard the sound of tires outside and looked through the door. "Oh, great. Here's *CNN.*" She sighed. "Well, I can't help it that those jerks you just tossed on their ass decided to go public." She rubbed her temple. "So now we have the press here, rabid about some story that's just bullshit."

"Should I let them in, ma'am?" Stacy eyed the gathering crowd outside the door.

"Not yet," Kerry said. "Alastair, what is it you would like me to tell the national press? You want me to refer them to you?" She listened. "That's not my place to tell them. In fact, you can't even tell me to tell them that because I don't work for you anymore."

"There's another news truck out there, ma'am?"

"Jesus." Kerry covered her eyes. "Alastair, you need to put out a press release. Is Hamilton there? He's on his way. Okay, well I'm sure the PR people didn't quit so you should have plenty of them there to write a press release explaining you've replaced the board."

"Is that Alastair McLean?" Stacy whispered. "Is he back in charge of things?"

Kerry nodded. "Against his will," she whispered back. "He's not happy about it. I volunteered him."

She listened again. "I can't do that. I know things are moving too fast and I kno—what?" She paused. "Okay so they'll file lawsuits, big news there but..." She paused again. "Oh hell, Alastair. It's too late. We're here. Dar's changes are already going in."

Kerry shot a quick glance at the door. "Alastair, we're out of time. You need to deal with the press. I need to get Dar out of here before they make an honest-to-god Federal case out of this. Get off your ass and call *CNN.* I'll try to get things normalized here." She hung the phone up and circled the desk. "Holy crap."

"Ma'am, you have brass ones," Stacy said in an awed tone.

Kerry stopped at the door and turned. "They already fired me. What exactly do you think he's going to do? Stall the press as long as you can." She yanked the door open, resetting the bolt so it would shut after her and headed down the corridor.

"Yes, ma'am." Stacy turned and put her hands on her desk as the door opened and a cavalcade of press and cameras and overcoated handsome men and women stumbled inside. "Hi," she said. "Welcome to ILS Mid Atlantic. What can I do for you?"

KERRY GOT TO the door to the operations room and peered through it, seeing techs very busy at their desks and Dar seated at the supervisor's raised platform on the phone. One of the supervisors was perched on the edge of the desk listening, the other was on the far side of the room, watching the monitor board.

She saw the board and it was looking ugly. Kerry knocked on the glass, attracting the attention of the supervisor near the desk. He hopped up to come open the door. Dar looked up as well, meeting her eyes.

Kerry smiled briefly as those blue orbs rolled expressively. The lock clicked from the other side and she pushed the door open and walked to the raised platform. "Hon?"

Dar held up one hand. "Yes, that's right. Just give it another fifteen minutes. Thanks." She hung up the phone and then ignored its insistent ringing as Kerry came up next to her. "Hey."

"What are...never mind." Kerry refused to let herself be distracted. "That was Alastair out there. He called here because we're not answering our phones."

Dar glanced at hers. "Not getting a signal in here. Not surprising with these metal walls and EMF. So what does he want?"

"What doesn't he want?" Kerry lowered her voice. "They kicked the board members out and they went public."

"Morons." Dar didn't look perturbed.

"Yes, who are intending on filing suit against him, against us, and against the Pope for deliberately disrupting operations."

"Can't prove any of that," Dar said.

"No, except here we are," Kerry said. "They told the press we did this just so we could disgrace them."

Dar rested her hands on the desk and drummed her fingers against its surface. "Hm. You know, that's the one single reason I might actually have done it. Unfortunately for them, we didn't."

"But we're fixing it."

"They're fixing it." Dar pointed at the consoles. "I just provided copies of the previous configuration to them."

"You didn't go in there?" Kerry's voice sounded surprised.

"Nope. Haven't touched a keyboard.

"There are about a hundred press people outside. They told them we were here and that we also deliberately did this so we could swing the contract away from ILS and make points with the government."

"Except for the deliberately, that's what we're here doing," Dar said. "You know, Ker, I don't know what else they could have done to preserve their reputations."

"Tank ours?" Kerry said sharply.

Dar lifted both hands up and let them drop.

"So what are we supposed to do?" Kerry half whispered. "Dar, we could get into some serious political and financial crap here."

Dar put her hand on Kerry's knee. "We might," she said. "But right now we're in flight here. We can't just turn off the engines."

Kerry looked around at the absorbed faces of the techs and their quick shifting of attention from the scribbled on pages to their screens. "Yeah, well that's what I told Alistair," she said. "I told him to get off his ass and have someone in PR call the press."

"Did you really tell him to get off his ass?"

"I did."

"Good girl." Dar took hold of Kerry's hand and brought it closer, giving the knuckles a quick kiss. "That's exactly what he needs to do. It's not our place to solve this press problem."

"But that doesn't help the fact they're all out there," Kerry said. "Or what the bastards told them."

Dar leaned back in her chair and lifted her shoulders in a mild shrug. "First thing;s first. Let's get this fixed." She glanced up at the monitor. "Type faster, folks." She raised her voice. "There's light at the end of the tunnel there, I see some greens."

The supervisors turned and looked. "Holy crap, there are."

Everyone looked up at the board and fell silent. The only sound in the room was the rattle of computer keyboards. It was odd and discordant, the heavy clicks echoing softly.

"Good old IBM keyboards," Dar commented after a long moment. "Noisiest input devices on the planet. I think the sound's patented."

Kerry kept watching the board, listening to the noise of the typing. As that slowly started to wind down and become less of a solid continuous sound, the map started to change. "Ah."

"What's going on?" The supervisor leaned toward her. "Is it...oh."

Reds and yellows morphed into yellows and greens. The keyboards went quiet as they watched the yellow fade and a flow of blue sweep across the big status monitor and started a gentle pulse.

"Son of a bitch," the supervisor standing at the desk said into all that quiet.

The techs all turned around and looked first at him, then at Dar, who stood up and put her hands on her hips.

It seemed anticlimactic. All those problems, all that trouble, and now..."Nice," Dar said. "Very nice."

"And that, people," Kerry said, "is why they pay her the big bucks."

"I haven't seen the board look like that in weeks," one of the techs said. "Did we really do that?"

"You did," Dar said. She walked down from the desk and moved in front of the consoles. "What you did was put things back the way they were before they got cocked up." She rested her hands on the steel edges of the old fashioned workspaces. "Good job, guys. Make sure you save the configs and put these someplace safe."

"Ms. Roberts, is it true those guys who made the change deleted everything?" one of the techs asked. "For real?"

"For real," Dar said. "To be fair to them, because I want to be fair, I do believe they did think the changes would make things—not necessarily better—but different and their own. "We architects are arrogant bastards and totally invested in our way of doing things."

Kerry blew a raspberry at her.

"It's true." Dar smiled anyway at the sound. "I completely believe with all my heart that's it's my way or the highway. Anyone here think that's not true?" She looked around at the techs, who smiled back. "Well, so did they."

"Yes, ma'am." Paul had re-entered. "But you were right and they weren't." He watched the board and saw the slow relaxation of bodies into chairs around the room. "What was worse, though, at least from our side, was that when something went wrong before, you all over in ops would own it."

Dar nodded. "Yes," she said. "I don't believe in shifting blame. That's why they paid me and Kerry the big bucks because those bucks stopped at our desks. If something got screwed up, if I rooted through it enough I could get it to come back to some decision I'd made that just hadn't been right."

"Even if that actually hadn't happened." Kerry interjected dryly. "Dar tends to the chivalric sometimes."

Dar blushed slightly. "I wouldn't say that. But I understood where my responsibility was." She looked over at Paul. "And that was to take the hit for things that happened in my organization. It's what management is for."

Paul shook his head. "It's what leadership is, ma'am. There's a difference."

"Yeah," one of the techs said. "That's it."

They all stood up, a spontaneous reaction that surprised Dar and made her take a step back, her brows lifting a little as they all started applauding. "Ah c'mon."

"That was pretty ace." Steve had been sitting in a corner and now approached Dar. "So it should all be working now? Can I call back to the office and tell 'em?"

"Sure." Dar smiled as the techs all surrounded her, offering handshakes and soft congratulations. Some brought up the notes they'd worked off and started asking questions.

Kerry smiled at the reaction, folding her arms across her chest and waiting as she watched Dar sheepishly accept the accolade. "Might as well enjoy the moment," she commented to the supervisor standing next to her. "I'm sure *CNN*'s not going to be clapping."

"Do you have to talk to them, ma'am?" the supervisor said. "We could sneak you out the back door, couldn't we? And then pretend we don't know what they're talking about when they ask us stuff?"

Kerry looked at him. "I've got six people from the government here and their limos parked outside. It's a little hard to miss," she said. "But thanks for the offer. I do appreciate it. Steve?" She motioned the man over. "We've got a problem outside."

He reached for the phone and started to dial. "What kind of problem?"

"When you're done there, let's get Bridges on the line and find out what he wants us to tell the press outside."

"Oh." Steve grimaced. "That kind of problem"

"Mmhm."

Chapter Fifteen

THEY WERE IN the small office that, once upon a time, Kerry had borrowed in her last visit to the office. Just a desk, a phone and a TV mounted on a wall that had never been changed since she'd left.

"Standby please, for Mr. Bridges." A quiet, female voice emerged from the speaker phone.

"Sure." Dar sat behind the desk, her chin resting on her fists.

Kerry was seated on the surface, a cup of water in her hands. If she stood up and looked out the small window, she knew she'd see a parking lot full of television trucks. The feeling of being under siege was undeniable. "Should I call Richard?"

"Not yet," Dar said. "Let's wait to see what he says."

"Regardless of what he says, Dar, the board's going to sue us. Shit. We'll be lucky if they don't end up making us shut the company down."

"Maybe it won't be so bad, now that everything's fixed."

"Dar."

"Yes?" Dar looked up at her with more than a hint of annoyance.

"Roberts?" The line opened abruptly. "You there?"

"We're here." Dar answered. "In the middle of a shit storm, unfortunately." She focused on the phone instead of the woman at her side.

Briggs grunted. "Just heard from the computer people. They're whoop-de-doing all over the place here because crap's working again. So congratudamnlations."

"Yeah, thanks," Dar said. "The jacktard former board members of ILS went to the press and blew their story out. So now half the planet's in the front parking lot wanting the rest of the story."

"Ah."

They waited in silence for a bit. "So what would you like us to do, since whatever we say will involve your organization." Kerry said, after the quiet had gone on too long. "And we're due back there for a demonstration."

"Hold your shorts, kid." Brigg growled. "I'm writing a memo. You'll go with the goons I sent there and don't say a damn thing. Just 'no comment' your asses out the door."

Dar and Kerry regarded each other somberly. "Just leave?" Dar said.

"What, did I start speaking Russian? Yes," Brigg said. "Go get the rest of those chimps and head back here. I'm including all of you in a national security memorandum. Move it, people. Goodbye!"

The line went dead. Dar leaned back and folded her arms, her face twisting into a disturbed expression. "I guess that would get us out of this for now."

"It would." Kerry got up off the edge of the desk and went to the window, peering outside. "We don't say anything. We can go back there and let the government cover it all up. They seem pretty good at that sort of thing."

"Mm."

"After all, it's just going to be a 'we said, they said' anyway, Dar. They can't prove we touched anything, but we can't prove we didn't get someone else there to do it."

"Yeah."

Kerry heard the tone and grimaced a little. From the corner of her eye she saw the TV trucks, antennas angled up. It reminded her of the time when they'd been dependent on the technology.

Working in desperate times in service to what they considered the greater good. She leaned against the wall and watched Dar shift and steeple her long fingers, tapping the ends of them against her chin.

She remembered Dar working for hours, testing cables, providing leadership to their team and refusing to stop until they'd found the right ones, putting them in the right place. The only credit they'd received was the heartfelt thanks of the men they were helping. But it was the right thing to do.

Just like today, fixing the screw-up was the right thing to do. Kerry knew it the moment they'd headed to Herndon, the moment she'd seen the security guard's relief, the moment she'd seen that board clear and calm and seen the faces of the techs who'd done it.

It was right. It felt good. She watched the motion as Dar drew in a breath and her shoulders straightened up. It wouldn't have made sense to do anything else, no matter what the consequences eventually were.

Dar instinctively understood that.

Kerry saw the contention coming in the tension in Dar's back as she prepared to stand up and argue about something Kerry knew she wasn't going to win at.

Shouldn't win at. Sometimes consequences didn't matter. If they ended up out of business, ran out of town, living on the boat...shoot. How bad would that be?

She smiled and felt a sense of odd acceptance flow through her. "So are you going to give the interview, or you want me to?" She broke the silence and savored every word as she watched Dar's whole body relax and her shoulders jerk in a faint, silent laugh.

Dar turned around in the chair, meeting Kerry's eyes with a smile in return.

"We've been trying to walk away from this from the start, hon. That was wrong," Kerry said. "I was wrong in wanting you to stay clear. This was ours and we need to own it until it's done."

"No matter what happens."

"No matter what happens," Kerry echoed, feeling a sense of relief that almost made her sleepy.

Dar extended one hand. "C'mere. Let's go to hell together." She got up and as Kerry came over she wrapped her arms around her. She let her head rest against Kerry's. "I could no more walk away from this than I could walk away from you."

Kerry leaned against her and let it go. "Wherever we go from this, I'm right there with ya," she said. "So let's go get on camera."

Dar shouldered her messenger bag and took Kerry's hand in hers, heading for the door and what waited beyond.

"SO WHAT ARE we doing?" Steve asked as a pod of reporters filed into the ops center. "My office said we were supposed to be going back to The White House."

"We will," Kerry said. "We just need to do this short interview to wrap things up, then we can head back. "

"Okay," Steve said amiably. "I called back there and everything's running great. That sure was something to watch." He leaned back against the console. "Have to say, those guys are kinda okay. I'm glad now we're gonna hire them."

"They're okay," Kerry said. "Be right back." She left Steve by the wall and headed across the room to where Dar was standing with a reporter from *CNN* and one from *The Washington Post*. Two photographers were a few steps back taking pictures and the camera crew was setting up to shoot the supervisor's desk where Dar had taken up residence.

The techs were watching covertly. Paul and the two supervisors were around the far raised desk, content to watch the action as they stood under the big monitor board with its newly placid twilight shades.

There was a faint scent of garlic and cheese in the room and Kerry's stomach rumbled as she recognized the smell of fresh pizza nearby. She detoured over to the far desk and climbed up the tiers, returning the smiles as she approached. "Hi there."

"Ms. Stuart." Paul had a cup of coffee clasped between his hands. "This is the first time I haven't had my guts in knots for weeks."

"What he said," one of the supervisors said. "Look. My phone's quiet." He pointed at it. "No calls, no calls waiting, no notepad full of names and numbers for me to call back with excuses. God bless you guys."

Kerry smiled. "It was a team effort. And speaking of team efforts, do I smell a team pizza somewhere?"

Paul chuckled. "Yup...in the break room, c'mon." He motioned her toward a side door. "I had it brought in. Wasn't sure what we were going to end up with this afternoon. Thought I'd have to have the guys on the desk without a break."

Kerry followed him into a back room where a refrigerator and coffee machine held pride of place, along with several tables, one of which was covered with pizza boxes. "Ah. Score."

Paul handed her a plate and took one for himself. "Feels like twenty pounds off my shoulders. It's been so bad."

"I know it must have been," Kerry said, pleased to have a whole veggie pizza to herself. She bit into a piece and chewed it. "I wish the whole thing hadn't happened."

"Yeah, me too," he answered. "I don't know if I want to work for the government," he added. "My parents met at Woodstock. I don't think they'd forgive me for working for the Repugs."

Kerry swallowed reflectively, "I'm a Republican," she said. "I'm not sure it matters when you do what we do and I'm not sure there's much of a difference between working for the government or working for ILS."

"You're a Republican?"

Kerry nodded. "Dar's agnostic. She doesn't much like either party." She picked up another plate and plunked a piece of meat covered pizza on it. "And Paul, nothing says you have to work for the government. I'm sure there's a spot for you in ILS if you want to stay with them. They've lost enough staff over the last month."

"Yeah I know."

Kerry saluted him with her snack, then picked up the plate and headed out the door with it. She dodged a few cameramen as she made her way over to where Dar was settled behind the desk.

"So, Ms. Roberts, we do appreciate you sitting down and talking to us, especially after that press release from the former board of ILS," the reporter said. "I know you understand that I have to address the allegations they made."

"Sure." Dar glanced up as Kerry approached, her eyes lighting up a little at the sight of the plate she was carrying. "Whatcha got?"

"Pizza." Kerry put it down. "Take five minutes and scarf it. You know what that tastes like cold."

The door opened and two more journalists came in, joining them up on the dais. They were carrying microphones and had backpacks secured to their backs with gear inside. "Okay, we ready?" One of them asked, his microphone flag declaring him from *USA Today*. His companion had a local television station patch on his jacket.

Dar had wolfed down several bites and set her plate aside. She wiped her lips with the napkin Kerry handed her. "Ready," she said. "You've got fifteen minutes. Start talking."

"Start rolling," the *CNN* reporter said. "Ready?"

"Ready."

"All right. Dan Gartersberg here at the ILS facility in Herndon, Virginia," he said, facing the camera. "Earlier today, ousted board members of ILS issued a press release accusing former employees of engineering a malicious attack on their systems, causing widespread outages across the US and internationally, even affecting our armed services."

Dar waited for the camera to turn to her. She folded her hands on the desk and took a deep breath.

"We were tipped off that those ex-employees were, in fact, here in this facility and we've come here to ask them what their response is to these allegations and an explanation of what, actually, is going on." He turned smoothly and stepped back and the camera focused on Dar. "This is Dar Roberts, one of the accused. Ms. Roberts, what do you have to say about these allegations?"

Dar smiled at the camera. "A lot," she said. "But we don't have all day so I'll just say they're untrue and we can move on to your next question."

Dan Gartersberg nodded. "Very well then. Tell us about this supposed attack then." He looked around and the camera panned with him. "Here at this headquarters it seems very quiet."

The camera swung back. "Sure," Dar said. "Let me lay out the data points for you. I'll start with who I am, then move into why ILS got itself into this situation, who was responsible for it, and why I stepped in here today to make things right."

He smiled, off camera, and gave Dar a thumbs up. The print reporters were scribbling furiously, one whispering into a voice recorder.

"So let's get started."

THE RIDE BACK to the White House was very quiet. The two Marshals were playing cards in the back section and Steve was riding with them in the front, the two accountants busy studying papers spread out on their laps.

Kerry and Dar were sitting next to each other, lost in their own thoughts. The interview lasted a half hour and at the end of it they'd found it hard to tell if the reporters bought the story or not.

They'd ruined the story, Kerry realized, by having fixed it before the press arrived. It would have been so much more satisfying to them to have found things in chaos. Sweating men and red alerts going off were much better television than calm monitors and relaxed techs munching pizza.

Oh well.

They both had their phones turned off. Kerry had quickly sent a message to Richard Edgerton, though, and one to Maria. Now she wondered if they would even be let inside the executive building, much less get to demonstrate anything. "Hey, Dar?"

"Hm?"

"Anything you want to see here? As in tourist stuff?"

Dar pondered that as they pulled into The White House parking lot.

"The Air and Space Museum?"

Kerry smiled. "Just won ten bucks off myself."

They got out of the car and filed through the gate, the guards giving them respectful nods as they went into the building. Steve led them to the presentation room, then ducked out and left them without further word.

Kerry put her hands on the back of a chair. "Should I turn my phone back on? I'm pretty sure that low thrumming sound you hear is shit hitting the fan."

"Sure." Dar pulled her own out and switched it on. It had just synced up when the door slammed open and Bridges stormed in. "That didn't take long."

"You stupid son of a bitch," Bridges said. "What in the hell did you think you were doing? I told you to come straight back here! Do you have any idea what kind of chaos you caused by opening your yap to the press when I told you not to!"

"I decided otherwise," Dar responded, flatly.

"Oh you did, did you? Well take your decisions and get the hell out of here. Contract's scratched," Bridges said, visibly fuming. "Forget it. With that publicity there's no way you're going to do anything at all for this government."

"Okay." Dar picked up her bag. "C'mon, Ker. Glad we could fix everything and then get fucked up the ass as usual from some two bit moron with no sense." She indicated the door. "Let's go have dinner and go home."

He was between her and the door and she walked right at him, expecting him to move to one side. When he didn't she stopped and looked him right in the eye, her head level with his. "You said to get out. Mind moving your ass so I can?"

One of his gray eyebrows cocked upward. "Did you really just call me a two bit moron, Roberts?"

"Yes. Move," Dar said. "I've got things to do."

Kerry came around the other side of the table and stood watching them. "Yeah, no win scenario," she said. "We weren't going to walk out of there and not defend our reputations."

Bridges swung around on her. "Reputations?" He looked from her to Dar. "You two are idiots. You have no idea what business you're into."

"No, we do," Dar said. "I completely understand why you wanted us to just come back here. I'm just telling you I wasn't going to let that go unchallenged. That's my ego. My problem. Now get out of my way so I can get started on hiring lawyers for the crap that got shot my way for solving *your* problem."

"So you decided your reputation was more important than a bunch of major contracts your new business is based on?"

Dar looked him right in the eye. "Yes."

"You're an idiot." Bridges stepped aside. "Get the hell out."

Dar reached for the door, hauling up short as it swung inward and revealed the highly inconvenient and slightly rumpled form of the president. "Ah." She took a step back. "Hi there."

"Well, hello there, ladies." He came inside and shut the door. "Second time today I heard yelling coming from this room. What's the scoop?" He looked at Bridges. "Thought we were supposed to see that new computer thing today."

"Not today, sir," Bridges said. "I've decided to change companies. Didn't like what I saw from these here people."

"Yes, excuse us." Dar went to step around the president, stopping when he held a hand up.

"Now hold on," Bush said. "All I've been hearing this morning is how nifty this new thing is. Sounds like it was a success to me. So why make a change? What's the deal here?"

"Sir, we can discuss it later," Bridges said.

"Or we can discuss it now," the president countered.

Bridges looked frustrated and annoyed. Kerry got the sense he was used to getting his own way and was also used to having his suggestions accepted without question. She felt her Handspring buzz in her pocket, but left it where it was, waiting for Bridges to answer.

She didn't feel apprehensive either way, which was a little strange.

"Ladies, why don't you sit down here and let's just hear this out," Bush said. "Mike? I'm sure we've just got some kind of misunderstanding. Right?"

He pulled out a chair and waved Dar into it, then repeated the process for Kerry, seating himself between them as Bridges very grumpily took a seat across from them. "Now." He put his folded hands on the table. "What's the scoop?"

Bridges just stared moodily at him.

"You want the short version or the long one?" Dar finally said. "The short version is we were instructed to do something and we chose to do otherwise. Mr. Bridges did not appreciate that."

"How come?" The president asked, in a mild tone. "I mean, how come you didn't follow the instructions?"

"Because she's an idiot," Bridges said.

"Now, Mike, I don't think that's true," Bush said. "I know all about idiots, after all. I get called one often enough." He smiled at both Dar and Kerry. "So how come?"

Dar cleared her throat gently. "Because it went against my honor to do so."

Kerry felt the silence drop over the room. She watched the faces of the two men at the table and sensed Dar had selected just the right words. She saw the president's expression shift and Bridges move in his chair, settling more square onto it and folding his hands on the table.

"Well then," the president said, after a long moment. "I know a little about that, too." He eyed Bridges. "So, Mike, did this cause us a real hassle, or you just ticked off because you didn't get listened to?"

Bridges frowned. "It's a publicity thing," he said. "Could be a problem with Congress."

Bush shrugged. "Full moon rising could do that. Tell you what. Let me let these ladies show me their new computer thing and we let things lie quiet for a little while, see what shakes out," he said. "Something'll come along to distract 'em, and if it doesn't, we'll make something up."

Bridges sighed.

"Ladies?" Bush stood up and stepped back. "Don't you all worry. Mike's just got his nose out of joint. He gets that way sometimes. They don't give him enough bran in the staff mess." He opened the door and lifted his hand to wave. "Talk to you later, Mike."

"Sir." Bridges rested his head against his fist, letting out a grunt of irritation as the door closed behind them.

ANDREW STOOD BESIDE the loveseat Ceci was sitting on, watching the big screen television mounted on the far wall. His eyes were fastened on the angular face the camera was pinned on, listening intently to what Dar said. "Huh."

"I have no idea what the dickens that kid's talking about," Ceci said. "And neither does that reporter."

Andrew cleared his throat. "I do believe she just told that there feller something about that bank thing that broke yesterday."

"Hm." Ceci regarded the familiar figure. "She looks good on television, Andy. Maybe we should have taken her to acting class. Remember that agency that wanted her for commercials?"

Andy looked around at her, both eyebrows hiking up.

"Okay, maybe not." Ceci chuckled as Dar stopped talking, waiting for the next question. She was at some desk somewhere and she looked relaxed, her elbows resting on the surface and her hands folded.

She did look good on camera, the blandness of the cubicle walls making her dark hair and pale eyes stand out. When she started talking her speech was crisp and confident. You just got the feeling she knew what the hell she was talking about.

Dar always had. Even in the wretched youthful arrogance that drove Ceci insane, there was always an understanding, at least on her part, that as annoying and aggravating as it was there was always truth in what came out of that mouth. "Did she just tell that reporter the guy who replaced her there was a one balled unicorn?"

"Yeap."

"*CNN*'s getting bold in its old age."

"Yeap."

Ceci shook her head and went back to watching Dar field questions, shrugging off the accusations of the former board members, downplaying the chaos her mother knew was going on as long as a few hours previously.

Master of her element. Ceci smiled. "Sharp kid, our daughter."

Andy grinned wholeheartedly. "Sharp as mah old boot knife."

Ceci extended her legs and crossed them at the ankles, feeling a new sense of contentment as she watched the screen. The sight of Dar's face no longer igniting in her any feeling of regret over their mutual mixed history.

Dar glanced off camera briefly and smiled and it was easy to guess who she was looking at. "I thought she said they weren't going to get involved in all that stuff," Ceci said after a bit. "But that...they said they're at an ILS building, right?"

"That Virginia one. I recognize it," Andrew said. "Dar probably went out there to fix ever'thing up. Got tired of all the yapping."

"Maybe they'll leave her alone now."

"Maybe that there dog'll turn that tail around and fly off."

"Idiots."

Andrew snorted, then glanced up as he heard the doorbell ring. "Who all's that?"

Ceci craned her head around him and peered toward the door. "Oh damn it, my x-ray glasses are on the table. Can you toss them to me?"

"Lord." Andrew got up and went to the door, opening it and moving forward to stand in the opening. "Yeah?"

The young, copper haired girl on the landing took a step back. "Oh. Hello," she said in a doubtful tone. "I was looking for Ms. Roberts."

"She ain't here," Andrew said. "What'cha want with her?"

"Andy, stop scaring that kid." Ceci edged her slim form around his. "Well, you're the young lady from the Island Market, aren't you?"

The girl nodded. "My name's Kristie," she said. "Sorry to bother you. I'll come back." She started to back up. "Thanks."

"Eh eh eh." Ceci held up a hand. "Hold on there, kiddo. I think we need to talk to you."

Kristie stopped and eyed her uncertainly.

Ceci crooked her finger at her. "Don't worry. I won't kill ya. I just want to talk to you. I think you owe me that after the trouble you got my child into."

"I didn't mean to," Kristie said. "That's w...I mean, I wanted to apologize."

"C'mon in." Ceci pushed the door open. "Maybe you can do more than that."

"ALL RIGHT NOW, let's see what we got."

They were seated around the small work table on one side of the big office. Dar was showing the demo on her laptop, her screen turned so that the president could see it.

The surreal nature of the moment wasn't lost on Kerry. She was seated on the other side of the table, watching the man alternate his attention between the computer and Dar, head cocked slightly in an attitude of listening.

"So you can just ask it whatever you want to, right?"

"Right," Dar said.

"Sounds easy." The president inched over. "Can I try it?"

"Sure." Dar turned the keyboard over and pushed back in her chair, extending her legs under the table.

Kerry watched him peck out a question. "Eventually Dar wants to make it so you can just talk to it," she said. "Speech recognition is a little tough."

"'Specially when you sound like I do." The president looked up and winked at her.

"Any variance is tough," Dar said. "Unless you talk like Kerry does. But you can write algorithms that can deal with tonal variations." She glanced at the screen where the database was pondering a response. "I'll have it practice on my dad."

The screen cleared and returned some data. "So, what it says is it found nothing in the current data flow that referenced your name and the word jackass," Dar said. "Remember this is just a random test database."

The president chuckled. "Okay how about this." He pecked the keys again. "How about, tell me something about rockets and the US East Coast." He hit enter. The screen hesitated then responded, this time with a full page of detail. "Well now, look at that."

Dar nodded. "It found some email that referenced those terms and some song lyrics. The human operator will probably want to see some additional detail about the first, but maybe not the second."

Bush nodded and hit the key for the first return. "So this'll show me that actual mail, huh?"

Dar nodded.

"That's going to freak everybody out." He studied the screen. "Ain't it?"

Kerry sat forward and rested her elbows on her knees. "In reality, it's something that any Internet service provider can do right now," she said. "They see all your data so if the police wanted, they could have them capture all the traffic you send and receive and turn it over."

Bush blinked. "Really?"

"Sure," Dar said. "It's what I could have done when I was at ILS. Capture every bit of information going in and out of the Pentagon and sold it to the highest bidder."

The president sat back in his seat and regarded her. "I don't think I like that idea," he said. "Here's the problem with all this technology stuff. We don't have a handle on it. It's too wide open."

Dar considered the question. "It's true the Internet changed everything," she said. "It connected the world in a way that I don't think anyone was ready for. But the truth is, bad people do bad things and use whatever is available to do what they do."

Bush nodded. "That's right. I did a study on that, if you can believe it. Telegraph, telex, Morse code, fax modems, all that. But now this here everyone connected thing makes it too easy for them, too hard for us."

"So this is a tool to help counteract that," Kerry said. "But you have to put it in the hands of trusted people. Really trusted. This would be so easy to use for someone to persecute people for a lot of reasons not related to national security. You know what I mean?"

He produced a wry smile. "Lot of things can be used for good or bad," he remarked. "But I thought someone told me all this stuff was..." He frowned. "Encrypted? So you can't see it?"

"Technically that's true," Dar said.

"But there's a way around that?"

"Yes."

Bush nodded slowly. "Tell me something." He hunched forward, resting his elbows on his knees and clasping his hands together. "What do you ladies think? This thing a good thing for us to do?" He looked from Dar to Kerry. "This right?"

Silence fell as they all sat there, thinking.

Finally, it was Kerry who cleared her throat and spoke first. "The truth is, if someone wants to hurt us bad enough, they will. They'll find a way. If it's known that we can do this." She pointed at the computer. "They'll find a way around it."

Bush glanced aside, then back at her. "That's probably true."

"So what I think is you should tell everyone you decided not to do this," Kerry said. "Tell them either it can't be done, or it's not right, or whatever you want to make people think it's not being done."

The president watched her face thoughtfully. "But do it."

Kerry nodded. "That's what my father would have said to do. He would have called this playing to the beliefs of the people."

"What about you?" He glanced at Dar. "You think that's the thing?"

"I think you should do it because it can be done. And if we can do it, whoever's against us can do it, too. It's stupid not to," Dar said. "But I don't disagree with Ker's slant on it."

Another silence fell. Dar found herself wishing they were home. All the excitement she'd felt about demonstrating her program evaporated away into doubt and uncertainty of where they would be tomorrow and what new problems she'd face.

She felt a little down. She wasn't sure if she cared what they did with the app now. If they decided to just cancel it she sort of felt like she might be glad. In fact, if they finished up now she and Kerry could go see the Air and Space Museum.

That sounded like a hell of a lot more fun than doing a demo for Congress.

"Well," Bush finally said, after pondering to himself for a long time. "Here's what I think." He straightened up in his chair and leaned back, hiking up one ankle and putting it on his knee. "I think we're going to have to show this off, because if we say never mind, they're all going to think we're lying sacks of marbles."

Ah well. Dar sighed inwardly.

"I'll just have to come up with a good story about how we're gonna lock this up in the depths of the Pentagon and only allow access to it with a gun and a court order by Eagle Scouts," Bush concluded. "Or something like that."

"Will they buy that, sir?" Kerry asked, quietly.

"Doesn't matter," Bush said. "She's right about the cat being out of the bag. Can be done, so we gotta do it." He scratched the bridge of his nose. "Sometimes politics are a mess."

Kerry almost laughed. "I think my mother agrees with you."

"When I demo this for the senators, I'll skew it to show how the automatic processing works rather than have them ask questions of it," Dar said. "How it finds connections. I think that's less intimidating."

"Mike was right on that," the president said in a rueful tone. "I shoulda kept my yap shut. One of them poked the bear one too many times about us not knowing enough to stop those planes and I told 'em we had something to make that up now."

"I remember when it happened, right after, everyone was so angry and...I guess embarrassed." Kerry said. "I remember thinking, how could we let this happen."

Bush was staring past her. "Just be glad you weren't sitting in my chair," he said, then he straightened back up and clapped his hands together. "But that's water under the bridge, right? How about some coffee, ladies? 'Bout that time of day."

"That would be great," Kerry said. "We didn't get any sleep last night trying to fix that problem. It's been a long day."

The president got up and picked up a phone, which connected without him having to dial. "Hey, get me a tray with some coffee and some cookies in here, willya? For all of us? Thanks." He put the phone down. "Now, we got a minute here, tell me about that whole thing with the press. What's up with all that?"

Dar and Kerry exchanged glances. "It's a long story," Kerry said.

"Hey, I like stories." He sat back down. "Specially when they're being told by good looking women. Have at it."

"THAT WAS WEIRD." Kerry smiled politely at the guards as they left the office.

Dar eyed her. "Given what we've gone through in the last few hours, I don't know what part of that you're referring to."

"Yes," Kerry had to admit. "This is one of the stranger days I can recall."

They were being led down the hall by an aide. Dar finally took her phone out of her pocket and looked at it. "Ten missed calls. Glad this thing has a silencer."

Kerry checked hers. "Yep." She thumbed through the numbers. "Here's Richard. I better call him back once we're outside."

"Did you know you used to be able to listen to analog cell phones by tuning in a radio scanner?" Dar asked, as she put the phone away. "They were radio transmissions in the clear."

"You know this personally?"

"Yep."

Kerry digested that as they left the building and started down the sidewalk to the parking lot side by side.

"Roberts."

They turned to find Briggs jogging after them. He waved them forward. "Let me walk you ladies to your car."

"'Bout to get weirder," Kerry muttered as they cleared the gate. "I can just tell."

CECI TOOK A seat in the little garden, while Andy collected the dog toys and started tossing them. She regarded the girl sitting uncomfortably in the other chair. "You know we talked to your father."

She nodded, relaxing visibly. "Yeah he told me. I got really pissed off at him. I was so mad. He told me he was going to get them out of here, and you know that's not fair."

"No, it isn't," Ceci agreed. "That wasn't a nice way to pay Dar back for a good deed she did."

"I told him that it was so cool for her to come in and get in this guy's face and he should be thankful, you know? Not get all mean with her." Kristie looked around, then back at Ceci. "But he didn't get that. He thought maybe she did it just to get in with me."

Ceci shook her head. "Not my kid," she said, flatly. "Let me tell you from the perspective of someone who had to deal with raising Dar." She leaned an elbow on the table. "She's nuts. Not in a bad way, but she does crazy things for people because she's got some weird internal chivalry that makes her do it."

Kristie frowned. "What do you mean?"

"She would step in front of a bus for a complete stranger," Ceci said. "She got into that guy's face on your behalf just because jackasses offend her sense of what's right." She watched Christy's face closely. "Sorry to disappoint you."

Kristie looked away. "Well, that's not what my dad thinks."

"Therein lies the crux of the problem," Ceci said. "Because it's true and it's not fair of you, or your father to make assumptions like that.

The idiot who was going after you, he could have had a gun. She could have been shot getting involved in that and you know what, kid? You aren't worth it."

Kristie stared at her.

"Not to me, not to my husband, not to Kerry Stuart," Ceci said. "I would rather have seen you raped and beaten than have to have her get hurt doing something like that."

"That's harsh," Kristie said, bluntly.

"Life is, sometimes," Ceci said. "Your father telling us he intends to make it hard for us to live here until we leave is harsh, too, especially since the only reason he's doing that is because he thinks Dar's going to turn you gay."

Kristy turned bright red.

"You do know that's not how that happens, right?"

"I don't know anything about it, but that sounds really stupid," Kristie said. "You can't make people any way like that."

Ceci regarded her. "No, you can't. But you know, you can't all the time help who you're attracted to either."

Kristy gave her a suspicious look. "What do you mean?"

"Well, take me." Ceci suppressed a smile. "I grew up in a very rich family up north. My parents were willing to provide me with pretty much anything I wanted. They took a lot of pains to introduce me to young men who were in the same station of life I was and give me a chance to find a partner among people who were like we were."

Kristie paused and then nodded. "Yeah, I get that. My dad does that, too. He has me go with him to his club meetings and stuff like that."

"Right. So what did I do? Ran away to a Greyhound bus station and fell in love with the first guy in uniform waiting for a ride I found."

"Really?"

"Really." Ceci glanced fondly at Andrew, who was chasing Mocha across the grass. "Andy's from a very poor family in Alabama. We have exactly nothing in common. But that never stopped us from loving each other and making a life together. So when my daughter told us she wasn't going to have a conventional love life, it never fazed either her father or me."

"Did your parents freak out?" Kristie asked, curiously.

"They certainly did. I was disowned," Ceci said. "But I never cared. Andy was more important to me than they were. So I sympathize with you about your father."

"He's so stupid," Kristie said. "That's all he can think of—about that gay stuff. It had nothing to do with that, with sex or anything. I just thought it was cool what she did and I said so." She got it all out in a rush of words. "I didn't think he'd freak out like that."

Ceci studied her in silence, glancing up when Andy wandered back over and sat down next to her. "He's not religious?"

Kristie shook her head. "No, we don't go to church or anything like that. That's what I told them." She gestured vaguely in the direction of the condo. "He just doesn't like gay people."

"How come?" Andy asked.

"What?"

"How come he don't like gay folks?" he repeated. "He grow up with the church or what all?"

Kristie shrugged. "Most people don't. Right? It's weird. It's not...I mean it seems weird."

Andrew shrugged back. "I guess we got a different view on it. Never much bothered me." He cleared his throat gently. "Not with Dar, anyhow."

Ceci turned her head. "But you didn't like it when they hit on you. I remember that."

Kristie's eyes widened. "Hit on you...what do you mean?"

Andrew stroked Chino's head as the Labrador nuzzled him. "Had me some problems with that in the Navy," he said. "I got het up when folks talked bad about gay people, cause of Dar, and some folks took that to mean I went that way, too."

Kristie frowned. "But you were married, right?"

Ceci raised her hand. "E-yep," she agreed. "We're an old fashioned couple. We got married before I had Dar, strange as that probably seems to you young 'uns."

"And they still wanted to...uh...have you?" Kristie made a face. "Now see what I mean? That's gross."

Ceci had to internally agree that the kid might actually have a point there. She remembered the feeling she'd gotten when Andy indignantly told her of the advances. "That is kind of gross," she admitted. "But at the time I told Andy to just ignore it."

"But I did feel something bad. So I thought maybe your father had something like that go on," Andy said. "Put people off."

"I don't know." Kristie shook her head. "He never said anything like that. I think he just..." She paused and fell silent. "He just wants us to be normal."

"Ain't no such thing," Andrew said.

"I'm sorry we all got into this mess," Ceci said. "Especially since it all started with a relatively good deed. Any ideas on how we can get everyone's shorts out of a knot?"

They regarded each other in silence.

"SO LOOK." BRIDGES folded his arms and leaned back against their rental car. "Here's where we stand."

They were outside in the late afternoon sun, a cool breeze moving the air around them. Dar was seated on the hood of the car and Kerry was leaning next to her.

"I know where we stand," Dar said. "But if it means anything, sorry we pissed you off." She shifted a little on the hood. "Didn't mean to."

"What? Never mind that." Bridges waved his hand. "That boat's down the river. Something else came up," he said. "You'll be a footnote in an hour. Everyone got focused elsewhere."

"Great," Kerry said. "This needed to get more complicated."

Bridges peered at her. "You should be used to this, Stuart."

"I'm not. I went into high tech for a reason," Kerry told him. "I'd rather be home installing servers for the Dade County school system."

"What?"

Kerry rephrased her speech. "I want to go home. You can keep Congress."

"Thanks for nothing." Bridges turned back to Dar. "How close is this thing to being able to do something useful?"

Dar folded her arms. "Six months. We could start a limited deployment in probably four."

"Not fast enough."

"Do you want it to work?" Dar said. "I think I asked you that in our last meeting. If you want it to be this, a canned demo, you can take this and use it. Won't do anything useful though."

Bridges looked around. "We need this thing. Situation just came up, just after you left off talking to POTUS," he said. "I can't give any details, but let me tell you after that piece aired on Turner's butthole I got a call from some people who want to see this, as in, now."

Dar shrugged. "I'd be glad to show whoever wants to see this demo. But the real thing's just not ready. Writing code takes time."

"Not only that," Kerry said, "it's going to take time to get all the taps into all the ISPs for the collecting to start. This can't happen overnight."

Bridges pinched his lips with his fingertips. "Will throwing money at it help?" he asked. "Buy a bunch of bodies for you to use?"

"To an extent, sure," Dar said. "More people can code segments. But it's still not going to be overnight."

"I could find some other bunch of idiots to do this."

"You could." Dar's voice remained mild. "That's capitalism. There's always competition."

"Smart ass," Bridges said. "Tell you what, I'll quadruple the contract price. You get me something in four weeks."

Four weeks. Kerry looked at Dar, mentally doing the math and feeling a touch lightheaded at the amount they'd clear from it. She saw the thoughtful look in Dar's eyes and remembered their upcoming vacation, feeling a pang of regret.

Regret which lasted barely more than a microsecond.

"No," Dar said. "I've got something scheduled the next couple weeks I'm not going to back out of. I'll have my team work on it, but they'll finish it when they do." She got up off the car hood and unlocked the doors. "If that's not good enough let me know. We'll move on."

Bridges studied her. "You actually mean that." He seemed amazed.

"I do," Dar said. "I don't want to put my life on hold right now. Kerry and I are going to the Grand Canyon."

Bridges stared at her. "You're shitting me. You're going to blow me off for that?"

"Yes."

"What in the hell is wrong with you?"

"Excuse me, we've got an appointment with Congress." She opened the car door and slid behind the driver's seat as Kerry scooted around and got in on the other side. "Do me a favor and let us do this right. It's going to be damned embarrassing if you don't."

He put his hand on the door. "Roberts, if something happens that this thing could have prevented and didn't, it's on your head."

Dar met his eyes without flinching. "It is," she said. "Which is why I'm going to deliver it to you when it's ready. It's my reputation on the line."

For a moment she was sure he was going to slam the door on her. She made sure her body parts were inside, but he merely shut the door gently and patted it. Then he lifted a hand and walked off, heading back toward the gate with its stern guardians.

"I have no idea how that ended," Kerry admitted.

Dar started the car. "I think we're okay," she said. "And if not, screw it."

"I don't know, hon." Kerry settled back in her seat. "This is pretty deep."

"Honestly, I don't care." Dar backed up and started out of the lot. "I'm going my goddamned vacation and I don't care if the whole Western world falls on its ass while we're gone."

Kerry started to make a comment, then saw the line of Dar's jaw tighten and she merely reached over and tucked her hand around her Dar's arm. "Can we stop and grab a snack?" she said, instead. "I'd like to get something in my stomach first before I start returning these calls or talking to Congress."

"Sure."

Kerry leaned over and let her head rest against Dar's shoulder. "What a weird day."

Dar diligently searched the passing buildings for something edible, wishing the demo for the Senate was behind them. And more than that wishing they were on the way home. The events had left her more than a little unsettled. "Tacos okay?"

"Mm."

"How about fried chicken?"

"Mm."

"Jamba Juice?"

"That's the ticket," Kerry said. "My gut's not willing to deal with that other stuff right now." She kept her head where it was as Dar pulled off into a small strip mall and into a parking spot. "Thanks."

"Anything for you." Dar patted her cheek. "And there's a chicken wing place next door. Meet you back here?"

Kerry gave her arm a squeeze and released her. "You bet."

They got out of the car and split up, Kerry ducking into the smoothie shop and Dar making her way into the wing joint. It was moderately busy in both and Dar got in line and waited, thumbing through her messages.

One from Maria, hoping things were all right. Another from Colleen, congratulating her on the interview.

Dar smiled a little at both of them. She opened a third that had an attachment. She opened that to find a set of code snippets for her to review.

"Ma'am?"

Dar looked up to find the cashier waiting for her. "Sorry." She put the Handspring away. "Dozen wings hot and a large coke."

"Sure," the woman said. "Naked?"

"Yes." Dar responded, ignoring the sniggering of the two teen boys behind her. She paid the woman and moved down the counter and heard the door open. Without turning, she felt a sense of warmth on the side of her body facing the entrance and knew without looking that Kerry would be there.

"Hey." Kerry bumped her with an elbow. "I got you one, too. I thought it might counteract the wings."

Dar collected her wings and they went to a back table, sitting down together on the bench seats. Dar pushed the basket of wings in the center of the table and Kerry handed over a tall, blended smoothie. "Are there peaches in that?"

"Of course."

Dar pulled the cup over and contentedly sucked on the straw. "Thanks."

"Anytime." Kerry picked up a wing and nibbled on it. "I called Richard while I was waiting. I thought he'd have stacks of subpoenas for us so I figured I might as well find out the worst before we fly home."

"And?" Dar was divesting a wing of its meat, sucking at the bone with single minded intensity.

"And nothing," Kerry said. "He called the lawyer that was in that press release and the guy hung up on him."

Dar looked up and frowned.

"He thought it was pretty weird, too."

Dar's phone rang and she sighed, putting down her wing and fishing the gizmo out. "Dar Roberts," she said. "Who's this? What? Oh." She cleared her throat. "I've said everything I've got to say already about that."

"Uh oh." Kerry picked up another wing. "Hope they don't get a cell signal in the Grand Canyon."

Chapter Sixteen

THEY SAT IN the car parked in the lot outside the congressional office building finishing up their fruit smoothies, the windows rolled down as the late afternoon sun streamed through them.

They had ten minutes before their appointment. Dar leaned back in the driver's seat, one knee hiked up with her elbow resting on it. She was looking out the window, watching people walk down the sidewalk and turn up the steps to enter.

"Ready?" Kerry asked, putting her cup down. "Let's get this over with."

Dar nibbled on the straw from her smoothie and remained quiet for a moment. "Hm."

Kerry half turned and regarded her. "Hm? Hm what?"

"Not sure what I should tell these people," Dar said. "I've been thinking about that since we left The White House." She shifted a little and also half turned so they were facing each other. "I keep wondering if we got ourselves into something we shouldn't have."

"It's a little late for that, hon," Kerry said in a gentle tone. "We made a commitment to them."

"I know."

Kerry watched her profile, which was thoughtful and sort of somber. "Well," she finally said. "Regardless of what we end up doing, we probably should do this thing here and not blow them all off."

"Yeah," Dar said. "You're right."

Kerry waited. "But?" She prompted after another silence between them.

"But I realized when he was typing in questions into it that I'd overlooked something about this system," Dar said. "I've been thinking about it in the terms of having trusted people use it."

Kerry exhaled a little. "And you realized that trust is relative?"

"Outside you and me, yes," Dar said. "It's too enticing. You could find out anything about anyone who uses computers with this."

"That's true. But you also said it's technology that's out there in the wild. So it's going to happen anyway."

"Yeah," Dar said. "I don't know, Ker. I don't know what to do. My perspective's all turned around now." She put her cup down and opened the door, pressing the buttons to roll the windows up. "But you're right. We do have to go show them something."

Kerry got out and pulled her messenger bag from the back seat. She slung it over her shoulder as she joined Dar in the front of the car, and they walked toward the building entrance. They walked up the steps and through the door, walking across the floor to the reception desk.

Dar handed over her business card and the woman nodded, handing it back and pointing to the door behind her that had, once upon a time, been guarded by some big, hungry Marines. Kerry followed Dar through it, then took the lead on the way to the big room the intelligence committee met in.

Just outside they paused and Kerry reached up to twitch Dar's collar straight. "So, I'm sure —" Dar put two fingertips against her lips and Kerry looked up at her in surprise.

"Don't do that," Dar said, quietly.

Kerry's fair brows contracted. "Hm?"

"Be straight with me. You've been telling me what you thought I wanted to hear all day. Stop it."

Kerry was stunned speechless. She stood there just staring into Dar's eyes. Finally she took a breath. "I ju —"

"I know," Dar cut her off gently. "You just didn't want to piss me off and I was in a crap mood. I get it." She moved her fingers and cupped Kerry's cheek instead. "But don't do that. I don't want that between us. I don't want to wonder what you're thinking."

It was painful and not. It poked a pin in her heart and yet she felt a certain relief at Dar's words. That surprised her and yet as she thought about that, it didn't surprise her at all. She put her hands in her pockets and exhaled. "I think maybe this place does that to me."

Dar looked around, then back at her.

"I lived most of my life inside the mirror funhouse of politics," Kerry said. "Reality was whatever you convinced people it was." She felt her skin flush as a skittering of past memories flashed into her mind's eye. "I had to learn how to pitch everything."

Dar reached over and tweaked her nose. "Not with me, okay?"

Kerry looked up to find herself being watched with wry affection and a mature understanding that made her feel suddenly like a high school kid again. "Sorry."

"Don't be. I just don't want to ever start down that path with us."

Kerry's eyes dropped, then lifted. She reached over and took Dar's hand, lifting it to her lips and kissing the knuckles. "Thanks for being such a grownup."

Dar's eyes twinkled. "If my mother were here to see that, she'd be peeing herself."

"If anyone else in this building were here to see that they'd probably be peeing on us," Kerry admitted wryly. She released Dar's hand and took a breath.

"So level. What's your take on the demo?" Dar asked. "How should I play it?"

Kerry studied her face for a moment. Then a faint smile appeared. "Okay," she said. "What I think you should tell these people is the truth. Just lay it out. They're not idiots. They know the politics. Don't whitewash what could happen."

"Even if that kills the project?" Dar watched her intently. "They're going to freak out."

"Yes," Kerry said. "Because it's going to come out anyway. I'd rather get that out up front."

"Bridges is not going to be happy."

Kerry shrugged. "I think what matters is what makes us happy. Isn't that what this whole crazy last month has shown us?"

"Could be." Dar smiled. "But thanks. Glad to hear you say it."

"That's what you were going to do anyway, isn't it?" Kerry smiled back, then sobered. "It's the right thing for us to do. What stresses me out is that we have all those people back there depending on us now. It bothers me that we could do something that would result in them getting hurt."

"Isn't that what we just did, though?" Dar asked. "You and I decided to retire. Whole fucking planet stops in mid spin and half the country floats off into space. I think it's just part of our mojo."

"Mm."

"Anyway." Dar leaned forward and touched her forehead to Kerry's. "Don't ever hold back, okay? If you feel it, say it."

"Even if it pisses you off? I was trying not to do that, with all the craziness," Kerry admitted. "I wasn't bullshitting you, I just figured there was a better time to mouth off."

"Even if." Dar looked up as footsteps approached. "Ah."

Kerry glanced over her shoulder. "Ah," she repeated. "At least this wasn't in a dusty old stairwell. Hello, Mother."

"We'll continue the talk later." Dar squeezed her shoulder and turned as well. "Hi."

Cynthia Stuart arrived at their side and produced a smile. "Hello, there. How did your other meeting go?"

Dar turned and pushed open the door to the hearing chamber. "It went well." She stood back to let the other two enter. "It's been a busy day. Hope everyone's on time here."

"Oh, I have no doubt," Cynthia said. "Everyone is most interested in hearing about this. In fact it was the topic of conversation at a luncheon I just left. One of the senator's sons is part of the technology office in The White House and he was quite enthusiastic about it."

"Uh huh." Dar walked over to one of the tables, put her bag down, opened the top of it and pulled out the laptop. "Do you have a..." She looked around at the room. "No, probably not?"

"I think they last retrofitted it with electricity in place of gas lamps," Kerry said. She felt a flood of humor come through her body, making her feel giddy. "So if you're looking for a projector, hon, give it up."

"Mm."

"Did I tell you they had the Titanic hearings in this room?"

Dar looked up at her, hands still on the keyboard, eyebrows lifted.

Kerry winked at her, then went over and leaned against the table, facing the slowly filling room. She remembered the last time she'd been here and the face off she'd dealt with.

An evening of utter aggravation, stress and anxiety that ended peacefully in Dar's arms. She turned to watch her beloved partner mess with her demo, thinking about their conversation just moments ago.

Dar sensed the attention and glanced at her. "Something wrong?"

"Not a damned thing," Kerry said. "I was just reflecting on the fact that there is no luckier son of a bitch than me anywhere."

Dar's left eyebrow hiked up.

Kerry just smiled and turned around, moving away from the table and into the center of the chamber. "Ladies and gentlemen, if we could please get seated since we have a limited time for this demonstration and I know you all want plenty of time to ask questions."

There were some surprised looks and some annoyed looks, but Kerry returned a smile to all of them, waiting for the group to settle down behind their desks and grudgingly give her their attention. "The last time we had a conversation you were all wondering how we knew what we knew when we knew it," she said. "This time we're going to show you how much information is out there that people like us have access to, and people like you want access to."

Now she had their attention."Or you think you do," she added. "So let's get started."

IT WAS DARK outside the airplane windows as they flew along the east coast on the way home. Dar had the hood on her hoodie up surrounding her face and she was sound asleep in her seat, her long body relaxed.

Kerry was close to being the same, but her mind was slower in winding down and so she was quietly sipping some Kahlua and cream as she listened to the drone of the engines in the mostly silent plane.

The demo went fine. Dar answered questions in a calm and straightforward manner and therefore scared the living crap out of everyone in the room, up to and including Kerry's mother.

Outrage, shock, disbelief and calculated interest all wound up in a ball as both the positive and negative of the system's ability occurred to the distinguished audience in turn.

They'd shared all that with Gerry Easton, who thought the whole thing was hilariously funny. And she'd gotten a chance to spend time with Alabaster, the Labrador. It made her fiercely miss home and Chino and led to them to take a red eye home instead of waiting until the following morning.

So here they were, content to leave the politics to the politicians. She'd come around to the decision that whatever happened did. Dar said if they lost the contracts, there would be others and the staff they had on board would shift over to those.

And if no other contracts were found and it turned out they needed to shrink rather than grow, then that's what would happen.

They would go on their vacation. They would let the chips fall where they may. And since they both tended to potato chips and not gambling chips, the fallen ones would be taken care of by the tongues of two Labradors. So in the end, what would be, would be. Kerry put her cup down and let her eyes close, turning her head to the right to face her sleeping partner.

The sounds around her shifted a little and took on a hint of echo and she felt herself start to fade out, glad of a chance to get a nap before they landed and would have to drive home.

Two flight attendants in the galley just forward of their seats were talking in low tones. Curiously the words sharpened in her hearing as she hovered on the brink of sleep.

"Boy, I'm glad that computer glitch got cleared up."

"No kidding! It's been a nightmare with flight ops the past two weeks. What was it, two hundred cancels, and those four near bang ups on the ground? Sheesh."

"They couldn't schedule half the planes yesterday. But it was smooth tonight."

"Sure was. Don said everything's running like normal again. Glad they figured out what the problem was, but damn it took them a long time."

"Sure did."

Kerry opened her eyes and studied Dar's sleeping profile as the words faded and the attendants moved off down the aisle. They did that, she and Dar. Two anonymous women sprawled in seats at the front of a half empty airplane.

Should they have done it sooner? Could they have? Kerry sighed and closed her eyes, shaking her head slightly. It didn't really matter, did it?

Water under the bridge. That was in the past. She couldn't change it, so they just had to carry on and take each moment as it came.

"GOOD MORNING, KERRISITA." Maria waved at Kerry as she passed the open door to her office. "Did you have a nice trip back?"

"We did." Kerry paused in the doorway, a cup of coffee in her hand. "Very quiet flight and no traffic when we drove back to the island." She paused to take a sip. "Which reminds me, I've got to find a real estate agent and have them come in this afternoon. Dar and I are going to find a place somewhere around here to live."

Maria looked surprised. "I thought you very much liked the place you have?"

Kerry shrugged. "It's a condo," she said. "We want a house with a yard. Some place the dogs can run around and we can personalize more. Dar used to live around here, matter of fact."

. "That is so nice. Would you like me to make those arrangements?" Maria asked. "I have how you call them, the contacts?"

"Sure." Kerry smiled. "That would be awesome, Maria. You know us," she said. "Something on the waterfront with a slip for the boat and a yard."

"Si." Maria nodded. "I will have my cousin come in to talk with you. She and her husband have many clients in this town and also, Coral Gables."

"Sounds good." Kerry toasted her with her coffee cup and headed off to her office. "Good morning Mayte," she said, entering the outer chamber. "You ready to move down the hall?"

There were boxes scattered around, half full. "Ah, Kerry, yes." Mayte paused in the act of putting papers in one of them. "I like the new office very much but I will miss being around here with you and my mama."

"You needed your own space," Kerry said. "Dar and I will be just fine here, right Zoe?"

The younger girl smiled from her place kneeling in front of another box. "Yes, ma'am," she answered. "I will do my best."

Kerry smiled and entered her own office and its sedate sunniness. There was a distinct scent of waxed wood from the floors and fresh paint from the walls, and as she crossed through the beams of light from the window she felt a sense of contentment.

She heard Dar's voice on the phone from the room next door. A moment later her presence was detected and Chino came trotting in with Mocha at her heels. "Hey, kids."

Chino came over and sat down next to her chair, tail wagging.

Kerry sat behind her desk and put her cup down, reaching for her mouse to wake up her desktop system. She studied her screen and chuckled, starting on the first of her list of new mail, glancing up at footsteps to see Mark entering. "Hey."

"Hey." He came over and sat down, picking up Mocha to pet him as the puppy came pattering over. "Guess what?"

"What?" Kerry started sorting through her mail.

"Pete got a call from the old place," Mark said. "They told him they were straightening stuff out and did he want to come back." He scratched Mocha behind his ears and the puppy yowped, tilting his head back and poking his tongue out. "He said he told them thanks, but no thanks. But at least they sounded sane again."

"It must help that things are working again," Kerry said. "And boy am I glad that's done."

Mark nodded. "The way the big D did it—that was slick, you know? Got those guys in Herndon to do it. And they recorded the whole thing."

Kerry nodded. "I don't blame you for not wanting to touch that, by the way," she said. "I was glad Dar didn't either, though at the time I was ready for it to get done any way she could."

"I felt like a chickenshit," Mark admitted. "But man, I so didn't want to go in there. It gave me creeps just standing at security, even though those guys were totally cool and would have let me up if I asked them to."

"The guys at Herndon were pretty glad to see us, too," Kerry said. "Until I told them the government wanted to hire them." She shook her head. "Not sure how that's all going to work out."

"They really going to take all those contracts?"

Kerry glanced up at him and nodded. "They lost trust," she said. "I still can't believe they were that stupid."

"Wow." Mark said.

"Speaking of stupid." Dar came to stand in the connecting door, leaning against the frame of it. "Hamilton just called. He said he's got a meeting with the lawyer from the ousted board members in about a half hour. He'll let us know what comes out of it."

"Tell him to tell Richard." Kerry took a sip of her coffee. "Maria said no process servers have shown up here yet so who knows what's going on." She pushed a folded newspaper across the desk toward Dar. "No sign of anything in the news."

"Which is probably good news," Dar said. "So let's move on." She winked at them then returned to her office, with Chino at her heels.

"She's right," Kerry said. "So, I got your note about the data center. Dar and I talked about not doing that, but now I think we should. Talk to me about the location."

"Sure." Mark got up and came over to the desk and put down a folder. "So here's the deal, it's a giant freaking datacenter that one of the big boxes put up and then the county tanked 'em. So it's all ready for us."

"You guys can get this rolling while Dar and I are on vacation, right?"

"You bet."

KERRY WRIGGLED A little into the base of sand she was lying on, gazing up at the canopy of stars overhead and listening to the breeze stirring the sabal palms and palmetto bushes, surrounding the small beach on Dar's little offshore island.

She felt mellow and relaxed, tired from a long day of diving and swimming. She was content to lie where she was, being warmed by a nearby campfire and waiting for the sounds of Dar coming up out of the ocean where she was busy collecting them some dinner.

That would mean she would need to stir and go cook whatever it was Dar came up with. Until then it was just her and the salt-tinged night air and the gentle sounds of the Dixie riding at anchor nearby.

The weather was perfect. Not too cold, but not muggily hot either. The air was full of the smell of the ocean, the seaweed on the shore and the wood smoke from palm branch fire.

Here there was no sound of civilization to bother them and only the threat of a curious crab to disturb them. Kerry was glad of the isolation and the opportunity to spend some time with her family without interruption.

She stretched her arms out and her fingertips brushed Chino's damp fur, feeling the twitching of the sleeping animal's dreams as she looked up at the stars and thought about the past little while.

What had Ceci called it? A cycle of change. Kerry pondered for a moment whether the change had ended for a while, or would continue on.

The sound of something emerging from the waves made her lift her head and peer past the fire, smiling a little as the moonlight revealed the outline of Dar's tall form as she trudged up out of the surf. She had a shortie wetsuit on and a tank. She turned and sat down on one of the picnic benches to take them both off, dropping her fins and mask on the table's surface.

"Ah, the primordial huntress returns," Kerry said.

Dar gave her a droll look, then held up her catch bag. "I have critters for you."

Kerry amiably got up and brushed herself off, then walked over and took the bag, handing Dar a towel in return. "It feels like there's a lobster in here."

"Dos." Dar roughly toweled her head dry, walking over to the folding table and donning the dive coat lying across it. "Nice under there. You can see the moon almost to the bottom." She draped her towel over a hook under the umbrella covering the table and ran her fingers through her hair.

Kerry hung the bag on another hook, then turned and shifted a big pot of water onto the fire's sturdy grate. She stepped back as the flames bathed the bottom of it and it hissed gently.

The heat of the fire toasted her, a counterpoint to the cool breeze coming off the water and through the rough underbrush of the little island that had once been Dar's hideaway and still had no real name.

Dar fished a bottle of ginger ale from the cooler under the table and opened it, then settled into a hanging rope chair with a satisfied sigh. "Nice." She rested her hand on one knee and took a swallow of the cold soda, rinsing it around inside her mouth before swallowing. "What a beautiful night."

Kerry took out covered side dishes that had come with them on the Dixie and grinned. "Glad you thought of coming out here." She kept an eye on the pot, waiting for it to boil, and got out the plates and cups they'd likewise brought.

"C'mere, little man." Dar picked up Mocha and set him on her lap, where the sleepy puppy yawned and plopped down, idly chewing on her fingers. "I saw an octopus."

"Did you? Damn. Now I'm sorry I didn't tag along." Kerry observed the water starting to bubble and took the catch bag off the hook, positioning it over the pot and turning the lever that let it latch on to the edges. "Wish I'd remembered my ear plugs."

Dar chuckled as she swiveled a little and watched Kerry grimace in reflex as she unlocked the bottom of the catch bag, dumping its contents into the pot. The glow from the fire outlined her beautifully, catching highlights in her hair as she cautiously removed the bag.

There were no sounds save the hiss of the water droplets hitting the fire. Kerry popped the lid onto the pot and went back to fixing their plates up.

"No screams?" Dar asked.

"Pfft." Kerry came over with a plate of cut fruit and offered her some. "One more week and we're off to river rafting. Dar, I can't wait. Even if we end up sleeping on rocks I don't care."

"I care." Dar selected a piece of watermelon and bit into it. "These are supposed to be high class campsites. We better the hell get air mattresses at the least."

"Sissy."

"Hey, shortie. I've camped rough. Have you?"

Kerry chuckled. "Closest thing to rough camping I've done is sleeping on the floor of your office. So, no. But I'm sure we'll be fine. I was thinking before about going to sleep and being able to see all the stars in the world overhead. Not like here. I want to see the Milky Way."

"Me too." Dar rested her head against the rope and rocked back and forth gently. "My dad once told me he'd been to places where you could see stars like that. In the desert and all. But he said you would always wish for clouds because for them it was the darker the better."

"Sure." Kerry rocked along with her in the next chair. "But I can't wait to just go do that. Spend time looking at stuff I've never seen and the rafting. I want to get out of my head space for a while."

Dar remained quiet for a bit, just nodding slightly as she scratched Mocha under the chin.

The wash of the waves was broken suddenly by the sound of a boat engine growing slowly louder. Dar looked over her shoulder, then got up and went to the shore. She walked along peering out over the ruffled waters.

"Of course, our life can't stay perfect for more than fifteen minutes," Kerry said, getting up and going over to the fire. She removed the pot lid and peered inside, then put it back down, going over to the table and getting it set.

"Cutter," Dar called back over her shoulder. "Heading this way.

I'm going to go over and get on the boat radio before they assume we're illegal aliens."

"Okay." Kerry got the tops off the side dishes and portioned them out. "Don't take too long. Lobster'll be ready in about five minutes."

"Won't take more than two." Dar jogged along the shore and hopped up onto the floating dock that extended out to the anchored yacht bobbing at the end of it. She got to the side of the boat and vaulted up and over the railing, moving quickly across the deck and into the cabin where the inside radio system was.

She'd just picked up the microphone when searchlights lit up the outside of the Dixie and she stepped halfway out of the boat, shading her eyes from it. "Dixieland Yankee to Coast Guard cutter, Coast Guard cutter off my port side. What's the problem?"

The light outlined her a moment more, then cut off and the radio crackled. "Cutter Avalon—sorry about that Dixieland Yankee. Is that Captain Roberts?"

Dar felt her brain quietly explode at the title. "Uh. Yes," she said after a moment. "It is."

"Standby, Captain. We're coming in."

Dar put the mic down and went onto the back deck, standing with her hands in the pockets of her dive coat as she watched the cutter rumble closer.

She saw several men standing on deck and two were getting into their pontoon launch, which was lowered into the water and shortly speeding her way. "Over here." She pointed them around the front of the Dixie and a moment later they were alongside the floating dock, hopping out.

Dar got onto the dock to meet them. "What's up?"

One of the men stepped forward. "Lieutenant Davis, we met a bit ago down south."

"I remember. Did I look suspicious again?" Dar asked, with a smile.

He half shrugged. "You know how it is."

Dar nodded. She did. "We were just having a cookout. I've been coming to this little spot in the ocean since I was around fifteen."

He nodded. "I have a spot like that about ten nautical south from here. But ah..." He glanced past her to the fire lit beach scene. "Mine's not nearly so nice." He had his hands in his pockets. "But I'm glad I bumped into you because your name came across the wire not long ago."

"It did?"

Davis nodded. "One of our other ships picked up a body the other week. Guy apparently drowned, but no one seemed to know how he got into the water," he said. "It was just off that island you live on. Apparently he lived there, too."

Dar felt a chill. "His name Billy?"

The lieutenant looked hard at her. "Yeah. So you knew him?"

The dock rocked slightly and they looked over to see Kerry approaching. "In a manner of speaking, I guess," Dar said. "He was a jackass I ran into on the island and had an argument with."

"What's up?" Kerry asked

"Well, we heard that some guy on the island told the cops about that and that they should find you and ask about it," he said. "About that argument, I mean. He told the cops there was bad blood there and maybe you knew what happened to him."

"What?" Kerry said, sharply.

"They found the missing guy. The one who was after Kristie," Dar said. "And I'm willing to bet it was her father who told the cops to come looking for me about it."

Kerry looked at her, then at the two Coast Guard officers, then back at her. "Son of a biscuit," she said in a crisp clear tone. "If there's anyone who might have done something to him it would be that bastard, Jim. The developer, who owns that place."

To both of their surprise, the Coast Guard officer nodded. "That's why I'm glad we ran into you, because I've got some intel on that guy and it's not good. You should watch out. The cops ran everyone's records and the guy who was talking to me told me that guy's bad news."

"What kind of bad news?" Dar asked. "Criminal background?"

Davis shrugged. "That I don't know. He didn't say."

"What a bastard," Kerry said. "What happened was, Billy threatened Kristie, the cashier in the island market. She's Jim's daughter. Dar happened to be there and got in his face and he left."

The officer frowned. "Okay, but why is that guy Jim sending the cops off after you then? Sounds to me like you did him a favor."

Dar sighed. "Long story," she said. "But thanks for the warning. I'll be sure to keep my eyes open. Do the cops want to talk to us?"

Davis shrugged. "Not my area. It was just coffee machine convo, you know? At the base, because anything that happens on that island gets chewed over. I listened because I heard your name and we'd just met."

"I appreciate that," Dar said. "Jim has a problem with us, so I guess he thought this was a good opportunity to get us in some hot water."

"Is it possible the guy just actually drowned?" Kerry asked. "He seemed like a guy who liked to party."

"Yeah, that's what the cops said," Davis agreed. "Who knows? Anyway, just be careful, okay? Especially out here like this in the middle of nowhere." He lifted his hand in a wave and got back in his pontoon boat, making a gesture to the seaman who was driving it.

Dar and Kerry watched them putter off and then they both sighed. "Well, poo," Kerry said. "I didn't need to hear that."

"Me either." Dar put her arm around Kerry's shoulders. "Let's go have our lobster."

They walked down the dock back to the beach where Chino and Mocha were waiting. Kerry went over to the pot and took its top off, releasing a cloud of bay leaf and spice scented steam into the air.

As she worked she thought about Billy. To hear something had happened to him seemed sad, in an impersonal kind of way, because as much of a jerk as he was, jerkiness didn't deserve death.

To hear that they'd been blamed didn't surprise her at all. From the time the security guards had asked her and Dar if they'd seen him that time, in the back of her mind she'd suspected something was in the works.

Sucks. Kerry got their dinner plated, then glanced up to see Dar standing on the shore, hands in pockets, staring off at the dark horizon. She put the plates down, covered them and walked over, nudging Chino aside as she put her arm around Dar's back. "Hey."

"Hey."

Kerry looked up, spotting tears rolling down Dar's face. "Oh, hon."

Dar shook her head and lifted one hand to wipe her eyes. "Last time I do someone a favor," she said, clearing her throat. "Bastard."

Kerry put her other arm around her and gave her a hug.

"What's the point in doing the right thing if all it gets you is kicked in the ass?"

"Ah, Dar." Kerry felt the ache in her heart for her. "It's not always like that." She rocked them both a little. "A lot of people love you for your doing the right thing. I sure do."

Dar sighed.

"Your mom picked the right name for you, honey. You are a Paladin," Kerry said. "You have such a polished, white soul."

Dar blew a raspberry at her. "I tried to do right by ILS, and it gets me lawsuits. I do a favor for some kid and I get thrown under the bus when some guy croaks. What's the damn point?"

Kerry patted her on the stomach and hugged her again. "The point is, it's who you are."

"Ugh."

"You told me not to talk smack at you," Kerry said. "So I'm not. Dar, you are who you are. Don't even contemplate changing that."

"Growf." Chino added commentary.

"Ahh. Screw it." Dar wiped her eyes again. "Let's go have dinner." She walked arm-in-arm with Kerry back up the beach, circling the fire and dropping into the chairs dug into the sand on either side of the table.

Kerry uncovered the plates and handed her one, then pulled her own over and they ate in companionable silence for a few minutes. "I've got apples baking over there when we're done."

A faint smile appeared on Dar's face as she concentrated on divesting her lobster from its shell. "I can smell them," she said. "Thanks, Ker."

"Anytime. I can make them in the oven but there's something about a campfire that makes them extra good," Kerry replied. "Not sure what it is."

"Everything tastes better over a campfire."

"Well, that's probably true but I have to admit I'm glad I don't have to gather wood every time we make coffee."

Dar chuckled softly.

"Feel better?"

Dar shrugged. "I just decided to hell with it. Let them come talk to us. By the time we're done with Jim and that island, they'll be sorry they messed with us."

Kerry chuckled. "You mean because we're giving the condo to your folks?"

"My mom'll run for condo association president and my father'll use that golf course for target practice. They're screwed. All we did was bring our dog in the gym."

"And love each other," Kerry reminded her. "That's our biggest offense."

Dar picked up the cup of apple juice and toasted her with it. "That, I plead guilty to." She waited for Kerry to lift her own cup and touch it to hers. "For all time."

"Likewise," Kerry said. "To hell with what anyone thinks about it."

The End (for now)

OTHER MELISSA GOOD TITLES

Tropical Storm

From bestselling author Melissa Good comes a tale of heartache, longing, family strife, lust for love, and redemption. *Tropical Storm* took the lesbian reading world by storm when it was first written...now read this exciting revised "author's cut" edition.

Dar Roberts, corporate raider for a multi-national tech company is cold, practical, and merciless. She does her job with a razor-sharp accuracy. Friends are a luxury she cannot allow herself, and love is something she knows she'll never attain.

Kerry Stuart left Michigan for Florida in an attempt to get away from her domineering politician father and the constraints of the overly conservative life her family forced upon her. After college she worked her way into supervision at a small tech company, only to have it taken over by Dar Roberts' organization. Her association with Dar begins in disbelief, hatred, and disappointment, but when Dar unexpectedly hires Kerry as her work assistant, the dynamics of their relationship change. Over time, a bond begins to form.

But can Dar overcome years of habit and conditioning to open herself up to the uncertainty of love? And will Kerry escape from the clutches of her powerful father in order to live a better life?

ISBN 978-1-932300-60-4
eISBN 978-1-935053-75-0

Hurricane Watch

In this sequel to *Tropical Storm*, Dar and Kerry are back and making their relationship permanent. But an ambitious new colleague threatens to divide them — and out them. He wants Dar's head and her job, and he's willing to use Kerry to do it. Can their home life survive the office power play?

Dar and Kerry are redefining themselves and their priorities to build a life and a family together. But with the scheming colleagues and old flames trying to drive them apart and bring them down, the two women must overcome fear, prejudice, and their own pasts to protect the company and each other. Does their relationship have enough trust to survive the storm?

ISBN 978-1-935053-00
eISBN 978-1-935053-76-7

Eye of the Storm

Eye of the Storm picks up the story of Dar Roberts and Kerry Stuart a few months after *Hurricane Watch* ends. At first it looks like they are settling into their lives together but, as readers of this series have learned, life is never simple around Dar and Kerry. Surrounded by endless corporate intrigue, Dar experiences personal discoveries that force her to deal with issues that she had buried long ago and Kerry finally faces the consequences of her own actions. As always, they help each other through these personal challenges that, in the end, strengthen them as individuals and as a couple.

ISBN 978-1-932300-13-0
eISBN 978-1-935053-77-4

Red Sky At Morning

A connection others don't understand...
A love that won't be denied...
Danger they can sense but cannot see...

Dar Roberts was always ruthless and single-minded...until she met Kerry Stuart.

Kerry was oppressed by her family's wealth and politics. But Dar saved her from that.

Now new dangers confront them from all sides. While traveling to Chicago, Kerry's plane is struck by lightning. Dar, in New York for a stockholders' meeting, senses Kerry is in trouble. They simultaneously experience feelings that are new, sensations that both are reluctant to admit when they are finally back together. Back in Miami, a cover-up of the worst kind, problems with the military, and unexpected betrayals will cause more danger. Can Kerry help as Dar has to examine her life and loyalties and call into question all she's believed in since childhood? Will their relationship deepen through it all? Or will it be destroyed?

ISBN 978-1-932300-80-2
eISBN 978-1-935053-71-2

Thicker Than Water

This fifth entry in the continuing saga of Dar Roberts and Kerry Stuart starts off with Kerry involved in mentoring a church group of girls. Kerry is forced to acknowledge her own feelings toward and experiences with her parents as she and Dar assist a teenager from the group who gets jailed because her parents tossed her out onto the streets when they found out she is gay. While trying to help the teenagers adjust to real world situations, Kerry gets a call concerning her father's health. Kerry flies to her family's side as her father dies, putting the family in crisis. Caught up in an international problem, Dar abandons the issue to go to Michigan, determined to support Kerry in the face of grief and hatred. Dar and Kerry face down Kerry's extended family with a little help from their own, and return home, where they decide to leave work and the world behind for a while for some time to themselves.

ISBN 978-1-932300-24-6
eISBN 978-1-935053-72-9

Terrors of the High Seas

After the stress of a long Navy project and Kerry's father's death, Dar and Kerry decide to take their first long vacation together. A cruise in the eastern Caribbean is just the nice, peaceful time they need—until they get involved in a family feud, an old murder, and come face to face with pirates as their vacation turns into a race to find the key to a decades old puzzle.

ISBN 978-1-932300-45-1
eISBN 978-1-935053-73-6

Tropical Convergence

There's trouble on the horizon for ILS when a rival challenges them head on, and their best weapons, Dar and Kerry, are distracted by life instead of focusing on the business. Add to that an old flame, and an aggressive entrepreneur throwing down the gauntlet and Dar at least is ready to throw in the towel. Is Kerry ready to follow suit, or will she decide to step out from behind Dar's shadow and step up to the challenges they both face?

ISBN 978-1-935053-18-7
eISBN 978-1-935053-74-3

Stormy Waters

As Kerry begins work on the cruise ship project, Dar is attempting to produce a program to stop the hackers she has been chasing through cyberspace. When it appears that one of their cruise ship project rivals is behind the attempts to gain access to their system, things get more stressful than ever. Add in an unrelenting reporter who stalks them for her own agenda, an employee who is being paid to steal data for a competitor, and Army intelligence becoming involved and Dar and Kerry feel more off balance than ever. As the situation heats up, they consider again whether they want to stay with ILS or strike out on their own, but they know they must first finish the ship project.

ISBN 978-1-61929-082-2
eISBN 978-1-61929-083-9

Moving Target

Dar and Kerry both feel the cruise ship project seems off somehow, but they can't quite grasp what is wrong with the whole scenario. Things continue to go wrong and their competitors still look to be the culprits behind the problems. Then new information leads them to discover a plot that everyone finds difficult to believe. Out of her comfort zone yet again, Dar refuses to lose and launches a new plan that will be a win-win, only to find another major twist thrown in her path. With everyone believing Dar can somehow win the day, can Dar and Kerry pull off another miracle finish? Do they want to?

ISBN 978-1-61929-150-8
eISBN 978-1-61929-151-5

Storm Surge

It's fall. Dar and Kerry are traveling — Dar overseas to clinch a deal with their new ship owner partners in England, and Kerry on a reluctant visit home for her high school reunion. In the midst of corporate deals and personal conflict, their world goes unexpectedly out of control when an early morning spurt of unusual alarms turns out to be the beginning of a shocking nightmare neither expected. Can they win the race against time to save their company and themselves?

Book One: ISBN 978-1-935053-28-6
eISBN 978-1-61929-000-6

Book Two: ISBN 978-1-935053-39-2
eISBN 978-1-61929-000-6

Partners

After a massive volcanic eruption puts earth into nuclear winter, the planet is cloaked in clouds and no sun penetrates. Seas cover most of the land areas except high elevations which exist as islands where the remaining humans have learned to make do with much less. People survive on what they can take from the sea and with foodstuffs supplemented from an orbiting set of space stations.

Jess Drake is an agent for Interforce, a small and exclusive special forces organization that still possesses access to technology. Her job is to protect and serve the citizens of the American continent who are in conflict with those left on the European continent. The struggle for resources is brutal, and when a rogue agent nearly destroys everything, Interforce decides to trust no one. They send Jess a biologically-created agent who has been artificially devised and given knowledge using specialized brain programming techniques.

Instead of the mindless automaton one might expect, Biological Alternative NM-Dev-1 proves to be human and attractive. Against all odds, Jess and the new agent are swept into a relationship neither expected. Can they survive in these strange circumstances? And will they even be able to stay alive in this bleak new world?

Book One: ISBN 978-1-61929-118-8
eISBN 978-1-61929-119-5

Book Two: ISBN 978-1-61929-190-4
eISBN 978-1-61929-189-8

Other Yellow Rose books you may enjoy:

Struck! A Titanic Love Story
by Tonie Chacon

Their hearts were struck long before the ship hit the iceberg.

Megan Mahoney, the apprentice ticket agent who stumbles across an unused ticket and takes a leap of faith to create a chance for a new life and love in America.

Emily and Ethan Westbrooke, American shipping magnates, twins who were sent away from their home and family in order to hide the shame of their sexual desires.

Frances Cheswick, the spoiled darling of the Cheswick family. She's too young for love, but she knows what she wants. And, Frances always gets what she wants.

Alice Pearce, goddaughter to Frances's mother. Her ticket for a second-class berth makes her question her place in the family and in society at large, but what she finds there makes a permanent place in her heart.

It was the adventure of a lifetime on the maiden voyage of the luxurious *Titanic*. Their hearts, like the ship, were on a collision course with destiny.

ISBN 978-1-61929-226-0
eISBN 978-1-61929-225-3

199 Steps to Love
by Pauline George

At 61, Lucy finds herself divorced and decides to go on holiday to Whitby. There she meets the gallery owner, a woman named Jamie, who she is drawn to in ways she can't yet understand.

Jamie is also drawn to Lucy, despite the advice of her best friend against lusting after a straight woman.

But just as they come together, Lucy leaves without explanation, not only putting a physical distance between them, but an emotional one as well.

Can they overcome the distances and find each other? Or is it more than just the miles that's keeping them apart?

ISBN 978-1-61929-214-7
eISBN 978-1-61929-213-0

In the Midnight Hour
by Brenda Adcock

What happens when you wake up to find the woman of your dreams in your bed? All-night radio hostess Desdemona, Queen of the Night draws her listening audience with her sultry, seductive voice, the only thing of value she possesses. During the day she becomes an insecure, unattractive woman named Marsha Barrett, living in a world with too many mirrors. She is comfortable with her obscurity until she meets Colleen Walters, a tall, attractive woman hired to expand her listening audience by selling Desdemona to new markets. When she wakes up in bed with Colleen after a night at a club, Marsha is terrified. A woman like Colleen would never go to bed with a woman like Marsha. She might dream about such a thing, but in the harsh reality of daylight, it would never happen. Beauty is only drawn to beauty and Marsha refuses to believe beauty could ever be drawn to anyone who looks like her. Just as she begins to believe happiness may be possible, the past returns determined to destroy them.

ISBN 978-1-61929-188-1
eISBN 978-1-61929-187-4

It's Elementary, Too
by Jennifer Jackson

What happens when personal and spiritual confusion lead to intimacy apathy?

It's Elementary, Too, follows Jessica and Victoria through the emotional and psychological aftermath of a recent school shooting.

As an elementary school teacher, Jessica was held hostage, her life threatened, and she witnessed the assailant assassinated before her. Initially suffering from Post Traumatic Stress and survivor's guilt, her denial of emotional struggles eventually spawns even greater issues.

Victoria tries to maintain the act as stoic protector, but it weighs heavy on her emotional stability. After numerous rejections, she turns her back on teaching and her life in Austin and finds a separate path full of inviting promises.

Studies show most primary relationships falter after traumatic life events. This story examines the gradual emotional and intimacy decline and the possible resurrection of Jessica and Victoria's relationship. The ultimate question: is love really enough?

ISBN 978-1-61929-218-5
eISBN 978-1-61929-217-8

OTHER YELLOW ROSE PUBLICATIONS

Be sure to check out our other imprints,
Mystic Books, Quest Books, Silver Dragon Books,
Troubadour Books, Young Adult Books, and Blue Beacon Books.

About the author

Melissa Good is an IT professional and network engineer who works and lives in South Florida with a skillion lizards and Mocha the dog.

VISIT US ONLINE AT
www.regalcrest.biz

At the Regal Crest Website You'll Find

- The latest news about forthcoming titles and new releases

- Our complete backlist of romance, mystery, thriller and adventure titles

- Information about your favorite authors

- Current bestsellers

- Media tearsheets to print and take with you when you shop

- Which books are also available as eBooks.

Regal Crest print titles are available from all progressive booksellers including numerous sources online. Our distributors are Bella Distribution and Ingram.

CPSIA information can be obtained at www.ICGtesting.com
Printed in the USA
BVOW02s1334160715

408908BV00002B/225/P